TANGLED
TRUTH

ALSO BY THE AUTHOR

Fiction by Rebecca Carey Lyles

PRISONERS OF HOPE SERIES

Shattered Dream (Book One)

Tangled Truth (Book Two)

Hidden Path (Book Three)

KATE NEILSON SERIES

Winds of Hope (Prequel)

Winds of Wyoming (Book One)

Winds of Freedom (Book Two)

Winds of Change (Book Three)

Short Stories by Rebecca Carey Lyles & Friends

Passageways: A Short Story Collection

Nonfiction by Becky Lyles & Friends

It's a God Thing! Inspiring Stories of Life-Changing Friendships

On a Wing and a Prayer: Stories from Freedom Fellowship, a Prison Ministry

PRISONERS OF HOPE SERIES
BOOK TWO

TANGLED TRUTH

REBECCA CAREY LYLES

PERPEDIT ✓ PUBLISHING, INK

COPYRIGHT © 2019

Perpedit Publishing, Ink
PO Box 190246
Boise, Idaho 83719

http://www.perpedit.com

First eBook Edition: 2019
First Paperback Edition: 2019
ISBN: 978-1-7341439-2-8 (ebook)
ISBN: 978-1-7341439-3-5 (print)

This is a work of fiction. Names, characters, places, organizations and events portrayed in this novel are either products of the author's imagination or are used fictitiously.

Cover design by Ken Koeberlein of Koeber Designs

Published in the United States of America
Perpedit Publishing, Ink

DEDICATION

The first novel in the PRISONERS OF HOPE SERIES, *Shattered Dream*, was dedicated to the former cult members who graciously shared their stories with me. This second novel, *Tangled Truth*, is dedicated to those who have yet to escape but feel drawn to flee high-demand organizations and controlling individuals. May God lead you into glorious, joyous freedom.

THE SYSTEM

"I know that false teachers, like vicious wolves, will come in among you after I leave, not sparing the flock." (Acts 20:29 NLT)

"When the system starts seeking goals that are out of line with individual values, the individual, who is usually trapped in the system, can either get hurt or survive by lying. We all like to survive and people lie all the time because of this. People in oppressive state systems learn to lie as a normal part of their lives, simply to get along."
("What It Is Like to Go to War" by Karl Marlantes)

"As mere mortals who can't grasp the incomprehensible, we limp along with allegiances to various stepped-down versions of the incomprehensible that seem to suit us, such as the Marine Corps, the family, France, the Baptist Church, or the Order of the Eastern Star. We must strive, however, always to see these smaller entities as only pieces of the larger one we'll never comprehend." ("What It Is Like to Go to War" by Karl Marlantes)

"Truth has perished; it has vanished from their lips."
(Jeremiah 7:28b NIV)

CHAPTER ONE

I buckle the seatbelt and cover my face with my hands. What have I done? Did I just make the worst decision of my life? I've made so many bad choices, but this...

Deputy Manning hits the gas, and the SUV shoots up the highway, slamming me against the backseat. He gave me two options—the detention center or Olivia and Owen Pritchards' place. I'd rather go back to jail than return to their hostile household and horrid so-called church, Faithful Followers of the Way. Yet, I've chosen the warped world I escaped not that long ago.

For a brief moment, I was my real self again, Cassie Anita True. But for the next year, I'll be called Cassandra Turner, my church-approved name. The thought is so depressing, I lift my head and look out the window, so I don't start crying.

The SUV zips along the deserted two-lane highway. Fence posts with their rumpled moon shadows whip past my backseat view. I have a feeling the deputy is exceeding the speed limit by at least twenty miles per hour.

I clamp my teeth to keep from screaming, *Stop! I changed my mind!* I've come up with some dumb ideas while under the influence. But right now, I'm stone-cold sober—and craving cheap whiskey to rescue me from the reality that lies ahead.

In some ways, Followers' lives are worse than those of inmates. Instead of steel bars, mental and emotional bars block their freedom. I'm jumping right back into the "frying pan" I fled last night, solely for the purpose of helping FFOW members escape the hellhole. I'm not sure how I'll do it, but I trust I'll have more opportunities to do so outside jail than inside.

Way too soon, the deputy brakes to a halt in the middle of the road, directly across from the floodlit "Fellowship Neighborhood" sign.

I unbuckle my seatbelt and reach for the door handle.

"I'll get your door," he says.

How could I have forgotten? Backdoors in patrol cars don't have handles on the inside.

He steps from the front and opens my door.

I start to get out, but my feet stick to the rubber mat. I suck in a breath.

"What's wrong?" He sounds impatient.

Biting my lip to keep from crying out, I pull one foot at a time off the floormat. The pain is incredible and even worse when I maneuver from the vehicle and shift my full weight onto my feet. I moan and grab the door.

Manning frowns. I'm sure he's thinking, *What's your problem?*

I slide the mat out of the car and hold it so it catches the light.

He stares at my bloody footprints and then at my feet. "You can't walk like that. I'll drive you to the door."

"No!" My voice in the quiet night is louder than I intended. "We can't be seen together." I'm already worried someone coming home from an all-night work project or leaving early for a Saturday-morning project will see us. I hand him the mat and close the door. "You'll want to rinse it first chance you get. Thank you for the ride."

I start to hobble across the road but stop and look at him over my shoulder. "Don't forget your promise."

"I'll be on it the instant my shift ends." He glances at the mountains, which are now edged with light, and opens the hatchback. "Sorry about your feet." Laying the mat inside, he pushes the door down and is about to leave, when he says, "The least I can do is help you to the sidewalk." Taking my arm, he slowly walks me to the curb.

I flinch with every footstep. But with his assistance, I'm able to step up onto the smooth, cool cement.

"Good luck." He releases my arm. "You'll need it." With that, he trots to his vehicle and takes off.

I watch the taillights fade into the distance and am turning to go when a reflection on the floodlit sidewalk catches my eye. Bloody footprints—mine. Kneeling, I use the bottom of the robe to wipe them from the concrete as best I can. I don't dare leave behind clues of my nocturnal wanderings.

I sidestep from the sidewalk onto the night-chilled grass. It feels wonderful under my feet. With any luck, it'll also hide my messy trail. Of course, Followers don't believe in luck, despite what Deputy Manning said.

Actually, I have to agree, which may be a first for me since I joined the church. Better to trust God than vague, elusive luck. I breathe a quick prayer and break into an awkward, painful run across immaculate lawns. Not because I'm anxious to return, but because the sun is rising. I can't be seen in my nightgown. The residents would be scandalized. Dread replaces the freedom I relished mere hours earlier. The grass, which felt good at first, now stabs my raw feet.

Finally, as the first rays of sunlight touch the treetops, I reach the Pritchards' property and stagger behind the garage. Olivia didn't bother to tell me the keypad code when I moved in, but Owen did. I've never used it and hope and pray I remember it correctly.

I punch in the number. The deadbolt releases. *Thank you, Jesus.* Slowly, ever so slowly, I twist the knob and slip inside. The garage smells of rubber and engines, but not of garbage, which is *never* to be left inside the garage. I shut the door as soundlessly as possible, lock it, and aim for the kitchen door. Each silent stumbling step across the cold cement is soothing yet excruciating. I'm grateful my bedroom is the first one at the top of the stairs. I'll have to make the climb on my knees.

Trusting the code is the same for all outer doors, I tap it into the keypad by the kitchen door. The lock clicks, thank God, and I turn the knob, millimeter by millimeter, all the while questioning the wisdom of returning to this house and these people. If I were smart, I would...

What exactly would I do? Now that daylight is breaking, what *could* I do in my nightclothes with trashed feet? I blow out a long breath. I've made my bed with the Followers. I've got to lie in it, for better or worse—probably worse.

I push the door, barely opening it. Chicken and cauliflower aromas from last night's meal sift through the crack. Soon, those odors will be replaced by coffee and bacon and other breakfast smells. The thought triggers mixed emotions.

First come happy memories of Saturday morning breakfasts at my grandparents' Oregon farm and Sunday morning breakfasts with my family in town. But those sweet recollections are soured by a vision of Olivia marching through the kitchen, telling each person how to do his or her task better. None of us can do anything right, in her lofty opinion.

I open the door farther and peek inside. I can see the kitchen, the stairs to the second floor, and by craning my neck, the doorway to the basement stairs. The Pritchards must have left the door open. No lights are on, and no one is in the kitchen. Maybe Olivia and Owen gave up on me and went back to bed. The mere thought of Olivia turns my stomach. Owen isn't so bad, but Olivia...

The gloom below triggers another vision, this one of little Zachary imprisoned at the far end of the house, huddled alone and afraid in the cold dark basement. My foot pain is nothing compared to his suffering. I burst into tears, biting my knuckle to keep from sobbing out loud. Oh, how I'd love to whisper to him, "Hang on, little guy. Help is on the way." But Olivia has probably posted a guard—or a camera.

"God," I whisper under my breath, "help Deputy Manning keep his promise."

I wipe my eyes with a sleeve and step inside. Quietly closing the door behind me, I'm about to crawl up the stairs when a desperate thirst assaults my parched throat. I was thirsty when the deputy found me and should have asked if he carried bottled water. But I was too distracted to pay attention to my bodily needs until now.

Cringing with each step, I cross to the cupboard, swipe at my nose, and reach for a glass. I fill it, down the water fast and am filling it again, when I hear, "Cas-sandra Turner!"

I jerk, sloshing water on the counter, and turn my head.

Like a ghost in a white flannel nightgown, Olivia hovers in the dim opening between the dining room and kitchen. "You slut, where have you been?"

Can't say she's not upfront about her feelings. I wipe the counter with the dishcloth and finish filling the glass.

Olivia comes closer. "I–asked–you–a–question."

I drink the water, every last drop, and set the glass on the counter. My feet are burning, and I fear they'll stick to the floor if I don't move soon. I stare out the kitchen window, where dawn is seeping through the darkness and returning color to the grass and trees. "I have no idea."

Officer Manning's words ring in my head. *We Followers are first-rate liars.*

"What?" She scurries around to stand before me. "You can't be that stupid. You know where you were." Switching on the light over the sink, she peers at my face. "Why are you crying?"

I dry my cheeks with my sleeve. "I was worried about Zachary, plus I had an upset stomach and couldn't sleep. I don't know what happened. I lost it, I guess, and started walking, without paying attention to where I was."

My feet throb.

"You're from Bozeman. You knew where you were."

"I'm from Oregon, Olivia. In Bozeman, I was either in school or tending a dying husband—or out of my mind drunk. I had no idea the church or this neighborhood existed. Tonight, I walked a long way and, eventually, found myself here." I shrug. "What more can I say?"

"Don't do it again." Olivia looks me over from head to toe. Her perpetual scowl deepens. "What's on your robe?"

"Blood."

"How did you get blood—?" She spots the prints marking my path from the door to the counter. "Disgusting. Clean the floor, now, before the blood dries." Lifting her feet, she checks the bottoms of her slippers. "Use paper towels and disinfectant from the cupboard under the sink. And put plastic grocery sacks on your feet, so you don't make a worse mess. Then get dressed. Ruby Jade will no doubt want to speak with you first thing. You caused me and Leadership, and Owen, to lose hours of sleep."

What about the little boy who spent the night shivering in your basement prison, too frightened and heartbroken to sleep? Keeping my thoughts to myself, I ask, "Where are the bags?"

"You should know."

I don't respond.

She rummages through the pantry, straightens and tosses two sacks at me. "Who did you talk to?"

Balanced on one foot, I fight the pulsing pain and lean against the counter to pull a bag over my other foot. "Who did I talk to?"

"While you were gone."

"Who would I talk to in this neighborhood in the middle of the night? I don't know anyone outside this household.'

"You know Sebastian."

"I have no idea where he lives. Besides, I wouldn't go looking for my boss late at night."

"Are you sure?" She arches an eyebrow.

I ignore her insinuation and put the second bag on the other foot. My feet feel as though they're on fire.

"You have friends in Bozeman."

"In Bozeman, not out here in the boondocks." I hold out a foot. "You think this happened while I was visiting with someone?"

Olivia bristles. "Don't get sassy with me." She huffs into the dining room, probably on her way to update Leadership regarding my sassy mouth.

One by one, I rip paper towels from the roll that hangs beneath the upper cupboard.

My hands-and-knees ascent up the uncarpeted stairs takes forever, but at least I'm off my feet. In the bedroom, early morning light filters through the open blinds. I crawl past the beds, trying not to rattle the grocery sacks and wake Marcela.

She stirs. "Cassandra, what…? Are you okay?"

"I've been better." I veer into the bathroom. "Sorry to wake you."

She follows me in and turns on the light. Straight out of bed, with her strawberry-blonde hair going every which way and her green eyes half open, Marcela somehow manages to look as pretty as always. Her eyebrows are creased with concern.

I pull myself onto the edge of the bathtub and turn the faucet. Once I get the temperature adjusted, I'll plug the drain and fill the tub with a couple inches of warm water.

Marcela stares at my sack-covered feet. "Anything I can do to help you?"

"You could put the trashcan over here, so I can throw these grocery bags away." I peel the first sack off my foot.

She gasps. "Your foot, it's…"

I turn it so I can see the bottom. "Yeah, it's shredded. No wonder it hurts like the dickens."

She frowns. "Cassandra…"

"One of my grandpa's favorite words." I squirt shower gel into the running water.

"You shouldn't say it. It means devil."

I snicker. "Not *devious* devil?"

"Cassandra…" Marcela waggles her finger at me then takes the trashcan from the cabinet under the sink and sets it beside me.

I drop in the bag and tug at the other sack.

Marcela grimaces. "What happened? Olivia came to our room, looking for you in the middle of the night. Where were you?"

"Long story." The fewer details she knows, the safer she is. "I was upset about Zachary and couldn't sleep, so I started walking."

Her mouth drops open.

"Yeah, I know. Not my smartest move.'"

I put both feet in the water. The razor-sharp sting steals my breath. I gasp and grab the tub spout, huffing one fast breath after another. To get my mind off the pain, I whisper, "I have good news for you."

She raises an eyebrow.

Motioning her close, I murmur in her ear, "We've figured a way for you to talk to your family."

"You have?" Her eyes brighten. "But who is *we*?"

"Corban and Logan Dahlstrom. I work with them sometimes."

"I can't wait!" She claps her hands. "What do I need to do?"

At the sound of the bedroom door opening, she clamps her hand over her mouth and sits back.

"Do we have any hydrogen peroxide in the cabinet?" I ask. "I should disinfect my feet after I soak them. And gauze. I'll probably need lots of gauze or big bandages."

Marcela opens the cabinet door just before Olivia walks in. "What are you doing out of bed, Marcela?"

Marcela looks over at her. "Helping Cassandra."

"She made a mess," Olivia states, her features impassive, "she cleans the mess. Go back to bed."

Marcela hands me a brown bottle and is getting to her feet, when her alarm clock buzzes, followed quickly by the alarm on my "Time to Serve Jesus" clock.

Olivia stomps out, slamming the bedroom door hard enough to wake the entire household.

"I'll get the alarms," Marcela says.

I lift a foot, shake off water and pour peroxide over the sole. The pain shoots up my leg like a Taser zap. Sucking in a ragged breath, I douse the other foot before I can chicken out.

When Marcela returns, I'm panting and clutching the bathtub edge. She asks, "You all right?"

I puff my cheeks and blow out a long stream of air. "The peroxide was worse than I expected."

"Your feet look like raw hamburger." She hands me a towel and a small tube. "I don't see any gauze under there, but I did find this antibiotic ointment. Want me to ask Olivia if she has gauze?"

I dab at my feet with the towel. They have a wet skin smell. "She's so mad, she wouldn't tell you if she did have it."

"You're probably right." She lowers her voice. "But as my granddad used to say, there's more than one way to skin a cat."

I blink. Is my rebellious spirit rubbing off on my roommate?

"I'll be back." She darts out the door. In less than a minute, she returns with a roll of white gauze-like material. "This is cheesecloth from the pantry," she whispers. "I've never seen it used, so take as much as you need. I'll cut it with my hair scissors."

After I dab the medicinal-smelling ointment on my feet, she helps me wrap them and slip on socks to hold the cheesecloth in place. I tuck in the edges to hide the pilfered fabric from Olivia's prying eyes.

The long night begins to catch up with me. "I need to go to bed, Marcela." I touch her arm. "Thanks for all your help. I'll get out of your way, so you can get ready for work."

"This is Saturday."

"Oh, right. We're supposed to return to the lady's house today to paint it." I slide off the bathtub and fumble on hands and knees toward my bed. "Don't think I'll be much help."

"I'll run this to the kitchen and bring you breakfast later."

"Thank you."

"Give me your robe, so I can put it in cold water to soak out the blood."

I remove the bathrobe and hand it to her. "You're the best, Marcela." Climbing onto my bed without using my feet is a challenge, but I manage and am barely beneath the covers before I fall asleep.

The next thing I know, Marcela is shaking me awake. "Here's some orange juice," she whispers. "Drink it fast, and I'll refill the glass with water. Olivia won't let me bring you breakfast. She says you should have eaten with the rest of us."

"She's all heart." I push to a seated position.

"Shh." Marcela sets the juice on my nightstand, raises the blinds on the window above our beds and opens it. "Fresh air will do you good."

I'm tempted to tell her how wonderful the air smelled last night but decide to save my illicit memories for another day. I take a long sip of the fresh-squeezed orange juice. It's a taste of heaven that soothes my throat. I didn't realize how dehydrated I was. I down the entire contents and hand the glass to Marcela. "Just what I needed. Thank you."

She hurries to the bathroom, runs the water and returns. "The van leaves in a couple minutes." Setting the glass on my nightstand, she asks, "Anything else I can do for you before I go? I'll wring out your robe and hang it to dry when we get back."

"You've done plenty for me already." I glance at the window. "Looks like a beautiful day to work outside. Who all is going?"

"Almost everyone, even the children. They love to paint. Candice is staying home with Tristen. He's teething and running a fever." She opens one of her dresser drawers. "Olivia has a meeting this morning, so she won't be going, either."

I raise my eyebrows. "Should I guess who the meeting is with?"

"She didn't say, but…"

"You know what?" I lower my voice. "I'm so tired, I don't care. They're going to do what they're going to do. So be it." *And help me, God.* If Olivia insists I go with her to the Fearsome Threesome meeting, I won't budge an inch.

Marcela lifts a white bundle from a drawer and shakes it out.

Coveralls? "Are you allowed to wear those?"

"Only over our clothing for protection, and only when we're at a jobsite."

"I understand. Those are way too sexy to wear in public."

She peeks at the camera. "Cassandra…"

I motion her over, and she moves to the foot of my bed, her back to the camera. "If the brothers are there," I whisper, "ask for details."

"I will." Her eyes sparkle. I love seeing her come alive.

One of the kids calls her name from the base of the stairs.

"Do you want the door left open or closed?" she asks.

"Open." I want to hear what's going on in the household, especially if authorities come for Zachary.

She waves and races down the stairs, coveralls in her arms.

I fall onto my pillow, wishing for more orange juice and imagining it might taste even better with vanilla extract in it.

Without vodka, the combination would be as close as I might come to creating a screwdriver cocktail in the Pritchards' house.

On the other hand, maybe it's a good thing Olivia and Candice are here—or I might spend the morning concocting mixed drinks. I stare at the ceiling. The idea of being one of two peons subject to Olivia's whims makes me cringe. Candice is probably thinking the same thing. Neither of us is a match for our household guardian's temper.

If she takes off before the authorities come—and I pray they do come—how will they get to Zachary without a key? Like me, Candice probably has no idea where the keys are. I'd hate for the cops to kick the door in and scare Zachary. The poor little guy has endured so much.

About to come unglued imagining all that could go wrong, I force my eyes shut. God's got this. He doesn't need me to point out potential potholes ahead.

CHAPTER TWO

I'm nodding off, when through the open window, I hear a vehicle on the driveway. Olivia must be leaving for her meeting. I push the covers aside and struggle to my knees on the bed, groaning every time I bump my feet. I don't know why I'm going to all this trouble. If she stays, she'll find a way to make my life hell. If she goes, she and Leadership will find a way to make my life hell. I guess I just want to know where she is, so I'm halfway prepared for what might happen next.

One forearm balanced on the window ledge, I lower the blinds and open the slats. A sheriff's department SUV is parking on the driveway below my window and two unmarked or maybe civilian cars are pulling alongside it.

My heart begins to thump.

The vehicles stop and two uniformed deputies exit the SUV, a man and a woman. The man has a paper in his hand. Another uniformed deputy gets out of a car and helps a woman from it. *Deputy Manning.* I smile. He kept his promise. *Thank you, Jesus!* Must be Zachary's mom with him.

Two women appear from the other car. They're both wearing navy blazers, but one has on pants and the other a pencil skirt. The group is assembling near the deputies' vehicle, when one of the garage doors rattles and Olivia's van backs onto the driveway and stops at a distance from the others.

A moment later, she's striding across the drive. "Can I help you, officers?" Her saccharine voice reaches me loud and clear. "I was just leaving for a meeting."

My guess is she thinks they have the wrong house—or that they're here to arrest the household slut, as she calls me. Reaching behind the blinds, I quietly push the window all the way open. The camera perverts can think what they want. I don't plan to miss a word.

The first two deputies step forward. "Good morning." The female officer is speaking. "I'm Deputy Forbes, and this is Deputy Hansen. We're looking for Mr. and Mrs. Pritchard."

"I'm Olivia Pritchard." Her voice and demeanor morph from kind and sweet to cautious and harsh. "What's this regarding?"

"An eight-year-old boy named Zachary Russell. Red hair, green eyes."

I clap a silent clap.

She takes a step backward.

"He's missing," Forbes says, "and we have reason to believe he's in this house." Her voice is firm, unyielding.

The other deputy widens his stance.

Olivia pushes her fingers into her hair, her actions jerky and robotic.

"Zachary Russell is a resident here," the officer continues. "Correct?"

"Uh, well, I…"

"Is he a resident in this home?" Forbes lifts her chin. "Yes or no."

"Yes, but…"

"But what, Mrs. Pritchard?"

"He's not here."

"Where is he?"

"Uh, well, he's in school. You can go find him there."

"It's Saturday. School is not in session."

"A, uh, a special makeup class. He missed a couple days."

"What school?" Forbes asks.

"Triumphant Way Elementary School." Olivia seems to be regaining her confidence.

Deputy Forbes turns to Deputy Hansen. "Ask the captain to send someone to the school."

"You can't..." Hands at her side, Olivia spreads her fingers wide. "He can't do that."

Forbes peers at her. "Why not?"

"They would...they would disturb the children, strike fear in their hearts."

Forbes and Hansen look at each other and then at Olivia. Neither one speaks.

"Oh," Olivia says, "I just remembered. He's not there today. He's sick."

"So, he's in the house?" Deputy Forbes folds her arms.

"Uh, actually, yes." Olivia twitches. "But he can't be disturbed."

"Is someone watching over him?"

"Well, no. I mean, his eyes... He has to be a dark room."

I–am–amazed. My mother always said one lie leads to another. Olivia is digging herself in deep.

"Take us to him. Now." The deputy's voice leaves no room for argument.

Even so, Olivia throws her shoulders back and defies the officer. "I can't. He's in timeout."

"Timeout?"

"Yes, because he's a *brat*." She practically shouts the word. "He has sin in his heart."

The woman with Deputy Manning rears, mouth open, like she's about to retort. But Manning puts his arm around her, whispers in her ear, and she closes her mouth.

"Where is this timeout?"

Olivia flails her arms. "I need to make a phone call."

I can only imagine how hard this is for her without Leadership direction.

"Where–is–the–boy?"

Olivia mumbles something I can't hear.

"Speak up." Forbes rests her hands on her duty belt.

Deputy Hansen places a hand on the butt of his Taser and tilts his head, as if trying to better hear Olivia.

"Uh, well…downstairs." Her voice trembles, and she nods over and over, reminding me of her husband with his bobbing head.

"If you would please lead us to Zachary, Mrs. Pritchard, you would save us all time." The officer indicates the others. "My apologies. I should have introduced those with us. This is Ms. Trina Russell, Zachary's mother."

"I know who she is!" Olivia snaps, sounding more like her normal self. "She's not allowed on my property."

"Zachary Russell's mother isn't *allowed* where he lives?"

"Ruby Jade ordered—"

"Whoa." Forbes raises her palm. "Are you speaking of Ruby Jade Paradise?"

"Yes, of course."

A breeze blows through the blinds. Though the wooden slats don't budge, the draft ruffles my hair and cools my face. I touch my cheeks. Until now, I hadn't noticed they feel hot. The flannel gown is warming me from head to toe.

"As I understand it," the officer says, "she's a pastor, not a judge. Therefore, her alleged order is irrelevant to a parent-child relationship."

"B-b-but," Olivia sputters, "she's—"

"This gentleman," Forbes continues, "is Deputy Manning, Ms. Russell's fiancé."

Olivia looks as though she's about to respond, but the officer raises her palm. "These two individuals, Ms. Randolph…"

The one wearing the skirt lifts her hand.

"And Ms. Lloyd…are specialists with Child Protective Services."

The other woman nods.

Hansen holds out the paper he's been holding. "This warrant authorizes us to search your home."

"Judge Snow would never—"

"Signed by Judge William Bock." Forbes smiles. "He's new to our court and happy to provide assistance to a needy child."

Olivia rips the warrant from the deputy's hand, crumples it into a ball and tosses it aside. "Zachary Russell is not needy. We take good—"

Hansen retrieves the paper, smooths and folds it, and slides it into his shirt pocket.

Forbes crosses her arms again. "Time to take us to the boy, Mrs. Pritchard."

I bet the others are holding their breath, like I'm doing, and wondering what the angry woman will do next.

"Will you lead us, Mrs. Pritchard, or shall we find our own way?"

I can't see Olivia's eyes, but I'm positive they're shooting daggers at the officers. "I'll get him and bring him out to you." She starts for the house.

"We'll go with you," Forbes says. My guess is she wants to see Zachary's "timeout" location as well as prevent Olivia from making phone calls or running away—or possibly obtaining a weapon.

Olivia looks at her watch. Sunlight glints off the face, and the jewels sparkle like those on Ruby Jade's behemoth timepiece. "I have a meeting to attend."

"A child's welfare is our only concern right now."

"I should call to let them know I'll be late."

"First things first. Let's go."

"I tell you, he's a troublemaker. He has sin in his heart."

"That's a lie!" Trina Russell leaps at Olivia. "My Zachary is a good boy."

Manning grabs her arm.

She resists for only a moment, her FFOW training quickly returning her to submission—an assumption on my part. Could be her response is due to her respect for her fiancé. Or maybe she knows creating a scene won't help her son.

Forbes motions to the others. "The specialist directly assigned to this child will accompany us. Everyone else, please wait here while Officer Hansen and I accompany Mrs. Pritchard into the house."

Ms. Lloyd joins the two officers. They walk to the house together, then out of view beneath the porch roof. They're barely inside, as far as I can tell, when Candice appears from where they disappeared and hurries toward the group, her baby in her arms.

I clap again, silently. She's going to tell them about Mylea. Smart move. I can't hear her because her back is to me and she's speaking softly. She talks to Manning, then to Trina, and then to Ms. Randolph. They all nod, the social worker pats her arm, and she hastens toward the porch.

Weird. She didn't talk very long. I chew at my lip. Maybe they plan to meet with her later about her daughter.

Trina peers at the house and then at the garage, hands clasped. I'm relieved to see how anxious she is to reunite with her son. She looks a lot like him, although her hair is a darker shade of red than Zachary's.

He'll be so happy to see her. But will they let her take him home with her, or will he have to go to foster care? I don't have any idea of her history. If she has a drug problem, who knows what a judge will decide.

From my bedroom at the head of the stairs, I can hear Olivia's voice through the open door. She must be on the landing between the two sets of stairs. She doesn't sound happy. "He's down there."

I assume they made her get the keys to the basement rooms on their way through the house.

"Please lead the way." Forbes is pleasant enough, despite the hint of irritation in her voice. Olivia being Olivia, has probably dragged her heels all the way.

Smiling, I sit back on the bed, resting on my own heels. I can't wait to watch Zachary's reunion with his mother. "Almost there, Zachary," I whisper. "You'll see your mama soon."

I hear a knock and whip around, heart pounding and pain stealing my breath. Is it Olivia? She won't appreciate me spying on her. But Candice is the one who peeks in from the hallway. Tristen is asleep on her shoulder. She whispers, "I was afraid I might wake you."

I motion for her to come in.

"I wondered if you knew sheriff's deputies are out front." She sits across from me on Marcela's bed. "You look hot, Cassandra. Your cheeks are red."

"This nightgown is really warm." Normally, I'd be appalled to be in pervert view without my robe, but at the moment, I'm too hot to care.

She sighs. "Flannel in summer is hard, even with air-conditioning."

I settle onto my bed, one ear tuned to what's happening outside. "I've been watching."

"What do you think—?"

Beneath my breath, I whisper, "Camera," and flick my chin toward it.

"Uh-huh." She nods like she knows exactly what I mean, which is too bad. Twenty-four-seven surveillance should not be the norm in an American household. Or any household.

I smile and lean to the side to study Tristen's face. "He's adorable." Scratching my cheek, I murmur, "I saw you out there."

"I wanted them to know Zachary is a nice boy, not bad, like Olivia says."

"Good for you. They need to hear the truth. Did you mention Mylea?"

"I thought of it, but…"

"But what?" I can't imagine why she would pass up a rare chance to talk with law enforcement *and* CPS.

She whispers, "What if it's not God's will?"

"Are you kidding me? God gave you your little girl, not—"

"Shh." She aims a side glance at the camera.

"This is your chance," I hiss. "Sheriff's deputies and Child Protective Services are right outside the door."

She doesn't respond.

Hearing a commotion downstairs, I turn my head to listen. Zachary's cries rise above the sound of shuffling feet. "I want my mama, I want my—"

"Yeah, buddy, I know." Hansen's voice. "You'll see your mom soon." Zachary must have shied away from the social worker. After what he's been through, he may never trust women again.

"Is this an exit?" Forbes asks.

"Yes. To the garage." Olivia's words are clipped and toneless. "Walk out through here, and I'll go to my meeting. Late."

"Is Mr. Pritchard at his place of employment today?" Forbes asks.

"No. He's painting a house."

"Where is the house located?"

"In town. Why do you want to know?"

"What's the address?"

"I have no idea."

For a long moment, all I hear is Zachary crying for his mother. Is this a standoff? Olivia finally says, "Across from Cooper Park."

"I'd like to take this child to his mom." Hansen is speaking.

"Right," Forbes says. "Then let dispatch know Mr. Pritchard's location."

"I don't understand," Olivia says. "Why—?"

"Mrs. Pritchard…" Forbes's voice. "Let's step outside to join the others."

"I have a meeting to attend."

No response. The door opens and closes, and Zachary's sobs fade.

I maneuver onto my knees and reach for the windowsill. "We can watch Zachary reunite with his mother."

Candice lays her baby on Marcela's bed and joins me at the window. She smells like baby powder.

I open the slats a little farther.

"They can see us," she murmurs.

"Everyone down there is too focused to—"

"Behind us, Cassandra."

I snort. "Gives 'em something interesting—"

"Zach!"

"Mama!"

Mother and son race across the driveway. The little boy leaps into his mama's arms. They hug and hug and hug, whispering into each other's ears. I swipe at my wet cheeks with my nightgown sleeve. What a sweet reunion. Well worth every blister and bruise on my feet.

Everyone, even the men, are wiping their eyes—everyone, that is, except Olivia, who has distanced herself from the deputies and the social worker. Based on her red face, rigid shoulders and clenched fists, I'd guess her blood is boiling.

Forbes, who's now wearing disposable gloves, is holding a metal bucket in one hand and a ratty gray blanket in the other. She throws the blanket across her shoulder, walks over to a flower bed and dumps the bucket's contents.

Hansen lifts the radio mic attached to his shirt and speaks into it. I can't hear what he's saying.

Ms. Lloyd joins her CPS coworker, but Olivia stomps toward her vehicle, apparently still determined to join the leadership meeting—or maybe, more determined than ever.

Releasing the mic, Hansen takes two strides and steps in front of her. "We didn't give you permission to leave."

"I don't need your permission, you devil man." She swats at him, like he's an annoying insect.

Forbes sets the blanket and bucket on the pavement and joins Hansen. "You *do* need our permission. Olivia Pritchard, you are under arrest."

I look at Candice, who returns my gaze, eyes wide.

Olivia yells, "You can't arrest me! I'm a—"

We flip back to the scene below us.

"I repeat." A new element, possibly controlled anger, shades Forbes's voice. "You are under arrest."

Olivia appears to be gauging the distance to the van.

Forbes jerks her chin and Manning joins them. The three officers form a triangle around Olivia, feet wide, hands poised at their sides.

Motioning to the others, Forbes calls, "Get down behind your cars." I can't imagine the deputies will resort to violence, but they must want to protect Zachary and the women from whatever might go wrong.

The three women duck behind the bumpers. Trina holds her son to her chest. Zachary buries his face in her shoulder and clings to her like he'll never let go. I wonder if he has any idea his tormentor is about to be taken to jail.

"Get away from me," Olivia yells, arms waving. "Get out of my space, you devil people."

"Mrs. Pritchard." Forbes' firm voice breaks through the noise. "I'm sure you don't want to add assaulting officers to the child-abuse charge."

"Child abuse? I did no such thing!"

"An eight-year-old child lying on a cold concrete floor in a dark, locked, empty, basement room. No furniture. Only a solitary threadbare blanket—" She jabs a finger at the blanket and bucket. "A stinking, filthy bucket for a latrine…" Her voice rises. "No sign of food or water."

Forbes, I can tell, is incensed but trying to control her fury. "I believe it's called child abuse. And I suspect the judge will agree."

"Ha." Olivia throws her head back. "That's what you think. You can't prove a thing, and even if you did, the judge—"

"We have evidence, pictures and witnesses." Forbes peels off the gloves and stuffs them in her pants pockets. "Kidnapping may also be included in the charges. For your information, your husband is being arrested on the same charges."

"But…" Olivia deflates like a punctured tire. "You don't understand. We only did what we were told to do. God tells Ruby Jade—"

"I understand you broke the law, the reason for your arrest."

"I'm calling my attorney." Olivia folds her arms.

No doubt, all she has to do is call Ruby Jade, and a church lawyer will come running.

"You can phone your attorney from the jail."

Deputy Hansen pulls out a card and begins to read from it. "You have the right to remain silent—"

"I will *not* remain silent. I will have you fired for this infringement on my freedom as an American citizen."

"Anything you say can and will be used against you in a court of law. You have the right to have an attorney—"

"I *have* an attorney. I'll call him now."

"If you cannot afford one—"

"I can *very well* afford an attorney."

Forbes raises a hand to silence her.

I can quote the warning by heart, having heard it so often. But Olivia evidently doesn't understand this is routine, not something specially composed for her.

Finally, Hansen finishes, steps to the SUV and opens door. He motions to Olivia. "Have a seat."

She lifts her chin. "I will do no such thing."

"Do you want to be charged with resisting arrest in addition to the other charges?" Forbes asks.

"I am not resisting arrest." Hands on her waist, she insists, "I will drive myself."

"This is the last time I will ask before we cuff you."

"I need to make a phone call."

"You may call from jail."

"I can't go." Olivia's vigorous headshake reminds me of a dog shaking a stuffed toy. "I have children. I have responsibilities."

The three officers close in on her again.

Olivia looks from one to the other. I'd swear she's planning to bolt. Instead, she bursts into tears. "This is wrong," she sobs. "So very wrong. The slut belongs in jail, not me."

The officers glance at each other and shrug.

Candice whispers, "Who's she talking about?"

"Me." I give her a wry smile. "She hates me."

"Mama, are they taking her to jail?" Zachary asks.

Olivia screams, "Shut up, brat," and climbs into the SUV.

"She also hates Zachary," I whisper. "God only knows why. He's a sweet kid."

Hansen slams the door and wipes his hands on his pants, as if removing grime.

Zachary climbs off Trina's lap. The two of them stand, along with the CPS women.

"Am I a brat?" Zachary asks. "All the time, she calls me a brat."

"Don't listen to her." Trina pulls her son close. "You're a good boy, a very good boy. She's a bad lady who's going to jail 'cause she did terrible things to you. I wish I hadn't let her take you away from me."

"I'm thirsty, Mama."

"Oh, of course you are. I'm so sorry. I have a water bottle in the car. I'll get it for you."

Manning says, "I'll get it."

I can hear Olivia's muffled cries and see her scrabbling at the door panel. Reality is hitting home. If she were anyone else, I might empathize with her predicament. I've sat where she's seated. But she deserves to suffer consequences for her callous abuse, whether or not she admits what she did was wrong.

You knew better, lady. I'd love to say those words to her face.

Candice nudges me. "Should we call the office to tell Leadership what happened?"

"Huh-uh." I shake my head. "Olivia has to be the one to break the news. She needs to feel the full weight of her crime. Believe me, I speak from experience."

CHAPTER THREE

I watch Hansen and Forbes slide into the SUV's front seat. Zachary's rescue and Olivia's arrest are worthy of trumpet fanfare and fireworks, but all I can do is cheer inwardly. Maybe when she's sentenced, I'll be able to celebrate openly.

During the brief time the deputies' doors are open, Olivia's loud harangue spills out, spewing insults and swear words into the quiet morning. I snicker. If only our fearsome leader could hear her protégé now. The SUV swings a wide U-turn, spurts up the long driveway and surges onto the road. I bet Deputy Forbes exceeds the speed limit all the way to the detention center.

The women come out from behind the vehicles. Trina is holding Zachary's hand. Deputy Manning joins them, unscrews the water bottle lid and hands it to Zachary. The parched child drinks and drinks—and drinks.

"Whoa, buddy," Manning says. "Easy does it. I have more in the car."

Zachary lowers the bottle and draws in a long breath before he takes another drink.

Clipboard in hand, Ms. Lloyd says, "As discussed earlier, supervision and protection are under our jurisdiction." She's a tall woman with short hair and glasses. "We're allowing you temporary, conditional custody, Ms. Russell. Your son may reside with you, but you may not live on Faithful Followers of the Way property or with church members."

"My brother and his wife live in town," Trina says. "They have two bedrooms waiting, one for Zachary and one for me. They've never been FFOW members."

"FFOW?"

"That's what we call Faithful Followers of the Way."

"I see." She makes a note. "Is this the couple your son lived with during your incarceration?"

"Are we going to Aunt Shawna and Uncle Dale's house?" Zachary looks excited.

"Yes." Trina smiles. "Yes, to both questions."

"I miss them so much." Zachary hugs her waist. "They were nice to me, not mean like…"

Ms. Lloyd peers down at him. "Mean like who?"

He lowers his head.

"It's okay. You don't have to tell me." She points her pen at Trina. "Brother's address the same?"

Trina nods.

"I'll call them to let them know to expect a visit from me this afternoon." She slips a paper from the clipboard and hands it to Trina. "This is a copy of what you signed earlier."

"Thank you."

"You must vacate your dormitory residence within—"

"We'll stop by the women's dorm next," Deputy Manning says. His voice rings with authority. "I'll take a couple minutes to load Trina's things in my car and drive directly to her brother's house."

Trina glances at him. "You have time?"

"Sure." He smiles at her. "Glad to help however I can."

Good for Deputy Manning. He's probably dead tired after working all night, but he's going the extra mile for Trina and Zachary.

"Men aren't allowed in the dorm," she says. "They might—"

He shrugs. "This uniform opens a lot of doors."

"If you run into problems," the specialist says, "call me. The housing requirement must be met."

She turns to Trina. "Your brother's home was previously approved but is only temporary approved at this point until we make our inspection. Also, Zachary is allowed a week to adjust to this change of circumstances." Flipping a page on her clipboard, she continues. "During that time, you must make arrangements for him to attend a different elementary school. He must not return to the Triumphant Way Elementary school or to the Faithful Followers of the Way church or property or play with church members' children."

Her voice rises. "And he must never, *never* be subjected to a cleanse, as I believe the shouting and beatings are termed—or spanked. Is that clear?"

Zachary buries his face in his mother's side. The woman's words must have triggered traumatic memories. I wonder if his mother has any idea what happened to him at the school. I feel for him, but I'm so happy he's going home with her to an aunt and uncle he obviously adores.

"Yes." Trina puts her hand on her son's shoulder. "I agree completely and will comply."

"Even if you don't agree with something we ask of you, you *must* comply. Do you understand?"

"Yes."

"As Zachary's guardian…" The woman's voice is firm. "You *will* attend parenting classes sponsored by the department."

Manning lifts a finger. "May I attend with Trina?"

"In what capacity?"

"As her fiancé."

"By all means." She makes a notation. "Good for the family."

Zachary stares up at him. "Are you a daddy?"

"No, but I hope to become a daddy soon."

"Cool." Zachary grins.

Candice smiles.

I give the deputy a discrete thumbs-up. *You're an okay guy, Lawrence Manning.*

The case worker motions to Trina. "Both you and Zachary will receive counseling per our department requirements. Understood?"

Trina nods.

"Any questions?"

"What about Zach's clothes and toys?" Trina asks. "I sent everything he had with him to the Pritchards' house."

Huh? I don't remember seeing him with a toy. In fact, I don't remember any of the children playing with toys.

Zachary seems surprised by the request, as if he'd forgotten he once had toys.

"We'll send someone over to retrieve them." She glances at the house and jots another note. "Any other questions?"

"No, not right now."

"I gave you my card. Please feel free to call any time day or night."

"Thank you so much for all you've done." Trina rubs Zachary's curly red hair. "To be reunited with my son so suddenly is mindboggling." She beams. "I'm about to bubble over with joy."

"Looks like Zach boy is a happy camper too," Manning says.

The other CPS woman smiles. "We're always pleased when we have happy endings." She peers at Manning's vehicle. "Do you have a booster seat? State law requires—"

"Yes, ma'am. In the backseat."

I whisper to Candice. "Olivia's van doesn't have booster seats."

"She says they're a nuisance."

"Maybe after this experience, she'll no longer believe she's above the law."

Candice's expression says what we're both thinking. *That'll be the day.* Still, I hope she doesn't go blabbing my rebel comments to Leadership.

The specialist promises to see them later, and the two women get in their car. Manning opens his car's backdoor, helps Zachary onto the booster seat and assists him with the seatbelt. Trina sits in the backseat beside her son.

Following the CPS car off the property, Manning drives my little friend away from the Pritchards' house of horrors. Unlike me, Zachary will never return. I'm excited for him and more than a little envious.

"Amazing," I whisper. "We saw a miracle I'd have trouble believing, if I hadn't seen it with my own eyes."

Candice nods.

"The best part was seeing Zachary with his mom. They were both so happy." I smile at the memory.

"It was sweet." Her voice is subdued.

I turn to her. "You can have the same—"

As if on cue, Tristen begins to fuss. She reaches for him, whispering, "Careful, Cassandra."

I glance at the camera. "Think about it."

"I'll talk to Scott."

"I'll be glad to help."

"What can you do?" She gives me the zombie stare.

"I don't know, but I'm willing to find out." I consider offering her Manning's phone number. However, I'm not sure she's ready. Also, handing out his information so soon after my disappearance last night might not be a wise move on my part.

Baby on her shoulder, she murmurs, "Better go change his diaper," and walks out the door.

I gaze at the empty doorway. How can she see Zachary's longing for his mother and not think of Mylea? The little girl must feel abandoned by her parents and miss them terribly. Has Candice turned off her love for her daughter? Is she pouring all her affection into Tristen?

Child Protective Services would help her, like they did Trina and Zachary. But she bypassed a perfect opportunity to get their attention. Candice once told me her parents joined FFOW when she was ten. Could be she's so entrenched she can't imagine a different life, a better life, even for her children.

I yawn, amazed by how sleepy I am, and slide under the covers. I should be enjoying Olivia's absence, but I can barely keep my eyes open. Besides, without use of my feet, what can I do other than sleep?

"Cassandra..."

Someone is calling my name, but I can't answer. I'm too drowsy.

"Cassandra, wake up."

Annoyed I'm responding to my non-name, I open my eyelids just far enough to see who it is.

Marcela is kneeling beside my bed.

I should have recognized her voice—and the smell of her green-apple shampoo. I must have been sleeping extra hard.

"Did you hear?" she asks, her voice low but urgent.

"Hear what?" My voice is froggy and I'm so hot I throw off the covers. The perverts have already gotten a good look at my nightgown.

"Olivia and Owen were arrested." She's breathing hard. "I saw sheriff's deputies take Owen away. You'll never guess why." Before I can respond, she says, "CPS found Zachary, and they accused the Pritchards of kidnapping him and abusing him. He was downstairs in timeout, that's all. Isn't it awful they put Olivia and Owen in jail?"

I frown. "The Pritchards imprisoned a small child. That's what's awful." I roll onto my side. "I watched Olivia's arrest."

"Oh…" Her mouth drops.

"Zachary's mom was here with two CPS women who gave her conditional custody of her son and…" I drop my voice. "And ordered her to keep him away from the school and the church."

"Misuse of government power, for sure." She scowls. "Trina and Zachary have rights. They have freedom of religion." Eyebrows low, she peers at me. "How did they know about Zachary?"

"The deputies didn't say, but they came with a search warrant." I yawn and remind myself to tell the story as if I don't know the background. "At first, Olivia wouldn't tell them where Zachary was, but eventually she did."

I brush hair from my face. "I can't believe he was in the basement all those hours, poor baby. After they brought him out of the house, he ran straight into his mother's arms. They hugged and hugged. Made me cry to see how happy they were."

"Is Trina leaving FFOW?" Marcela seems more concerned about Trina's FFOW attendance than Zachary's wellbeing.

"You know her?"

"She works nights at the factory. Sometimes, we pass each other during shift changes."

"You work at the same place as Zachary's mom, but you didn't tell me?" I can't believe she kept the information from me.

She gives the camera a side glance and whispers, "What good would it have done?"

"I would have—"

Marcela interrupts me. "Is she abandoning the program?"

I blow out an exasperated breath. I can't wait to have a normal conversation again. "The case worker said she has to move off the FFOW campus."

"Oh…" She frowns. "Leadership won't like it."

"So?"

"Cassandra." She gives me the "stop being a bad girl" stare, but I refuse to retract my response.

"Well, anyway," she continues, "they arrested Owen right in front of us. He and Olivia might go to prison—"

"Please help me to the bathroom." I push upright. "My feet hurt. I need to change the dressing and add more ointment."

She gives me a strange look before she helps me out of the bed and onto my sore feet. I should probably crawl, but I have to start standing sometime.

The moment we're in the bathroom, I turn on the tub water.

She kneels beside me, and I murmur into her hair. "The Pritchards had no legal authority to take Zachary from his mother. In addition, they kept a child in solitary confinement. The officers said he was in a dark room with only a blanket and a stinking bucket to pee in. No food, no water. It's called child abuse, Marcela."

"Ruby Jade must have told them to do it."

"If I told you to steal a car and you did it, which one of us would go to jail because she broke the law?" I adjust the water temperature before I plug the bathtub drain.

"Well, I guess I would. But Owen is such a nice man. I hate for him to suffer when—"

"What about Zachary's suffering?"

"Well…"

"And the fact all Owen had to do was say 'no.'"

"We can't ever say 'no' around here, or…"

"Or what?" I unwind the gauze from my feet.

Marcela sets the trashcan by the bathtub. "He would have been sent to the men's dorm, for months, or maybe even a year."

I drop the gauze into the garbage can. "And because he agreed to break the law and abuse a little boy, he may be sent to prison for five, ten, maybe twenty years." I stop the water and lower my feet into it. Like before, the sting takes my breath away.

"Ruby Jade says God's law is above man's law."

"Marcela..." I twist so we're eye-to-eye. "Stop being a parrot and think for yourself. Other than the fact Ruby Jade is *not* God and her law is *not* God's law, a little boy's heart was shattered when he was stolen from his mother. He suffered Olivia's mistreatment *every day* he was here, culminating in illegal imprisonment. In case you forgot, abuse breaks God's law *and* man's law."

"But it was to teach him a lesson."

"And what was the lesson?" I clutch the edge of the tub.

"He has to submit to cleanses, or he'll go to hell."

"Besides the fact I know you don't really believe what you just said, do you really want to be the kind of teacher who allows her students to beat on each other? What if Zachary was your brother or sister—or your child?"

Her gaze flicks from one side of the room to the other. "I, I guess... I mean, if they let go of Jesus..."

"Marcela..." I give her the same "stop being a bad girl" stare she gave me, except I'm thinking, *quit acting like a puppet.*

She turns away.

I'm as frustrated with her as I was with Candice and tempted to shake her until common sense rattles loose from whatever mental shelf she relegated it to. I know she knows better. All I can think is seeing her household guardian arrested unsettled her and she's toeing the party line as some form of self-protection.

Someone knocks on the bedroom door, and she gets up to answer it. *Good timing, Lord. I was about to throttle my roommate.*

"Hi, Candice," Marcela says.

"Cassandra's boss is downstairs. He wants to talk with her. She needs to come to the living room."

"I'll tell her."

Whoops. I never once thought of letting Sebastian know I'm bedridden. But it's Saturday. Am I supposed to work weekends?

Marcela returns to the bathroom. "Did you hear her?"

"Yes. I should have called Sebastian. Can I borrow your robe?" Mine is hanging from the shower rod and still damp.

"Sure." She hurries to the closet, brings the robe and helps me slip it over my gown.

"I don't have time for gauze," I whisper. "I'll have to crawl to the bed. Can you go down and lead him up here?"

"But men aren't allowed—"

"He can stand at the door."

"Your feet, they're…" She grimaces.

"Sebastian told me he fought in the Vietnam War. He's seen worse."

Although I'm expecting him, when my boss appears at the doorway, I'm suddenly shy. Seeing him outside of work feels awkward and strange. I say, "Hi, sorry you had to wait," and adjust the pillow behind my back.

He stops, hat in hand. "Cat True, what are you doing in bed on a nice day like this?"

I'm trying to think how to warn him about the camera and how to ask him not to use my nickname, when he exclaims, "What in tarnation?" His eyes focused on my feet, he steps to the end of my bed. "Have you seen a doctor?"

"No." I glance at the camera. "But I soaked my feet and put hydrogen peroxide and antibiotic cream on them."

"I'm taking you to the emergency room."

"I can't afford—"

He moves to the side of the bed and slips his hands beneath me. Before I can object, he lifts me, pillow and all, declaring, "I'm your boss, and I say you need to see a doctor. You can't work with feet like cube steak. You're hot and feverish, which means they're sure as heck infected. The Pritchards should have seen to it you received proper medical care."

"The Pritchards are—"

"Yeah, I heard." He looks directly at the camera. "Anyone with questions about this woman's medical care can talk with me. You have my number."

We pass wide-eyed residents on our way out the living room door. They're seated around the big room, awkward expressions on their faces, like they don't know what to do with themselves on a Saturday afternoon. With no meeting to attend, no new project to tackle, and no Pritchards to tell them what to do, they're as lost as newborn puppies with their eyelids sealed shut.

Yet, a hint of peace has slipped into the room, as if a dark cloud has lifted. Even Olivia and Owen's children seem happier. I'm tempted to shout, "Now's your chance, people. Pack your things and leave while you can."

Sebastian has me twist the doorknob to open the door, and then he whisks me out onto the front porch. I don't even have a chance to say goodbye, not that my housemates care if I go or stay. He settles me in his ancient pickup, and with gentle, careful motions, places the pillow beneath my feet. Closing the door, he goes to the other side to slide behind the wheel. His truck smells manly, like old leather mixed with bare metal.

He turns the key and the motor sputters to life. After a U-turn, we traverse the long driveway to the street. Over the motor's rumble, I tell him, "I'm sorry I missed work. I should have called you. But I'm pretty sure I don't have your number."

"It's Saturday, Cat. You didn't miss work."

"Then how did you know about me?"

"Logan and Corban mowed today. I went over to work on the rose garden and run interference in case Vance hassled them—no love lost between him and those two."

"They already heard about my feet?"

"Rumors spread amongst the Followers like measles in a one-room schoolhouse. They'd heard you disappeared and then came back. They didn't mention your feet, but I got a feeling in my gut I'd better check on you."

I gaze out the window. We're driving the same road I jogged last night. I'll remember those few moments of freedom for a long time.

"What happened to your feet?"

"I ran on a road. Barefoot."

"Were you running away?"

"Yes and no." I think of telling him how I discovered Zachary, how I ran for help, how the deputy found me—how the Pritchards were arrested. But the deputy and I made a pact, and I know Sebastian tries to stay out of Ruby Jade's business, so I tell him the same story I told Olivia.

I finish my story about the time we pull under the covered entrance to the hospital emergency room. He shoves the gearshift into park, switches off the noisy engine and gives me a "yeah, sure" look. "I have a sneaky feeling," he says, "there's more to the story."

"Let's just say…" I try to suppress a grin but fail. "As I see it, Ruby Jade set a trap for me, but it caught the Pritchards instead."

"Way to go, Cat True." He high-fives me. "Tickles my gizzard when a Follower pulls one over on Leadership. From what I heard back at the house, Ruby Jade is spittin' mad, furious as a cornered cougar. Be warned, she'll growl and swing her purple claws at you, but don't let her scare you into admitting something you'll regret later."

"Thanks for the warning."

He lifts a finger. "I know for a fact she tried to post bail for the Pritchards, but Judge Snow is out of town and the other judge isn't answering his phone. His voice message says he won't be available until Monday afternoon. Looks like a couple of Followers will be spending Easter Sunday in jail."

"How ironic." I unbuckle my seatbelt. "They don't celebrate the holiday, so it's not a huge deal to miss it. But I bet they're upset about missing the special concert tonight."

"Ah, yes." He snorts. "The not-so-special bruhaha that keeps the locals hooting."

I give him a side glance. "I take it they're not impressed."

"One old timer hit the nail on the head when he said, 'Any cowboy can carry a tune. The trouble comes when he tries to unload it.'"

I laugh. "Thanks, Sebastian. I needed a good laugh."

Chapter Four

Two hours later, a male nurse named Drew wheels me out of the hospital. Despite his attempts to distract me with dog stories—he trains dogs on the side—I'm shaky and exhausted. I'm also grateful the ordeal is over, and I can return to my bed.

Drew chuckles at the bumper sticker plastered to the tailgate of Sebastian's faded-green pickup. *Is there life after death? Touch my truck and find out.*

I laugh, too, mostly because my boss is such a softy. He wouldn't hurt a soul.

Sebastian opens the creaky door for us. "Gotta discourage the riffraff. This old gal doesn't look good in fingerprints."

"Can't argue with that." Drew helps me into the pickup. "Remember, drink lots of fluids and get plenty of rest. Stay off your feet and be sure to see Dr. Vasquez at her office on Monday."

He closes the door and leans in the open window. "Better get some food in your system. Your stomach growled the whole time we were working on you." He smiles, salutes Sebastian and returns to the hospital.

The sunshine-warmed cab and the hot seat feel like heaven after the cold hospital. I drop my head against the back window and breathe in the warm leather smell, not certain I have the energy to fasten my seatbelt.

Sebastian starts the engine. "You look a bit peaked. Rough going in there?"

I blow out a long breath. "I never want to experience that level of pain again." Somehow, I manage to muster the strength to click the seatbelt ends together. "My mother would be proud. The soles of my feet are now the cleanest they've been since I was born, if there's any skin left."

He grimaces. "What's this about fluids and food?"

"I've had one glass of orange juice and two glasses of water today. They said I was dehydrated. In addition to the IV drip, I was told I need to eat a meal and drink lots of water."

"Will you get food and water at the Pritchards' house?"

"Probably not. Olivia wouldn't let Marcela take breakfast up to me this morning."

"Olivia is gone."

"But not for long, I fear. She'll return, and then…"

"And then all hell will break loose." A fierce expression crosses his face. "We've gotta take those church bullies by their horns and prepare to be tossed around."

"I didn't mean to pull you into this, Sebastian. Ruby Jade is your boss, and I know you don't want to get involved in her stuff. The fact is, none of the leaders like me, including Olivia. I've ticked them all off, one way or another."

"We'll worry about R.J. and her cronies later. Right now, we're gonna fill your belly."

He exits the hospital parking lot and drives onto a busy street. A warm wind blows in the open windows. I close my eyes and lean my head back. All too soon, he slows and turns into a drive-in restaurant. "After we eat, we'll find somewhere to fill your prescription."

I glance at the papers in my hand. I must still be traumatized because I'm gripping the hospital's paperwork almost as hard as I clutched the bedsheet in the emergency room. "The doctor gave me two prescriptions."

Separating the crumpled prescriptions from the other papers, I reread the instructions. Dr. Vasquez explained how to use the salve and how often to take the antibiotic, but I was too out of it to grasp much of what she said.

Sebastian bypasses the drive-through speaker and takes us directly to the pickup window. A teenage girl leaning on her forearms gives us a questioning look.

Sebastian rests an elbow on the truck's window frame. "You still have that prime-rib special going on?"

"Uh-huh." She nods. "Today is the last day."

He turns to me. "You like prime rib?"

"Yes, but—"

"We'll take two prime-rib meals and two large waters."

Our wait is surprisingly short. Sebastian pays, telling the girl to keep the change. By her shocked expression, I gather the tip is generous. I'm not the only recipient of my boss's kindness.

He hands both take-out containers to me and pulls forward. I peek inside the top one. It has a nice-size steak, au jus, a large baked potato, green beans and a garden salad. "This smells wonderful, Sebastian. I'm surprised a drive-in has prime rib."

"They only offer the meal deal now and then. I check their sign most every time I come to town." He parks under a tree. "If you don't mind, I'll cut the meat on the tailgate. It's tender. However, slicing Styrofoam on our laps may make a mess worse'n a cow with diarrhea."

"Ew." I groan. "Not an appetizing analogy."

He chuckles and exits the truck with our meals plus a plastic knife and fork, which came with the food. "This wannabe knife should work," he says. "If not, I'll use my pocketknife."

"You can skip my steak." I've seen him clean his fingernails with his knife. "I don't need any more dirt in my system."

"Ah, but that's what those pills are for." He smirks and walks to the rear of the truck.

All I can do is shake my head.

When he returns with our food, which tastes as good as it smells, I thank him for feeding me and for cutting my meat. I don't ask which knife he used. "I also appreciate the fact you didn't take me to a sit-down restaurant in my nightgown. They might have kicked me out."

He glances at me. "Oh, yeah. I forgot. I was thinking about your feet, not your clothes." He stabs a piece of meat with his fork. "You up to workin' Monday?"

"I'd like to, but the doctor said to stay off my feet."

"You need to get out of the house."

"You're telling me. If it hadn't been for the excitement this morning, I'd be going stir-crazy already. I have absolutely nothing to do but sleep. No books to read, no movies, no television, no music..."

"I'll pick you up. You can sit on your backside and finish planting the annuals."

My immediate thought is Vance. "Will you be there?"

"Most of the time." He eyes me. "There a problem?"

I look away. I hate for him to have to babysit me because I'm afraid to tangle with Ruby Jade's jerk son.

"Cat..."

I turn to him. "The other day when you were away, Ruby Jade laid into me as she was leaving, and then Vance tried to get me to go to the basement with him." I don't repeat the nasty names they called me or tell him his boss wants to bleach my skin.

Sebastian pounds the steering wheel. "Lowdown slimy snakes."

"I feel a little more vulnerable now with my feet like this. Actually, a lot more vulnerable. But I don't want to make a big deal about it, for you to have to arrange your life around me."

"I have more rosebushes to plant, so I'll be around. And I'll feed you three squares every day."

"Just because you're my boss, you don't have to—"

"Just because I'm your boss, I've got to make sure you and the others I oversee are treated well."

"You spoil us."

Sebastian leaves me in his pickup and knocks on the Pritchards' front door. No one answers, so he tries the knob. The door is locked. When he returns to the truck, I tell him the code and he punches it into the keypad beside the garage door. The door clatters upward.

He drives inside, cuts the motor and glances around the mostly empty garage. "Where's everyone? Off on another work project?"

"Or…" I look at my watch. "At church, getting ready for the concert."

He gets out and opens my door. "You sorry you'll miss the big shebang?"

"Not at all. Like the neighbor you mentioned, the loud singing and lack of harmony drive me nuts."

Sebastian laughs. "You saying they sound like a pack of wolves howlin' at the moon?"

"Exactly."

He props the kitchen door then carries me up the stairs and sets me on my bed. Before he leaves, he grabs my water glass. "I'll fill this for you."

While he's getting the water in the bathroom, I lean my pillow on the wall, arrange my nightgown and Marcela's robe over my legs and lean back. I can't believe I'm still wearing bedclothes. But getting dressed would take a lot of energy, and I'm ready for another nap.

Sebastian eases between the twin beds, hands me the water and sits on Marcela's bed. "Note on the mirror says to text your roommate," he murmurs. "They'll send someone with a wheelchair."

I groan. "I'm so tired…"

"Idiots." He grunts. "You were at the ER, not a spa." Louder, he says, "I understood the doctor to say she wants you to stay in bed until you see her on Monday." He stands. "I'll be glad to drive you to the appointment. Anything else I can get for you?"

"Nothing comes to mind. Thanks for everything you've done for me today."

"See you bright and early Monday morning." He aims a finger at me. "Take care and stay in bed, or I'll dock your pay." He grins and walks out, closing the door behind him.

I awaken to the sound of a commotion below. Ah, the troops have returned, for better or for worse. The room is bathed in a twilight haze.

I push upright and switch on the lamp so Marcela will know I'm awake. She'll want to tell me all about the service. I'll have to ask if Ruby Jade ranted about the Pritchards' arrest or my rebellion. Missing a special concert is supposedly as socially unacceptable as being late for an audience with the pope.

Marcela opens the door and peeks in. "Cassandra, you're awake." She steps into the room. "Did you get my message?"

What happened to, *Hi, how are you? Feeling better? What did the doctor say?*

"Sorry." I shrug. "My phone is off. Not sure when I last checked it."

She glances at the camera. "I mean the written note I left in the bathroom."

"Sebastian plopped me down on this bed, and I've been sleeping ever since. Woke up when I heard everyone come in the door."

"That's too bad." She frowns. "Scott and Candice offered to bring a wheelchair to take you to church. You missed the special concert."

"Oh, right. It was tonight. But I couldn't have gone, even with a wheelchair. The doctor told me to stay in bed."

"Yes, but—"

"Did you forget I spent the afternoon in the emergency room?"

"No, but—"

"But what?"

"Ruby Jade wanted you at church."

"I'm fairly certain she's aware of my injuries. If she needs more info, she can talk to Sebastian, or to me." God forbid I ever have to speak to the woman again. "How was the concert?"

Marcela, who seems hesitant to drop the subject of my absence, sits on her bed. "I think it went okay. We had a few visitors." She pauses. "Somehow, the atmosphere seemed more subdued than usual."

"Because of the Pritchards' arrest?"

"I guess. Hard to say."

"From my own experience with concerts, you can't always put your finger on what was different about an event." So much more I'd like to say. No doubt the arrests unnerved the Faithful, but they should have applauded the Pritchards' incarceration.

Does the news make Inez Curtis nervous? She was a partner in the crime, maybe the instigator. Could be, she was arrested, too, or will be soon.

"Tomorrow, then." She gives me a bright smile. "Scott loaded a wheelchair in the van, so you can go to Sunday school and church with us."

Sleep is a long time in coming. Back when Eric's life was ebbing away, I'd get up to read or watch television or write in my journal. Sometimes I'd pluck a quiet melody on my guitar. I can't do any of those things here—or even celebrate Olivia's absence with a nip of vanilla extract. Could my life be any crazier?

Yes, it could be. Marcela's forced separation from her husband and family is beyond crazy. It's horrendous. Logan's fiancée being stolen from him is as savage as marauding barbarians kidnapping girls to be their brides. Corban not being allowed to attend his fiancée's funeral, and Mylea and Zachary being torn from their parents are cruel, evil acts. Acts done in the name of Ruby Jade's warped version of God.

Still, I feel as though my life is spiraling out of control. If I stay, this lifestyle, this environment, these off-kilter people and their senseless capitulation to Leadership dominance will suck my soul dry. I've been there with Eric's death, and I don't want to walk through an emotional desert another time.

The old questions resurface. To stay or not to stay. To play the FFOW game as long as I have to and then move on. Or forget the game and move on. One thing's for sure, I'm not going to church tomorrow. I will protect my feet, whatever it takes.

The next morning, I crawl to the bathroom and follow my usual routine the best I can. I'm making my way to the bed, when Marcela says, "You need to get dressed. We'll be leaving for church soon."

"I'm not going."

"We'll help you."

"I like having feet, and I'll follow doctor's order to preserve them."

"But Ruby Jade wants you there." She's pleading with her eyes.

In other words, you'll be blamed if I don't show. "Please give my regrets to Ruby Jade, but I have to follow the doctor's directives. I can't be a good Follower without healthy feet." I nearly gag on my smarmy words. "The sooner I heal, the sooner I'll be back to work."

Marcela rushes out of the room, and I settle on my bed, prepared for a long boring day alone with nothing to do. Within minutes, she returns with a food tray and sets it on my lap.

"Oh, wow, I, uh…" I'm so astounded I'm almost speechless. Finally, I say, "Thank you, Marcela," and pick up the fork.

"As soon as you eat," she says, "I'll help you get dressed. Then Scott will carry you to the van."

I give her my most gracious smile. "As I mentioned earlier, I won't be going." Ruby Jade must be pushing hard.

"You have to. You can't miss—"

"I'm sure I'll be much better by next Sunday."

She reaches for the tray. I clutch the plate with both hands, breathing in the wonderful smell of bacon and eggs. She can have the tray, but she can't have my plate. "Thank you for breakfast, Marcela. I, uh, hope everything goes well for you today at church." *And I pray Ruby Jade doesn't do something awful to you again.*

The moment I no longer hear the van's tires on the driveway, I put my phone in the robe pocket and climb off the bed. I crawl to my dresser to gather clean underwear before I maneuver into the closet. There, stretching as far as I can reach from my lowly position, I slip a top off a hanger and pants off the rack of polyesters.

Once inside the bathroom, I close the door and lock it. Knowing the surveillance perverts are aware I'm alone makes me more cautious than usual.

Balanced on my knees, I brush my teeth and wash my face, but I sit on the floor to change the dressing on my feet. Thank God, Marcela left me lots of cheesecloth. Finally, I remove the gown and robe I've worn for way too many hours and wriggle into the clean clothes.

Getting dressed for the day seems to have taken hours—and sapped all my energy. I'm tempted to go back to bed. Instead, I dial my mom.

She answers after the second ring. "Cassie?"

"Hi, Mom." I try to sound enthused, despite my exhaustion. "I'm glad I caught you before you left for church."

"I'm lounging on the patio with an ice pack this morning."

"Oh, no! What happened?"

"You're not going to believe this." She makes a disgusted noise. "While I was gardening yesterday, a wasp bit my neck below my ear. The side of my neck and face swelled like a balloon. I look ridiculous."

"How terrible, Mom. I'm so sorry."

"Could have been worse." She sighs. "I could have been stung on both sides."

"Is Dad taking good care of you?"

"He wanted to stay home with me, but he's still teaching the junior high boys' Sunday school class, as he has for years. I told him I'd be fine without him for a couple hours, although I do hate to miss the Easter service."

She asks what time I'm going to church. I tell her I have a headache. Once again, I'm lying to my mother. No way can I tell her the truth about my bizarre weekend. She says she's sorry about my headache and that I won't be wearing her favorite sundress to church. I know she's talking about the yellow one with the huge orange and pink flowers and magenta bolero jacket.

I picture myself walking into Sunday school in the dress and sandals and almost laugh out loud. The women's eyes would pop and their mouths would drop. Inez's face would turn red, and she'd start screaming about my ridiculous outfit and all the skin I was revealing. Such a rebellious act would trigger a cleanse, for sure.

I push the FFOW thoughts away and ask about my parents' redecorating progress and what they've heard from Kip. She asks about the rehab program and my teacher's aide job and is probably frowning at my vague, evasive answers. I salve my conscience with Sebastian's promise to check into the stalled

Transformation Way rehab program. Maybe the next time I speak with my parents I can be more truthful.

The conversation is winding down when I hear a knock on the bedroom door. My heart skips a beat. I thought everyone was in church. "Hang on, Mom. Someone is knocking." I open the bathroom door and lean out. "Who is it?"

"Seb," comes the muffled reply. "Came to see how you're doing."

"Give me a minute."

"Mom..." I speak into the phone again. "I need to go. I'm so glad we got to talk, and I hope the swelling goes down soon."

"Thank you, dear. It's a good excuse to be lazy."

"Yeah, sure, Mom. You don't have a lazy cell in your body. I love you. Give my love to Dad."

"I love you, too, and I'll pray your headache subsides. Bye."

"Bye." Maybe God will apply her prayer for my head to my feet. But why would he, when I lied about the headache?

Pushing my bedclothes to the side, I crawl into the bedroom and stop outside the bathroom door. My back against the wall, I call, "Come in."

Sebastian opens the door, sticks his head in and scans the room. "There you are. I thought maybe you'd skipped town."

"Not much skipping I can do with these feet. How did...?"

Out of camera range, he mimics punching a code then asks, "How're you doing?"

"Better, I think. Just got dressed."

"You look better. Sleep good?"

"Yes."

"How about food."

"Marcela brought me breakfast."

"Good for her."

I don't mention it was a bribe, of sorts. Or that she tried to take it from me.

He comes into the room, a paper bag in one hand and a to-go cup in the other. "Hope you like bagels and cream cheese."

"I love bagels and cream cheese."

"Good." He lifts the cup. "In case you're not a coffee drinker, I brought you green tea."

"Perfect. I drink both, but tea sounds good with a bagel."

"Want me to help you to your bed?"

"I'll sit here for now. Should be easier to eat on a flat surface than in bed."

Balanced on his heels, he crouches beside me, his back to the camera. "Threw in a couple honey and jam packets plus napkins and a plastic spoon and knife." He's dressed in his usual attire—jeans, plaid western shirt, boots and cowboy hat. But the boots are polished, and the jeans and shirt look new. His spicy aftershave awakens my sleep-dulled senses.

Lowering his voice, he says, "Caught sight of the van mentioned the other day." He waits until I catch his drift. "Headed this direction."

"Why on a Sunday?" I murmur. "Everyone's at church."

He quirks an eyebrow. "Solitary target?"

I think of my conversation with Mom, but I don't remember either of us saying anything that might trigger Ruby Jade's temper. Will anyone notice I lied to my mother? Or care? "When?" I ask.

"Just now."

"Thanks." Unless the snoops were around earlier, they missed my phone conversation.

"I'm off to the races." He gets to his feet, knees popping. "Need to head to town for church."

"Thanks for the bagel and tea." I lift the sack. "This is an amazing treat. I can't wait to dive in."

"Call if you need anything." He tips his hat and leaves, shutting the door behind him.

I remove the top from the cup and sip the hot tea. *Thank you, God, for giving me the world's best boss. I hate to imagine how broken and discouraged I'd be without him.*

CHAPTER FIVE

Since she returned from church, Marcela's been so quiet
I finally ask, "Everything okay?"

She moves from the closet, where she's hanging
her church clothes, to stand between me and the camera. "The,
um, you-know-who are—to use my mom's word—prickly
today."

"Uh-oh." I lower my voice. "Any mention of arrests?"

"We were told members have been attacked by the devious
devil and persecuted for Jesus."

"How about the victim?"

She shrugs.

"He's happy and safe now." I fold my arms. "That's all that
matters."

Hands on her waist, she bends toward me. "The service
started fifteen minutes late, Cassandra, because I was in a private
room, being grilled by Leadership—all three of them. They
called me a liar when I said I didn't know where you were Friday
night and didn't even know you'd left the room."

Her voice is growing louder. "All I could—"

I put my finger to my lips.

"All I could say," she whispers, "was 'look at the tapes.'" She narrows her eyes. "I don't know *what* you were doing out of bed in the middle of the night, but it got *me* into hot water."

"They should've talked to me, not—"

"They would have talked to you, not me, if you hadn't skipped church." For a long moment, she scowls at me. "I'm going to go help with lunch." Shoulders stiff, she strides out of the room.

Saddened by this breach in our friendship, I sigh. I'm sorry Leadership pressure has made her doubt my story, just like they doubt hers. Then again, my story is a crazy one. But as long as Deputy Manning and Zachary don't rat on me, I'll stick with it.

I'm surprised but grateful when she brings me a tuna sandwich and chips plus a fresh glass of water. "Thank you, Marcela," I whisper. "I feel awful you had to take the heat for me. You've been through enough—"

She interrupts with, "Then go tonight."

Before I can tell her I can't, she exits the room.

When I'm finished, I set the tray aside and crawl into the bathroom to call my brother. Kip actually answers his phone. I'm grateful he takes a hint from my reticence and doesn't ask about the issues I mentioned earlier. Our call is short, maybe not within the fifteen-minute limit, but short compared to our norm.

I doze off and on all afternoon. My body seems to be compensating for days of sleep deprivation as well as my midnight run. Now and again, I remember this is Easter Sunday and breathe a prayer of thanks to God for sending Jesus. I thank him for accepting his Son's sacrifice on my behalf—as well as for all mankind. All I had to do in return was ask him to be my Savior.

I praise him for raising Jesus from the dead to share his resurrection power and his Holy Spirit with me. I'm not powerless and life isn't hopeless, even when my circumstances might suggest otherwise. It's what Easter is all about.

Candice delivers my supper tray. When she comes to retrieve it, she says, "We'll be leaving soon for evening church. Scott and I will be happy to help you down the stairs and into the van."

"Please thank him for me, but my answer hasn't changed. I'll continue to do what the doctor said."

"Ruby Jade says the Great Physician doesn't need human doctors."

"I've heard Leadership tell people to go to human doctors."

"Yes, but Ruby Jade—"

I finish for her. "Is not a doctor, nor is she the Great Physician."

She blinks, obviously shocked at my audacity. Yet, she makes another effort to persuade me. "We have a wheelchair for you."

"I appreciate your thoughtfulness and may use it later."

The house quiets when my housemates depart. For a change of scenery, I crawl into the hallway to call my dad. I have no idea if the black van is still in the area, but I plan to watch my words.

He answers, his voice as cheerful as always. "Hey, it's my girl."

"It's my dad," I say. "The one and only."

"Well, I should hope so." He chuckles. "Your mom and I are climbing the foothills. I trust the reception holds. Wish you were here."

"I'd love to be there." The thought of hiking a rocky trail makes me cringe, but to be with them would be wonderful.

"We saw a doe with twin fawns a couple minutes ago."

"Wow, how cool. Mom must be feeling better to be out walking."

"She says this distracts her. She's wearing her biggest garden hat and sunglasses, trying to be incognito. Truth is, she's always wanted to be a private eye."

"Edward." My mother's voice. "I'm protecting the swollen area from the sun. My skin is very tender right now."

"The good news," Dad says, "is the swelling is going down. But I'm sad I can't call her Homer Simpson any longer."

"Dad, you didn't."

"Mea culpa. But only once. Your mother has a mean backhand."

"Dad..." I roll my eyes. "On another subject, how's Grandma doing?"

"Well..." He hesitates. "I'm no doctor, but—"

The doorbell chimes above me. I jerk, and my heart hiccups.

"Did I hear a bell?" Dad asks.

"Yes, a doorbell. Uh, maybe someone will get it." Who could be here? I'm pretty sure the entire neighborhood is at church. And Sebastian, my only non-Follower acquaintance, knows the code.

The doorbell rings a second time, and loud pounding resounds from downstairs. Someone is determined to get inside. A muffled shout comes through the bedroom window. "Cas-san-dra, open the door. I know you're in there."

Vance...

"Uh, Dad, you're breaking up." Now, I've lied to both parents. On Easter, no less.

"Is this better?"

"I think so."

I crawl into the room and onto the bed to peer at the driveway. I can't see Vance, but I see his car and hear his singsong call. "Cas-san-dra, open the door. Tonight's our night." His speech is slurred. He's been drinking again.

"Cassie, are you there?" Dad asks.

At the sound of breaking glass, I hit "end" and dial 911. I'm not about to deal with Vance Longpre on my own. The dispatcher answers before the first ring ends. "Is this an emergency?"

"Yes, someone just broke into the house where I live." My voice quivers. "I heard glass shattering downstairs."

"What's your location?"

I whisper the Pritchards' address. "In the Fellowship Neighborhood outside of town."

"Bozeman?"

"Yes."

She has me repeat the address and then asks for my phone number. "Are you alone?"

"Yes."

"Please stay on the line. Deputies are on the way. What's your name?"

I tell her my real name, which seems the legal thing to do.

Vance calls my FFOW name again. He sounds closer now, like he's at the base of the stairs.

I roll off the bed, somehow managing to land on my knees.

"I heard a voice," the dispatcher says. "Where's the intruder?"

Phone at my ear, I crawl to the door and close it most of the way.

She repeats the question.

A loud thump and then another are followed by slurred swearwords.

"He's coming up the stairs."

"Are you able to move to a secure location?"

I shut the door. The latch clicks in place, making more noise than I intended. Maybe Vance is too drunk to notice. I lock the door with trembling fingers. "In my bedroom," I whisper. "Just locked the door."

"Good. The deputies will be there soon. Does he have a weapon?"

"I don't know." I turn toward the bathroom to put one more barrier between me and Vance.

"Are you acquainted with the intruder?"

"I can't see him, but he sounds like a guy named Vance Longpre."

Inside the bathroom, I'm maneuvering around to close the door when Vance shouts, "I know you're in there." He hammers the door. "Come out, or I'll kick…" His words dribble into a mumble.

"Hang on, Cassie," the dispatcher says. "The deputies are in your neighborhood. They'll be there soon."

I lock the bathroom door and sit with my back against it, shaking so hard I fear I might drop the phone. "The outside doors have keypads."

"What's the code?"

For a second, I can't remember the code, but then it comes to me.

Vance slams against the door.

My breath comes in ragged spurts. Where are the deputies? When people called the cops on me, they were there in seconds, maybe minutes, at the most. That's how it felt, anyway.

Hearing shouts and a commotion, I whisper into the phone, "I think they're here."

Vance is belligerent and loud. But it isn't long before the noise fades and the dispatcher says, "Deputy Henricks needs to speak with you. Can you open your bedroom door?"

"Give me a minute." I crawl from the bathroom to the door and unlock it. When I open it, all I see are tan-clad knees. Glancing upward, a duty belt comes in view, then a brown shirt and a badge—and a woman's chin.

Hand on her gun, she steps back, a puzzled expression on her face. "Ms. True?"

I nod. "Yes."

"I'm Officer Thornton." She kneels. "Are you injured?"

"Yes, but it happened earlier."

"Can I help you up?" She extends a hand.

"Thank you, but I can't stand right now. I'll crawl to my bed."

"Okay..." She straightens. "I'll get a statement from you after you're comfortable."

When my housemates walk in the kitchen door after the evening service, I hear a kid ask, "Is that Vance's car in the driveway?"

"Looks like it." Deanna's voice.

"I wonder what it's doing here." I think her son is the one speaking.

"Maybe he's visiting Cassandra." The voice belongs to Deanna's oldest daughter.

I grimace. What did Sebastian say about the FFOW rumor mill? Followers would have a rollicking good time with such a juicy tidbit.

"He may be Ruby Jade's son, but he shouldn't be..." A male voice. Deanna's husband, Michael. "Heidi, you check the living room. Marcela, check your bedroom."

The thump of footsteps bounding up the stairs halts outside the open door. "Cassandra..." Marcela peeks into the room. "Are you, uh, alone?"

"Of course, I'm alone." Though her question angers me, I'm still unsettled enough my voice wavers and my hands shake. I thought I was over the intrusion, but I'm not there yet. I push upward, my back on the wall.

She steps into the room. "I was afraid Vance... I mean, his car—"

A cry from below interrupts her.

"Dad, Mom—the door window, it's broken. There's dirt and glass everywhere. And a cactus. It's broken too."

Marcela waits, listening for more and then turns to me. "Did Vance..." She winces.

"No. I called the sheriff the moment I heard glass break. Vance was about to kick our bedroom door in…" I swallow. "But the deputies got here before he did and took him away."

"Oh." She pauses. "Ruby Jade will be upset when she learns he was arrested."

"What about me?" My voice breaks. "He was coming after *me*."

She edges in front of the camera, whispering, "You're not her son, who can do no wrong."

The others gather behind her.

"What do you know about Vance's car?" Deanna asks. "And the shattered window?" By the sound of her voice, you'd think I was the one who broke it.

"I don't know much." I clear my throat, but my voice and my hands continue to tremble. "I heard glass breaking and called the sheriff."

A chorus of groans accentuated by frowns follows.

Michael's forehead furrows. "Followers don't involve the authorities in their affairs."

I'm not a Follower, I'd like to say. *I have a brain—and I use it.* What about the sheriff's department "authority" Ruby Jade sent to find me Friday night?

"I was alone and unable to walk or defend myself," I tell them. "I had no idea what was happening downstairs. I heard glass shatter, assumed a thief was breaking in—a logical assumption, by the way, and I thought my life was in danger."

"You should have called the church."

More people crowd into the room.

The Pritchards' youngest daughter, Rosaline, says, "She should have been in church."

Heaven help us. A mommy clone. I pull the covers over my knees. "Even if I had a number for the church office, which I don't, would someone have answered it during the service?"

"You could have called one of us," Deanna says.

"I don't have your numbers. Besides, God only knows what would have happened in the time it took someone to drive all the way over here."

They gawk at me, unblinking.

I cross my arms. "What would *you* have done?"

They side glance each other and then look away, reminding me of puppets without a puppeteer. Maybe they're hoping the other person will answer, but no one responds.

"Nothing? You would have done nothing? Knowing an unscrupulousness individual or individuals were breaking into this place, you would have let them do whatever they wanted, not only to the house, but to you and your families?"

I gaze from person to person. "I had no idea how many people were down there or what their intentions were, but I could tell they weren't selling magazines. Besides, in case you don't know, forced entry is illegal."

Still, no response, only glazed-over stares.

"Scott and Michael, you wouldn't have protected the families in this home? Candice and Deanna, you wouldn't have protected your children?"

"Well," Olivia's mother, Alice, says, "it was Vance, not a Gentile."

Not a Gentile?

A different kind of adrenalin surges through me, and my fear is replaced by exasperation. "And that makes it okay for him to break into this house and threaten me?"

No one responds.

"Just so you have the whole picture…" I ball my fists, frustrated by their determination to blame me and exonerate their leader's son. "After the deputies arrested Vance, one of them came up here to make sure I hadn't been harmed." I pause to let the fact sink into their thick skulls that a *Gentile* cared enough to ask about my wellbeing.

The only change in their expressions is a hint of curiosity. I sigh and continue my story. "After she interviewed me, the officer said Vance evidently found a potted plant on the front porch and threw it through the front door window. All he had to do then was reach inside and unlock the door. She also told me he was inebriated, which explained his slurred threats."

Their eyes widen.

"Oh, dear…" Candice puts her hand to her mouth.

Their collective body heat fills the small room, intensifying perfumes and body odors and making me hot and anxious for their departure. I'm tempted to toss back the covers and rip off my clothes. It would make me feel better and make them scatter like startled rabbits.

Scott lowers his brow. "Ruby Jade won't like it."

"Won't like what?"

"She won't like people learning her son was drunk and you had him arrested."

"Based on my parents' experience with my drunkenness, I believe they'd say she should worry about her son, not about what people think. And to set the facts straight, I did *not* have him arrested. I called 911 to ask for protection. They took it from there."

Candice chews her lip. Deanna rubs her neck. The others gaze at their hands. Finally, Michael says, "We'd better go clean the glass out of the carpet and cover the window with something."

"Ruby Jade will disapprove," Alice is quick to say. "It'll make us look like a bunch of hillbillies and reflect poorly on the Followers."

God forbid we appear less than perfect. "Does anyone in the church have a glass business?" I ask.

"Tom does," Scott says. "Tom Hastings."

"Maybe he could replace the glass first thing tomorrow morning, provided he has a decorative piece to fit the oval."

Scott and Michael look at each other.

"We'd have to get Ruby Jade's approval," Deanna says. "She oversees all household renovations."

"You need her approval to replace a broken window?" I'm shocked, but not really. The woman controls almost every aspect of their lives. And if I'm honest with myself, of my life, too.

"It's the Pritchards' house." Scott says. "Their insurance will cover the cost."

"Actually…" I hold out my hands. "Vance should pay for it."

Their shocked expressions are laughable.

"He's the one who broke the window *and* the law." I fold my arms. "It's called breaking and entering."

Almost in unison, they eye the camera and then each other. Nervous tics I hadn't noticed before appear—on a cheek here, the corner of a mouth there, an eyelid, a shoulder, a pinky finger.

"You shouldn't…" Deanna whispers. "You're speaking out of turn."

I bury my face in my hands. "I give up." I'd love to see her tell a judge expecting restitution is *speaking out of turn*.

At the sound of shuffling feet, I raise my head. One by one, they leave the bedroom and filter down the stairs.

"We should notify Olivia." Alice's voice.

"Is she allowed phone calls in jail?" Scott asks.

"I don't know," Alice says. "Maybe we should ask Ruby Jade."

"I'm afraid she has her hands full, with Vance's situation and all." Scott again. "You know she doesn't like to be disturbed unless it's a life-and-death matter."

"I heard she plans to post bail for Owen and Olivia tomorrow afternoon," Michael says. "They can decide what to do with the window when they come home."

"This is so awful," one of the girls whines. "All our members are in jail."

"Three people is not *all* the Followers, Heidi." Deanna sounds stern. "You know how Ruby Jade hates exaggeration. It's of the devious devil."

All I can do is shake my head.

True to his promise, Sebastian arrives at a quarter to eight Monday morning to pick me up for work. Literally. He carries me down the stairs and through the kitchen, where Candice is washing a baby bottle. He stops at the windowless front door he evidently left open. "Rough night at the homestead?"

"I'll tell you about it on the way."

Once we're in the truck, he hands me an energy bar and a bottle of water. "How's everyone doing without Olivia and Owen?"

I inhale the bar's sweet fragrance. "Just the smell of these energizes me. To answer your question, things are a bit awkward. The residents aren't sure what to do without..."

"Without Olivia riding herd?"

"Uh-huh."

"I bet they could figure it out fast."

"A few days on our own, and the house could become a pleasant place to live." I open the water bottle. "You've probably heard about Vance by now."

"Yep." He shakes his head. "The fool. But R.J. won't leave him, or the Pritchards, in the slammer for long."

"And then..." I sigh. "As you said, all hell will break loose. My housemates assure me Ruby Jade is furious I called the cops on her son. She'll blame me for his arrest."

"Yep, she's so dadgum ticked her son and two FFOW members are behind bars, you'd think she squatted with her spurs on. I heard her ranting at someone on the phone this morning." He toggles a finger and mimics his boss. "Is the sheriff not paying attention? Does he not remember who funds his campaigns?"

"Wow…"

"Yeah, but don't let her get under your skin. You have the upper hand now, whether she knows it or not. God gave you leverage with Vance's high jinks. Keep it."

"I wish I wasn't so closely connected with his arrest." And with the Pritchards' arrest. Apparently, Inez hasn't been arrested yet. Could be the Pritchards are protecting her because she's part of the leadership team.

"Keep your innocence front and center, Cat True, propped between your horse's ears. R.J. has a way of unraveling self-esteem to the point Followers doubt themselves and will admit to anything to end the pressure."

He exits the neighborhood and turns the truck toward town. "Doctor first, and then we'll aim for the courthouse to do a little arm-twisting. Nonviolent, of course."

"I hope so. I'd hate to be involved in another controversy." Cranking the handle, I lower my window. "Did you tell Vance's dad?" I suck in the fresh morning air.

"About the break-in?"

"Yeah." Sebastian's perpetual good humor fades from his face. "Quentin isn't doing too good." He blows out a breath. "No one around here is aware he has a terminal heart condition, not even Vance. In fact, Quentin doesn't want either Vance or R.J. to know because they'll go after his business, which has only recently recovered from when she gutted it years ago."

He works his jaw, and I get the feeling whatever she did to his brother still angers him.

"That's too bad."

"Yeah, he's a good guy who got a raw deal."

We drive in silence for a while before I ask, "How do you know so much about what goes on at FFOW if you're not a church member? I understand you overhear Ruby Jade talking now and then, but my guess is she's not your only source of information."

"You're too smart for your britches." Sebastian chuckles. "I keep my eyes and ears open. Also helps to have a beer now and then with a couple ex-Followers who have contacts on the inside. And my buddies, the Dahlstroms, they do their best to keep me updated."

I'm about to ask why he stays, why he cares, but we've arrived at the doctor's office. Sebastian gets a wheelchair from inside and rolls me into the waiting room. Because I'm the first patient of the morning, a nurse takes me directly to an exam room, which smells like disinfectant.

She helps me climb onto the hard exam table and remove my socks. Slowly and cautiously, she unwinds the gauze the ER staff wrapped around my feet and deposits it in a trashcan. As she leaves, she says, "I'll let the doctor know you're here."

I check the soles of my feet, one at a time. Hard to tell, but I think they've improved.

Less than a minute later, Dr. Vasquez, a dark-haired woman about my age, walks in. "Hi, Cassie. You're looking much livelier than the last time I saw you."

She examines my feet and is pleased with my progress. "You can walk," she says, "but only if you're wear cotton socks and well-padded slippers." After applying fresh ointment and gauze, she tells me I can replace the gauze the next time I change socks. And I should return for a follow-up visit in a week.

"We were extra busy when you were admitted to the ER." She opens a drawer, pulls out gauze packets and ointment tubes and sets them on the counter. "I was running three directions at once and didn't catch how you injured your feet. I knew you walked or ran a long distance while barefoot, but I didn't hear why you weren't wearing shoes."

I tell her about Zachary's disappearance from my household and how I was upset no one would tell me where he was. I couldn't sleep, so I wandered outside. I also tell her deputies found the little boy locked in the basement.

She asks about the people I live with, how long I've lived there, why so many people live together, and what I do for a living. Eventually, I tell her about Faithful Followers of the Way and the control, which governs every aspect of our lives.

I'm not surprised when she asks, "Why do you stay?" Her probing gaze is kind and her voice gentle. I imagine this is how she speaks to women in domestic violence situations.

"Court order."

"You're kidding." She narrows her eyes. "A judge ordered you to go to a certain church and to live with people who lock children in basements?"

"I'm an alcoholic who's been sentenced to the church's rehabilitation program for a year." I don't tell her Transformation Way temporarily closed its doors. For all I know, the program could start again next week. "The judge probably doesn't know everything that goes on at the church."

"I'll write a letter today. Which judge?"

"Judge Snow. Good luck."

She lifts her chin. "What do you mean?"

"He's not a church member, but he's an ally, of sorts."

"I'll 'cc' the sheriff and the chief of police."

I place my hands behind me on the exam table and lean back. "From what I've heard, they're also under the leader's thumb." I'm convinced Zachary was rescued because Deputy Manning bypassed the sheriff and went directly to Child Protective Services. When CPS requested the department's help to locate a missing child, the sheriff was forced to cooperate. Ruby Jade has likely given him a loud and painful earful by now.

"I've been told the Faithful Follower church is more authoritarian than most, but I had no idea of the level of control." She makes a note on my chart before looking me in the eyes. "When you're ready to separate from the church, Cassie, let me know. Doesn't matter whether your year is up or not. As your doctor, I'll support you, even testify in court, if necessary."

"Thank you, Dr. Vasquez."

"Please call me Brianna."

I smile. "Thank you, Brianna. I won't forget your offer." Even if I never ask for her help, knowing she cares about my predicament calms my spirit and reminds me I'm not alone in the battle for a future outside FFOW.

My stomach clenches when the courthouse comes into view, the way it did the day I was sentenced to two years in jail. I stare at the tall building, remembering the austere courtroom and pompous Judge Snow. From everything I've learned since he switched my incarceration from GCDC to Transformation Way, he's wedged inside Ruby Jade's back pocket—or, more likely, her pocketbook.

Sebastian parks beneath overhanging tree branches. "Sorry my truck doesn't have air conditioning, but I won't be gone long, and you should be cool in the shade." He crosses the street and disappears inside the courthouse.

What my boss believes he can accomplish at the courthouse for my cause, I don't know. But I appreciate his willingness to fight for me, like my sweet doctor offered to do.

I rest my head against the seatback and put my feet on the dash. No matter how much I sleep, I always need more, it seems. I've barely closed my eyes, when I hear a familiar voice. Random thoughts tumble through my half-asleep brain. *No, it can't be. Yes, it can. Where am I? What if she sees me?*

Without moving my head, I peer through lowered lids. Ruby Jade and a man I've never seen before are walking toward the pickup. Surely, she'll recognize it. They're tilted toward one another, talking, and don't look my direction. I drop my feet to the floor, stifle a groan at the pain, and slide lower in the seat. I hope the shade or the reflection of leaves on the windshield prevents them from seeing me, but I can't be sure.

"This is such a waste of time," Ruby Jade is saying. "We already know what the judge is going to do."

"We have to go through the motions," he says. "Keep it on the up and up."

The sound of their voices changes. I push high enough to see they've turned and are crossing the street, headed toward the courthouse. *Thank you, Jesus, for keeping them from seeing me. Please don't let them run into my boss.*

I'm wide awake now and couldn't nap if I tried. The man's words run through my head. *We have to go through the motions, keep it on the up and up.* What were they talking about?

Less than fifteen minutes later, Sebastian comes sauntering across the street. He doesn't look like he has a care in the world. Maybe he and Ruby Jade didn't cross paths, after all.

The moment he opens the door, I ask, "Did you see Ruby Jade?"

"Yeah, but she didn't see me. She was too busy scheming with her lowlife attorney."

"Good…I mean, good she didn't see you."

He plops onto the driver's seat. "Mission accomplished. I spoke with a prosecuting attorney and left messages for both judges, telling them about the defunct rehab program."

"Won't it endanger your employment?"

"No skin off my back." He shoves his key into the ignition. "R.J. can fire me anytime she wants, but sure as the Montana sky is blue, she'll think twice before she does."

"I thought you stayed out of her business, other than managing her property."

"My dad always said, 'Don't mess with somethin' that ain't botherin' you.' Well this is bothering me—this catch-22 you're stuck in. You don't have family around to cover your back. So, I made it my business. If R.J. doesn't like it, so be it.

"Truth is…" He chuckles. "She won't know the source. I signed the notes to the judges 'concerned relative.' And the prosecuting attorney? He's new in town. Doesn't know me from Adam."

"He could describe you."

"Yeah, I s'pose. But how many other yahoos in this county look like me?"

I glance at Sebastian's worn jeans, plaid western shirt, rolled sleeves, cowboy hat, salt-and-pepper mustache and weathered tan. He might stand out on the streets of New York, but here in Bozeman, he's just another rancher running errands in town. "Concerned relative, huh?"

"Yeah, you can call me Uncle Seb."

"Think I will." I try it out. "Uncle Seb. I like the sound of it."

He laughs. "Vance has never called me 'uncle,' but it's okay by me. I don't claim him, either."

"So, Uncle, now that you've publicly expressed your opinion regarding Transformation Way, tell me—why haven't I met anyone else in the program?"

"Has anyone made a point to introduce you around?"

"No. If anything, Followers avoid me."

"Take my word, the FFOW tactic is to divide and conquer. The fewer friendships, alliances and family ties among the members, the more power and control Leadership has."

"Now that you mention it, Corban and Logan are the only ones who've reached out to me."

"They're not only on the inside but also on the outside looking in—and they have family support, which is key to right-thinking in the church."

"At least their family is still together, unlike my roommate's family."

"Be careful how closely you interact with your roommate or with Corban and Logan at church. Or even on the property when I'm not around to run interference. One wrong move, and you'll never see them again."

CHAPTER SIX

When Sebastian pulls into Ruby Jade's mostly empty garage, I ask about the older model car at the far end.

"Belongs to the maid. She's a retired woman doing penance for watching television."

"Penance?"

"Housecleaning for R.J. Her version of penance tends to involve free labor."

"Myrtle Mae told me her daughter has a television in her bedroom. Must kill the maid to dust it for her."

"It's not the only TV." Sebastian turns off the engine. "She has one in the kitchen, one in her office, and one in the living room behind a painting. And Vance has two or three downstairs."

"It's so…" I sputter, "so hypocritical."

"Yeah, and only the beginning of their double dealings."

"If you know so much about them, why do you—?'

"Let's just say I don't go digging under the outhouse for water."

"Okay…" I'll have to think about that one.

He settles me by the rose garden and then goes to get the sunhat, gloves and gardening tools. The sound of riding mowers in the backyard makes me smile. The Dahlstrom brothers are already hard at it. They must have parked behind the house. I can't wait to talk with them during our break.

Seated on the ground, planting annuals around the perimeter of the rose garden, I miss my mom more than ever. She'd love to help me arrange the pansies in a pretty pattern. But she wouldn't understand the Followers' deference to Ruby Jade and the other leaders—or why I'm still here. She's independent, and she taught me to be independent.

Yet, here I am, totally dependent on FFOW. I groan with disgust. I have no one to blame for my predicament but myself and my disastrous love affair with alcohol. The reason why I'm still here.

In the early days of my battle with booze, I thought I was the one who had to get me clean. However, after multiple futile attempts, I know better. Only God can restore me to wholeness and health. I thought the Transformation Way program would be the means he'd use, but right now, I'm having my doubts.

At breaktime, Corban and Logan come around the corner with a big green garden wagon to deliver me to the picnic table. I feel like a little kid, bumping along with my knees at my chest. But their thoughtfulness makes me smile. Logan pulls the wagon, and Corban pushes.

Head near mine, he murmurs, "Sorry about your feet, Cassie."

I enjoy hearing him huff in my ear.

"It was my fault." My voice vibrates with the ride over the wide expanse of lawn. The grass isn't rough, but it's not exactly smooth, either.

"Your fault?"

"I'll explain later."

"Heard you had lots of excitement at your house—a trip to the emergency room, the Pritchards' arrest, Vance's break-in."

"Longest weekend of my life."

Myrtle Mae is standing by the picnic table when we arrive. She waits until the guys lift me onto the bench before she comes around the table to give me a big hug. "I'm so glad to see you," she says. "When Sebastian told me about your feet, I was afraid I wouldn't see you for weeks."

"I'm happy to see you, too, and to get out of the house. Even with Olivia absent, it's an oppressive place."

"What did the doctor say this morning?"

"She said I can walk if I wear cotton socks and padded slippers."

"Wonderful news." She beams. My dad would call her smile a million-watt grin.

From across the table, Corban lifts his hand for a high-five, and we smack palms. Logan gives me a thumbs-up.

"Hey," I say, "weren't you the one who told me to watch my sign language?"

"Yeah, well…"

Myrtle Mae walks to the other side of the table and places her hands on the brothers' shoulders. "May I?"

They help her sit between them, although she doesn't need their help. She's spry for her age. Hands folded on the table, she says, "Please tell us all about your exciting adventures, Cassie."

I run my fingers through my hair. "The last few days may have been exciting at times, but I'm not sure I'd call them adventures." I tell them the same version of my midnight wanderings I told Sebastian and the doctor. I also tell them about Zachary's reunion with his mom and how Olivia fought her arrest.

"And Vance?" Corban asks. I can almost see Logan's antenna rising.

"I was the only one home Sunday night, which seemed like the perfect time to call my dad." I lean on my forearms. "Olivia has a way of interrupting whenever I try to talk with my family."

Logan snorts. "She has Leadership's sixth sense."

"While we were talking, I heard someone pound on the living room door and yell for me to open it. And then I heard glass breaking. Apparently, Vance threw a potted plant through the front-door window. That's when I ended the phone call and dialed 911."

"Smart move." Now, Corban's the one to give me a thumbs-up.

Myrtle Mae nods her approval.

"Before the deputies took Vance away, they told me he was drunk."

Logan stretches his back. "Not the first time he's been hammered."

"Thank God you weren't harmed." Myrtle Mae reaches across to squeeze my hand.

"Oh, Myrtle Mae…" I cover her hand with mine. "I'm so sorry. I keep forgetting Vance is your grandson."

She gives me a sad smile. "He is what he is. I pray for him every day."

Sebastian comes with grapes and lemonade—and Francis and Fenwick. The dogs stand on their back legs and rest their front paws on the bench, wiggling and whining for attention.

I'm trying to pet them both, when Sebastian says, "Down boys."

They drop to all fours and run to the other side of the table. Corban and Logan lift them onto their laps, where they continue to wriggle until Sebastian tells them to sit.

I scoot over to give him room. "Does Vance have a drinking problem?"

He sets the tray on the table. "For years, R.J. has used her influence to sweep his *little habit*, as she calls it, under the rug. Until yesterday, she managed to keep him out of the slammer."

"The word is out," Logan says. "I hear he made the evening news."

Corban is quick to add, "Hearsay only."

"Of course." I raise my eyebrows.

Fenwick licks Corban's chin. He laughs. "Fenwick understands. He must watch the news with his owner."

Sebastian settles at the end of the bench and hands out the lemonade before he starts the grape bowl around the table.

"Followers won't be told," Myrtle Mae says. "Or they'll get a twisted version, which blames someone else for his arrest."

"Yeah…" I raise my hand. "Someone like me."

"The truth will get around fast enough." Logan pops a grape in his mouth and speaks around it. "I may plant a few seeds myself."

Myrtle Mae presses her hand to her collarbone. "You wouldn't."

His brow furrows. "If you think I shouldn't…"

"Just pulling your leg." She slaps his shoulder. "I'm for slipping truth into Followers' heads every chance we get."

For a moment, our little group is quiet, as if we're all calculating the consequences of Vance's arrest. Will Ruby Jade disown her son? Never. Will she have the deputies who arrested him fired? Maybe. Will she reprimand the sheriff? Probably.

The silence is broken by a bird chirping above us.

"You're right, Cassie," Corban says, "she'll blame you, not Vance."

"I'm sorry." Myrtle Mae pats my arm. "I wish I could do something to help you, but she doesn't listen to me."

Sebastian grunts. "You don't have to take it sitting down, Cat."

"Oh, but I do, if I want to remain in the program."

"When you're boxed in a canyon, you either bushwhack a trail to the top or shoot your way out."

I look to the others for an explanation. All three have puzzled expressions on their faces, yet they give me encouraging nods.

I smile at Sebastian. "Whatever you say."

Later, after Myrtle Mae and Sebastian take the dogs to her house for their bean treats, I ask the guys about their plan to connect Marcela with her family.

"Everything is in place for a phone call from either or both of her parents tomorrow," Corban says. "I called her yesterday when her boss was gone to let her know."

"Is she excited?"

"Excited is an understatement." He laughs. "I'm surprised she didn't drop the phone and do cartwheels."

"I'm thrilled for her." I picture Marcela's shining eyes and elated smile. "Will Rodrigo be able to call her?"

"Yes," Logan says. "I've figured a way to arrange the produce boxes, so he's not only hidden, but muffled. I was able to give him a quick heads-up last time I delivered there." He grins. "Should have seen him. It was like a light switched on and he came alive."

"Wonderful. Marcela will be so happy."

"Their calls will have to be short, but it's a start."

Sebastian is driving me home after work when we see Vance's car coming our direction. I stifle a swear word and shrink into the corner. "They let him out."

Sebastian waves, but Vance stares straight ahead.

"I guarantee..." Sebastian's voice is as grim as his eyes. "The dude's gonna be pricklier than a porcupine."

A few minutes later, we turn onto the Pritchards' long driveway. Ruby Jade's car is parked in front of their house. She's standing under a tree, talking with Owen and Olivia.

"Must a driven all three of them here herself," Sebastian says, "after she posted bail."

The way they watch Sebastian's truck roll toward them makes me wonder if they're waiting for me. My stomach clamps and I clasp my hands in my lap.

"Appears to me to be bad timing." He stops the truck and shifts into reverse. "Better go find us a bite to eat." One hand on the steering wheel and an arm across the seatback, he cranes his neck and backs out of the driveway.

Ruby Jade waves and calls, but if he's aware, he doesn't show it or slow our retreat.

Once we're out on the highway, he chortles. "She's gonna pitch a whopper of a hissy fit."

"I can only imagine." My heart thumps at the thought. "How do you handle it when she gets ticked with you?" Maybe he can give me some pointers. I have a feeling I won't come out of the weekend crises unscathed.

"I always give her a reason she can't refute, even when she tries. This time, I'll tell her I forgot to pick up the socks and slippers the doctor told you to get."

"I have socks and slippers."

"Are the socks cotton?"

"No, I don't think so."

"Are the slippers padded?"

"They're a bit like walking on cardboard, but they're brand new. I'm only allowed to wear them in my bedroom, so I don't wear them at all. They'll do."

"No, they won't. Next stop, the mall."

Sebastian parks outside JCPenney and walks around to my open window. I expect him to tell me he'll find a wheelchair and return in a jiffy. Instead, he says, "S'cuse my reach," and sticks his arm inside to open the glovebox. He pulls out a tape measure. "Set your foot on the dash."

I do as he asks, and he stretches the tape along the length of my foot. So like a man. Why ask about size when one can get exact measurements? Eric, my dad and my brother would have done the same thing. I try not to snicker.

He straightens. "Any color preference?"

"No, but I can do without bunny heads or meowing cats—or bear claws. Those freak me out."

"Never heard of such a thing."

"The life of a bachelor."

He starts for the store then stops and turns around. "Any idea where I should head?"

"You might try the shoe department first. If you don't find slippers there, then women's sleepwear."

"Oh…" He sounds unsure.

"Ask a clerk for help."

I watch him amble toward the entrance, looking for all the world like a rancher going out to check the livestock rather than to a mall to purchase slippers for a female employee. Not many bosses would do as much. *Thank you, Lord, for Sebastian. He's a good guy, a good uncle—even if he works for the Wicked Witch of the West, something I still don't understand.*

Forty-five minutes later, Sebastian returns with a big grin on his face. "Found a treasure." He reaches into the bag and pulls out a gray t-shirt. "Saw this after I bought the socks and slippers. Hope it fits."

He unfolds the shirt and holds it out. It has a tabby cat printed on it. Pink lettering beneath the cat reads, "I Am the Cat's Meow."

"You like it?" He's as eager as a child offering a mud pie to his mom. "It's perfect for you."

"I love it. Very cute. I can't wait to wear it, but for now, you'll have to keep it in your hideout. Olivia would steal it the minute I hung it in the closet."

"Look at these beauties." He holds up a pair of tiger-striped open-heel slippers. "They're called 'Kat-a-Pillers.' Again, perfect for you. And…" He squeezes one. "They don't meow. I tested 'em."

"Those are amazing, Sebastian. Thank you." I try not to giggle at his enthusiasm.

He hands me a package of socks. "Put on a pair, and I'll help you get out to see if these fit." Sliding his pocketknife from his jeans, he cuts the plastic tie, which holds the slippers together. "The medium size seemed closest to the measurement I took."

I remove my Noreen-purchased nylon socks and work the new ones over the gauze.

He extends his arm.

With his help, I climb out of the truck and step into the slippers, my weight on my feet for the first time in…what's it been, three days? "They fit, Sebastian, and they feel good. Thank you. I'll pay you back when—"

"You'll do no such thing. Venturing into the women's section was an adventure for me—not one I care to repeat, but I need to try new things. Keeps me young." He digs into the bag. "One more thing. I've been meaning to get a pair of sunglasses for you. What do you think of these?"

"They're wonderful." I slip them on. "You are too good to me, Uncle Seb."

"Let's go grab some grub. How does Tex-Mex strike your fancy?"

By the time we arrive at the Pritchards' house, Ruby Jade's car is gone. However, the atmosphere inside is as tense as if she were there. The fact is apparent the moment Sebastian and I step from the garage into the frigid kitchen. Olivia has obviously retaken control of household affairs—and the thermostat.

She's standing in the kitchen. "Well, look who the cat dragged in..."

I know she's not referring to my worldly nickname. Determined to take the high road, I manage to choke out, "Welcome home, Olivia."

Behind her, Candice shoots me a don't-push-it frown.

One of the girls walks in with a stack of dishes. They must be cleaning the table after everyone ate supper. Thank God, Sebastian fed me.

"I'll help you up the stairs," Sebastian says. The going is slow, but I make it to the upper landing without dropping to my knees. We stop at my bedroom door.

"I'll be here at a quarter to eight again tomorrow," he says. "Your maiden run in the slippers went slick as a whistle, but you're not ready to hoof it to R.J.'s house."

"Thank you for all you've done for me today."

He lowers his voice. "The storm cloud hanging over this place is likely to burst tonight. Keep in mind you're a child of the King, no matter what some misguided folks might say."

"I'll try."

"You gotta do more than try. Don't let them box you in."

I lift my chin and square my shoulders. "I'm a daughter of the King of kings."

"That's my girl." He salutes and bounces down the stairs. At the bottom, he doffs his hat in the direction of the kitchen, but I don't hear anyone say goodbye to him.

I shuffle into the bedroom and then into the bathroom, where I sit on the toilet seat to rest before I brush my teeth and get ready for bed.

The sun hasn't set, but I have nothing to do—no book to read, no movie to watch, no guitar to play. And with the chilly reception downstairs, I have no desire to mingle with the others. Besides, I'm tired.

I hear a knock on the bathroom door. "Yes?"

"It's me, Marcela. You have a special visitor."

"A visitor at this time of night?"

"Yes, she's waiting in the hallway."

Her monotone delivery tells me this is not a wanted visitor, no matter how *special* she is. Has to be one of the Fearsome Threesome. Can't say Sebastian didn't warn me. "I'll be out in a minute."

I stand, stare at myself in the mirror and whisper, "You're a daughter of the King of kings, Cassie True, the Creator of the universe. Don't forget."

CHAPTER SEVEN

I flush the toilet, run the water in the sink for several seconds, wait a moment and then open the door. Ruby Jade is seated straight across from me on my bed. I must have stirred the hive to warrant a personal visit from the queen bee herself, though I doubt she's bringing me honey. She pops something into her mouth, twists a cap onto an amber pill bottle and drops it into her purse.

I force my mouth into a smile. "Hello."

Dressed in a purple pantsuit and wearing a three-strand pearl choker about her wide neck, Ruby Jade is denting my mattress big time. I hope the depression isn't permanent, or I'll have a horrific backache tomorrow.

A faint smile twists her purple lips into a sinister curl. "I see you're on your feet again, Cassandra." She lifts her arm to glance at her watch, and I catch a glimpse of red up her sleeve. I thought her rash would be gone by now. Not that I care, but she has plenty of money to get professional help and buy medicated creams.

"I saw the doctor this morning." Arms folded, I lean a shoulder on the bathroom doorjamb, my pathetic attempt to appear relaxed. "She said I've begun to heal and can walk a little in slippers."

"Let me see."

I shuffle around Marcela's bed into a cloud of rosewater perfume, which makes my eyes water. I cough.

One glance at my tiger-striped slippers and Ruby Jade rears back like she just saw a real-live tiger. "Where did you get those gaudy things? Surely, Noreen knew better than to—"

"Sebastian bought them for me. The reason why he left the driveway earlier. He remembered the doctor said I can walk, if I wear cotton socks and padded slippers."

"So, you picked the ugliest, sleaziest ones you could find."

"Sebastian did the shopping. I stayed in his pickup."

"He's a single man. He shouldn't—"

"Shopping was his idea, not mine."

"You should have refused."

"No one else offered to take me to the doctor or buy me slippers. I told him I'll pay him back, if I ever get a paycheck."

Sparks flash at the backs of her eyes. "That's enough impudence out of you." She points toward the door. "Marcela—"

I turn. Marcela is standing in the doorway, hands clenched, face white.

"Tell the others to gather in the living room."

"Yes, ma'am." She disappears.

Ruby Jade returns her attention to me. "Have a seat, Cassandra." She motions to Marcela's bed.

I sit across from her, pulling my feet inward so the toes of my slippers don't touch her purple-and-white stilettos.

Her violet eyes soften. Hands folded in her lap, her thumbs begin to turn, over and under, over and under. "You can tell me," she says.

I tilt my head. "Tell you what?"

"Tell me where you've been."

"Okay." I shrug. "After work, Sebastian drove to the mall—following a quick stop here, as you know—to buy the socks and slippers. And then he stopped by—"

"No, no, no." Her voice is gentle and her smile sweet. "Friday night, when you damaged your feet." Her pupils are mere pinpricks, which is odd, considering the lighting in the room isn't very bright. "Where did..." Her words slur. "You...go?" She blinks, shakes her head and straightens.

"I'm not sure." My jail-honed poker face set like flint, as my grandpa used to say, I give a vague wave of my hand. "Somewhere around here."

"You knew. You knew."

"I was hot, and I didn't feel good. And I was upset about Zachary's disappearance. All I know is I walked and cried and walked and cried. Eventually, I found myself back here."

Her gaze hardens. "Downstairs with you. Now." She jumps to her feet, bumping my toes.

I suck in a gasp.

"Stop being a baby." She stomps out the door, heels striking hard enough to put holes in the floor.

My heart hammers my ribs, yet I contemplate ignoring her command just to see if she'd throw me over her shoulder and haul me to the living room. Thanks to my throbbing feet, I decide to save my rebellion for another day.

One foot at a time, I work my way down the stairs and across the kitchen and dining room. At the opening between the dining room and living room, I stop to assess the situation. Every member of the household is there, including the children.

By their somber expressions and restless fidgets, I'm fairly certain this isn't a party. Not that Followers ever party. They wouldn't celebrate my graduation from crawling to walking upright, but you'd think the Pritchards' return from jail would be cause for high spirits.

Marcela and Candice avoid eye contact with me. The others glance at me and quickly look away. I plaster a smile on my face to show them they don't have to be nervous for me.

From her recliner "throne," Ruby Jade motions to the folding chair in the middle of the room. "Have a seat."

Sebastian's words pound with my pulse, which drums my ears. "You're a child of the King, no matter what some misguided folks might say. Don't let them box you in."

I slowly make my way to the designated chair. My focus on my housemates, I picture the word MISGUIDED on each forehead, including the children's foreheads. When I get to Olivia and Ruby Jade, I envision a different word— CHARLATAN, written in red and underlined twice. Finally, I sit in the chair, place my hands in my lap and plant both feet flat on the floor.

Everyone looks so tired. I wish I could gift them with the freedom to go to bed and sleep as long as they need. A good night's sleep is such a luxury in this house.

Their usual guardedness has been replaced by an anxious wariness. Jaws clamped, hands fisted, their bodies appear motionless, yet their gazes flick about the room. Beneath the stillness, their muscles shift in constant but barely discernable tremors. Sweat intermingles with the rosewater.

They're edgy, but why? I'm the one on the hot seat, not them. Still, they probably know better than I do what this "gathering" is about.

Owen, pale and bewildered after his night in the pokey, is seated on the couch directly in front of me. His head wobble is small but persistent. Scott and Candice are beside him. Ruby Jade is next to Candice in Owen's recliner.

Candice holds Tristen. Sprigs of hair spike from the baby's head. He coos and waves his arms. I vow to think of him and his sister and how I might help them have a better future, no matter what happens tonight.

Olivia, who's in her usual recliner, glares at me. But, what's new? She licks her lips as if she's about to devour my hide, which is probably not far from the truth. What did Sebastian say about a storm brewing over this household?

Like everyone else, I'm wearing a long-sleeved top, yet the Arctic-level air-conditioning raises chill bumps. No one else is shivering or rubbing their arms, so I refrain from hugging myself to stay warm. Could be the others know better than to question the temperature, especially with Ruby Jade present.

Marcela's fingers twitch in her lap. The silent children try to mask their fear, but their endless glances from me to Ruby Jade speak volumes. The teens are more successful with their attempts at nonchalance than the younger ones. Years of practice, I suppose.

I feel for them. As with Zachary, I'm the cause of the trauma they must endure, something I deeply regret. Why not send them to bed and let the adults deal with my supposed offenses?

Other than her twirling thumbs, Ruby Jade appears relaxed and at home. "Cassandra Turner..." Her thumbs stop and twirl the opposite direction. "You are new to the Faithful. You may not understand our ways."

You mean YOUR ways, don't you?

"We placed you in this household so members well-versed in our ways could teach you the difference between right and wrong, good and evil, transparency and deviousness. Unlike other churches, we don't hide our secret sins or pretend we're something we're not."

I nearly choke. The Great Pretender telling me not to pretend.

"As the Bible commands, we confess our sins to one another." Her lavender eyes bore into me. If I let her, she'd drill to the center of my being, remove my core personality, and leave me a shell of a person—an obedient, submissive, empty shell.

I wonder where her comments are leading and how they relate to 1 John 1:9, which says we confess our sins to God, and he forgives and cleanses us. I fight the urge to turn away. As Sebastian warned, I can't let her scare me into saying or doing something I'll regret. I *can* let her think she has the upper hand, that she's in control of the situation.

"This, my sugar plum," she purrs, "is an opportunity for you to confess your failings and sins."

I have a feeling she means more than listing the times I've exceeded the speed limit. And if she calls me *sugar plum* one more time, I'll gag.

"Tell us…" She twirls her thumbs the opposite direction. "Tell us what happened when you left this house, your sanctuary, without permission Friday night."

"I told you all about it when you were upstairs." I clasp my hands in my lap. "I also told Olivia."

Her eyes flash. "But you didn't tell us everything."

"I told you everything I remember." Once again, I put on my poker face.

Our fearsome leader's face clouds like a darkening sky before a thunderclap. Those around me, young and old, shrink into their seats. Tristen is the only oblivious one, yet he stops his coos and watches his mother's face.

Ruby Jade screeches, "Liar!"

I jerk, as startled as if I'd been slapped.

Tristen bursts into terrorized screams.

Candice pulls her baby to her chest, muffling his cries.

Ruby Jade swings her direction. "Give him to me."

"I can quiet him, Ruby Jade," Candice pleads. "He just needs a minute."

"Now, Candice…" She's no longer yelling, but the threat smoldering below the surface is unmistakable.

Candice glances at Scott's impassive face, stands and bends over the recliner to give Tristen to the angry woman.

Ruby Jade grabs the baby below his armpits and thrusts him into the air.

Candice reaches for him, gets the evil eye from Ruby Jade, and quickly backsteps.

"Shut up, you devil child!" Ruby Jade shakes him, over and over, shouting, "Shut up, shut up, shut up!"

Wide-eyed, the baby stiffens, stares at her for a long, unblinking moment and then shrieks. Turning his head, he reaches his arms toward his mother, crying louder than I've ever heard him cry. If he could talk, I know he'd be calling for his mama.

Paralyzed by shock, I'm slow to react. But now that I comprehend what's happening, I slide to the edge of the folding chair, ready to jump up and shout, *Give him back to his mother!*

Before I find my voice, Ruby Jade shoves the hysterical red-faced baby at Candice. "I was the first to bond with this one at his birth," she shouts. "But he's rejecting my spirit, which means he's rejecting God's Spirit. Put the devil baby in his crib, close the door and return at once. I will not allow him to disturb this meeting."

Once again, I'm painfully aware I'm responsible for the trauma a child is suffering. He needs to be held and comforted by a loving parent, not abandoned to cry out his confusion and fear alone in his bed.

Her face as white as the walls, Candice hurries into the dining room.

Ruby Jade calls after her, "Leadership will rid him of his demons later and discuss integrating him into a home where the parents have more control."

Candice gasps, stops, and then hurries away.

Scott looks straight ahead.

Leave Tristen alone. He's doing what babies do. And leave Candice and Scott alone. You're terrifying us all. Of course, terror is probably her intent.

She whips around, a long purple fingernail pointed at me.

I can almost feel it poke my chest.

"You..." She punctuates her words with nail stabs. "Will–submit–to–God's–holy–will." She flips her hand over, palm up and raises it toward the ceiling. Her sleeve slides to her elbow, revealing the red rash I noticed earlier on her forearm. In a voice heavy with assumed authority, she orders, "All rise."

The others stand. I follow their lead, half expecting a judge to walk in.

Ruby Jade barks, "Not you, stupid."

I slowly sit. Even without a judge, this feels like a courtroom—other than the fact I've never been called "stupid" in court.

Still seated, Ruby Jade says, "Deliver the truth, Faithful Ones."

The others close in on me, children at the forefront, almost touching me. I pull my feet under the chair. The adults hover above the kids, their glazed eyes hard and unreadable, except Olivia's, which burn with hatred. Her daughters are at my knees. She ogles me from over their heads, as if I'm a bug she's about to squash.

"Tell us the truth, tell us the truth," the girls cry, shaking their fists at me.

The others pick up the chant. "Tell us the truth, tell us the truth." They brandish their fists in time with their words, their shouts reverberating between the walls. The loud screams hurt my ears, but I don't dare cover them. Over and over, they shout, "Tell us the truth, tell us the truth. Submit to God's holy will, submit..."

The chill I felt earlier is replaced by head-to-foot heat and sweat. My heart pounds. I can hardly breathe. All around me, my personal space has been invaded by their hot frenzied bodies. I clasp my trembling hands together, desperate to push through the group to get a full breath of air. Is this what claustrophobia feels like?

Olivia squeezes the girls' shoulders. They hush and drop their hands. The others follow suit. She juts her chin at me. "You went to the police about Zachary."

I shake my head.

"I can't hear you!" Ruby Jade shouts. From the sound of it, she hasn't left the recliner.

I speak louder. "I did not go to the police."

"You called the police," Olivia insists.

"I did not. You can check my phone."

She pushes her girls aside and gets in my face, shouting, "Liar!" Her breath is atrocious. I wish she'd had one of the mints she keeps on her kitchen desk before this started. "You're a deceiver, a seductive sinner." Her saliva sprays my face.

"Liar, deceiver," the others yell. "Seductive sinner."

"What would I have told them? I didn't—"

"Impertinent." She slaps my face.

I jolt backward, squinting at her, comprehension dawning. This must be a cleanse.

The others shout, "Impertinent, impertinent, impertinent."

I'm about to shove Olivia away, when Ruby Jade takes control again. "Stop." She waits until the chants die away. "Owen," she orders, "speak up."

After a brief hesitation, he leans toward me over a child's head. "You left bloody footprints in the garage, Cassandra." His voice is quiet, his eyes vacant. "You should have wiped them before they dried."

"Olivia told me to clean the kitchen floor and go to bed."

"Impudent." She slaps my other cheek. "Don't blame me for your sins."

"You went out seducing men." Deanna shakes her finger in my face. "In your nightgown."

"Not true."

"A woman of the night. You're a woman of the night."

I stare at her, having no idea of cleanse protocol. If I respond, I get slapped. If I don't—

"Confess, Cassandra," Ruby Jade yells.

"I am not a woman of the night."

"You called the police," someone shouts.

"I did not."

"You failed to clean the garage floor," yells another. "You should be ashamed."

"True." I lift my head and declare at the top of my voice, "I confess I did not clean the garage floor."

"You were out seducing men, stealing them from their wives."

"I did not and would *never* do that."

They're shoving their fists at me, not hitting me yet coming too close for comfort. I lurch from side to side, evading their thrusts. *Tristen, Mylea. This is for you.*

"Tell the truth," Ruby Jade calls. "You're a streetwalker who returned to your old ways."

"I lived on the streets, but I was not a prostitute. I've always been faithful to my husband. I honor his memory by remaining celibate."

Someone screams at the top of their lungs, "You're a liar, Cassandra Turner!" My ears ring. For the first time, the universal Follower hoarseness makes sense.

Olivia's mother yells, "You're a slut," and punches my arm. Through her narrowed eyelids, she somehow manages to project the same hatred her daughter has for me.

One of the boys hollers, "You're lazy. You made a mess and didn't clean it up."

"You ran away without permission," cries the youngest girl. She pounds my thighs with her fists. I remember Zachary and thank God he's not part of this coldhearted chaos.

The accusations come so fast I no longer have time to respond. I gasp for breath, fearing my housemates' body heat may smother me.

"Confess your sins, Cassandra Turner," Ruby Jade shouts. "Get the demons out."

Though I can't see the woman, she must be directing the cleanse. Lucky me.

A moment later, she's in front of me, inches from my nose. "What a blessing this is for you, Cassandra." Her breath is as bad as Olivia's. "How your household members must care for your soul. This is your chance to come clean, to get a breakthrough and find God's will for your life. Ask Jesus to help you expel the demons."

I pull away from her. "What demons?"

She stays in my face. "The demons within."

"I don't—"

"The rebellion demon, the lust demon, the temptress demon…" The purple fingernail appears again, so close I'd go cross-eyed if I looked directly at it. "The falsehood demon, the betrayal demon, the, uh, demon of…" She's apparently out of demons.

Olivia is quick to help her out. "The demon of uncleanliness, of filth."

"Yes," Ruby Jade nods her head in agreement. "Confess and they will come out of you."

"I don't, I can't—"

Ruby Jade's face reddens. She snorts and backs away. "Marcela, Candice, time for truth serum."

Before I can ask what truth serum is, first one side of my face and then the other is splattered with spittle. I fight the urge to wipe it away—and then something wet hits the top of my head.

"Mother," Olivia snarls. "Enough. Ruby Jade did not ask for your participation."

Someone slaps the back of my head, knocking me forward.

Olivia's eyes flash. "Mother, I said that's enough."

"Cassandra Turner, confess your sins to your sisters and brothers." Ruby Jade waves her arms. "Get the demons out."

"Tell us your sins," Owen says, "and release them, so we can help you." A gentleness has come into his eyes, like he wants to help me end the abuse.

"You're holding back," Olivia screeches, "leading others to the devil's lair. Repent. Cry out to God."

Ruby Jade looks from side to side. "Marcela, Candice, what sins have you seen this woman commit?"

Neither woman responds.

"What sins," demands Ruby Jade, her face a deeper red than before, "have you seen this woman commit?"

"She seduced Sebastian," Candice says. "She had him carry her to his truck. He was forced to touch her inappropriately."

I choke. "He did no such—"

"Shut up." Olivia slaps me. Her evil grin reminds me of Disney villains.

The others chant, "Seducer, seducer, seducer."

"Marcela." Ruby Jade again. "What sins have you seen this woman commit?"

"Hypocrisy," Marcela shouts. "And mockery. She pretends to be a good Follower, but she mocks us behind our backs. She used us to get out of jail."

I drop my mouth in horror. How could she? I stare at her, but she's not there. Her eyes are blank. Why did she turn on me? I thought we were friends. She knows I've been trying to help her.

As one, the older members shrink backward, like I coughed devious demons in their faces.

Their chant interrupted, the children look confused.

I'm now so hot and the smell of sweat and bad breath is so strong, I think I might pass out. *Help me, God. I don't know how much more I can take.*

"Spit on her, Marcela," Ruby Jade demands. "She spit on the face of God by mocking his servants. She's an abomination. Unless she repents and confesses, she'll burn in hell."

Marcela bends toward me.

I close my eyes.

Moisture dribbles down my cheek.

CHAPTER EIGHT

The screams fade into a distant roar, like I'm under water. I have a sensation of floating, not in water but on the ceiling, as if I'm merely an observer of the happenings below. I see myself in the chair surrounded by angry people who shout and flail in slow motion.

But all I feel is peace—and a cooling breeze. *Thank you, Jesus.*

"Ruby Jade," someone yells above the ruckus. "Ruby Jade!"

Her eyes blaze. Teeth bared, she scans the group. "You know better than to interrupt me. Who said that?"

Silence shutters the cacophony. No one dares to breathe. From upstairs comes the faint sound of Tristen's wails. Poor baby. I glance at Candice. She looks stricken. I can tell she's fighting tears.

The brave person, one of the teen boys, whispers, "A sheriff's car is coming up the driveway."

Ruby Jade's purple eyes and mouth form circles. "Oh." She straightens, jerking side to side, reminding me of an off-balance bird. "Everyone, go to your rooms. Olivia and Owen, you stay here."

As one, the group rises. I struggle to return to my body.

The others scatter like cockroaches in the light. Even in my befuddled state, I wonder if the analogy speaks to the reality.

"Move it, Cassandra," Olivia yells. "Get upstairs."

After a long, trembling breath, I slowly push to my tender feet and hobble into the dining room. I feel shaky inside, as though I came through a ferocious storm. And maybe that's what it was, a FFOW storm.

Should I have told them to get lost and refused to sit in the chair? But where could I have gone? If I didn't cooperate, would Ruby Jade have asked the judge to return me to jail?

Ahead of me, our fearsome leader is scuttling into the kitchen, high heels clomping. The floor jitters. Without looking back, she flings open the door and stomps into the garage. Deanna rushes to close the door.

My head begins to clear. Why is Ruby Jade in such a hurry? Is she running from the law?

Hearing tires on the pavement, I peer out the kitchen window. A deputy in a sheriff's department SUV is parking in front of the house. He gets out, and I step out of his view. He scans the area then walks toward the front door.

I slip behind the partial wall that divides the kitchen from the dining room. From there, I can see into the living room. If someone catches me snooping on the Pritchards' conversation, I could get into big trouble. I'll take my chances. The deputy might have an update regarding Zachary.

The doorbell rings. I peek around the wall.

Owen opens the door. "Hello, Officer." His voice falters, and he clears his throat. "What can I do for you?"

I'm impressed that Owen, a guy released from jail only hours ago, is congenial and polite. Olivia stands behind him, wringing her hands.

"Good evening." I can't see the deputy's face, but I can hear him. "I'm looking for Olivia Pritchard, Owen Pritchard, and a, uh, Ruby Jade Paradise." His voice holds a smirk, as if he finds her name amusing. I would too, if I didn't know the woman.

"We're the Pritchards," Owen says. "And Ruby Jade…" He glances around. "She was just here."

Olivia punctuates her words with nods. "She left a few minutes ago."

"I was told I could find her here."

"You would have, if you'd come a half hour earlier." Owen tips his head. "I'm sorry you missed her."

"Is she returning to her home?"

"I have no idea." Owen looks at Olivia, who shrugs. "She didn't say."

The officer grunts and extends two packets. "These are for the two of you. Child Protective Services has requested your attendance at a Preliminary Protective Hearing."

My guess is the hearing is about Zachary. Is the deputy trying to serve Ruby Jade papers for the same hearing? Inez was the one who helped Olivia lock Zachary in the basement.

The officer departs. Owen shuts the door behind him, and he and Olivia open their envelopes.

I slip across the kitchen to catch a glimpse of the deputy through the window above the sink. From what I can tell, he has two, maybe three packets in his hand. Are they all for Ruby Jade?

Hearing footsteps on the stairs, I grab a glass from the cupboard. Holding it with an unsteady hand, I'm filling it with water when Marcela comes into the kitchen.

"There you are," she whispers. "I thought maybe your feet hurt too much to climb the stairs. I can help you."

The person who ratted on me now wants to help me? "I'm slow as a snail," I murmur, "but I think I can do it."

At the sound of cursing in the living room, we both freeze.

"This says we're required to be at CPS at eight a.m. tomorrow." Anger constricts Olivia's voice. "I have hair and nail appointments I can't break. I need to call somebody, the judge, maybe."

I watch the SUV turn around in the driveway.

"It's a fact-finding hearing," Owen says. "We should be there, with our attorney, to make sure they get the facts straight. Besides, I doubt we have a choice as to whether or not to attend."

The moment the vehicle reaches the street, I hear a garage door open and see Ruby Jade's car back onto the driveway. Interesting. Pastor, Prophetess and Psalmist Ruby Jade Paradise hiding from the law after an attempt to force me to confess all my secret sins. Interesting.

Following Marcela up the stairs one careful step at a time, I consider asking her what happens when a cleanse is interrupted. But then I remember Zachary's ill-treatment and decide I'd rather not know.

I can't wait to wash away the "cleanse" I just experienced. For the sake of my feet, I decide to bathe rather than shower. I'm settling into a full tub of warm water, when I hear a knock on the door and Marcela's voice. "Cassandra, it's me."

"You can come in," I say. "The shower curtain is pulled, but I'm not sure what accusations might—"

"I'm moving out and need to get my things." Once again, her voice is hoarse. Now, I know why.

"Moving? Right now?"

"Ruby Jade sent me a text." The latch clicks, and Marcela comes into the bathroom. "She says you're a negative influence and I have to move to another household. I'm supposed to be there in forty-five minutes."

She opens and closes drawers.

I peek around the curtain.

Her face a mask, she tosses toiletries one after another into a cardboard box.

"I'm sorry you have to move because of me." Seems like I cause trouble for everyone. "I'll miss you."

"Maybe we'll see each other around, but..." She lowers her voice. "We won't be allowed to talk."

"That's terrible. We have to find a way to stay in touch." I think of the Dahlstrom brothers' plot to connect her with her family. "Will you have the same job?"

"As far as I know."

"Good." I consider how to say my next words. "I, uh, heard about tomorrow."

She smiles. "I'm excited."

"It'll be good." I sigh. "I was looking forward to hearing all about it."

She leans close and whispers, "I'm sorry I said those terrible things about you. When Ruby Jade singled me out, I knew I had to come up with something. Or she would have decided I let go of Jesus and made me have a cleanse, too."

"Marcela." I groan. "She has a twisted view of God. Once you accept Jesus as your Savior, he makes you a child of God forever. He'll never *ever* let go of you. Promise me you'll allow your family to help you escape this crazy place. You should be moving in with your husband, not to another household."

She backs away. "I'd better finish packing."

"Marcela…"

She turns to go.

"I know it's scary, but it'll be easier, after—"

"I hope so." She closes the door.

I join the others for breakfast. As usual, they ignore me. I wish I could say the same for Ruby Jade, whose eyes in the picture on the opposite wall appear to follow my every move. Her sardonic smile suggests to me, if no one else, that she's the cat and we're the mice.

Marcela's empty chair makes me sad, though I'm excited she'll receive calls from her parents this morning, the first step toward her exit. I try to stifle my jealousy. At the rate things are going, I might be kicked out before she makes her outward move.

Olivia's furtive glances my way suggest barely suppressed hostility. Her glinting eyes and the hard set of her mouth remind me of an eagle eyeing its prey. Evidently, screaming in my face last night didn't deplete the rage I trigger in her.

Hell hath no fury like a woman scorned, they say. In Olivia's case, hell hath no fury like a woman caught red-handed.

As he promised, Sebastian gives me a ride to work again. "You're walking better, and you're not bruised and battered," he says. "Did they let you off easy last night?"

"Not for a moment."

He gives me a second glance. "Did Olivia go on the warpath?"

"Olivia and friends, directed by Chief Ruby Jade Paradise."

He grunts. "I presume she fired up a cleanse session specially for you."

"Your presumption is correct."

"Had a feeling you were in for it."

"I hate to tell you, but your name was dragged into the accusations."

He raises an eyebrow. "What did I do this time?"

"You inappropriately touched me when you carried me to and from your truck. Actually, I supposedly encouraged you."

"It'd be nice if Followers would get their minds out of the gutter." His mouth twitches with disgust.

"Ruby Jade heard what they said. Did she say anything to you?"

"Not yet, and I doubt she will. She knows it's hogwash. In fact, I think she gets a kick out of whipping her underlings into a frenzy."

I picture her bemused expression in the dining room picture. "You're putting your neck on the chopping block for me. I appreciate it, but—"

"Like I said, you don't have loved ones to run interference, so good ol' Uncle Seb is stepping in to take their place."

"Thank you, Uncle Seb." I feel silly calling him *uncle*, but the big grin on his face tells me he loves it. "I can't begin to explain how grateful I am to know I don't have to face the Followers on my own."

The days blur past. Every morning, I shift from my household's physical and emotional chill to Ruby Jade's yard. Sunshine and mellow breezes thaw my body while enjoyable work and caring friends warm my soul. I'm grateful for an opportunity to defrost each day, yet I feel like my psyche is splitting in two. How long I can keep my true self intact, I'm not sure.

Over iced tea with lemon slices one afternoon, Myrtle Mae asks about my family.

"My parents have been married almost thirty-five years," I tell her. "They're wonderful, both of them, and have supported me through a lot of crazy times."

"Did they approve of your husband?"

"They adored him. I think they miss him as much as I do."

"How sweet." She pats my arm. "Tragic but sweet. Do you have any siblings?"

"One brother, Kip. He's two years older than I am and single." I swirl the ice cubes in my glass. "I wish I could visit them."

"You could borrow my car."

"Very generous of you, Myrtle Mae. I'd love to take you up on your offer, but the fact is, I'm court-ordered to be here. This place is my—I finger quote—*jail* for the next year." I sip my lemonade. "Actually, it's a worse jail than the detention center in a lot of ways, but I ignored the red flags and let Noreen convince me Transformation Way would change my life. I have to live with my choice—and the judge's decision."

"I believe they call it 'false advertising.'"

"True, but I might never have met you or Sebastian or Marcela—or the Dahlstrom brothers. And I've been able to…" I pause, carefully choosing my words. "Encourage others to seek a better life."

"Good for you, sweetie. I'm glad to hear you're blooming where you're planted, as they say. But back to your family. Surely, the judge would allow them to come see you." Her forehead wrinkles and her smile fades.

"What?" I ask. "What's wrong?"

"My thoughtless daughter cut ties with my family—our family—and expects all the Followers to do the same. She wouldn't approve of a visit from your loved ones."

"You've mentioned a brother…"

"Norman and I reconnected a few years back. But as I said, Ruby Jade hates him, so I don't see a whole lot of him. Once in a while, he'll sneak over at night, and Sebastian lets him know when she's out of town. Those are the times we can relax and enjoy each other's company. How about your family? Does she allow you to call them?"

"Yes, but…" I stare out the window.

"Now it's my turn," she says." But what?"

"Phone calls are hard. Either Olivia tells me to hang up or she puts me to work. Or some other interruption forces me to cut the calls short." I push my hair behind my ears. "I hate to admit it, but I've been lying to my parents, making up stories, because I can't bring myself to tell them I'm not in the rehab program."

I sigh. "I don't know how much longer I can maintain the charade, with my parents or the judge."

"One of the worst things my daughter does is divide families or she destroys them entirely." Tears well in her eyes. "So many divorces, so many broken homes…"

"I'm thinking it'd be easier not to talk with my parents and my brother."

She gives me a questioning look.

"I used to tell them all about my life. We had an open relationship...well, except when I was deep into alcoholism. I'm not sure what I told them then."

"I'd hate to see you stop communicating." Her forehead wrinkles. "To this day, I mourn the loss of my family, most of whom have now passed away. I wouldn't wish such agony for you and your family."

Corban and Logan are mowing, Sebastian is pruning, and I'm deadheading flowers beneath a shade tree, contemplating how much I miss Marcela. I remember my best friends from high school and college. We did everything together, from studying to hanging out to painting each other's fingernails.

Eric was my best friend, until he died, and then my neighbor and I grew close. But only as drinking buddies. God only knows what kind of nonsense we told each other. Marcela and I could have had a best-friend kind of relationship, under different circumstances.

Now, I may never see her again. If we meet at church, we can't talk. I flick a bug off my arm and tell myself to stop thinking like a victim and find a way to scale the canyon wall. After Marcela and Rodrigo escape FFOW, as I hope they will, and I graduate from the program, as I hope I will, I'll find a way to renew our friendship.

Corban steers his mower my direction. I get to my feet and brush off my jeans, prepared to stand aside while he mows around the flowerbed. But he stops, switches off the engine and sidesteps from the seat onto the grass. "Hey, Cassie True."

"Hi, Corban Dahlstrom." His presence reminds me I'm not alone in the battle. I have four faithful friends right here in Ruby Jade's backyard, ironic as it is. Yet, speaking with any of them at length in view of her house makes me nervous. I glance at the windows.

"They took off a few minutes ago," Corban says. "In Ruby Jade's car. Vance was wearing an expensive suit. I know because I occasionally work the men's department at the store. And his haircut looks recent. I have a sneaky suspicion he has a court appearance this morning."

"Thank God, I wasn't called to testify."

"It could still happen."

"Probably depends on whether he pleads guilty or not."

"Or his mom buys his way out." He eyes my feet. "Fancy slippers."

I wriggle my sock-covered toes. "Sebastian got these for me. Ruby Jade had a fit when she saw them. Called them ugly and sleazy."

"That's hilarious." He laughs. "Good for Sebastian. Are your feet better?"

"Much better. Thanks for asking. I'll see the doctor again on Monday. She'll probably tell me I can return to my normal life."

His brow puckers. "Not as if this life is normal."

"Sometimes I'm tempted to accept this as my norm, to make the next year easier."

"But would it?" He lifts his ballcap, runs his fingers through his dark hair and replaces the hat. "The so-called norm around here comes with constant demands, constant demeaning, constant upheaval, constant stress. And don't forget the cleanses."

"I had half a one the other night. It was enough for me."

"Half a cleanse?"

"A deputy came by to serve papers to the Pritchards and Ruby Jade. His arrival cut short the cleanse—not that I minded." I push hair out of my eyes. "Seemed odd Ruby Jade hid in the garage until he left."

"Rumor has it she's involved in several court cases, but she has this crazy idea if they don't serve her, she doesn't have to show up for court." He snorts. "Actually, crazy is *her* norm." He returns to the mower seat. "I'd better get to work. Just wanted to check on you."

"Thanks, Corban. When we have a chance, I'd like to talk with you about something, in private, if possible…"

"We can walk the path in the trees after lunch. It's not very long, but long enough to talk for a few minutes." He glances at my feet. "Sorry. I forgot…."

"Can I walk it in my slippers?"

"The trail is flat and doesn't have a lot of rocks."

"Worth a try."

He starts the engine but then motions me over. "Just so you know, an incomplete cleanse is as if you never had a cleanse at all. You haven't seen the end of it."

"I had a feeling…"

CHAPTER NINE

As always, lunch with my friends is relaxing, unlike meals with my housemates. Birds cluster, circle and swoop above the trees, a beautiful, carefree dance that lifts my spirit and moves me to prayer. *God, you are so good to me. You knew these people and this place would be what I need to help me survive FFOW.*

Corban downs two turkey rollups and a handful of chips before he says, "Cassie, want to go for a walk in the trees before we get back to work?"

Logan's eyebrows lift, but Sebastian doesn't flinch a muscle.

"Sure. I've been wanting to explore in there. It's like a mini forest." I wipe my mouth with a napkin and pick up my water bottle. "Thanks, Uncle Seb. Delicious, as always."

"Uncle Seb?" Logan eyes us both.

I lift my chin. "He's been taking care of me, like an uncle would do."

"You couldn't ask for a better surrogate relative." Corban says.

Logan snorts. "Maybe a better-looking one."

Sebastian scowls at him.

"Spoken like a true FFOW member." I laugh. "Where it's all about appearance."

"And tattling." Corban stands and steps over the bench seat. "We're supposed to bond to the group, not to family, and tattle on everyone, whether or not they're blood relatives."

"I swear..." Sebastian raises his hand. "No fancy duds and no snitching."

"What a relief." Water bottle in hand, I stand and follow Corban toward a stand of trees.

He leads me onto a sand-covered path winding through sun-warmed evergreens. I breathe in the heady pine aroma. "Wow, Corban, this is beautiful."

"Yeah, I like it back here. The trail is short but private. What's on your mind?"

I hesitate, not sure where to begin. Finally, I nudge a pinecone off the trail with the side of my slipper. "You know I was married, right?"

He nods and starts walking, but not so fast I can't keep up. "Logan told me about the night Noreen brought you into the dining hall and took you up on stage. He said you lost your husband to cancer. Must have been a rough time for you, for both of you."

"Yes, it was." I match my steps to his. "Marcela says you went through something similar with your fiancée. Her name was Shelby, right?"

He looks surprised. "No one mentions her anymore."

"I hope I haven't caused you pain—"

"No, you haven't. It's good to hear her name again. She died suddenly. Only sick a week or so. Ruby Jade was ticked with her parents because they took her to a hospital and didn't ask for a healing ceremony. She wouldn't let them have the funeral at FFOW, so they had it at another church. Since then, no one dares talk about Shelby, except my family. It's almost as though she never existed."

"The shock must have rocked your world and your plans for the future."

He stuffs his hands in his pockets. "For a long time after, I felt as if I was in a dark cloud, like I couldn't see a foot in front of me. You must have felt something similar."

"I did, although booze had a lot to do with my dark cloud. How did you survive the pain? I assume alcohol wasn't an option for you."

"I had a different addiction, one not only accepted but encouraged by Leadership."

"Really?" I slow my steps. "What was it?"

"Work." He stops and jams his hands in his back pockets. "I volunteered for every possible work project, which kept me too tired to think or feel. I couldn't dwell on what might have been or even the fact Shelby was gone. To be honest, it felt good to be bone-tired day in and day out."

"Does that mean you haven't processed your loss?" We're face to face now. "I mean, I'm just now coming to the place where I don't have to rely on liquor to dull the pain."

"If my parents hadn't broken my round-the-clock work cycle..." He shakes his head. "I'd probably be dead."

"I assume their intervention was without Ruby Jade's approval."

"Right." He snaps a pine needle from a tree and slips it between his teeth. "Better than a toothpick."

"If you say so." I have a feeling it doesn't taste all that great. "How did they convince you to stop?"

"My mother pulled the mom card on me."

"Oh, yeah?" I tilt my head.

"Early one morning, four a.m. to be exact..." He chuckles. "I returned from a work project and slipped into the house, hoping to catch a shower and a couple hours of sleep before I started another project at eight.

"But Mom, who was waiting for me in the living room, had a different plan. She switched on a lamp and told me to sit. Scared the daylights out of me."

I laugh. "Bet it did."

"First off, I didn't know she was there, and secondly, she hadn't used that tone of voice with me since I was young. I fell into a chair across from her, wondering what in the world I'd done to upset her.

"She got right to the point, said I had to cut way back on work projects. She also said I had to face my loss and ride the waves of pain, which were sure to come. I was so tired I didn't argue with her. I got up, went to bed and slept for almost two days straight. Then my parents sent me to counseling—*secret* counseling, of course. Ruby Jade would have had a cow. We're supposed to take all our problems to our esteemed leaders."

He shudders and continues. "The short answer is my family and the therapist helped me accept Shelby's death and move forward, helped me stop expecting to run into her at church."

"One reason I dropped out of college," I tell him, "was I kept seeing Eric ahead of me in the halls or turning a corner. I'd go chasing after him, but it would never be him."

"Crazy..." He shakes his head. "How our minds can trick us."

We start walking again.

"People must have thought I was crazy, and maybe I was for a while." I pause, remembering how scattered and lost I felt. "I've seen you volunteering at Ruby Jade's house and at the widow's house, the one with the bird nest in the gutter—and at the Saturday market. Are you sure you've cut back?"

"Believe me, you're seeing the scaled-down version."

"Marcela told me you weren't allowed to attend Shelby's funeral service."

"My biggest regret..." He rubs the stubble on his chin. "My family's biggest regret is we let Ruby Jade dictate our actions. Followers are warned to never step foot into other churches, for any reason. But we should have been there, we should have followed our hearts."

His face darkens. "Did Marcela tell you Ruby Jade and her minions attended Shelby's funeral?"

"Uh-huh."

"Still gets under my skin." He kicks a stone. It ricochets off a tree. "The counselor said being at the service would have provided closure and helped with the grief."

"Oh, Corban, I'm so sorry." I blink away tears. "Eric's funeral was the absolute worst thing I've ever endured." For a brief moment, I allow myself to recall the agony of the awful day. "But even worse would have been to miss it."

"There's a silver lining." His smile is sad, but his gaze holds something different, maybe hope or optimism. "That's when the lightbulb clicked on for my family and we began to pull away from FFOW."

We're looping back through the trees. I can see the others ahead.

"I wanted to talk with you…" I touch his arm. "To say I'm sorry for what happened to Shelby, and also to say I understand. The emptiness, loneliness and pain can feel so endless. What you experienced was tragic. I totally get it. If you ever need to talk, we'll find a private place to chat." I look up into the trees. "Like here."

"Thanks, Cassie. I appreciate sharing something so personal with you, even if it's hard to talk about." He ducks his head. "I hope we can take more walks, longer walks." With a shy grin, he adds, "That is, if you want to."

"I'd love to get to know you better, Corban. Making friends is a challenge around here."

"You're telling me. If I didn't have Logan and my parents, I'd go nuts. Ruby Jade has tried multiple times to separate us, but refuse. If it wasn't for our contributions to the offering plate—and to her jewelry fund, if you get my drift—she'd have kicked us out long ago."

"Might not be such a bad thing."

"Logan and I are waiting for our parents to figure out the mortgage situation. We want to be around to support them when the volcano blows."

We're nearing the picnic table.

I have one more question to ask him. "Has Marcela been able to talk to her parents and Rodrigo?"

"Yes." He grins. "The calls went through without a hitch."

"Wonderful. I'm so happy for her." Someday, not today, but someday, I'll be able to share her joy with her.

Sebastian is gathering the lunch items. He asks, "What's this about calls?"

Logan explains how the three of us created a way for Marcela to communicate with her husband and parents. He finishes with a big smile and a wide flourish. "So far, the plan is working great."

"Good job." Sebastian shakes each of our hands. "I'm britches-bustin' proud of you three."

Corban grimaces. "You don't need to be that proud."

"You're fighting the system and standing up for what's right. Cat True, it won't be long until your friend makes the big break."

"I hope so."

"She's had a taste of freedom."

Other than peeling and slicing cucumbers for lunch, I don't have any other Saturday duties, mostly because Olivia is in bed with a migraine. Dread of a potential prison sentence must be getting to her. Everyone seems to breathe easier when she's not around. However, her absence doesn't compel my housemates to be any friendlier toward me.

After lunch, most of the others go to a neighbor's backyard to clean flowerbeds and thin overgrown blackberry bushes. They don't ask me to accompany them and I don't volunteer. They won't be compensated for their hard work—pruning prickly blackberry bushes is difficult, to say the least. Yet, the property owner will be obligated to pay the church. So much for Christian charity.

Alone in my upstairs bedroom—Ruby Jade has yet to assign another roommate—I have to admit I'm bored. I'd almost rather be cleaning house than sitting on my bed with nothing to do. I could call home, but as much as I'd love to talk with my parents, I hesitate.

How long can I maintain the charade? I was evasive with them during my early days on the street. They eventually caught on and called my bluff. If I don't connect while I have a chance, they'll worry about me and might even come to see for themselves what my life is all about.

I go into the bathroom, close the door and dial my mom.

She answers immediately. "Cassie, sweetheart—so good to see your name on my phone screen."

"I'm happy to hear your voice, Mom."

"What have you been doing lately?"

"Today, I'm enjoying a day off, putting my feet up."

"Are you still working and attending sessions at the rehab center?"

"Mm-hmm."

"Is the counseling helpful?"

"Uh-huh." My talks with Myrtle Mae and Sebastian and my walk with Corban surely count for therapy. "They're keeping my head screwed on straight."

She laughs. "Good for them."

We talk about her volunteer work and Kip's latest antics, and then she gets a call. "Cassie, I'd better take this. I'm at a coffee shop, waiting for a friend. She's the one calling."

"I'll let you go, Mom, and catch up with you later."

We say our goodbyes and I hit the end button, relieved. The shorter our talks, the less likely I'll be to spill the beans.

Kip doesn't answer. He and his buddies are probably scaling a mountain right now, or maybe they're already at the top, taking macho selfies. I envy him, yet I'm happy he can live out his passion with friends who share his enthusiasm for a view above the world's craziness, one I can only imagine.

Saturday night, the household Faithful follow their usual rituals to make themselves shiny and pretty. No one asks me to help, so I stay in my bedroom out of the way. I try Kip one more time. And again, no answer.

Sunday morning, I fix my hair and apply the requisite makeup, including the all-important eye makeup as well as nutmeg foundation. I put on pants rather than a dress, fairly certain my doctor-ordered foot attire would not contribute to the altogether look Noreen advocates. No one comments on my outfit at breakfast. In fact, they don't acknowledge my existence except when they want me to pass the salt or the butter.

However, when I trail them into the garage and over to the big van, Olivia, who's in the front passenger seat with the window down, does a doubletake. "You can't walk into church like that."

I look from my flowered jacket and blue blouse to my black pants, white socks and tiger slippers and then up at her.

"Why not?" Owen asks. "She's clothed."

My thoughts, exactly.

"Not my point," Olivia snarls. "Her attire is entirely inappropriate for our sanctuary, our sacred place."

Sacred place? I fold my arms. *Sacred as a Roman colosseum packed with bloodthirsty throngs cheering believers' deaths.*

She glances at her watch and scowls at me. "You have one minute to put on a dress, take off those stupid socks, and change into real shoes."

The Alquist family, along with Scott, Candice and baby Tristen, hurry to their cars. I bet they're glad they don't have to ride in the Pritchards' van. It's big, but it can't hold all nineteen household members—seventeen since Zachary and Marcela left.

"That would go against doctor's orders," I tell her. "I'll stay here."

"You can't..." Conflicting emotions battle on her red face.

The others hold their collective breaths.

Owen taps the steering wheel. Tap...tap...tap... "Olivia, we need to go, or we'll be late."

She swears.

Eyebrows raise.

The kids ogle each other.

"You slut." She jabs her forefinger at me. "You're determined to ruin my life."

"For Pete's sake, Olivia." Owen slaps the dash. "Isn't that a bit melodramatic?"

She whips around. "I'm going to report you for taking an apostle's name in vain."

"You just took God's name in vain."

"I did not."

He aims a thumb behind them. "We have witnesses."

She swivels. I can't see her glare, but it must be fiery because the others all turn away.

Owen starts the engine.

Staring straight ahead, Olivia growls, "Get in."

I search for a handhold, unsure how to pull myself up and into the van.

The Pritchards' oldest son, Jeffrey, climbs out and helps me into a seat by the door. I murmur a grateful, "Thank you." Takes a lot of courage for a teenager to chance provoking his volatile mother. Maybe his father's uncharacteristic boldness inspired him.

The ride to church is quiet. Even the children stare straight ahead. When we arrive, Olivia bounds from the van—I didn't know she had it in her—and marches into the building. I swear steam is spewing from the top of her head.

Jeffrey helps me to the pavement. But from then on, I'm on my own, other than a mumbled "sorry" from Owen as he trots past. No one walks with me or opens a door for me. I take it my housemates don't want to be seen with such an inappropriately dressed person.

Inside the building, my inclination is to disappear in a secluded corner and skip Sunday school. But, really, where can I hide? This place has cameras everywhere. And my absence from the class would probably trigger another cleanse.

I slide onto a metal folding chair in the single women's classroom just before Inez struts in. At the sound of her heels rat-tat-tatting across the floor, the women stop talking and sit taller, hands in their laps. The smell of hairspray hangs in the air. I can taste it.

Clasping my hands, I pray Inez has a full agenda, one which doesn't include ridiculing the members of her Sunday school class. But, no such luck. The first thing our fearsome leader does is point out a run in a woman's nylon.

"I'm sorry, Inez," the woman grovels. "It happened when I was carrying my husband's music stand into the church."

"You should be more careful."

"I should be."

"Tell your husband to carry the music stand. You will carry his instrument."

"His horn is heavy. That's why—"

"Do as I say. And keep an extra pair of pantyhose in your purse."

"What a wonderful idea. I'll put a pair in my purse the instant I get home."

In my jaded opinion, the woman is overly eager.

Inez's long pause triggers fidgeting amongst the onlookers. "You let go of Jesus, Gloria."

"I didn't mean to."

"What if you dropped over dead right then?" Her voice rises. "You would have gone straight–to–hell." Inez's wicked snigger is straight from hell.

Gloria covers her mouth. "Oh, no…"

Inez's lips twist. "Think about it."

I want to jump up and shout, "That's a lie!" But I haven't forgotten the last time I contradicted Inez. If I rise, she might somehow see my slippers and chew me out. I shove my feet under my chair.

Like a vacuum, fear has sucked all noise from the room. No one moves. But then a buzz invades the stillness. I picture an angry hornet on the prowl. The women peer at their purses by their feet, each one obviously wondering if *her* phone is the culprit.

Who would call a FFOW member on a Sunday morning? They rarely, if ever, speak with relatives who don't attend the church, and their FFOW friends and family members are all in Sunday school classes.

Inez raises a palm to silence the mute group and places her other hand over her ever-present Bluetooth. "Yes?" After a moment, she says, "I'll be happy to do that." She smirks. "It'll be a good accountability reminder for the class."

Uh-oh. Her words sound ominous.

All around me, heads jerk, eyelids quiver, shoulders twitch, fingers flutter. I'm not the only one concerned about what Inez is "happy to do."

Hands folded on the lectern, she leans toward the class. "Ladies, we have a problem, one we must deal with immediately." She releases a long sigh. "I hate that I can't share the lesson I prepared for you. It's truly inspired by God. But it will keep until next week. Or, I may call a special session just for us. Wouldn't it be marvelous?"

When no one responds, threat tinges her voice. "Wouldn't it be *marvelous?*"

A woman shouts, "Amen." Another calls out, "Hallelujah, bring it on." The resulting laughter lessens the tension in the room.

"Time to get down to business." Inez checks the man-size jeweled watch on her wrist. "Cassandra Turner. Come to the front."

I blink, surprised to hear my name slip from her glossy lips. I'm a slimy worm in her world. But then her command registers in my brain. I stand and shuffle to the front.

Inez stares at my feet, like they're bugs she's about to stomp.

I stop several feet from her stiletto heels.

Statue-still, the wide-eyed women watch us, wary anticipation on their faces. All but one woman, that is. Seated near the window, Myrtle Mae's eyes are closed, her lips are moving, and her hands are folded beneath her chin. Her beautiful hair, which is loose today, glows in the sunlight.

Assured her prayers to God are with me in this godless environment, I focus on Inez and wait.

She swivels the wooden podium to face me. "I'm told your cleanse last week was incomplete."

I clasp my hands behind my back. "I wouldn't know. It was my first experience."

"If you'll recall, you interrupted Zachary Russell's cleanse."

"As I recall, I stopped his classmates from beating him black and blue."

The woman in the first row who's been eyeing my tiger slippers gasps.

Inez's face darkens.

"However," I quickly add, "I did not interrupt my own, uh, experience." I can't bring myself to say cleanse. Jesus is the only one who can cleanse my soul. "The sheriff's deputies did the interrupting."

Inez's nostrils flare.

All around the room, women draw in air, and I remember they have no idea what goes on in other households—or in the rest of the world, for that matter. The atmosphere tingles with their excitement as well as their perfume-infused sweat. They shift, ever so slightly, closer to the edges of their seats. I imagine them thinking, *This is going to be interesting.* They may ignore me and keep their distance, but I add spice to their sad, dreary lives.

While thoughts bounce like racquetballs about my brain, Inez clenches and unclenches her fists. I'm pretty sure she'd love to yank my hair out by the roots. Has she noticed I'm wearing makeup today? I even included eye makeup—sans eye shadow. Her expression tells me she's not impressed.

"Lucille." She spits out the name, and the front-row woman jolts to attention.

"Yes, Inez?"

"Place a chair in the corner for our cleansee to sit on."

I raise an eyebrow. *Cleansee?*

Lucille leaps up, does as she was ordered, and returns to her seat.

Inez thrusts her index finger at me. "Sit."

CHAPTER TEN

I hate being treated like a dog, yet I obediently slipper-slide over to the chair. Sebastian's words replay in my head. *You're a child of the King, no matter what some misguided folks might say.* Whatever they say or do to me, I will remember they are pathetic, ignorant puppets. I write *Puppet* in blue on the women's foreheads and *CHARLATAN* in red on Inez's forehead.

Similar to Olivia, she's furious. God only knows why. I picture red-hot lava erupting from the top of her head, spilling over her highlighted hair and dripping down her white suit.

"To your feet, troops!" She motions to the class. "Time to fight God's battle. We will be victorious this time! We will prevail! The demons will bow before us!" She's nearly frothing at the mouth, working the others into a frenzy.

"We will prevail, we will prevail!"

Someone shouts, "Banish the denizens of Hades."

"Yes, yes, Jesus."

"Thy will be done. Thy will be done."

Pushing away chairs to make room, they advance toward me like a pack of hungry wolves. Some have hard faces and angry eyes. Others have empty eyes and blank faces. None of them blink.

Inez mounts a chair behind them, yelling, "Cassandra Turner, you disobey the phone rules and talk too often and too long with the uncircumcised!"

Uncircumcised? I give her a confused look. "I occasionally talk with my parents and my brother. They're the only people I call or who call me."

"Exactly. You're listening to liars."

I shake my head.

The women close in. One of them bumps my toes. I swallow the pain and pull my feet beneath the chair.

"Confess, Cassandra," someone calls.

Others chant, "Listening to liars, listening to liars, listening—"

"You missed four church services!" Inez shouts. "You turned your back on God."

"I was injured and following doctor's orders."

She snarls, "Your demon doctor is not one of us."

"Demon doctor" becomes the new mantra. "Demon doctor, demon doctor, demon doctor…"

Inez waves her arms. "You were injured because you ran away from God."

"I did not run away from God."

"If you hadn't let go of Jesus, your feet would be fine today."

I stop arguing with her. What's the use?

"You let go of Jesus!" the women scream, inches from my face. Saliva splatters my cheeks. They shake their fists at me.

Eyes full of fury, a teenage girl shouts, "You let go of Jesus!" and slaps my cheek.

"Evil whore!" Inez rages at the top of her lungs, her face bordering on purple. "You watched Olivia's arrest without authorization."

Her statement drains the noise from the room. In the void left behind, the women gape from Inez to me. They obviously don't know what she's talking about.

Inez scowls. "You viewed an arrest without Leadership authorization. You celebrated the arrest, you arrogant pig."

The women glance at each other, obviously confused.

Myrtle Mae's voice plays in my head. *Pay no mind to Inez. She's a heartless twit who tears others down to build herself up.*

"You cheered one of the worst travesties to come upon this church."

Worse than destroying families and abusing children?

"Without authorization," the group shouts. "Travesty, travesty."

"Arrogant pig, arrogant pig." Someone kicks my shin.

"You should have mourned!" Inez screams, "not cheered."

Accusations and slaps fly at me from all sides. They hit my face, my shoulders, the back of my head. Once again, I feel my spirit leave the chair. This time, I float behind and above my body.

Their shrieks fade. I no longer smell their fear, their sweat, their shampoos, soaps and perfumes. I no longer feel their spit or their slaps and kicks. From a distance, their actions are silly and robotic, their faces contorted.

I'm at peace, yet I'm not. I can't defend myself because I don't know what's expected of me. Should I say something? Or simply return lifeless stare for lifeless stare?

"Confess, Cassandra," they cry. "Confess, confess, confess."

My mantra becomes a song. *I'm a child of the King, to his promises I'll cling. I'm a child of the King, all his praises I'll sing. I'm a child of the King—*

Inez, still standing on the chair, raises her arms. "Quiet." She turns. "Myrtle Mae, why are you still in your chair?"

Myrtle Mae opens her eyes. "You know I don't approve of cleanses, Inez."

"Whether or not," Inez barks, "whether or not you, in your ungodly condition approve, cleanses are the standard in this community and an opportunity for the cleansee to escape hell."

"I beg to differ." My sweet friend lifts her chin, daring to contradict Inez.

"I'll speak with Ruby Jade about this. You'll have to face her wrath."

"I've been facing my daughter's wrath for years. I'm sorry she cloned you to be—"

"Hush your mouth." Inez spins back to the women. "Carry on."

I glance at the clock. Almost time for the church service.

"What do you hear?" a young woman calls. "What is God telling you?"

A woman shouts, "Don't resist what God has for you!"

I don't know how it happens, but I return to my body and raise my arms.

They stop—and wait, eyes wide, mouths open, shallow breaths silent.

"I confess…" Forcing what I hope is a penitent facade onto my face and into my voice, I cry, "I confess I did not mourn Olivia's arrest."

"Don't mention her name," Inez orders.

"I identified with her, for I've been in her shoes, but I did not mourn." I close my eyes and rock back and forth, back and forth.

"Come out demons of arrogance and selfishness," demands an older woman.

"I confess I call my parents and my brother more than once a month." I open my eyes. "And I do not watch how many minutes I'm on each call." I lower my hands.

"Demon of disobedience, be gone!" Inez shouts. In almost the same breath, she adds in a normal tone, "Time for church. Wrap it up, girls."

"Be gone demons, be gone demons, be gone demons…" As one, they pivot, fluttering their hands toward the window while they make their way to their chairs. My guess is they're ushering the imagined evil spirits out of the building.

Without as much as a glance at me, they grab their purses and follow Inez from the room—everyone except Myrtle Mae.

I take a deep breath and slowly blow it out, gathering my wits and calming my spirit. Thank God that's over. Maybe I won't have to endure another such session for a while.

Myrtle Mae gets to her feet and walks my direction. She bumps into a chair on her way from the corner. Considering her vision, one stumble isn't bad. Even so, I'm sad she can't see clearly. I feel like I should help her, but I'm trembling, and my muscles are noodles.

When she's near enough to touch my arm, she whispers, "I'm so sorry they put you through one of their so-called cleanses. Are you okay, sweetie?"

"I think so." I stand on wobbly legs and, one hand on a chairback for support, give her a weak hug. "I'm a bit shaky, but I remembered encouraging things you and Sebastian have said to me. And I could tell you were praying for me, which helped, a lot."

"I was praying, like I do for all of Inez's victims." She chuckles. "Good timing with the confession."

"I kept my eye on the clock. I knew I couldn't peek at my watch."

"I'll walk with you to the sanctuary."

"Are you sure? No one else wants to get within ten feet of me."

"We'll make a show of you leading me there." She reaches for my arm.

"Can we stop by the restroom? They didn't intentionally spit on me, at least I don't think they did, but I was sprayed." I shudder. "I have a silly urge to wash my face." Maybe I can dab at it with a paper towel, so the makeup doesn't come off. I wouldn't want to get castigated for revealing bare skin in church.

We find two seats near the aisle in the women's section and sit. I fold my hands in my lap and prepare to appear attentive.

"Excuse me."

The voice is familiar.

I turn.

Hank is standing in the aisle, his hand out. "Phone check. I'll take your phone, after you enter your password."

I stare at him like he's lost his mind.

The woman on the other side of Myrtle Mae reaches past her to grab my sleeve. "Just give him your phone. Don't try to hide from God and create another scene."

She thinks I created the Sunday school fiasco? These people are nuts.

I snap the pink purse open, pull out the phone and turn it on. After I tap in the code, I hand it to him, praying he won't find anything offensive.

A moment later, he gives it back and turns to a man on the other side of the aisle.

"He's making sure you don't have any photos," Myrtle Mae whispers. "Whether they're of family members, pets or friends, they're considered false idols. Even scenery is off-limits. Only pagans worship God's creation rather than God himself."

I sigh. Every minute is a new revelation.

The service begins with music led by a group of perfectly attired teenagers, boys in the top two rows, girls in the front two. Too wrung out from the cleanse and the phone stress to sing, I mouth *rhubarb* over and over. My high-school choir director told us to do that when we forgot the words.

To still my frazzled mind, I think of a Sunday school song from childhood. *Jesus loves me, this I know, for the Bible tells me so. Yes, Jesus loves me, yes...* Yes, he does love me.

The music stops. I close my mouth, and we all sit.

Noreen strides across the stage in her "altogether" outfit of green heels, ankle-length green-and-yellow suit and green earrings. She steps behind the pulpit. "I have two very special announcements this morning." Her smile is so big I fear her red lips will split. Not a pretty picture. "Very exciting," she says.

Myrtle Mae elbows me. "Hang onto your seat."

I don't know if she's warning me or being facetious. I sneak a sidelong glance at my elderly friend. By the crease in her cheek, I'd guess the latter.

"We have hired..." Noreen drags out her words. "A new director...for our Transformation Way program!"

"Hallelujah!" the people shout. "Glory to God!"

She waits until the pandemonium settles. "He's a very qualified man with a PhD in psychology. In addition..." Her focus glides from one side of the room to the other. "We've hired an addiction counselor. Transformation Way is now fully staffed, PGIH!"

"PGIH, PGIH, PGIH!"

I should be applauding with the others. After all, I'll become well acquainted with the staff—if Ruby Jade allows me into the program. Even with a judge's order, I know I'm at her mercy, or lack thereof. Rather than cheering, I'm thinking, *fully staffed with only two people?*

"And..." She raises her hand to quiet the over-exuberant crowd. "Transformation Way reopens its doors at eight a.m. tomorrow morning."

"Glory be," Myrtle Mae whispers. "About time, daughter."

The congregation rises in a rush of wind, roaring their approval. Myrtle Mae and I are a bit slower to get to our feet and join the clapping.

Eight a.m. Huh. Seems I would have been informed. I'll have to tell Sebastian. Wasn't it just a few days ago he stopped by the courthouse? Now, I'm curious. What did the judge say to Ruby Jade? And how did she find replacement staff so quickly?

The applause stops. Noreen exits one of the platform's side doors and Ruby Jade enters from the other. Today, she's dressed in black with red accents. Her updo includes a sparkly red tiara.

"To further elaborate on Noreen's announcement, her wonderful announcement..." She smiles her most benevolent smile. "Dr. Hoffman, the director, will be flying in from Seattle two days a week, and Ms. Montoya, our counselor, will be driving over from Billings three days a week."

I frown. The two-hour drive each way won't be fun—or safe—in the winter. And as a veteran of other programs, I'm horrified they won't have fulltime onsite staff. What if someone has a meltdown or a rough withdrawal? Or falls off the wagon?

Maybe they'll utilize an on-call nurse. But now that I think about it, why would they? The school doesn't have a nurse on staff.

"You can be assured," Ruby Jade adds, "we'll encourage both individuals to move here and join our congregation as soon as possible."

Oh, I bet you will.

Noreen stops me on the way out of church.

My stomach jumps to my throat. One-on-one encounters with any member of the Fearsome Threesome are never good.

"Just to make sure you understand, Cassandra..." She shakes her finger at me. "You *will be* participating in Transformation Way, no matter the condition of your feet."

And here I was worried Ruby Jade wouldn't let me attend.

"Judge's orders. You must comply. Eight o'clock sharp tomorrow morning. Be there."

Funny how she's shifting their noncompliance onto my shoulders.

"I don't have transportation. How will I get here from the Pritchards' house?"

"Oh…" She scratches her neck. "I'll discuss the situation with Leadership and let you know."

I would suggest Olivia drop me off when she drives the kids to school, but I'd rather not be in the same vehicle with her, if I can avoid it. "Does this mean I'll no longer help Sebastian Longpre maintain Ruby Jade's property?"

"I'm, I'm sure…" Her eyes flick from side to side. "As I said, I'll let you know." Head high, she tap-tap-taps on her tall green heels down the long hallway.

As before, Jeffrey helps me into the van before he closes the door and sits in the back. I'm fastening my seatbelt when Olivia's phone dings. She listens and then turns, a happy smile lighting her face.

"Cassandra, you're moving to the women's dormitory this afternoon."

She's so gleeful, I'm surprised she doesn't add, "Good riddance to bad rubbish."

"You will attend Transformation Way every morning and do yardwork at Ruby Jade's home every afternoon."

I'm about to ask how I'll get to Ruby Jade's yard, when she adds, "Sebastian Longpre, Ruby Jade's property manager, will pick you up at twelve-fifteen each weekday and deliver you directly to the dormitory after work." Without giving me a chance to respond or ask questions, she turns around.

"Thank you, Olivia."

No reply. Why Noreen can't call me, I don't know. But at least I now have a vague idea of what my future holds.

Biting my lip to contain my joy, I revel in how my life has once again changed for the better, despite the chaos the FFOW control freaks create. I'm moving out of the Pritchards' house, happy I won't be leaving either Zachary or Marcela behind, and happy they're both on a path to freedom. I'm finally, finally, *finally* beginning the program that's *my* path to freedom and a future. And I'm staying at a job I love.

I'll be able to see Sebastian and Myrtle Mae every day and Corban and Logan now and then. I may have to endure more cleanses, but I'm grateful I can be with my friends and stop lying to my parents. *Thank you, Jesus.*

The moment the lunch dishes are cleared, Deanna appears at the opening between the dining room and kitchen with a cardboard box in each hand. "I'll drop these by your door."

"You have one-half hour to pack." Olivia turns from wiping the counter. "And to clean the bedroom *and* the bathroom. You will leave them spotless, or else." She doesn't elaborate on the "or else."

I consider asking, "What's the rush?" But I'm as anxious to go as she is to get rid of me.

On my way through the kitchen to the stairs, I grab grocery bags from the pantry. Olivia watches but says nothing. In the bathroom, I throw my toiletries and jewelry into the bags. My bath towel, hand towel and washcloth go in the bottom of one box and the shoes in the bottom of the other. Over those items, I pile clothes from my dresser and the closet. Olivia can keep her hangers. If she found even one missing, I might land in jail again. Or, at the very least, it'd trigger another cleanse.

All the while, I'm wondering if I should mention the boxes my mom sent, which I hope are in the basement. Should I stir that pot? Or let it be for the time-being? I hate to leave my guitar behind, but temperature-wise, it's in a safe place. If it's where I think it is.

"Cassandra," Olivia calls up the stairs. "Time's up. Scott and Michael will carry your things to the van. Whatever you leave behind will be burned."

Wow, she must want to purge this house of all signs of my existence. She'll probably wipe the walls with disinfectant and bleach the bedding. I keep the bedroom and bathroom clean, so the "or else" shouldn't be an issue, but you never know with Olivia.

"Ready?" The men are at the door.

"Ready." I grab my pink purse and the two grocery bags. "All packed."

From behind Michael's back, Scott gives me a sympathetic look.

They carry my boxes to the van. Candice and Deanna are already in the van. I presume they'd rather I not be alone with their husbands, slut that I am. The older women must be watching their kids. No other residents appear in the garage to wave goodbye or say they'll see me at church.

Climbing into the van with my purse and bags, I'm almost disappointed Olivia isn't taking the opportunity to send me away with a parting sarcasm.

CHAPTER ELEVEN

I take one last look at the Pritchards' house, happy to go but sad to leave behind my guitar—and the vanilla extract. The place seems normal from the outside. Are all FFOW homes as abnormal as this one is? I hope not.

I'm fairly certain Olivia is observing my departure from behind the blinds of the very window through which I watched her arrest and departure to jail. What will she do to celebrate? Have a swig from the big vanilla bottle in the cupboard? She needs something to smooth her jagged edges, but it'll take an elixir stronger than vanilla extract to accomplish such a challenging task.

I wave to let her know I know she's there. And to give her one more irritant to add to the many ways I've ruined her life.

Silence reigns supreme on the ride from Fellowship Neighborhood to the FFOW complex. After the gate, we navigate the treelined road, rolling past the buildings I've been inside—the church, the school and the dining hall. We continue to the three tall-short-tall buildings I noticed when I first came to FFOW.

Michael turns onto the street that runs between a hill on one side and the mini campus on the other. The buildings sit some distance apart, with grass all around. I wonder if Corban and Logan mow these lawns too.

Deanna acts as tour guide. "The first building is the men's dorm. Women are to maintain a twenty-foot distance at all times."

I stare at the two-story brick structure, not at all shocked women are forbidden to get close—or that she was quick to inform me of yet another rule. God forbid I might slip a toe inside the male-only zone. The dorm faces the other two buildings, and several cars are parked in front of it.

A dark-haired man walks from the dorm to a car. I don't know many people here, but he looks familiar. And then realization strikes—it's Rodrigo.

Candice, who's seated beside me, whispers, "Don't be lusting after Marcela's husband, Cassandra."

I squint at her—*what's wrong with you, woman?*—and whisper back, "I was trying to figure out where I'd seen him before. Is he in the rehab program?"

She shakes her head.

"The middle building is the Transformation Way center," Deanna continues. "You'll be spending a lot of time there, when you're not working or volunteering or attending services, of course."

Of course.

The center is one level and sided with dull red brick, same as the dorms. The front doors face several empty parking slots and the street beyond.

"The far building is where the women reside," Deanna continues. "No men allowed within twenty feet." *At least the ridiculous rule is fair, not favoring one gender over the other.* Like the men's dorm, the women's front doors are oriented toward the rehab center. Bushes, flowers and trees serve as boundaries between buildings. Sidewalks connect the dorms to the center, but none go directly between the dorms.

Michael pulls into a parking slot in front of the women's dorm. I gather my purse and grocery bags. Scott helps me and the other women from the van, holding my elbow only long enough for me to gain firm footing on the asphalt. Then he and Michael retrieve my boxes from the back.

Deanna and Candice hold the double glass doors for the men. I follow them into the lobby. A set of stairs is in front of us, with a hallway behind it. The walls are white, and the place has the same flowery smell as the sanctuary. I glance around. Sure enough, a beige vase of fake but perfumed pastel blossoms sits in a corner.

Closed doors with windows on the upper half anchor each side of the small foyer. Deanna rings the doorbell beside the door with a dark curtain blocking the window. A faint chime sounds, and a moment later, a tall fiftyish woman opens the door. Behind her, I catch a glimpse of a recliner and a television. *Television?*

She peers at us through tortoise-shell Harry Potter glasses and in a nasal voice, says, "May I help you?"

"Eunice," Deanna says, "this is Cassandra Turner." To me, she says, "Cassandra, this is Eunice Zaforris, household guardian for Transformation Way's women's dormitory."

Eunice is at least six-feet tall and big-boned, though not heavyset. Her straight iron-gray hair flips this way and that at about jaw level. The smudged round lenses lessen the severity of her angular face but amplify her eyes—one green and one mostly brown. They have a wildness about them unrelated to color. A result of too many years at FFOW, perhaps?

Her tan t-shirt is stained, her brown polyester pants snagged, her socks dingy, and her torn tennis shoes runover. She smells like Vicks. Do the leaders realize she lacks the altogether look? Maybe, similar to the Seattle director and the Montana therapist, she's not a Follower.

I step closer and extend my hand. "Nice to meet you, Ms. Zaforris."

Eunice is eyeing the men and the boxes. "This is as far as you go," she insists with her nasal voice. "No men allowed in the dorm rooms. In fact, you've already crossed the twenty-foot line."

"We understand," Michael says. "Leadership gave us permission to drive here and carry the boxes into the building. Our wives are prepared to carry them to the room." He gives the box he's holding to Deanna and Candice, who each take an end.

Candice smiles at Eunice. "Lead the way, and we'll follow."

Eunice, who's still inside her apartment, shuts the door.

Deanna and Candice stare at each other over the box.

We wait. And wait. Scott and the women set the boxes on the floor. I place my bags on a stair. Deanna is about to ring the doorbell again, when Eunice opens the door.

She's now wearing a lanyard around her neck with a ring of keys hanging from it. As if she's never seen us before, she studies our faces, one person at a time. Apparently satisfied we're the same people she saw earlier, she steps out of the apartment, pivots and locks the door.

I gather my purse and the bags. Candice and Deanna lift the box. Eunice scowls at the men. "You two stay here."

"We will," Scott assures her. "We'll be here when you return."

Her eyebrow flicks, as if she doesn't believe him, but she starts up the wooden stairway. It has a landing halfway up, where the stairs turn. Like the foyer, the railings and the walls are white.

At the top landing, closed doors line the long hallway, which runs both directions. Unadorned windows let in light at the far ends. The dormitory reminds me of a hotel. However, a hotel would have wallpaper and pictures plus a colorful carpet, not plain vinyl tile.

Eunice leads us to the rooms on the left. Midway along the hall, she stops to sort through the keys. The jangle is loud in the quiet hallway. After much searching, she picks one. Evidently, it's the correct key because the door unlocks with her first try.

She steps aside, and Candice and Deanna make their way into the room. I follow.

The room has white walls, no surprise, and a vinyl-tiled floor. It smells musty. Maybe it hasn't been aired out in a while.

I'm happy to see the narrow room has only one bed. I don't mind roommates, and I miss Marcela, but I have to admit the solitude I've experienced these last few days has been good for my jittery soul. The dark-blue bedspread matches the curtains on the solitary window. The closet looks adequate, and a chest of drawers with a small lamp on top hunkers in the corner. But I don't see a bathroom door—or a camera. Is it possible?

Candice and Deanna set the box on the floor and straighten. Deanna says, "We'll get the other box and then be out of your hair." She talks to Eunice without looking at me. My non-person status with the Pritchard household prevails, even when they're getting rid of me.

I walk to the window and push aside a curtain to check the view. Ahh, the cemetery. It's beautiful, with acres of green grass, bushes and trees surrounded by a short split-rail fence.

From what I can see, the headstones are simple and uniform in shape and color—no mismatched tombstones in the FFOW graveyard. I can't tell from here, but my guess is the engravings are limited to names plus birth and death dates. Creative epitaphs and etched designs are undoubtedly of the arrogance or pride demon.

The ornate granite slab that designates Eric's gravesite in the windswept Wyoming cemetery where his parents buried him would stand out like a sore thumb here. They interred him there because I couldn't afford funeral costs. I've only visited his grave once, and it was shortly after he died. The experience was so heartrending I haven't returned.

I turn to Eunice, who has a faraway expression in her mismatched eyes. "The view from here is pretty."

She blinks. "What did you say?" Each time she speaks, her nasal voice catches me off-guard. Could be she has sinus issues, which would explain the Vicks.

"The view is pretty." While I have her attention, I ask where the bathroom is.

She points to the open doorway. "Through the door and to the right—across from the stairs. Five toilets, five sinks, five showers."

"Great." No more private bathroom for me, but I survived the communal restrooms in jail. This can't be any worse. "How long have you been doing this?"

"Doing what?"

"Serving as a household guardian."

She rubs her chin bristles. "Two-and-a-half days...or is it three-and-a-half?"

"What?" I drop my jaw. "I expected you to say years or months, not days."

"I was told the previous household guardian disappeared."

If I could, I'd disappear too.

"Ran away with the guy who was the household guardian for the men's dorm."

I'm not sure how to respond, but I definitely understand the urge to flee this place.

"That's what I heard." She shrugs. "Don't quote me."

Visiting with someone who actually talks to me and who doesn't measure every word against WWRJS—what would Ruby Jade say—is refreshing. "Were you hired from the congregation?" I ask.

"I don't go to this church, or any church. When I was ten-years old, I decided religion isn't for me."

"Oh, I see."

"I came from transitional housing in town. Moved here eight months ago to live with my niece and her family. Then she and her boyfriend started having trouble. Actually, I think they were having trouble all along, but he blamed me, like my ex-husband blamed me for everything. So, I left—both places."

"That's too bad."

"I only had a few days of transitional housing left when this position came open. Now, I have a disability check, a place to live and three meals a day. What more can I ask for?"

A paycheck would be good. I'm wondering if she'd mind if I asked about her disability, when Candice and Deanna return with the other box. They place it on the floor beside the first box, stand and swipe their hands on their pantlegs, as if the boxes are dirty. Or maybe it's because they contain my trashy stuff.

"We'll be on our way," Deanna says.

"Thank you." I smile. "And please thank your husbands for me. You have all been very kind."

She pivots toward the doorway.

Candice whispers, "Goodbye, Cassandra."

I respond by mouthing, *Do it.*

She looks away, but I know she knows what I mean. Next time I'm near her in church, I'll slip her the deputy's phone number.

I watch them go. In any other setting, I would have hugged both women and said, "See you at church." But not here. "Your children," I murmur. "Think of your children."

"What?" Eunice comes to stand beside me.

"I'm sorry." I turn to her. "I was thinking about their families."

"They seem like nice people."

"Uh-huh." Nice, maybe, but misguided, for sure. "Do you have any idea how many people are in the rehab program?"

"A woman just moved out…"

I'd bet my pink purse it was Trina.

"But with you replacing her, the women still outnumber the men two to one. Six women and three men."

I rear back. "That's all?"

"All I know of." She walks to the door. "You can unpack now. Supper is served in the cafeteria in two hours."

"Is the cafeteria downstairs?"

"The breakfast area is downstairs in the room opposite my apartment." She points at the floor. "It's stocked with cereal, milk, yogurt, bananas and such, but lunch and dinner are over at the center."

"I see. Does anyone live on the first floor, other than you? I saw a hallway—"

"No." She shakes her head. "For some reason, they want everyone upstairs, in this wing." Before she leaves, she says, "Stop by my apartment on your way to supper, and I'll walk you over there."

"Thank you. I'll do that."

With a little wave, she steps into the hallway and disappears.

Surprised by her thoughtfulness, I find myself near tears. She not only talked with me, she offered to walk me to the cafeteria. After the Pritchard household, she's a breath of fresh air to my battered spirit. I am doubly blessed to have escaped Olivia and gained a kindhearted dorm mom.

I'm also pleased to know Transformation Way has a cafeteria. I hadn't thought about what I'd eat once I left the Pritchards' household. The cafeteria will be a great place to get to know the other program participants.

The dorm, which could hold far more than six women, is so quiet I feel as though I'm the last person on earth. I open the window to hear birdsong and be reassured I'm not the only living creature around. I also leave my door ajar while I unpack my things in the hope someone will stop by.

However, the floor doesn't come alive until dinnertime. Hearing voices and doors open and close, I peek into the hall. Three women are to my right, headed for the stairs, and two are coming my way from the other direction.

I step out of my room. "May I walk with you?"

One of the women, a beautiful black lady with long dreads who looks to be in her forties, yawns and says, "Excuse me." She offers her hand. "Yes, please join us. I'm Shakyra."

I shake her hand. "I'm Cassie…well, Cassandra around here. I love your hair, but I'm surprised. Ruby Jade doesn't strike me as someone who'd approve of dreads."

"You're right. She's not happy with my hair. I told her the options were to shave my head or to have my hair stick straight out. It's thick and bushy." Shakyra chuckles. "You should have seen the look on her face. Neither option appealed to her, so she let me keep my dreads, but she said I had to remove the pagan beads—her term, not mine."

"Oh…" Having just met Shakyra, I'm not sure what to say.

The other woman introduces herself. "Welcome to the dorm, Cassandra. My name is Merikay." She's younger and shorter than Shakyra, maybe thirty-five or so, with some Asian heritage in her background. Her porcelain skin is flawless, and her red lips are perfect, like a doll's. Her jaw-length brown bob reflects the hall light. She rubs her eyes. "That was the first nap I've had in ages."

"Yeah." Shakyra stretches her arms. "I had trouble relaxing, for fear I was late to a work project. But once I fell asleep, I went deep. Didn't know a thing until the alarm clock jarred me awake."

Are Shakyra and Merikay their real names or names Ruby Jade gave them? I pull my door closed. "I should lock this, but I don't have a key. I forgot to ask for one."

They snicker.

I raise a questioning eyebrow.

"We aren't issued keys because we're not supposed to lock our doors," Merikay says. "The rule is for our safety in case of fire, we've been told. Also, if you ever mistakenly lock your door or need to get into the storage room, be forewarned Eunice tends to lose her set of keys."

"The big bunch around her neck?"

"Somehow, they disappear in her little two-room apartment. And she won't let us help her search for them."

On the way out, we stop by Eunice's place. I knock, and she opens the door right away, keys still dangling from her neck. She doesn't say anything, just closes and locks the door.

She can lock her door, but we can't lock ours? Citing the same "in case of fire" logic, the Pritchards insisted we not lock our bedroom doors. They even did random checks. But this is not a home. It's a dorm, a huge, empty, isolated dorm. I've slept in too many risky places to feel at ease behind an unlocked door.

Walking to the center doesn't take long. Shakyra and Merikay give me a quick tour before we join the others. Though Eunice follows behind, she doesn't say much. I believe I'm going to appreciate this household guardian. She's the polar opposite of Olivia.

Unlike other rehab facilities, no motivational posters adorn the foyer. Instead, scripture verses are painted in large flowing script on two of the white walls. On one side: "There is a way which seemeth right unto a man, but the end thereof are the ways of death." Added in a smaller font is the source, "Proverbs 14:12 KJV."

Oh, yes, the King James Version. How could I forget it's the only translation allowed at FFOW? And how is the verse supposed to encourage us?

The scripture on the other wall is Proverbs 13:18, again from the KJV. "Poverty and shame shall be to him that refuseth instruction; but he that regardeth reproof shall be honoured."

At least it has a positive twist.

The offices off the foyer are empty, but I imagine they'll bustle with activity tomorrow morning. The center also has an auditorium, several classrooms, a chapel, kitchen and dining hall. Whatever is cooking smells spicy and wonderful. Mexican, maybe?

More verses are stenciled on the dining hall walls. On the far wall, a Proverbs 31 passage reads: "It is not for kings to drink wine, nor for princes strong drink, lest they drink and forget the law."

When I drank, I didn't forget the law. Rather, I was too hammered to care whether I obeyed it or not. Besides, I wasn't a king or a prince. I turn to the opposite wall and a Romans 13 verse. "Let us walk honestly, as in the day, not in rioting and drunkenness."

The back wall lists the evils of alcohol, according to Proverbs 20:1. "Wine is a mocker, strong drink is raging, and whosoever is deceived thereby is not wise."

I know from experience the truth of those words. I have been deceived by wine and strong drink. But couldn't something inspiring from the Bible be added, like Jeremiah 29:11? *"For I know the plans I have for you," declares the Lord, "plans to prosper you and not to harm you, plans to give you hope and a future."*

Plenty of wall space is available for encouraging thoughts. Oh, well. I'm obviously not the one in charge.

The others are already seated near the front at separate round tables—four men at one and three women at another. Two empty tables separate them. Talk about segregation. Beyond those tables are fifteen or twenty more tables with seating for six at each. Like the dorm's empty rooms, they suggest Leadership optimism regarding the expected number of participants.

Through the serving window, I'm introduced to Ronald, the cook, a slender balding man with kind eyes and S–E–L–F and M–A–D–E tattoos on the backs of his fingers. Due to his long sleeves, I can't tell if he has tatts on his arms, but I bet he does. He seems nice.

Then I meet the other men. Joseph, the household guardian, is Hispanic and appears to be way past retirement age. Before Ruby Jade got her talons into him, he probably went by "Jose´." He has thin graying hair and a salt-and-pepper goatee. Huh, I thought facial hair was off-limits for Followers.

I ask how long he's been the men's household guardian, and he says, "Three or four days. I just moved here from Idaho."

Maybe it's true the previous guardians ran off with each other. I give him a questioning look. "You're not from this church?"

"I'm a retired pastor, but I'd never heard of this place before."

Did Ruby Jade hire outside the Follower ranks because she was desperate, or is this the norm?

A middle-aged man, Italian by his looks and accent, tells me his name is Marco. He quickly corrects himself. "I mean, Marcus." Samuel and Bentley, both in their twenties, could have come straight from the Montana wheat fields. Their white foreheads and the permanent dents in their short sandy hair suggest they've spent a lot of time outdoors wearing hats. Samuel is taller than Bentley, but Bentley seems to be the more outgoing of the two.

At the women's table, I meet Liliana, a lovely Native American woman about my age with big brown eyes and silky black hair. Dana Marie is a stocky woman who looks as if she could wrestle a steer to the ground without much effort. She and Joleen, like Samuel and Bentley, are Caucasian and in their early twenties, but they have highlights in their dishwater-blond hair rather than hat dents.

I pull out a chair at the women's table. Just as I sit, Ronald calls, "Food's getting cold. Time to pray."

Joseph pushes away his chair and stands. "Let us pray." One arm high, palm facing the ceiling, he begins. "Almighty God..."

I suppress a groan, certain this will be one of those Sunday morning pastoral prayers that goes on and on. My stomach growls and a faint rustling circles the table. I'm not the only restless person here.

"Thank you for Ronald, who prepared this delicious-smelling meal for us," Joseph says. "We are grateful for the nourishment you provide. Bless our conversation and the service this evening."

Rats. I have to return to church tonight. For a sweet mindless moment, I thought I'd escaped to a more congenial environment. Silly me. I wonder how I'll get to church, but then I remember I'm now within walking distance, if my feet can manage it.

"I pray this in your precious Son's name, Amen."

A chorus of loud amens is followed by the scrape of chair legs against the floor. Everyone stands and forms a line to the serving window, women first. The quick reaction suggests the others are as thankful for a short prayer as I am. Either that, or everyone is extra hungry.

The food is surprisingly good, the best I've tasted in a long while—chicken enchiladas with Spanish rice and a cucumber-tomato salad. I'm included in the conversation around the table, another first at Faithful Followers of the Way. I may be stuck here for a year, but this is the most hopeful I've felt since I came.

Like Shakyra and Merikay, the others voice amazement they had no work assignment this afternoon. And like them, they spent the afternoon napping. For my dormmates to be so tired says a lot about FFOW exploitation.

Liliana wonders if the lack of a volunteer job was an oversight.

"Whatever it was…" Dana Marie stands, plate in hand. "I hope it happens again, every weekend. Anyone else want to get another enchilada with me? They're so good, I can't resist."

On our way to the dorm, Eunice asks about my slippers. I tell her I hurt my feet but they're better and I have a follow-up appointment with the doctor tomorrow afternoon. "Thanks for asking. I'm hoping the doctor will tell me I can wear shoes."

I can see the church sanctuary from where we're walking. It sits on the far side of a wide expanse of grass and trees. Any other time, I'd be glad to walk there. But I don't yet have the doctor's okay for long strolls. "I may have to skip church tonight. I'm not supposed to walk very far."

"I can drive you," Joleen says. She seems excited to do something so ordinary.

"Remember," Shakyra interjects with a sweet smile, "we need permission to drive."

"For such a short distance?" Joleen huffs. "We wouldn't leave church property."

"I'll take Cassandra over there," Eunice says. "I don't want you to get into trouble, Joleen."

I give Eunice a curious look. "I thought you didn't go to church."

"I'll drop you off and pick you up. You can call me."

"I'll need your phone number."

"One of these days..." Joleen spreads her arms and lifts her face to the sky. "This place will be a bad dream I forgot and I can—"

Shakyra elbows her. "Shh."

Thanks to the evening service's predictable format, I'm able to ponder the changes in my life since this morning's service. It all began when Noreen announced Transformation Way was re-opening its doors. Shortly after, I moved out of the Pritchards' house and into a much more pleasant environment, not that my few hours at T.W. prove anything at this point other than I've escaped Olivia.

However, the food is better, and the people are nicer. And my bedroom does *not* have a video camera in the corner. Best of all, the rehab program begins tomorrow. I don't know anything about it, but it satisfies the judge's order.

While the others sing unfamiliar songs, I mouth "rhubarb" over and over. Careful to move only my eyes, I search the single women's section for Myrtle Mae, but I don't see her. Could be she doesn't attend evening services. I'm anxious to tell her I'm now living in the dorm. She knows about my feet and about Vance's break-in and T.W. reopening tomorrow, but she doesn't know I moved out of the Pritchards' house.

Turning my head ever so slightly the other way, I search for Corban on the stage. Logan is seated in the front row beside a burly trumpet player, but I don't see his brother. The big guy must be obscuring him. I'm so disappointed we can't make eye contact I feel like crying, which is crazy.

We'll connect soon, I'm sure—except he and Logan usually mow early in the day, and I'll be working afternoons. I may have to resort to the junior-high tactic of sending messages through Sebastian or Myrtle Mae. Now that I've moved on campus, I can meet him in the cemetery greenhouse, like he suggested when we both worked at the school. We can plan rescues together and maybe help a lot of people do what Joleen wants to do—relegate this nightmare to the forgotten past, where it belongs.

"Transformation Way participants, please stand."

CHAPTER TWELVE

I jolt to attention.

Ruby Jade is at the podium, arms extended.

Dana Marie, who's seated beside me, elbows my ribs and jumps to her feet.

I follow her lead. People are staring at us. What did we do? The last place I want to be singled out is in this sanctuary. Sunday school was bad enough.

"These, my Faithful Followers, are the first participants in the Transformation Way reboot." Ruby Jade giggles. "I love that word from the computer world. It fits our situation perfectly. Let's encourage these precious individuals who are about to transform from serving the devil to serving the Lord."

She waves her arms, encompassing the standing men and women on each side of the auditorium. The others look as uncomfortable as I feel. Ruby Jade claps, and the congregation shouts, "Hallelujah, PGIH, PGIH!"

"Smile," Dana Marie whispers through a cheesy grin.

I manage a weak, equally bogus smile. If anyone is serving the devil, it's the devil woman herself. But I can't buck the system, not when Transformation Way is finally opening its doors. I'm learning to pick my battles.

When Eunice and I return to the dorm, I notice a keypad outside the double doors. "Does this mean the doors are locked at night?"

"I was told they automatically lock at ten-thirty and unlock at six-thirty in the morning."

"Good. What's the code?"

"I don't know the code."

"That's crazy. Why not?"

"I was told nobody needs it. Residents are to be inside the dormitory during those hours."

"But, what if—?"

"Rules are rules, according to Noreen."

"Crazy. I was given the code at my previous household. Why not here?"

She shrugs, and I quit asking questions. She knows less about the FFOW world than I do.

I say goodnight to Eunice at her door, and she reminds me breakfast is served from seven to seven-thirty in the small meeting room across from her apartment. "I make coffee at a quarter to seven."

I climb the stairs one at a time, weariness invading every cell of my body. Shuffling across the landing between flights of stairs, I checked the time on my phone. Ten-fifteen.

I'm tired, but I should inform my parents of my whereabouts and give them contact numbers. I see Kip tried to call. I'll call him back, but I have to keep my calls short. After all, not many hours ago, I confessed to talking too long on the company phone.

At the top of the stairs, the hallways each direction are empty and silent—and dim. Solitary bulbs in the middle of each ceiling provide the only lighting. I turn to the left, so tired I have to force myself to push one foot in front of the other.

Again, I get the feeling I'm the only person alive. The Pritchards' house was quiet, but not this quiet. Seven people living in a dormitory built for at least fifty. No wonder it feels like the abandoned warehouse I occasionally slept in back in the day. I shudder at the memory, grateful this is a vermin-free dwelling, as far as I know. With bunk beds, the two-story building could house eighty, ninety, maybe a hundred women. Is that the goal?

I'm a third of the way into the hallway, when I stop and glance from side to side, searching for a landmark in the barren expanse of floor, white walls, doors and ceiling. All the doors look the same, except for the numbers at the top. Try as I might, I can't remember my room number.

My first thought is to hobble down the stairs, knock on Eunice's door and hope she's not in bed. I hate to bother her, but she knows the number. I turn around and start for the stairs. This is going be another endless Follower night.

Wait! I flip around, the fastest I've moved since I injured my feet. All I have to do is peek inside rooms until I find mine. I left the boxes on the bed. Those will help me recognize my new quarters.

I carefully twist the knob on the closest door. It's locked. Does this mean someone broke the rules or are unoccupied rooms locked? I try the next door. It's also locked.

A deja vu feeling follows me along the hall. This is something like sneaking door to door in the Pritchards' basement, only I have a bit of light. And Olivia the Ogre isn't breathing down my neck.

The next doorknob releases. I inch the door open and peek inside. The dark room has a lived-in smell, a combination of well-used tennis shoes, dirty laundry and hair products. It also holds the snuffling sound of someone in a deep sleep. I pull the door shut and release the latch with only a hint of a click.

The door after that one also opens. Hearing nothing, I push it wider. Muted moonlight silhouettes the boxes. Sighing with relief, I check the number—sixteen—and step into the room. Home free, if such a thing is possible in this corrosive environment.

I close the door, letting the latch go with as much care as I released the previous latch. Then I lock it. This place is too creepy, and I've had too many bad experiences on the street. I'll take my chances with fire.

A breeze stirs the curtains, which makes me glad I left the window open. Moonglow draws me like an oasis in a desert. Kneeling before the window, I rest my forearms on the sill, my chin on my hands. Light from the half-moon sifts between branch shadows, weaving an ever-changing lace over the headstones.

If I were an artist, I'd paint the scene. It's restful, not macabre. Who knew I'd find peace in the FFOW cemetery?

"Thank you, God," I whisper, "for giving me a room on this side of the building. I was afraid painful memories would surface, but this is a balm to my soul."

Crickets fill the night with a unison melody. Unlike the Followers' music, the insects' song lifts my spirits. Between the budding branches, a light flickers in the distance. I watch it for several minutes and conclude it's stationary and must be on the greenhouse. I can't wait to meet Corban there to plan ways to help others escape.

A faint cry sounds somewhere nearby, maybe in the cemetery, and fades. I can't tell if it's an animal or a bird. Maybe it's a hunting call. This is the time of night nocturnal creatures begin stalking their prey.

Pine trees illuminated on the side of the mountain remind me of bristles on a brush. I'd love to hike to the top of Mount Killjoy with Corban. We'd help each other over rough areas, cool our feet in a gurgling creek, sit on a ledge holding hands and marveling at the view...

My pipedream bursts like a popped balloon. I cover my face with my hands. "Oh, Eric... I am so sorry. Here I am, imagining a special moment with another man, not with you. So wrong, so wrong."

My tears dampen my pantlegs, but my sobs are silent. I don't want to wake the others. When I'm cried out, I dig my hand towel from a box to wipe my face.

I didn't expect tears tonight or a longing for a drink. But that's how grief goes. It tends to hit when my defenses are down or when I think I'm done with crying.

A vision of Eric surfaces. He's on the couch, propped by pillows. I'm spoon-feeding him broth from a cup, the only substance he can tolerate. To this day, I can't handle the smell or taste of beef broth. After three spoonfuls, he shakes his head. "No more, Cat."

"But..." I refill the spoon, ready to tell him he needs to eat to keep his strength so he can continue to battle the cancer.

"No. More." The look in his eyes stops me, a look I haven't seen before. "Put the spoon down," he insists, "and give me your hands."

All through his illness, I've been quick to do his bidding, though his requests have been few and far between. Each time, I've jumped at the opportunity to help him. This time, I hesitate, afraid of what he's going to say. I don't want to hear it.

"Please, Cat, give me your hands." He's tired, yet I can tell he won't let this go, whatever it is.

I drop the spoon into the cup and set it on the homemade coffee table the neighbors left behind when they moved out. Running my fingers over the smooth finish, I remember how we sanded layer after layer of lacquer from the top. While we worked, we played loud, fast music on the stereo and devised crazy competitions, like who could sand the most area in ten minutes. Or who could remember the most words to a song. The varnish was thick, but we reached bare wood in a weekend. The next weekend, we painted it red and black to complement our eclectic college-student décor.

Placing my hands in my husband's thin weak fingers, I whisper, "I love you, Eric True."

He smiles. Not the wide grin that caught my attention the first night I saw him seated in the coffee-shop audience. But still, a smile. "I love *you*, Cat True," he says, "with all my heart."

For a long time, we gaze into each other's eyes. Gratitude to God wells in my soul. For once, I'm not railing at him for what Eric has to endure. I'm grateful he gave me such a loving man. Through health and sickness, good times and bad, my husband's love has never faltered. I cherish every moment we've had together.

"Cassie Anita True," Eric says, "you are my treasure above all things and all persons on this earth, a gift from our Creator."

"Funny, I was thinking the same thing about you."

"My illness has brought us even closer, something I didn't believe possible. God has been good to us."

"Huh-uh." I shake my head. "Cancer is not good."

"True." He squeezes my fingers. "But God is good."

"You can believe it, if you want." I shrug my shoulders. "But a good God wouldn't give you cancer."

"Cassie, Cassie, Cassie." He pushes an errant strand of hair behind my ear. "You'll see. Give him time." His hand drops onto the quilt covering his skeletal body.

"We've given him time. It's been—"

"Shh." He touches my lips. "That's not what I want to talk about."

I hush. With his energy level so low, even talking drains him.

Again, he takes my hands. "Because I love you so much, when I'm gone—"

Through tears, which erupt every time someone challenges my "Eric will beat this" fantasy, I cry, "Don't say that! You have to fight. You can't give up."

"When I'm gone, I want *you* to fight." He pauses to suck in a breath. "Don't give in to your grief. Move on with your life. You have many wonderful years ahead of you."

"I can't," I whisper. "I can't go on without you. Please stay." Tears stream down my face. I grip his hands, pleading, "Please, Eric...please stay."

He winces, and I loosen my grasp. "Sorry."

My husband stares at me for what feels like an eternity. "It'll be hard for a while, Cat. Very hard." He closes his eyes. Just when I think he's fallen asleep, he blinks. "I want you to open your soul, to grow deeper in your faith and allow yourself to experience a full life—without me."

I glare at him, unable to fathom any kind of life without him.

"Including..." His smile is gentle. "Another man's love."

I yank my hands from his and jump to my feet. "No, never!" Backing away from the couch, I stumble against the coffee table. The spoon clangs in the cup. "How can you say such a thing?"

"I say it because I love you more than life." He pats the couch cushion with his bone-thin fingers. "Sit, Cassie."

I pace the small room, back and forth, back and forth. His gaze never leaves me. Eventually, I give up and sit.

He wraps his hands around mine. "I love you so much..." Breathing in and out, he is slow to continue. "My heart fills with joy when I picture you in the arms of another man."

I rear back. Somehow, he manages to hold firm. I have no response to his preposterous idea. The pain drugs are making him hallucinate.

"I don't see the man," he says, "just his arms around you. Knowing you'll be loved and safe, that you'll have a companion for life..." He pauses to gather strength. "Maybe even a father for the children I'll never have with you...gives me great peace as well as joy. I'm happy for your future, Cassie."

He lets go of my hands. "I release you to live and to love."

"No, it's not what I want." I fall into his arms, sobbing. "Not what I want."

"I know." His voice is soft in my hair. The sickly-sweet smell that has come over him in recent weeks now has a rancid edge to it. "I know," he repeats. "It's not what I want, either." He rubs my back. "But you know what?"

"What?"

"I'm already looking forward to meeting you and your family in heaven someday."

Two days later, he died.

Tears rolling down my cheeks, I will the memory into oblivion and wipe my face with the towel. Grasping the windowsill for support, I slowly stand, move the boxes from the bed to the floor and set the alarm clock. Like my previous clock, an after-market label on top reads "time to serve Jesus."

I'll get up early to finish unpacking. Will that be considered serving Jesus? Probably not.

The next morning, I greet two sleepy-eyed women at the bathroom sinks and hear at least one other in the shower. No one has much to say. Back in my room, I dress and unpack my boxes. By six-fifty-five, all my FFOW-issued clothing is either in a drawer or on a hanger. Shoes and slippers are in a row on the closet floor and toiletries are in the dresser's top drawer. I flatten the boxes and slide them under the bed.

But I don't leave my room until doors open and close around me. When I step from number sixteen into the hallway, I'm greeted by the aroma of fresh coffee. Eunice is on duty, as promised.

The woman from the room beside mine is pulling her door closed. She turns to me with a smile on her face. "So, there's where they put you, Cassandra. Welcome to the T.W. reboot."

"Thanks." I don't tell her I peeked into her unlocked room last night.

"I'm Joleen, in case you forgot." She touches her toes and comes up into a backbend, hands clasped and stretched above her, index fingers pointed. "You had a lot of names thrown at you last night."

"It was all a bit of a blur, but I do remember you. Are you always this energetic in the morning?"

"Only when I've had a good night's sleep, which is a rare thing around here."

We follow the others to the breakfast room, where the smell of oranges and toast competes with that of coffee. Eunice is seated at the far end of a rectangular table, peeling an orange. She's wearing the same stained t-shirt she wore yesterday. A cell phone is on one side of her plate and a Bible on the other. She's already poured herself a cup of coffee and toasted a bagel.

The breakfast bar reminds me of a hotel continental breakfast, complete with a do-it-yourself waffle maker. Sparse as it is, it's more than I had on the streets. A couple of the women are making waffles. Joleen and I share the toaster.

She drops in a bagel half and I add a slice of wholegrain bread. While the toaster does its magic, I pour myself a cup of coffee and a half cup of orange juice and set them on the table. Then I butter the toast, add apricot jelly and grab a package of apple slices.

As I pull out a chair beside Eunice, I'm struck by how different this is from the big breakfasts at the Pritchards' place. And how much nicer the people are. A proverb my mother used to quote when Kip and I argued at the dinner table comes to mind. *Better a meal of vegetables where there is love than a fattened calf with hatred.*

I didn't get the meaning then, but Kip and I would quit bickering because we feared our next meal, breakfast, would be a pile of green beans or tomato slices. Today, the proverb makes perfect sense. I'd take this breakfast over my former household's spread any day.

Once we're all seated, Eunice says, "Let us pray." She folds her hands and bows her head.

The others lower their heads, but I stare at Eunice. I thought she said she's not religious. She slides a paper from the back of the Bible and reads aloud in her nasal voice. "Blessed Father in heaven, we thank you for your bountiful provision." Her plodding monotone delivery does not sound thankful. "May this food give us strength to resist the devious devil and to serve you and the Faithful Followers of the Way today. Amen."

When she opens her mismatched eyes, she sees me watching her but says nothing. I know I'm jaded, but common sense tells me she did not write the prayer.

She slips the paper into the Bible. "Now for the Scripture passage of the day." She finds her place and reads from Lamentations, chapter four. The gruesome description of starving people in a famine-ridden land is delivered without emotion or comment. I'm grateful the Followers only read three or four verses at a time.

Finished almost before she began, Eunice looks at us over her round glasses. "I've told each of you I'm not a religious person, which is God's truth."

I stifle a grin. What a paradox. A godless person proclaiming God's truth.

Across from me, Joleen's mouth twitches.

Eunice glances around the table. "My duties include saying a breakfast prayer and reading Scripture based on this chart—she holds up a paper—so you-all stay with the church's reading program. I am not, as you may suspect, being a phony. I'm merely following orders. I'm sure you understand.

"Also, for your information, I'm to observe your comings and goings and listen to your conversations. I've been asked to check your rooms, the hallways and the bathroom for cleanliness. And I'm to report my findings to the church office." She pauses, her gaze on the ceiling.

We wait. When her focus doesn't waver, I pick up the apple slices and open the package.

"In the name of full disclosure…" She's looking at us again, her eyes big behind her filmy glasses. "I don't want to do this. You're adults, but…" She sighs. "I have to do what I have to do."

I'd like to tell her full disclosure is not a Follower attribute. However, I don't know any of these women well enough to speak my mind. One of them might rat out my disloyalty.

"We understand." Shakyra flips her dreads behind her shoulder and gives Eunice a sweet smile.

"Thank you." Eunice reaches for her coffee.

Chatting with housemates who aren't hurrying off to work or school or to a FFOW project, I learn a bit about each of them. They were all in various stages of the program before the director and his wife left. Liliana and Merikay were nearing completion when the center shut its doors.

"What did you do?" I ask. "Go home?"

Merikay's bob swings when she shakes her head. "Ruby Jade wouldn't allow it. She put us to work, promising to reopen T.W., someday."

"How about you?" Liliana tucks her long dark hair behind her ears.

I hate to be the center of attention when I barely know these ladies, but the jail chaplain's words come to mind. *Transparency is the key to transformation.* And that's what I'm after. Transformation.

CHAPTER THIRTEEN

I smile and rest my forearms on the table. "If you were at the Wednesday potluck when Noreen introduced me, you know I came here from GCDC. Alcohol is my Achilles' heel, my downfall, my nemesis. Whatever you want to call it, it got me into a lot of trouble." I pause. "I *allowed* it to lead me into trouble. I was sentenced to two years and had served one year when I met Noreen, who offered to pull strings to get me into the program. Right after our talk, the judge released me and ordered me to serve the final year of my sentence here."

"Same thing happened to me," Liliana says, "except I was imprisoned on the Rez." She bumps Joleen's shoulder with her own. "This smart lady is the only one who didn't come from jail."

"What brought you here?" I sip my orange juice and try not to make a face. It's like drinking flavored water. I was told Ruby Jade wants Followers to drink fresh juice every morning to ward off illness. Evidently, T.W. participants don't warrant the real stuff.

"I've struggled with heroin addiction for years." Joleen sighs and rubs her temples, no longer the animated person she was earlier. "My aunt and uncle, who live in Bozeman, heard about T.W. and thought it might be a good place for me."

"Has it helped?" I'm excited to finally have an opportunity to ask about the program.

"The previous director and his wife were great people who…" Joleen looks around the table as if searching for opinions.

"Wonderful people," Merikay says. "Always encouraging."

"They didn't buy the party line." Joleen raises an eyebrow. "If you know what I mean."

We all nod, even Eunice.

"They'd tell me I'm a beloved, gifted child of God. But at church, I'd be subjected to a cleanse or called an addict, a loser, an embarrassment, stupid, a waste of humanity." Her face clouds. "The list goes on. Same words my stepmom screamed at me when I was a kid."

Tears spill over her eyelids. "Sometimes, I think the dual messages battling in my brain will make me crazy."

Now I understand why the previous staff left. They'd build up the participants, and Leadership would tear them down.

Liliana puts her arm around Joleen's shoulders.

I glance at Eunice. Is she going to report Liliana for inappropriate touch?

"For those of you new to this dorm…" Liliana smiles, her brown eyes bright. "Touching may be discouraged at church, but here, we don't hesitate to show our care and concern…when it's just us, that is."

I give her a thumbs-up. Finally, real people, not emotionless plastic mannikins fashioned from Ruby Jade's zombie mold.

I reach across the table to squeeze Joleen's arm. "I had a stable childhood," I tell her, "but those kinds of mixed messages would confuse me. Why do you stay?"

"Where would I go?" She wipes her face with a napkin. "I can't go back to my old friends or my boyfriend. They're all

users, and he's a dealer. Actually, he's no longer my boyfriend."
She makes a wry face. "Probably found someone else by now."

"What about your family?"

"They disowned me long ago, thanks to all the lies my
stepmom told them. Even my real mom hates me."

By the others' expressions, they totally get what she's saying.
I saw the same forlorn visages in jail.

Once again, I thank the Lord for my wonderful family, the
family I forgot to call last night. "I don't want to sound trite or
simple or give you a pat remedy for your pain, Joleen. I can tell it
runs deep. But the simple truth is Jesus loves you. He's not mean
and hateful like…"

By her expression, I can tell she knows who I'm talking
about.

"He loves you, he loves me." I look around the table. "He
loves all of us. I have to remind myself of his love every day
because sometimes I forget."

A bell chimes, and Eunice taps her phone. "Seven-thirty.
The Transformation Way doors open in one half-hour." She's
more tech savvy than I would have guessed.

We stand and take our plates and cups to the sink. Shakyra
says, "My turn to wash dishes."

"I can dry." I look for a dishtowel.

"No need." She smiles. "We let dishes air dry here."

Such laxity in a FFOW "household" makes me nervous, but
I don't argue. Instead, I hurry up the stairs as fast as my
slippered feet allow to brush my teeth, check my makeup and
run a brush through my hair. The others all wear makeup, so it
must be expected at T.W. too.

Back in my room, I unplug my cell phone from the charger.
If I had time, I'd call my mom and my brother. But the best I
can do at the moment is send a text. I address it to Mom, Dad
and Kip.

The program is ramping up. They can take that phrase however
they want. *I've moved into a Transformation Way dormitory on the church*

campus. And I changed jobs. I'll only work afternoons from now on. These are half-truths but better than the full-on lies I've been telling them.

In case of emergency, I can be contacted through the church or Transformation Way, but I don't know either phone number offhand. I give them Sebastian's cell number, which he gave me following the ER trip, and tell them he's my employer. *He's about your age, Dad, a super-nice man. I call him Uncle Seb.*

Along with the other T.W. women, I walk into the auditorium at seven-fifty-five. The men are two steps ahead of us. They sit on one side, and we sit on the other. I'm at the end of the women's aisle, directly across from Samuel, who's twisting his ballcap this way and that.

I check the auditorium. No cameras, thank God. I'm liking this place better all the time. But I don't understand the lack of surveillance. Seems Leadership would more likely play Big Brother here than in homes.

I'd also like to know why the program has such a large dining hall and auditorium plus two big dorms for a handful of participants. Maybe Ruby Jade has visions of many more participants and a much larger income. Or, could be the mini campus provides her with a tax write-off. Whatever the deal, I'm sure money is the baseline.

Similar to the dining hall, this room has Scripture verses from the King James Bible on three walls. Proverbs 23:31-32 is stenciled on one side. "Look not thou upon the wine when it is red, when it giveth his colour in the cup, when it moveth itself aright. At the last it biteth like a serpent and stingeth like an adder."

I resist the urge to roll my eyes. You'd think they'd use a contemporary translation, one which makes sense. From this version, wine appears to be a living force, masculine in gender. I get what it means, but still…

The back wall's warning comes from Isaiah five, verse eleven. "Woe unto them that rise up early in the morning, that they may follow strong drink; that continue until night, till wine inflame them!"

Yep, more uplifting thoughts to greet us each day.

The other wall has a hint of positive motivation from Ephesians. "Be not drunk with wine, wherein is excess; but be filled with the Spirit."

At exactly eight, according to my watch, all three members of Leadership step onto the platform at the front of the room. In a matter of seconds, a rosewater stench invades the auditorium. Some might appreciate the overpowering scent, but for me, it's a trigger for unpleasant memories and a harbinger of nasty things to come.

Silencing my phone, I slip it into my purse. Joleen, who's seated beside me, eyes it like she's never seen a shiny pink purse.

I whisper, "Noreen bought it for me."

She snickers. "Figures."

Ruby Jade stands beside the wooden lectern and begins with a whirl of purple nails. "Welcome, dear friends, to the Transformation Way reboot. We're so happy to have you with us. I know you heard the announcement Dr. Hoffman and Ms. Montoya will be joining us this week, Dr. Hoffman tomorrow, and Ms. Montoya on Wednesday. Beginning next week, he'll fly here twice a week from Seattle, and she'll drive over from Billings three times a week. What a joy to have such well-qualified individuals join our staff."

And on such short notice. I wonder if they have poor reputations in their hometowns and are desperate for work. I also wonder how long they'll last. As soon as the thought strikes my brainwaves, I regret it. If they don't stay, the program will die again. And I may never escape this place.

I sense the weight of Corban's solid hands on my shoulders, and I hear his voice. *Jesus is in this battered, rocking boat, right alongside us. He'll get us through this storm.*

Thank God for Corban. I needed his words today.

"This will be a morning of orientation and self-examination to prepare you for the hours you'll spend with our specialists," Ruby Jade says. "Hours dedicated to seeking forgiveness for deeds done in the flesh, for confession and repentance, contriteness of heart and humbleness of spirit."

She's waving her arms and getting louder, as if she's preaching to hundreds, not introducing a rehab program to a total of nine participants. "This is an incredible opportunity, Followers," she declares, "to cleanse your souls, to—"

She loses me at cleanse. What about healing from our pasts and focusing on our futures, for restoration, growth and renewal? For growing closer to God? For hope. What would be wrong with giving us hope?

Just when I fear I'll fall asleep listening to the same ole, same ole rhetoric, Ruby Jade says, "Inez will now explain the conditions of your participation in this program."

We all sit a bit taller, even the men across the aisle. Sure, some of us have to follow judges' orders, but I have a feeling their rulings aren't all Leadership has in mind.

"Good morning." Inez places a notebook on the podium and opens it. Her smile is forced, like she'd rather not be stuck in a room with a bunch of lowlifes. "Most of you are here by court order. You may not realize that with the order comes state funding to pay your way through the program."

Ah, the reason for no cameras. State inspections.

"Our beloved leader has designated a generous sum from the church treasury to ensure Transformation Way remains on solid footing. However, your participation is guaranteed by the State of Montana's contributions to the program."

She eyes each of us, one by one. Did I imagine it, or did she give me an extra hateful glare with her flinty eyes?

"Should you backslide into addiction," she continues, "disobey the rules or walk away, even for a few hours…"

I have a feeling those last words were meant for me.

"You will be discharged from the program, and we will lose your state funds. As a result, we will bill you for professional services, room, board, and any other expenses, including clothing purchases, incurred during your time with us."

I glance at my hands folded in my lap. My bracelet, my blouse, my pants, my underwear, my shoes and socks were purchased by Noreen. Except, I remind myself, the socks and slippers Sebastian bought for me. But basically, everything on my body and in my room is on loan, even the pink purse with the church-owned cell phone inside.

Inez arches an eyebrow. "I can tell by your expressions some of you aren't concerned about repaying your debt. Such thinking reveals an irresponsible, wicked attitude on your part, as well as a lack of understanding as to the sway we hold in the courts."

Leaning over the lectern, she grips the front. "We *will* get our money, one way or another." She smirks. "Count on it." With the barely veiled threat hanging in the air, she marches to her chair.

Wow, that was even more negative than Ruby Jade's speech. What happened to the biblical mandate to encourage one another?

Noreen stands and strides to the podium, high heels drumming the wood flooring. "In a minute," she says, "we will split the group for pastoral counseling sessions. The men will go to classroom A, where they'll meet with me and Inez, and the women will go to classroom D to meet with Ruby Jade."

A shared shudder washes over the women. This can't be good.

"Before we break..." She holds up paper and pens. "Samuel, please come to the podium."

Samuel unfolds his lanky frame and stands, a wary expression on his face. He sets his hat on his chair.

"Move it."

He hurries to the steps and climbs onto the stage. Somehow, dress pants and shoes don't look right on him. My guess is his normal attire includes jeans and cowboy boots.

"Give one set of labels to the men and one to the women. And give each person a pen."

He takes the sheets and trots down the stairs, his relief evident.

"Each of you peel off one label," she says, "and hand the sheet to the next person. Affix the labels to the backs of your cell phones. Then write your names on the labels and your PIN code."

"Not this again," whispers Merikay, who's seated beside Joleen.

A nervous murmur blows through our row. We pass the labels from woman to woman.

"Hurry." Noreen stomps a foot. "We must stay on schedule."

I grab my purse from the floor and pull out my phone.

The tap-tap-tap of her pen on the lectern has us all moving as fast as we can. I slap the label onto my phone, rub it to make sure it adheres and write my Follower name on it. And my PIN, against my better judgement.

"Samuel." Noreen's smirk has returned. "Please return to the podium."

Poor guy. He thought he was off the hook.

He approaches, cell phone and pen in hand.

She produces a plastic basket from inside the wooden podium. "Use this to collect the labels, pens and phones and bring them to me."

"Yes, this again," someone murmurs.

Once Noreen has our phones, she sets the box on the podium. "To help you concentrate on the program and not be distracted by outside interests and interruptions, we will store your phones for three months. At that time, we will evaluate each participant's progress to determine how much longer we should keep his or her phone."

Hands immediately go up. Marcus says, "My mother is extremely ill. I call every day to—"

She raises her palm. "I understand your concern. We will send your families letters explaining this phase of the Transformation Way program requires no outside communication. We will provide them with contact information for the church and for the school. In the event of an emergency, your family will notify us, and we will notify you."

My stomach churns. Not for one minute do I trust her words. If I hadn't sent my family a text with Sebastian's phone number earlier, they'd have no dependable way to contact me.

Other rehab programs sometimes require a communication blackout, but this is not a typical program. Leadership uses every means possible to separate us from our families and the rest of the world. I fear our phones will never be returned.

"But…" Marcus lifts his hand again.

With a ring of finality, she says, "That will be all. After a five-minute restroom break, report to your designated classrooms." She rejoins the other two leaders and they clomp off the stage.

Such generous charlatans you are to offer your warped version of counseling before the real counselors come on board.

I pause to reel in my attitude. Tuesday through Friday with the professionals will be better. Surely, they're not Leadership clones. I draw in a long breath and blow it out. I must, I must, I *must* focus on the future and keep my thoughts God-centered and under wraps.

I did it in jail. I'll do it here. I can do all things through Christ who gives me the strength I need to cope with the chaos.

After a quick dash to the restroom, the women reconvene in classroom D. Ruby Jade has us circle our chairs plus add an additional chair. I hate being this close to her, not only because of who she is but also because I'm sick of smelling rosewater.

One by one, she makes each woman tell her story of sin and shame, grilling those who gloss over their pasts—to bring them to a "place of uprightness," as she calls it. In actuality, she's highlighting their mistakes and misdeeds in order to humiliate them. All the while, her pupils remain small. Her eyes are almost fully violet. I've seen heroin addicts with constricted pupils, but Ruby Jade?

When she motions to me, the last person to tell my story, I strive to be straightforward, admitting how I let my husband's death and my neighbor's bad influence lead me into a miserable, selfish existence. I tell them about my alcoholism, my time on the streets, and my arrests, including the two-year sentence.

Finished, I sit back and wait for RJ to tear apart my words, which is what she did to the others. She badgered them until they cried, and then she mocked their tears. But she surprises me. Rather than address my story, she points to my feet. "I told you I detest those slippers. Why are you still wearing them?"

This again. Will she ever give it up? I'm tempted to say, "My feet are healing nicely. Thanks for asking." Instead, I say, "I'm wearing them because my doctor told me to."

"Knowing my disapproval..." She closes her eyes. "You..." Her breathing slows and her chin falls to her chest.

Joleen whispers, "What the...?"

The others look at me, and I shrug. I'm thinking of clearing my throat to wake her, when she lifts her head, blinks several times and continues where she left off. "You should have purchased a more modest pair."

Modest slippers?

"I have no money and no vehicle." Before she can respond, I add, "But I do have an appointment with the doctor this afternoon. I assume she'll say I can start wearing shoes again."

Ruby Jade frowns. "You're scheduled to work on my property this afternoon."

"Yes..." I nod. "I'll be *volunteering* there, as usual, with a short time off for the doctor visit."

Her lavender-tinted eyelids narrow. "Not only did you not receive Leadership permission for the appointment, you just said you don't have a car."

I lift my eyebrows. She knows I don't have a car. "Your property manager, Sebastian Longpre, said he'll drive me. I'm sure he'll work out the specifics with you."

With a noisy huff through her nose, she shakes her head and checks her big watch. "We have time for one more counseling session."

"Uh-oh," someone breaths. I'm sure we're all fearing we'll be the one to get two rounds with our relentless leader.

At the sound of a knock on the door, Ruby Jade says, "Come in, Eunice."

Oh, so she's the reason for the extra chair. Too bad. I wish she didn't have to go through this so-called counseling session with us.

The door opens and Eunice peeks in. I feel for the woman. She has no idea what she's in for. And she's no match for Ruby Jade's sharp tongue.

"Cassandra Turner!" Ruby Jade screeches.

I jerk to attention.

"Under no circumstances will the incident related to those vile slippers happen again." She jabs her fingernail at me. "If it does, I will have you jailed for the rest of your life." Her eyes are wild, her eyebrows scrunched. Her lips are taut, baring her teeth like a ferocious animal.

Because I left the Pritchard's house without your permission? Or does the real reason for your anger have something to do with your alcoholic son's arrest? I peer at her red face. Her reaction seems over the top, even for her. Does knowing she lost control of me for a few hours upset her? The thought makes me happy.

I suppress a smile, avoiding the other women's curious stares. They have to be wondering what in the world I did to make Ruby Jade so angry.

"I don't mean to interrupt," Eunice says from the doorway, her voice meek. "I can come back—"

"You're right on time," Ruby Jade insists. Her voice is at normal volume, with only a quake of rage. But her thumbs are twirling furiously. "We're ready for you. Please have a seat."

Eunice shuffles in, her eyes big and round behind her tortoise-shell glasses. She lowers her big-boned frame beside me.

Ruby Jade smiles at her. "Welcome, Eunice."

Eunice dips her head.

Beneath the Vicks smell, I detect coffee. Is it her breath or the fresh stain on her sleeve?

"I felt we should include our household guardians in this orientation for our residents because both you and Joseph are new to our community." Ruby Jade pauses, thumbs twirling the opposite direction. "Tell us your background, Sugar Pie."

Sugar Pie? Her voice is now gentle. Just like that, she switched off her madwoman demeanor and became a nice person. Talk about a Jekyll-and-Hyde personality.

Eunice tilts her head. "I already told you—"

"For the sake of these program participants, please."

"Well, okay." Eunice raises her gaze to the ceiling. A soft smile forms on her lips. "I was raised on a ranch in southeastern Wyoming near a small town called Chugwater. I had a wonderful childhood out on the ranch. I loved the animals, both wild and domestic, the seasons, the sound of the wind in the cottonwoods, the scent of rain coming across the prairie—"

"Get on with it, woman." Ruby Jade waves a hand. "We don't have all day."

"Oh." Eunice blinks back to reality. I'm sorry she can't continue to tell us her childhood memories. The ranch sounds wonderful. I'll have to ask her about it later.

"After I graduated from high school, I attended the University of Wyoming, where I earned a master's degree in psychology. Later, I received a doctorate in theology from a Colorado seminary."

CHAPTER FOURTEEN

I clamp my jaw to keep it from dropping. Judging by appearance, I assumed Eunice might not even have a GED. I mentally slap myself. After similar revelations by people I met on the street and in jail, I should know not to be so quick to stereotype. I study her face. *A ThD, but you don't do church. Interesting.*

"I've worked in a number of—"

"If what you say is true..." Ruby Jade scratches her arms. "Then you're highly educated, yet you came to us from a transitional living facility. What accounts for your indigence?"

Eunice shrugs. "Life happens."

Ruby Jade's eyes spark. "What kind of answer is that?"

"The truth." Eunice juts her chin.

"The truth is, you left your husband." Ruby Jade pulls a small bottle from her purse, squeezes out lotion and rubs it on her arms.

"He beat me."

"That's your story."

Eunice gapes at Ruby Jade, as if she doesn't quite believe what she's hearing. "What I said is the truth." She raises her palm. "So help me God."

With a sneer and a head waggle, Ruby Jade singsongs, "And you're sticking with it." She pokes a purple fingernail at Eunice. "The truth is, you left Lander, Wyoming, and came to Bozeman, Montana, to live with your niece, but she didn't want you."

"No, that's not what happened. Her boyfriend was jealous we were close and—"

"Enough." Ruby Jade taps her watch, a different one than I've seen before. This one is circled with silver and gold rings studded with sapphires. "We have more important matters to discuss."

By now, Eunice's hands are shaking and a stain I can smell forms beneath her armpit. I hurt for her. The rest of us have seen both sides of Ruby Jade and have learned to steel ourselves for the attacks.

"Eunice." Ruby Jade straightens. "Do you enjoy living here and eating at the Transformation Way dining hall?"

"Yes." Eunice rubs her palms over her pilled polyester pants.

"If you'd like to continue your employment with us, you must fulfill certain requirements."

"Okay…"

Why, I wonder, didn't she tell her the requirements when she hired her? I answer my own question. Because she wanted to lure her in, the same way Noreen lured me.

"We'll begin with your attire, which is inappropriate for a professional and for a FFOW member."

"But I'm not—"

"You will not only become a member, you will attend every church service and social event. My associate, Noreen Nystrom, will assist you with your clothing selection. She, with my approval, will determine what clothing items and accessories provide the altogether look for which we are known—as well as what best exhibits the gift of God within you."

"I can't afford—"

"Noreen will help you set up a payment schedule." Ruby Jade flips a dismissive hand. "Have you been reading the daily scriptures to the residents?"

"Yes."

"Saying a prayer before breakfast?"

"Yes."

"Checking the bedrooms and bathroom for tidiness?"

"Yes." With each "yes," she seems to gain confidence.

"I haven't seen any write-ups."

"Write-ups?"

"I told you to turn in a report to the office detailing the condition of each room and the tidiness infringements."

"The rooms are always clean."

"Come on, Eunice." Ruby Jade scowls. "These women have come off the streets, from prisons and jails. Cleanliness is foreign to them."

Cleanliness is foreign to us? Why does she assume we're dirty? We were expected to keep our assigned spaces neat in jail. And she has no idea how much a street person longs for a shower and a vermin-free place to sleep. I clench my fists, ready to defend my new friends. The ridicule and humiliation have gone on long enough.

Across from me, Joleen's eyes flash and her face contorts. Just as quickly, she squeezes her eyes shut and lets her features go slack, blowing out silent breath after silent breath. Following her example, I unclench my fists and bite my tongue. *Someday, Ruby Jade Paradise, I will tell you what I think of you and your intimidation tactics. That's a promise.*

"Do the white-glove test," Ruby Jade says. "I want to see a report every day detailing the smallest of infractions, the tiniest of dust bunnies. And be especially alert for illegal electronic devices and books or paperwork unrelated to this program."

"I, uh, had no idea." Eunice grips her thighs so hard I fear she's bruising them.

"You should have asked."

Such a typical Leadership response. I clamp my jaw to keep from jumping to Eunice's defense.

Perfumed sweat swirls about the tight circle. We shift in our seats. My guess is everyone is rooting for Eunice, hoping the excruciating interrogation ends soon.

"Is your television tuned to the weather station," Ruby Jade asks. "And only the weather station?"

"Well, yes, because it won't switch—"

"Good." Ruby Jade bends toward Eunice. "Do you observe the residents at night to be sure their hands are outside their covers?"

"I…" Eunice looks confused. "I don't understand about hands… How would I see them? If I turn on a light, they'll wake up."

"Use the flashlight in the breakfast room. We keep it there for power outages. By monitoring the women two or three times a night, you'll protect them from the demon of desire."

Eunice's chin jerks upward. "What?"

"And you'll also be able to ensure their doors are unlocked and their windows closed."

Eunice gawks at her.

"Time's up." Ruby Jade jumps to her feet. The hefty woman's agility always astounds me. "Lunch is served in the dining hall." Her violet eyes shine. "I hear Ronald is serving peach cobbler for dessert." She struts toward the exit. The others get up and start to follow.

At the door, Ruby Jade whips around, almost hitting the woman behind her. "The two stupidest comments I've ever heard—*life happens* and—" She sucks air through her flared nostrils, her chest expanding like a supervillain. "We'll begin with *life happens*. Followers are not victims of life. They take the reins. They're leaders, not lemmings."

I come close to snorting. *Since when?*

"And the second?" She scowls at me. "*My doctor told me to.* Followers are not puppets to be manipulated by the medical establishment."

Spoken by a master manipulator. I have a feeling she doesn't appreciate someone else horning in on her perceived "territory."

Not knowing whether she expects a response or not, I say nothing.

She shakes a finger at us. "Think, people, think."

By now, I know the last thing she wants is for us to think for ourselves.

She pivots, muttering, "Idiots..." The sound of her heels echoes along the hallway. I picture her drilling holes in the floor the way she drills holes in people's souls. She laughs an empty wicked cackle. The sound trails after her like tin cans clattering behind a car.

My dormmates glance at each other, eyes wide. But no one speaks as they straggle out of the room.

I check my watch. Twelve noon. I need to hurry to the dorm to close my window—in case Ruby Jade decides to do a personal inspection—and dress for work. But I can't abandon Eunice. She's still seated in her chair, staring straight ahead.

"Eunice..." I touch her arm. "You don't want to miss lunch."

She blinks and makes a valiant attempt to give me her attention, but I can tell she's bewildered.

I offer a sad smile. "If I'd known you were coming over, I would've warned you. Ruby Jade has two sides, and you got a taste of both. Mostly the nasty."

She slowly stands. "Wasn't expecting that."

"The woman has a talent," I whisper, "for blindsiding people."

"I don't get the hands thing." Eunice rubs her neck.

"Of course not. You have an innocent mind, unlike these perverted people."

She gives me a funny look.

Though I glimpse no cameras, I whisper anyway. "They have a real hang-up about, uh, intimate activity around here."

Eunice nods, yet the skin between her eyebrows remains puckered. "I don't want to…"

"We don't want you to. It's an invasion of privacy. Plus, I hate for you to lose so much sleep, if you could sleep at all." *And I don't want to close my window at night.*

Corban once told me after a while the bizarre seems normal, even to Followers who haven't grown up in the closed community. Eunice questions the absurdity, which is good. Maybe she and I can keep each other from succumbing to the bizarre.

As always, Sebastian has a lunch waiting for me. This time, it's a tuna sandwich on wholegrain bread with multigrain chips. I eat while he drives me to the doctor's office. "This is an amazing sandwich, Uncle Seb. Not many people can make tuna taste good. What's your trick?"

"Cottage cheese and capers."

"Really?" I hold the sandwich so I can see the filling between the bread slices. "That's all you add to the tuna?"

"No. I use other ingredients, like mayonnaise, but the cottage cheese and capers are what give it a different taste."

"I'll have to remember your secret. By the way, thank you for making waves at the courthouse about the rehab program. I have a feeling you're the reason why it reopened today."

"Didn't do much, but if it spurred R.J. to action, it was time well spent." He slows for a fox, which chose this moment to dash across the highway. "How was your first T.W. morning?"

I watch the bushytailed creature disappear in the tall grass. Such a beautiful animal. I haven't seen a fox in a long time.

"This morning might have been good…" I turn to him. "If the Fearsome Threesome hadn't decided to conduct their version of counseling sessions. The professionals don't come until tomorrow, so this was Leadership's chance to dribble a little more fear into our psyches."

He groans. "I can only imagine."

"Could have been worse. The men were stuck with both Noreen and Inez. Must have been hell. Ruby Jade took the six of us women and only had fifteen minutes to skewer each of us, thank God. Plus, she used some of the time to humiliate our dorm mom, someone she hired off the street a few days ago."

He shakes his head. "Couldn't resist stickin' it to her."

"Her name is Eunice, and she got it the worst. The poor woman had no idea what was coming, or what your boss is capable of doing to a person's self-esteem."

"Way to go, Cat." He pounds the steering wheel. "I'm glad to hear you say that."

"What?" I stare at him. "You can't mean—"

"You're tossing the hogwash out in the sunshine. Means R.J. and her cronies haven't bamboozled you. I know they've tried, but you get their game. And you're sensitive to those they're conning."

"I want to help people escape, but I need to do it in a way that's not obvious."

"You and the Dahlstrom brothers."

"Right. First thing I want to find out when I see them is how Marcela's communication with her family is going."

"Ah." He adjusts his cowboy hat. "Corban asked me to tell you your friend is… How did he put it?" He snaps his fingers. "Waking up. I believe he said she's waking up and making up for lost time."

"How exciting." I clap my hands. "Exactly what we were hoping for."

"Never met her," he says, "but I predict she'll skedaddle in no time."

Dr. Vasquez—Brianna—is pleased with my feet. "You can upgrade to tennis shoes…" She grins. "If one can call tennis shoes an upgrade from those fancy slippers."

I scowl and try to act offended but can't help but laugh.

"Be sure to wear socks with the shoes, for added padding and to reduce friction. But limit your walking and standing. If your feet begin to hurt, I want you to sit, kneel, lie down…whatever works for you right then. Don't walk on bare feet or wear dress shoes, especially heels, for the next two weeks. After that, you should be good to go, ready to return to your normal routine."

Inez will have a fit when I saunter into Sunday school in tennis shoes, but so be it. And Ruby Jade may believe bowing to a doctor's wishes is the height of idiocy, but as I keep telling the Followers, I value my feet and my ability to walk.

"I will not need to see you again," she says. "However, I want to keep in touch."

I'm about to tell her I surrendered my phone this morning, but then decide not to.

She studies me. "If possible…" Taking a business card from a counter display, she says, "This has my office number and email address." She turns it over and pulls a pen out of her jacket pocket. "I'll add my cell number and personal email on the back."

Sharing private info with me is super nice of her, but where am I going to hide the card?

"I'm not just saying this." She hands me the card. "I am here for you. Call anytime. I've been asking around town. What you told me has been verified over and over, sometimes with even worse horror stories."

She slaps the counter. "It's wrong!"

I jump. "I know—"

"Controlling and manipulating people for personal gain is *wrong*. Humiliation is *wrong*." Her eyes flash. "Humiliation in the name of God is even *worse*." She slaps the counter again. "Imprisoning young men and boys is *wrong*, and beating defenseless, vulnerable children is–so–very *wrong*." Slap, slap. "The sooner you get away from those vile people, the better."

I nod. "I know, but—"

She raises a hand. "I understand your situation, Cassie. However, I plan to keep an eye on the group. I'll also ask the physicians' association to find a legal, nonthreatening way to learn our patients' religious backgrounds. If we had that information, we could watch for symptoms of abuse in patients who come from your church."

I cringe at *your church*, but the fact is, I'm a member, whether I admit it or not. "I hate to tell you this, but I've been told several area doctors attend FFOW."

"No..." She groans and walks to the window. Shoving her hands into the pockets of her white jacket, she stares through the open blinds. "Turns my stomach." After a long pause, she says, "I'm new in town, fresh out of med school. Part of the oath my class took at graduation included a vow to have the courage to act when we witness injustice. Yet, those doctors are participating in the injustice, whether actively or by turning a blind eye."

Almost as if to herself, she asks, "What's in it for them?"

"A guaranteed steady flow of patients from the church?"

"Must be something more." She turns to me, her expression a mix of sadness and curiosity.

I reach for my socks. "Wouldn't surprise me."

Sebastian pays for the office visit, like he paid for the previous visit and the hospital charges. Outside the office, I thank him for covering my medical bills.

"My pleasure," he says. "I have very few expenses of my own, so I'm happy to help out a fellow rebel."

"Oh, so now I'm a rebel." I squint at him in the sunshine. "You must have been talking with Ruby Jade."

He chuckles. "When in doubt, let your horse do the thinkin'."

"Are you calling Ruby Jade a horse?"

"If the horseshoe fits…"

After I quit laughing, I say, "I can't see you letting Ruby Jade think for you."

"If the day ever comes…" He grunts. "Lock me up and throw away the key."

I pat his shoulder. "It'll never happen."

He opens the truck door for me, and I climb inside. The leather seat is warm, but not too warm. I set the business card on the metal dash, grab one of the tennis shoes I brought with me and slip it on. Finally, I can wear shoes.

He slides behind the wheel. "Must have been a good doctor visit."

"Two weeks in these and then, sad to say, I'm free to dress FFOW-style for church again."

"That's how the mop flops."

"Huh?" I look over at him. "What are you talking about?"

"I reckon you have to take the good with the bad, flip the coin to see both sides."

"Right." I put the second shoe on. "Feels great, although I'd rather wear sandals this time of year."

"Some folks can't be pleased."

I give him a dirty look, tie my shoes and sit back.

But he doesn't start the engine. Instead, he says, "Ever drive a stick shift?"

"Eric and I had an old truck we mostly used for hauling our canoe and kayaks. Sold it to pay medical bills."

"Think you could drive this one?"

"Sure, but why?"

"I'm headed to California Friday afternoon to be with my brother. Appears he's in the last stages of his illness."

"I'm so sorry. This is a sad time, for both of you."

"I'd like you to drop me off at the airport and use the truck to drive to and from the property while I'm gone—and anywhere else you want to go. Could be a while."

"How nice of you. Thank you." But what about Vance? How will I fend him off? Maybe I can borrow money from one of my dormmates to buy pepper spray.

Sebastian must read my mind because he says, "Vance and Ruby Jade are catching the flight after mine on Friday, no doubt to make sure he gets his dadgum paws on Quentin's money." He grunts. "Sure as shootin', they're not planning to hold my brother's hand and whisper niceties in his ear."

"Does he want to see them?"

"Do they care what he wants?"

"You're right. His wishes won't stop them."

The card falls from the dash, and I bend to pick it up. "I don't know what to do with this."

"What is it?"

"The doctor gave me her personal information. She's heard rumors and is concerned about me being at Transformation Way. Wants me to stay in touch."

"Good for her."

"But I can't keep this card. Ruby Jade told the dorm mom to search our stuff. She's a nice lady, and she doesn't want to do it, but…"

"But they'll turn her into a tyrant in no time."

"I hope not." I like Eunice and don't want to see her sweet spirit destroyed.

"Stick it in the glovebox," he says. "Ruby Jade never touches my stuff."

"She might, if she sees me driving your truck."

"I doubt it. She gives this thing a wide berth. Probably thinks it'll smear rust on her fancy Sunday go-to-meetin' clothes."

Sebastian and I walk Francis and Fenwick to Myrtle Mae's little house for our afternoon break. Actually, Sebastian and I walk. The dogs scamper here and there. They nose the grass and bushes and chase a squirrel. When it dashes up a tree, they sit at the base and bark. Moments later, evidently satisfied they've sufficiently warned the intruder against invading their territory again, they charge for the cottage's back door. They're sitting on the stoop when we arrive.

"Check out those tails," Sebastian says, "wagging like long johns on a clothesline in a windstorm."

Myrtle Mae is talking to the dogs through the screen. "I have a special treat for you boys, but you must be gentlemen."

"Gentlemen?" Sebastian nudges me. "Those two?"

"Hello, Cassie. Hello, Sebastian." I can barely see Myrtle Mae, but I hear the welcoming smile in her voice. "Come in, come in," she says. "Sebastian, if you don't mind, would you please put the leashes on the boys? We're not quite ready…"

We?

Sebastian hooks the leashes into the dogs' diamond-studded collars and holds them steady, so I can enter the house first. I blink to adjust to the lighting. Dressed in a yellow blouse and gray pants, Myrtle Mae is standing before me, a broad smile on her face—and an orange-striped kitten nestled in her arms.

CHAPTER FIFTEEN

"Myrtle Mae, how sweet." I reach to touch the tiny purring creature, but the dogs charge into the room, barking and bouncing at Myrtle Mae's feet. The cat hisses and swats at the dogs from its safe perch.

Myrtle Mae backs away.

"Down, boys, down." Sebastian yanks their leashes. "Behave yourselves."

"Do you want your beans?" Myrtle Mae asks.

Trembling with anticipation, Francis and Fenwick sit.

She hands the kitten to me. It's all claws and hisses but too small to do much but scratch my hands. I take it into the living room. Standing so it can't see the dogs, but I can see Myrtle Mae and Sebastian, I hold it close to my heart. I run my fingers over its head and neck and along its soft back. It shuts its eyes and begins to purr again. I breathe in its baby kitten smell.

Sebastian raises a kitchen table leg off the floor, slips both leash loops onto it and sets it down. "This'll keep 'em from being a nuisance. They're curious fellows who won't do any harm. But the little critter has had enough trauma for one day."

"Give them the treats I bought," Myrtle Mae says. She comes into the living room. "I was afraid they'd be jealous, so I got them something to chew on. Supposed to be good for their teeth." Head angled, she peers into my arms. I know she's trying to focus on the kitten. "Ah," she says, "you have the touch."

"All it needed was to feel safe." I know the need. "What kind of trauma did your kitten experience?"

"Got kit-napped from the litter this morning." Sebastian gives the dogs the chew toys and comes into the living room. "The shelter volunteer said the cat was ready, but you'd never know it by the ruckus we heard all the way here."

"This one was the runt," Myrtle Mae says. "Couldn't help myself. I've always taken to the underdog."

"Male or female?" I ask.

"Female."

"Have you named her?" I rub the white spot above the kitten's nose.

"No, not yet."

"You should ask R.J." Sebastian's eyes twinkle. "She's got a knack for giving people new names."

Myrtle Mae snorts. "People who already have perfectly good names."

He chuckles. "You should call her Citrine."

She stares at him, eyebrows bunched. "Where in the world did you get that name, Sebastian Longpre? Did you make it up?"

"I'll have you know it's the name of a gemstone." He squares his shoulders. "I was into rocks when I was a kid. Citrine can be yellow or orange or both."

"Nice." I trace the kitten's orange stripes. "Fits this cat, for sure."

"Sounds too much like *latrine* to me." Myrtle Mae frowns. "Not a good name for a sweet little kitty."

He grunts. "You'll have second thoughts when the critter does its business on your fancy carpet." He eyes the round area rug, which occupies a good portion of the living room floor.

I laugh. "You can work with the name, Myrtle Mae. Citrus is kind of cute and would fit, or maybe Citrina or Citriana."

"I've got it," Sebastian exclaims.

We give him our attention, but I can tell Myrtle Mae is as leery as I am. I had no idea he could get excited about naming a cat.

"Citronella." He appears quite pleased with himself. "You know, like the fairytale."

"Citronella?" I laugh. "Isn't that what they put in candles to repel mosquitos?"

"Cats repel mice. Gotta be a correlation there somewhere."

Myrtle Mae shakes her head. "Too big of a name for this tiny little thing. I'll go with Citrus."

I'm glad she likes my idea, but I tell her, "You can pick your own name. Citrus was only a suggestion to prime the pump, as my grandpa would say."

"I think it's perfect. Citrus it is."

I touch the kitten's pink nose. "Citrus, baby, you are going to be so happy living in this peaceful little cottage with the sweetest lady in Montana." The kitten opens its eyes and stretches, as if to say, "I know, I know."

"Thank you for helping me name her, dear." Myrtle Mae touches my cheek. "I hope you and Citrus can spend a lot of time together."

"Since you don't appreciate my ideas..." Sebastian turns toward the kitchen. "I'll take the boys and go."

"Don't be silly." Myrtle Mae grabs his arm. "You can't go yet. We haven't had our iced tea, and we haven't told Cassie our other surprise."

"Two in one day?" I grin. "Don't know if I can handle it." I've had several jolts today, many of them negative, but the kitten is wonderful. I'm delighted Myrtle Mae now has a companion to keep her company, and I trust her other news will also be good.

She tells me I can put Citrus in the box in the corner, but the kitten is content in the crook of my arm, and I'm enjoying her soft warm fur and the purrs vibrating my ribs. I slowly lower to the couch. If the kitten wakes and wants to explore, she'll have roaming room yet be out of the dogs' sight.

Sebastian settles into an easy chair.

Myrtle Mae goes into the kitchen. "Cassie, sugar and a squirt of lemon?"

"Just lemon, please."

Sebastian doesn't wait for her to ask. "Same for me."

A moment later, she places coasters and tea on the end tables beside me and Sebastian. "Be right back."

When she returns with her own glass, she joins me on the couch. "Is our little miss asleep again?"

"Yes." I stroke the kitten's paw. "Like a baby and like a cat. We should all be so relaxed." I lean to pick up the tea, but the kitten doesn't rouse. "Tell me your other news. I'm dying of curiosity."

She puts her hand to her mouth. "Oh, dear."

"What's wrong?"

"I was so excited to show you the kitten I forgot to ask about your first morning at Transformation Way. How was it? Good, I hope."

When I hesitate, she amends her words. "Maybe I should say *as good as can be expected*, considering its connection with my daughter's church."

"Actually, it was worse than expected. Neither the director nor the therapist could be there today—probably due to short notice. So, Leadership decided to do their twisted version of what they call counseling."

She frowns.

"But," I quickly add, "the first session is over and done with—and tomorrow's a new day. Plus, something wonderful happened to me yesterday afternoon. I moved from the Pritchards' house into the women's dorm."

"Hallelujah." Myrtle Mae waves a hand in the air. "No more Olivia Pritchard nonsense for you."

"Amen to that." Sebastian gives me two thumbs-up.

"What's the other news you two have for me?" I set my glass down. "This cute kitten is enough good news for one day, but you said you have more."

"Sebastian helped me purchase a cell phone with big buttons before we went to the shelter and found sweet little Citrus." She smiles. "Citrus... I love the sound of it."

"Me, too. Seems to fit her. I'm excited you have a cell phone. Now you can talk with your brother and your friends."

"And with you, although I'm aware Followers have to limit their calls."

"Please don't try to call me. Noreen took our phones this morning, plus our passwords."

Sebastian splutters into his tea and lowers his glass. "Of all the lowdown…"

"Actually, as you probably know, limiting outside communication for several weeks or months is common in rehab programs. But according to Noreen, after three months, Leadership will *review our progress* to determine whether they should return our phones. In the meantime, they'll be reading our texts and listening to our messages."

I shake my head. "Not only is phone use something the staff should decide, the FT will likely find excuse after excuse to deny us the ability to talk with our families."

Myrtle Mae lifts an eyebrow. "FT?"

"Fearsome Threesome."

Understanding lights her eyes. "Appropriate."

"Noreen promised to let our families know we won't be in contact for a while, but they'll inform us of emergencies." I pause. "But I don't trust anything coming out of Leadership mouths. One man's mom is seriously ill. I'm afraid he won't be notified regarding her condition." I turn to Myrtle Mae. "Sorry. I know Ruby Jade is your daughter. I don't—"

"I understand, dear." She sighs. "As I've said before, it's not how I raised her. Please feel free to use my phone whenever you need. And don't worry about the minutes. I can well afford to buy more."

"Good thing we picked up the cell phone," Sebastian says. "You can let your family know they'll be able to reach you through Myrtle Mae's number. Or mine. My phone is available anytime you're here."

"Reminds me." I push hair out of my eyes. "Before they took our phones, I texted your number to my family, for emergencies. I hope you don't mind."

"Not at all. That's what uncles are for." He swirls the ice cubes in his glass. "I'll be glad to relay messages."

I turn to Myrtle Mae. "Sebastian adopted me as his niece."

"How wonderful, dear." She grins. "He'll take good care of you. Before we get distracted, you should call your parents to let them know my number."

"Good idea." I glance around the room. "Where's your phone?"

"In my purse on the kitchen counter. I'll find a hiding place for it later." She lifts her chin. "Mind you, I'm not afraid of my daughter, but I'd rather she not know I have a phone. Let her think she's cut off my contact with the outside world. My brother and my friends will learn I'll call when I'm able."

How sad. Even Myrtle Mae's friendships are affected by her daughter's craziness. "Do you know your phone number?"

"Yes." She rattles it off, as if she's had the number for years. "And my PIN is MT1babe."

"Wow, your memory is impressive." I hand Citrus to her and stand. "Your PIN is perfect for you."

She grins.

"Here, I wrote down the number." Sebastian holds out a scrap of paper.

"Thanks." I take it from him and ask Myrtle Mae, "Mind if I go outside to talk?"

"Not at all."

The dogs wriggle and sniff my ankles as I pass, but I don't pet them. They'd smell Citrus on me and get excited all over again. At the door, I do an about-face and return to the living room. "The snooper van—can they hear me this far back on the property?"

"No need to worry," Sebastian says. "R.J. isn't monitored because she's above reproach, clean as a whistle, and her calls are top secret."

I laugh. "I can't believe you said that with a straight face."

Shaded by the carport roof, I lean against Myrtle Mae's car and debate whether I should send my parents and brother a group text. In this day and age, it's comparable to leaving a paper trail. Sure, their phone numbers can be traced, but a text is even more obvious.

I think of my FFOW cell phone, which is now in Leadership hands. I bet the first thing they did was check it for calls to the police about Zachary. Thank God they can't connect me with the Pritchards' arrest.

As far as I remember, my only calls have been to family members. And our texts to each other are innocuous. Or are they? Just this morning, I told them I call Sebastian "Uncle Seb." What will Leadership make of that? Will they decide we're too chummy and move me to another job? I wish I'd thought to delete my texts, but how was I to know I was about to lose my phone?

To save time and the mental energy required to explain the latest FFOW craziness without actually explaining it, I dial Mom and Dad's landline. Neither of them will be home right now. After a brief greeting, I tell them the staff took participants' phones for three months, the same as other rehab places have done. In an emergency, they can contact me through my boss.

"I sent his number in a text this morning, but I'll give it here to make sure you have it." I repeat the number. Thank God I remember it. "Or, you can call the phone I'm using right now. It will probably show up on your screen, but in case it doesn't..." I read Myrtle Mae's number from Sebastian's scribbles, memorizing it at the same time. "This phone belongs to a friend. I see her often, but not every day."

I'm about to hang up, when I remember my brother. "Please pass this number along to Kip. Thanks. I love you. Bye."

Despite the fact we all agree Ronald's lasagna is the best we've ever eaten, those at my table are subdued at supper. Talk at the men's table is also lowkey, like today's reminder of Leadership control has drained our hope and energy. Maybe we're all tired from an emotionally challenging morning and manual labor in the afternoon. Along with regular Followers, program participants build and paint houses, landscape and mow yards, serve as housekeepers in homes and motels, wait tables and wash dishes in restaurants, and toil in warehouses and factories. I hope tomorrow will be a better day, for all of us.

Thinking of the hard work everyone does, I ask, "Do you-all get paid at your jobs?"

"I do," Joleen says. "But I don't have much left after they deduct my tithe and car payment."

I frown. "Didn't know they could do that."

"Inez had me sign a paper to give them permission. A loan from the church was the only way I could afford a car."

"Noreen's husband owns a used car lot," Dana Marie says. "It's where we get our vehicles."

I silently vow to remain carless for the next year.

"Why are you asking?" Eunice gives me a quizzical look. "Don't you get paid?"

"I've been on volunteer status ever since I came." I shrug. "For all I know, I'll never receive a paycheck."

"We all do a lot of volunteering, in addition to our regular jobs." Dana Marie rubs her eyes. "Almost every night, usually late into the night or early morning. If the new staff gives us homework, I'm not sure when we'll do it."

"How do you get into the dorm?"

"What do you mean?"

"Eunice was told the doors lock at ten-thirty, but she wasn't given a code to open them. Right, Eunice?"

"Right, but I haven't..." I get the impression Eunice hasn't observed them returning late and has no idea how they deal with the code.

Shakyra rests her forearms on the table. "The guys who drive us to and from the jobsites have the code."

"You mean, our dorm mom doesn't have the code, and we can't have the code, but two *men* have it? Men who aren't supposed to come within twenty feet of the dorm?"

She holds her hands in the air. "What can I say?"

"Yet, we're not supposed to lock our doors at night." I glance around the table. "Which is asking for trouble."

"Shh." Liliana puts her finger to her lips. "Careful what you say."

"But—"

"They're the daytime security guards for the church," Dana Marie says. "Harmless old geezers."

"Hank and Pete?"

"You know them?"

"We've met. How do you know they're harmless?"

"I, well…" She shrugs. "They must have passed a background check to get the security job."

"Maybe, but I have a criminal record, and the first job I had here was in a third-grade classroom. I'd come from jail the day before and had no related experience."

"Change of subject." Shakyra glances around the table. "Anyone know anything about the new staff coming tomorrow?"

We all shake our heads, except for Eunice. "I was told they may not be Christ followers in the sense you-all are followers. I'm expected to attend sessions with you, so I can report their behavior to…what do you call them?"

"Leadership," Merikay says. "Is that the word you're searching for?"

"Right. They want me to tell them if the new people say or do anything…" She wrinkles her nose, and her big glasses raise and lower. "Of the devil."

"Like what?" Shakyra scrunches her dark eyebrows.

"They gave me a list of things to check."

"Can you tell us what's on the list?" I ask.

She pushes her glasses up her nose. "I'm to keep an eye on you-all, as well as the staff members, to watch for signs of rebellion." She smirks and lowers her voice. "I suggest you toe the line in my presence."

We snicker. And then stop. The consequences of suspected rebellion aren't laughable.

"But as for staff, no unholy words should issue from their mouths nor unholy actions occur with their hands, and they should dress professionally—no flipflops or plunging necklines."

Joleen snorts. "I certainly wouldn't want to see the director's chest hair."

Everyone laughs.

"What else?" prods Shakyra.

"They should not disparage Leadership or Follower ways."

"Okay."

"Or drink alcohol in your presence."

"Why," I ask, "would people hired to help us overcome addiction drink in front of us?"

"Seems the leaders are trying to cover all the bases," Eunice says. "The list is quite extensive."

"Good luck remembering everything." Merikay yawns. "They tend to add new rules every day."

We're a more enthusiastic group at breakfast, anxious to meet the new staff and dig into the program. "So, Eunice," I say, "I take it you'll be going over to the center with us this morning."

She sighs. "That's the plan."

"You don't sound too happy about it."

"I wasn't told spying would be one of my duties."

Someone gasps, and I raise my hand. "I'm gonna say something that might sound a bit radical, but please hear me out." I glance from person to person, and one by one, they nod. They may have second thoughts later, but right now, they're with me.

"Can we make a pact to protect our dorm mom? We don't want to lose her."

Dana Marie pushes still-damp hair from her forehead. "What do you mean?"

"First of all, what's said in this dorm stays in this dorm. Okay?"

They look dubious.

"I realize it's not the policy around here, but we all need a safe place, especially Eunice. She's the buffer between us and Leadership, and it's a tough position to be in."

"I agree." Dana Marie gives Eunice a thumbs-up. "I'm behind you all the way."

Eunice smiles.

"She's supposed to check our rooms and bathroom and hallways," I add. "If she doesn't report some kind of infringement, Ruby Jade will jump all over her."

"Let's take turns." Joleen comes alive. "We'll drop a tissue or a scrap of paper in the hallway, maybe dirty a sink or leave a soap bar in the shower. That way, no one person can be blamed, but Eunice will have something to report."

"Wonderful, Joleen." Liliana claps and her dark eyes shine. "Great idea."

I nod, though I know Ruby Jade will catch on fast. She needs victims to attack, to shriek at and dig her talons into.

"Very kind of you girls," Eunice says. "I've never been a tattletale, and this…this is different than anything I've ever encountered."

Just don't let the bizarre become your norm.

CHAPTER SIXTEEN

We meet in the auditorium again. Why am I not surprised all three FT members are on hand to welcome the new staff? I wonder if their presence is to remind us who's *really* in charge. Ruby Jade makes a big production of the introductions. Yet somehow, the ceremony, if you can call it such, becomes all about her.

"I looked far and wide," she proclaims, spreading her arms. Her hands quiver and her bracelets jangle, as if the search was so very difficult for her.

Yeah, I bet you looked far and wide. After the judge threatened to pull funding.

"And God led me straight to these two highly educated, highly recommended, well-trained, well-experienced individuals, praise Jesus. Your leadership team had an early morning orientation meeting with the new staff to acquaint them with our methods. I must say, we were very impressed. God has gifted us with the best of the best."

Is it the truth? Or did she happen across two people desperate for business—and in their desperation, responded to her desperation? I hate to be cynical, but really... Why would anyone choose to work here, let alone *travel* to work here? If they'd spent any time researching the place, they would have questioned why T.W. only has two staff members and why the previous staff left. Which brings me to the question that nags at me most. How long will they stay?

Ms. Montoya, the addiction counselor, is a nice-looking dark-haired woman of about forty. She seems to be a kindly person. And the blouse beneath her suit is buttoned almost to the base of her throat. No plunging neckline for her.

She also acts a bit bewildered. Is she wondering what she's gotten herself into? She asks us to call her by her first name, Jenica, and seems like she'll be easy to talk with. I hope she remembers to maintain client confidentiality, despite Leadership pressure to reveal our deep, dark secrets, which I'm sure will happen. And I hope she doesn't leave her notes in the building.

Dr. Andrew Hoffman appears to have had a rough early morning flight. But maybe his clothes are always dingy and askew. His beard is irregular in length and color, like his eyebrows and hair, where patches of white vie for dominance with faded orange-red locks. Behind his big aviator-style glasses, his eyelids droop over rheumy hazel eyes. He tells us we can call him "Doctor."

He's soft-spoken, yet I don't get the idea he's overwhelmed—or even impressed—by the charlatan and her clones. That's a good thing, but how long can he remain objective? The Fearsome Threesome have their ways of bringing everyone under their lacquered thumbnails.

From time to time, both Jenica and Doctor stare beyond our motley crew. I can tell by the way their eyebrows cluster and their heads angle that they're reading the verses stenciled on the walls. I wonder what they're thinking.

Finally, the Fearsome Threesome walk out. Their backward glances suggest reluctance to hand over the reins, but we all blow out sighs of relief and settle into our seats. Maybe it's the last we'll see of them for a while.

The fact the new staff was advised of FFOW methods bothers me. But surely these two have minds and wills of their own. And surely their professional counseling methods don't include the scream-and-demean approach.

"I want to get to know you better," Dr. Hoffman says, "and learn your expectations for the program. In a minute, we'll adjourn to the first classroom on the left and form a circle with the chairs. But first, I need to get my numbers straight. I was told the program currently has nine participants, but I count eleven of you. Did a couple of you register at the last minute?"

"Dr. Hoffman…" Joseph stands. "My name is Joseph Hildago, Reverend Jose´ Hildago, to be exact. I'm what you might call the dorm monitor for the men. And I'm about to go help paint a house. Ruby Jade asked me to meet you this morning, so you'd have a face to go with my position."

Doctor dips his head. "Nice to meet you, Reverend Hildago."

"Just call me Joseph." He smiles. "If you'll excuse me…"

"Do you have time to stay for the icebreaker?" Doctor asks. "It's a great way for all of us to become better acquainted."

"Sure, I'd be glad to."

Eunice stands. "My name is Eunice Zafforis. I, uh, manage the women's dorm, and I've been asked to observe the sessions here."

Doctor frowns. "Observe…"

She nods and sits.

He studies her for a moment. "Who asked you to observe?"

"Ruby Jade Paradise."

I love Eunice's transparency.

"I'll discuss this with her." His forehead furrows. "Much of what we do is confidential."

"I understand." Judging by the grin tugging at the corner of Eunice's mouth, his comment is music to her ears.

Bentley raises his hand. "You want both men and women in the circle?"

"Yes, men *and* women." He peers at Bentley from beneath bushy eyebrows. "Is that a problem for you?"

"No, not for me." Bentley folds his arms. "But it's not the policy around here."

"Policy?"

Joseph stands again. "It's what they do over at the church." He rubs his goatee and explains how separating genders appears to be a big deal at FFOW.

Dr. Hoffman listens intently, chin cocked, one scraggly eyebrow up and one down, and then says, "This is a rehab program, not a church."

Good luck convincing Leadership.

The icebreakers involve interviewing another person for five minutes to find out their birthplace, their favorite job and something surprising, unusual or funny about them. I'm paired with Marcus, and I'm tempted to say the surprising thing about me is I'm talking to a man in a FFOW facility.

But I don't. Instead, I tell him I was born in Salem, Oregon, and my favorite job was singing in a coffee shop. I stop and tap my lips. "The surprising, unusual or funny has me stumped, Marcus."

"Have you ever done anything dumb or taken any wild chances?"

"I've done a lot of stupid stuff, most of which I don't want to mention."

"How about contests? Have you ever won a contest?"

Other than music contests and my silly competitions with Eric, I can't think of anything. "Oh, yeah. I once had a pancake-eating contest with my big brother. He ate nineteen pancakes and I ate twenty-one."

"That's a good one," he says, "but didn't it make you sick?"

I laugh. "This may be TMI, but the short answer is those pancakes made a fast return trip."

The alarm on Doctor's watch buzzes, and we switch partners. This time, I'm with Liliana, and I'm asking the questions. She was born in Oklahoma, and her favorite job was cooking for a harvest crew. The most interesting thing about her is that her parents once traveled with a circus, training horses and performing with them. Sometimes, she was included in their acts. But when she turned six years old, they returned to Oklahoma and bought a farm, where they still live today.

We have a lot of fun and laughter with the ice breakers, and I'm liking the other participants more and more. Behind his absent-minded professor façade, Dr. Hoffman seems to have a sharp mind. And Jenica is sweet. From what I can tell, she's a caring person whose interest in helping us achieve our goal of sobriety is authentic.

For one of the activities, Doctor asks us to get out our cell phones. Of course, we have to tell him our phones were taken from us by Leadership for a minimum of three months. He raises his eyebrows but moves on to the next icebreaker without comment.

I'm wondering what he has planned for the remainder of the morning, when he announces he and Jenica are going to meet in his office to discuss the program. "Ms. Paradise gave us an overview," he says, "and the previous director left files and notes, but we haven't had a chance to study them. We need to familiarize ourselves with Transformation Way's history, as well as formulate a plan for the program's future."

I'm glad to know they want to create their own plan, although Ruby Jade may not give them the liberty they expect. At least for now, things are looking up.

"Joseph," Dr. Hoffman says, "you can go paint the house. And the rest of you are also free to go. Jenica will be here in the morning. I'll return on Thursday. I enjoyed getting to know each of you, and I believe we're going to have a good experience growing together."

Walking with my dormmates over to our dorm, I realize I haven't had real free time since I came to FFOW, and evidently, neither have the others.

"I hardly know what to do with myself." Dana Marie clasps her hands behind her head and stretches.

"Think I'll nap," Liliana wraps her long hair across one shoulder. "Another long night of cleaning is scheduled for the warehouse I'm assigned to."

"I'm not sure what I'll do without a cell phone." Joleen folds her arms. "Can't call or text anyone."

"A nap sounds good to me," Merikay says. "A rare opportunity." Shakyra and Dana Marie seem to like the idea, too. I don't say anything because this is my chance to explore the cemetery—and to test how much walking my feet can handle.

I check my watch. Two hours until Sebastian comes for me. Plenty of time.

We separate at the door to the dorm. "Where are you going?" Joleen asks.

"Just stretching my legs. The doctor gave me permission to walk more, but I'll have to take it slow, and I don't know how far I can go." I wave and keep walking, hoping no one asks to join me. "See you-all later."

Maybe it's silly, but I'd rather be alone with my memories. My emotions might get the best of me in a cemetery. Also, if I run into the caretaker, I want to tell him I'm a friend of Corban's and that we might meet there occasionally. If I dare. Corban said he's trustworthy, but I'm leery of most people associated with the church.

The FFOW graveyard is as beautiful in daylight as it was in moonlight, a perfect place for a stroll beneath tall cottonwoods. A gentle wind sways the branches and ripples the fledgling leaves above me. Their sharp woody smell holds a hint of sweetness.

The names and dates on the headstones intrigue me. A toddler here, an older person there. Five-year-old twins. I wonder what happened. None of the names are familiar. They might be common FFOW names, but I've met so few people at the church I can't connect any dots.

At the sound of tires rolling over gravel, I turn and see a golf cart coming my way. I wave. This is my chance to meet the caretaker. When he gets close, I see he's wearing a wide-brimmed black hat and a sports jacket, like the FFOW security crew. Odd attire for a cemetery caretaker, but it would be typical of Ruby Jade to require a uniform, just in case the governor wandered by.

I wait, and the cart stops beside me. "You again," the man says.

I peer beneath the hat brim. Hank from FFOW Security. Silly me. I should have known he'd somehow be alerted to my presence. Do they have cameras everywhere?

"Hank," I say, "what brings you clear over here?"

"You." He grunts. "I told you—"

"You told me I couldn't walk on the church lawn." I point at the path I'm standing on. "This is not grass."

"This is church property," he insists.

"And I'm a church member, as well as a participant in the Transformation Way program." I indicate the dorm. "I live right next door to this place, but you're telling me I can't walk here?"

"So…" He looks me over. "You're one of *them*."

"What does that mean?"

"All the more reason for you to stay off church property."

"Hank, I live in and on church property. This cemetery is part of my neighborhood." I wave my hand over the acres of headstones. "And these are my neighbors." I can't believe I said that.

He grimaces. "That's sick."

"My doctor ordered me to walk more, yet you're telling me I can't walk here?"

"Members need approval from Leadership to enter this cemetery, no matter the reason."

"Somebody grieving a lost loved one has to ask permission to visit their gravesite?"

"Yep." He nods.

"That's what's sick."

His brow lowers and he's about to speak, when the two-way on his belt crackles to life. "Hank, did you locate the intruder?"

Unclipping the radio, he raises it to his mouth. "Affirmative. Repeat offender."

"I'll submit a report," the man on the other end says. "Name?"

Hank eyes me. "I'll be there in a jiffy, Pete." He returns the radio to his belt and glances around. Leaning on the steering wheel, he crooks a finger at me.

I step closer.

"I shouldn't do this," he murmurs, "but so you can follow your doctor's orders, I'll give you a tip."

"Tip?"

"Go over the fence."

The squat split-rail fence is about hip-high and nothing like the fancy wrought-iron fences so many cemeteries have, probably because this is Montana, not Massachusetts. Even with sore feet, I'm sure I can get over the fence. "So, the only cameras are at the two entrances?"

"This cemetery has three entrances." He rubs his nose with his knuckle. "Cottonwoods make my nose itch. Who said anything about cameras…or motion detectors?"

I blink wide. "Oh…"

"Time for me to escort you out of here. Climb aboard." He points to the seat behind him, the one facing the opposite direction. Apparently, I'm not allowed to sit beside him and trigger endless FFOW rumors.

By now, I'm happy to get off my feet. What better time for a backward ride on a golf cart?

Maneuvering the electric cart through the cemetery, he says, "I'll tell Pete I gave you a warning, same as last time. But I'm actually going to give you two warnings."

I twist to see his face.

"First off, I don't want to *see*—" Staring straight ahead, he emphasizes the word. "I don't want to *see* you in here again. Secondly, if word gets out regarding a tip, I'll deny it to my grave. I'll tell Leadership you lied, and they'll believe me over you because I'm not the one in the rehab program."

"Gotcha." I can't argue with his logic.

"You were new at the school," he says, "and I assume you're new at T.W. I haven't driven you to any work projects yet."

"This is my first week."

"You're learning FFOW ways, like you learned about little boys and cleanses."

I bristle. I hate the lies that permeate this place, even in the cemetery. "Actually, Hank, the rest of the story is Child Protective Services discovered the same little boy locked in Olivia and Owen Pritchards' basement. His name is Zachary. CPS rescued him and returned him to his mother."

Leaning near his ear, I lower my voice. "With orders for her to *never* bring him near the school or the church again. I know all this because I lived with the Pritchards at the time and watched sheriff's deputies arrest Olivia when they rescued Zachary. Owen was arrested the same day."

"The Pritchards? Arrested?" He jerks his head. "Well, I'll be jiggered."

I laugh. "My grandpa used to say *I'll be jiggered.* I love it!"

"Uh-oh." He looks both ways. "I let go of Jesus. Shouldn't have said it."

"You did nothing wrong. Even if you did, you can't let go of Jesus because *he's* the one who holds you."

"Not true."

"Paul wrote in Romans that *nothing* in all of creation can separate us from God's love."

"Huh." He sounds surprised.

I want to say, *For Pete' sake, Hank, stop listening to Ruby Jade and read your Bible.* But I try a more politically correct approach. "Read your Bible. It'll encourage you."

Sebastian picks me up at twelve-fifteen. On the way to Ruby Jade's house, he tells me he has a phone conference with his brother's medical team this afternoon and another one with his brother's lawyers. "Myrtle Mae has been pestering me to let you two have an afternoon to paint the town red, so this is as good a time as any. You can drive her car."

I snicker. "Funny how I can't quite picture her partying around town."

"She wants to take you to some prissy place for tea and crumpets."

"Sounds fun."

"Maybe to you."

"What about Ruby Jade? What if she sees us?"

"I happen to know she'll be in court all afternoon. And no doubt her sidekicks will be with her."

"Is it about Zachary Russell?"

"I'm not sure, but I think it has something to do with property taxes. Remember, I don't ask questions. I merely keep my ears peeled."

"Right."

Myrtle Mae is beside herself with excitement. "This is going to be so much fun, Cassie."

I have trouble matching her enthusiasm. "How do you know someone won't see us and report me to Leadership? I don't want to get kicked out of the program."

"According to Sebastian, my daughter and her cronies are in court all afternoon. They're the only Followers allowed to go downtown, except the members who work there—and I hear those individuals are told not to linger in the devil's playground."

"If they can't go there, where do they shop?"

"Walmart. They buy everything there, including gas and groceries. Well, most everything other than their fancier clothes and shoes. Those they purchase at Macy's, or Noreen orders for them online."

"Makes sense. Walmart and Macy's are the only two stores I've been to with Followers. But if some of them work downtown…"

"I am prepared for the possibility." She giggles. "Follow me."

The kitten is asleep in a box in the corner. A hole at one end leads directly into a covered litterbox. I'm about to pick her up and carry her with me, when Myrtle Mae says, "Please don't wake Citrus. She'll start meowing, and then I'll feel terrible about leaving. She has food and water, so she'll be fine."

"Has she adjusted okay?"

"Other than wanting to be with me constantly. I have to wear an apron and put her in a pocket to calm her."

"Sounds like you need an afternoon out."

"That I do. And so do you." She takes me through the living room to her bedroom. "Welcome to my boudoir." The room is as charming and welcoming as the rest of her cozy home. Four small landscape paintings hang on one wall and a colorful star-patterned quilt adorns the bed. The oak dresser has a crocheted dresser scarf topped by perfume bottles and framed photographs.

I'm drawn to the pictures. "Myrtle Mae, is this you and your husband?"

She slides the flowered curtains back, letting sunlight into the room. "Yes, a long time ago. Kenneth and I were newlyweds.

One of his friends was getting into photography and asked us to pose for him."

Kenneth is a head taller than Myrtle Mae, and he has his arm around her. They both have dark hair. His is slicked back, and hers is long and straight. It's a black-and-white photo, yet her big eyes seem to glow and pull me into the picture.

"You were as beautiful then as you are now, and your husband was very handsome."

"Thank you. You're obviously overlooking the wrinkles."

I laugh and pick up another photo. "This must be the two of you with Ruby Jade…or, what did you say her real name is?"

"Marilyn June."

"She was a cute little girl." I hate to say those words out loud, but it's true. Dark, curly hair, alabaster skin, beautiful eyes, adorable smile. "She was a dark-haired Shirley Temple with Liz Taylor eyes."

"How do you know about those child actresses?" Myrtle Mae comes over to look at the picture with me.

"I used to watch old movies with my grandma."

She touches the picture. "You might not believe it, but back then, she was as sweet as she was adorable." A tear trickles down the side of her nose. "I miss my little girl."

"Must be hard for you to watch her now." I give her a hug.

"Every day, I pray she'll come to her senses."

"I hope she does." I know God can do it, but it'll require a miracle of the same magnitude as parting the Red Sea. I set the family picture on the dresser and pick up the third frame, which holds another black-and-white photo. "Are these your parents?"

"In a sense. They're actually my grandparents, but they're the ones who raised me."

"They look kind, very kind." I put the picture on the dresser. "One of these days, I'd love for you to tell me all about yourself. I hardly know anything about your history."

"Well…" The twinkle returns to her eyes. "Here's some history for you. A couple years ago, when I could still drive, a friend and I entered a costume party at the senior center and won because no one recognized us. We called ourselves the Hawaii babes."

"I can only imagine…" I laugh.

"You don't have to imagine." She pulls two floppy wide-brimmed hats from a closet shelf, one purple and one a neon pink, places them on the bed and takes out brightly flowered knee-length muumuu dresses. "These outfits plus sunglasses? No one will guess it's us."

CHAPTER SEVENTEEN

I giggle, beginning to catch Myrtle Mae's vision. "But my shoes and socks, they'll look weird with a muumuu."

"All the better, my dear, all the better."

"If you say so."

"Here's the clincher." She opens a drawer and produces two spray cans. "Purple hair or pink hair, which do you want?"

"I, uh, well… It's not something I think about every day."

She grins. "Take your time."

"Will it wash out? I mean, I can't return to the dorm with a weird hair color. Followers bleach and highlight their hair, but they don't do colors."

"Yes, sweetie, it'll wash out. We won't chance riling the nasties. Now, if you'd go place a chair in the middle of the kitchen floor and sit in it, I'll fetch a couple towels, and we can spray each other down."

I go for the pink spray because I know Myrtle Mae will look great in purple. For the sake of time and so our hair will dry faster, we streak wide swaths rather than color every inch. Myrtle Mae puts on socks and tennis shoes—to match me, she says.

Then we don the muumuus, hats and sunglasses, giggling the whole time.

For a final touch, we apply a thick layer of fuchsia lipstick. The effect is hilarious. Standing in front of her full-length mirror, I laugh out loud.

"Cassie." Myrtle Mae puts her finger to her colorful lips. "Don't wake Citrus." She tries to look stern, but her sparkling eyes give her away. She raises a finger. "Just thought of something." Sorting through the bottles on her dresser, she chooses one and sprays a cloud of White Shoulders over our heads. "We should reek like a spa."

I cough. "As long as it's not rosewater."

Once we're satisfied our disguises are complete, we tiptoe out of the house and under the carport to her older model light-blue car, which I'd put in the *classic* category. The shiny paint, including the white top, is in mint condition. We slide onto the slick vinyl seats and close our doors.

I run my hand over the smooth steering wheel. "What year is this car?"

"It's a 1972 Chrysler Newport. I inherited it from my parents when they passed." She pats the dashboard. "It's been a good vehicle."

"It's beautiful." I twist to glance at the backseat. "And in perfect condition."

"Thank you. Kenneth and I always took good care of our cars." She hands me the key. "Do you have your driver's license with you?"

I hold up my pink purse. "Only thing in here."

"Nice purse," she says. "Matches your hat—and your hair."

"That's a first." I slip the key into the ignition and turn it. The engine starts without hesitation. I roll down my window. It's true. We reek. I can barely breathe. "I haven't driven in a long while, Myrtle Mae. Are you sure you want to place your life and your car in my hands?"

"It'll come to you, dear." She pats my arm. "Like riding a bicycle."

I grin. "You're so cute in your Hawaii babe getup."

"Well, young lady, you're quite the eye-catcher yourself."

The turn-around area off the carport is barely wide enough for the big car. Thank God I don't have to back out the lengthy driveway on my first excursion in years behind the wheel.

"Although I no longer drive," Myrtle Mae says, "my brother takes this car in for maintenance now and then. The mechanic says it's in excellent running condition." She fastens her seatbelt. "I dusted it this morning and washed the windows. Hope they're not smeared."

"They look great to me." I'm impressed she didn't let her visual impairment stop her from tackling the big car's windows. Despite its age, the Chrysler is so clean and pristine you'd think we'd been transported to the seventies. Even the wooden cross hanging from the rearview mirror could have been carved yesterday.

If the car smells old and musty, I wouldn't know. All I can smell is White Shoulders.

We roll alongside Ruby Jade's garage, but I stare straight ahead, aiming for the street. If anyone is in the house, I hope and pray they don't see us. Passing the Pritchards' home, I do the same. Surely, they won't recognize me.

At the street's juncture with the highway, I stop, switch on the turn signal and secure my seatbelt. My relief at escaping Fellowship Neighborhood is replaced by another concern. "Highway speeds coming up, Myrtle Mae. You'd better pray."

"This jalopy needs to have the cobwebs blown out of it."

Because she's so relaxed, I decide to sit back and enjoy the ride. The car floats over the asphalt. "I love your car, Myrtle Mae. Such a quiet, smooth ride."

"Thank you, dear. It's old but reliable."

All too soon, the outskirts of town appear. The narrow downtown streets are likely to be crowded, as usual. Navigating them in this big car will be a challenge.

"I've reserved a special parking spot for us," Myrtle Mae says. "It's in an alley. Even if you could find a space on the street, you'd have to parallel park this boat. Other than the cost of tires, the only downside to this car is its size."

"Thank you for arranging an easier place for me to park. I hate to think how many tries I'd take to parallel park." Or how we'd explain our getup to a cop if I sideswiped another vehicle.

Arm in arm, we walk from the alleyway and around the block. FFOW life has been so confining I feel weird walking freely in public with my arms and legs exposed in the short-sleeved, knee-length dress—disguise or no disguise. "Myrtle Mae," I ask, "Are you positive Leadership won't come here to eat lunch or shop after court gets out?"

"From what I hear, they always eat at Restaurant des Delices because it's the most expensive one in town. As for shopping, they prefer bigger cities. Too much cowboy influence around here for their taste. They fly to Billings, Denver, Salt Lake, Seattle, San Francisco, even New York. Wherever my daughter gets the urge to visit after a big offering comes in."

I groan. "That's terrible."

"It's true. Every time she has the ushers pass the plates a second time, I know a shopping spree is coming up. And the Wednesday night potluck, which supposedly supports orphanages overseas? I overheard Noreen call those fees their fun-and-fashion money."

I'm about to kick a wall and scream my frustration to the world, when I catch sight of our reflections in a storefront and burst out laughing. We look ridiculous and so unlike ourselves no one would ever guess who we are or even that we're locals. I vow to forget FFOW for a couple hours and enjoy my sweet bubbly friend with the pinkish-purplish lips.

"My sight isn't good," Myrtle Mae says, "but a certain delicious chicken smell tells me we're nearing the tearoom."

"Your nose is correct." We're about ten steps from a blue door with a glass center. *Tanya's Tearoom* is printed on it in gold lettering. "Cute place. I love all the ivy on the wall." A wreath hanging from a hook beside the door is decorated with tulips, ribbons and Easter eggs.

"The inside is charming. You'll love it."

"But why does a tearoom smell like chicken?"

"You'll see."

I open the door for Myrtle Mae, and a bell tinkles overhead.

She whispers, "Do they still have the sign about the recipe above the counter? The one with the raven?"

The door closes behind us. Sure enough, on the opposite wall, amidst decorative plates, is a large wooden sign with a painted raven at the top. I read it out loud.

> *"Once upon a forenoon dreary,*
> *our cook labored, long and weary.*
> *Suddenly, there came a tapping,*
> *someone rapping his kitchen door.*
> *'Sir, this I ask, and nothing more.*
> *Chicken salad, a taste so rare.*
> *Please, please, your recipe to share.'*
> *'Never!' quoth the cook, eyes snapping.*
> *'Till death steals my breath,*
> *NEVERMORE!'"*

I chuckle at the abrupt ending. "So that's why I smell chicken."

"They're famous for their chicken salad croissants." Myrtle Mae is still whispering. "If you try one, you'll see why. They also have excellent quiche and finger sandwiches, as well as pastries. But their chicken salad..." She inhales deeply. "It's as good as it smells."

The tearoom is small and charming, with a deep pink counter front and creamy white walls. A corner cupboard displays teapots of all colors and sizes, and green tablecloths overlaid with lace cover the round tables. Set with delicate teacups and saucers, fresh flowers and linen napkins, the tables are inviting, and the effect is eclectic yet elegant. Mom would get a kick out of Tanya's Tearoom.

The only occupants are three middle-aged women seated at a table near the cupboard. They're too busy chatting to notice us. I'm relieved. They may not be from the church, but they might have snuck away, like I did. Of course, if that was the case, they wouldn't tattle. Or would they?

A dark-haired girl wearing a headband and dangling earrings comes from behind the counter, menus in her hand. She looks us up and down. Her nostrils flare, but her smile never falters. "Welcome to Tanya's Tearoom."

"Aloha." Myrtle Mae smiles sweetly.

"Thank you." I smile and nod, not sure how long I can playact with a straight face.

"You ladies came at a good time. Our lunch crowd has mostly dispersed, so you have a choice of tables."

"I always...I mean, I'd love a table by a window," Myrtle Mae says, acting rather prim and proper for a Hawaii babe. I assume she wants to ensure we have enough light to read the menus while wearing sunglasses. I'll probably have to help her.

The girl says, "Right this way."

After we're seated, Myrtle Mae says, "What is that delectable aroma I detect in this lovely tearoom?" She flips her purple-streaked hair behind her shoulder and purses her purple lips.

The girl's mouth twitches. "We're, uh, known for our chicken salad croissants. We roast the chickens ourselves. That's what the smell and the sign are all about."

"I cannot resist. I must try the croissant, dear."

"Wonderful." The waitress turns to me. "And, you?"

I rest my chin on the back of my hand. "I have a feeling..." I attempt to warble my voice, hoping I sound eccentric or old—

or at least unlike myself. "If I don't order the chicken salad, I fear I'll forever regret my decision."

"You won't be sorry." She hands us each a tea menu. "My name is Amanda. I'll get those croissants started for you and bring you some water. In the meantime, you can pick your tea, or whatever you want to drink." Leaving us, she goes to the ladies in the corner.

"Dear me." Myrtle Mae leans close. "Amanda has taken care of us when I've been here with my friends. Do you think she recognized me?"

"I don't recognize you." I chuckle. "I can't imagine how she could."

Amanda returns with the water and a small bowl of lemon slices. Myrtle Mae chooses an oolong tea, and I go for a fruity herbal infusion. Glancing from Myrtle Mae to me, Amanda asks, "Are you ladies from this area?"

I tilt my head. "I'm from the coast." Oregon is on the coast and where I grew up, so I figure it's somewhat close to the truth.

"I thought so," she says. "You definitely have the California look."

Myrtle Mae giggles and shrugs her shoulders.

Amanda heads for the kitchen, and I whisper to Myrtle Mae, "How are Hawaii babes supposed to act in a tearoom?"

"I have no idea." She snickers. "Silly, I guess. Lots of giggling."

I push a pink strand out of my eyes and under the hat. "If I look as funny to you as you do to me, we have plenty to laugh about."

My comment sends us into gales of giggles.

When she catches her breath, Myrtle Mae whispers, "Did you hear me? I about gave us away."

"When?"

"I started to say I always sit by the window."

"Yes, I did hear it, but you covered your slipup so well, I don't think she noticed."

Amanda returns with the sandwiches and pots of steeping tea. Apple slices sprinkled with cinnamon are artfully arranged at the sides of the dainty plates. The chicken, apples, cinnamon and tea all smell heavenly. Thank God I no longer smell our perfume.

My sandwich is as good as Myrtle Mae promised it would be. We're on our second cup of tea, when I see Vance walking toward us on the sidewalk. He'll pass right by our window. I should have known better than to throw caution to the wind and perch here like a mannequin on display.

"Myrtle Mae," I whisper. "Your grandson is coming our way. Pull the brim of your hat down."

She does as I ask, and I do the same, peeking around the rim to see if he notices us.

He stops, peers in and taps on the window.

We both freeze.

"Don't mind him," Amanda calls. "He's always trying to flirt with me, but I ignore him. He's a creep."

Don't I know it.

After a moment, he moves on, but my pulse pounds as if I just ran a marathon. I twist to watch him. I doubt he'll come into the tearoom, but if he does, I'll need to warn Myrtle Mae. Instead, he crosses the street, nearly getting creamed by a big pickup truck. The driver honks long and loud. Vince gives him the finger and enters a bar I used to frequent.

"Is he gone?" Myrtle Mae asks. "I'm getting a crick in my neck."

"Sorry. Yes, he's gone. I was watching to make sure he didn't come in here." I backpedal. "I mean, he's your grandson, but we would have had to work extra hard to stay in character if he sat at a nearby table."

She pats my arm. "I know he's obnoxious, but I would like to see him. He was a cute little guy when he was young, and I haven't seen him up close in months." She sighs. "I'm sorry to hear he's been pestering dear Amanda over there."

"Apparently she's given him the cold shoulder. He didn't come inside, which I assume means he took the hint." I don't tell her he chose the bar over the tearoom or that he's done worse than "pester" me.

Nearing the end of the delightful meal, Myrtle Mae says, "Next on the agenda, unless you object, is a visit to the theater we passed on the way here."

"A theater? Surely, your daughter wouldn't approve."

Her lavender eyes twinkle. "The theater shows oldies during the matinées. My brother said *Goldfinger* is playing this week. I haven't seen the movie in a hundred years."

"*Goldfinger?* You want to see *Goldfinger?*"

"I love James Bond movies. *Goldfinger* is my favorite."

"Maybe you are a Hawaii babe after all. What time is the movie?"

"Three p.m."

I check my watch. "Good thing the theater is nearby. We have eight minutes to find our seats."

Myrtle Mae graciously pays the bill plus adds a big tip, whispering to Amanda, "Treat yourself to something special, dear."

Amanda grins. "I will. Thank you."

Outside the tearoom, I thank Myrtle Mae for buying lunch.

"Like I said…" She pats my cheek. "You need to get away now and then to stay in touch with reality. And I need to get out of my little yellow house and have some fun."

We return to her little yellow house immediately after the movie. I hurry to change my clothes and wash the color out of my hair. When Sebastian comes for me, I'm in the bathroom dabbing at the fuchsia lipstick.

Before we part, I hug Myrtle Mae goodbye. "Thank you so much. You've given me the most fun I've had in years. That was a blast."

"Let's do it again sometime, shall we?"

"Can't wait. Next time, I'll be able to wear sandals." If Olivia returns my boxes by then. "And buy our lunch." If Ruby Jade starts paying me for my work.

Not until we're on the highway does Sebastian give me a questioning glance. "What did you two do today, or should I ask?"

"Probably best I don't tell you. Myrtle Mae has some surprising tricks up her sleeve."

"Your wet hair makes me suspicious."

I crank the window down. "I'd better air dry so no one asks questions at dinner."

"You could tell them you were caught by a sprinkler that came on when you weren't expecting it."

"I could..." I eye my boss. "But it would be one more lie to add to all the other lies I've uttered since coming to this place. Someone told me it's a way to survive, which is true, but I hate to develop another bad habit to break."

Come to think of it, was letting a waitress named Amanda believe we were from California also a lie? I'll be glad for the day when I can be me and live freely without deception.

At dinner, Eunice informs me I'm expected to join one of the work crews tonight.

"Sorry." I shrug. "My doctor told me I can walk, but I have to limit my time on my feet for two more weeks. I had a busy afternoon."

"Lucky you," Joleen mutters.

Eunice grimaces. "Means I have to call her back."

"Who?" I ask.

"Inez."

"I'm so sorry." I touch her arm. "I hate to put you in an awkward position."

"Since they took away your phones…" She groans. "Relaying messages has become part of my job description."

That night in my bedroom with the door locked and the window open, I replay the wonderful afternoon with my sweet friend. How did Ruby Jade turn into a monster when she has such a kindhearted, fun-loving mother? Lying on my back, I stare at the ceiling and recall every detail—the wonderful food, the movie, and especially the laughter as we sauntered about downtown in our silly outfits.

If we hadn't been giggling, I might have cried when I caught sight of Soroptimist Park on the other side of Main Street. The artsy little park was a great place to hang out with friends during college days. Eric and I used to perform there on my nights off from the coffee shop.

We played and sang together for the fun of it—and the enjoyment we saw on onlookers' faces. But it was nice when they threw enough money into Eric's open ukulele case that we could treat ourselves to a shared pita sandwich or a glass of wine. Those were the days.

A cry, like the one I heard the first night, drifts through the window. It sounds almost human. I sit up and peek out at the mountain. Someone once told me cougar screams can have a humanlike quality. A shiver shoots along my spine. I know I'm safe in my second-story bedroom, but still, the eerie shriek spooks me.

I lie down and roll onto my stomach, determined not to let sad memories or scary noises—or seeing Vance inches from my face—ruin a perfect afternoon. God has filled my lonely life with amazing friends, and I am grateful. Without them, I'd be lost. They provide balance to the FFOW craziness.

The next morning, Jenica has the entire group, men and women, move from the auditorium into a classroom. Rather than intermingle, the men sit at a table in the back, and we women sit in the front.

Jenica begins by handing us each a multi-page personality test and asking us to spread out across the classroom. "This is mostly for my benefit, not yours," she says. "You've likely done personality testing before, but this one is comprehensive and could require an hour or more to complete.

"There are no right and wrong answers," she explains. "Just mark those that best fit you. And don't feel rushed or like you're competing with anyone. We'll talk about the results in your private sessions."

Two hours later, following a restroom and coffee break—we're not allowed to eat or drink in the classrooms—Jenica has us form a circle. It includes all nine participants. But not Eunice. As she happily announced at breakfast, while wiping her glasses with her t-shirt, she's no longer required to join us. Instead, she'll provide childcare for a Follower couple.

I assume Dr. Hoffman must have spoken with Leadership about Eunice. I'm shocked the Fearsome Threesome acquiesced, but maybe they're biding their time, plotting another way to spy on us. I don't trust any of them.

"Yesterday's icebreakers were a lot of fun and helped us get acquainted with each other," Jenica says. "Let's continue the quest to know one another better by sharing our stories. I realize some of you know some of your stories, but you don't know all of them, and I don't know any of them. I'll start by telling you a bit about myself."

CHAPTER EIGHTEEN

I appreciate Jenica's approach, as if she's our equal rather than above us, a refreshing change of leadership attitude. I'm curious to know more about her. After being on the streets and in jail with other addicts, I can't help but wonder why anyone would make a career of working with people like me. We can be so belligerent and hell-bent at times, so determined to destroy ourselves.

Jenica tells us she was taken from her parents when she was three and placed in a foster home. "At such a young age, I didn't understand why. Later, I learned my parents were alcoholics who neglected me and my siblings.

"I never saw my parents again, and until recently, I hadn't seen my brother and sister, who are both older than I am. When we were removed from our home, we were sent to separate foster homes. Actually, I had no memory of either of my siblings. But my sister remembered me and our brother and searched until she found us."

She smiles, revealing a dimple I hadn't noticed before. "And then she organized a reunion, which included our families."

"How wonderful," Liliana claps. "When was that?"

"Last October. Having siblings is a new aspect to my life and a bit of an adjustment." She stares at the ceiling. "It's as if I had two holes in my heart I didn't know were there, but my siblings plugged them. Some days, interacting with my birth family seems too good to be true, yet I feel complete now, even without a connection to my parents."

She pauses, a thoughtful expression on her face. "Could be it's because I had long-term foster parents who filled the parent role for me. I have no desire to find my birth parents. On the other hand, my sister feels differently. She remembers our mother and father and is actively trying to locate them." With a shrug, Jenica adds, "You never know. I may meet them one of these days, if they're still living."

"Is that why you became a counselor?" Marcus asks.

"Maybe. I certainly spent plenty of time in school counselors' offices." She folds her hands but doesn't twirl her thumbs, I'm pleased to note.

"I didn't consider becoming a substance abuse counselor until I flunked my first year of college, thanks to partying more than I studied. In the midst of a starkly sober moment behind bars—yes, I've been there, done that, folks—I decided I didn't want to become my parents.

"I didn't know them or even remember them, yet I was following their footsteps. The thought blew my mind. I determined right then to find a different path.

"It wasn't easy…" She spreads her hands. "But it's why I'm here today, other than the fact I have three growing teenagers to feed and clothe. And who are all desperate to own the latest electronic devices. But that's another story."

We laugh and clap.

"Okay," she says, "Enough about me. Who's next?"

I raise my hand, anxious to get my contribution over and done with. I tell the same story the women all heard from me on Monday when we met with Ruby Jade. But this time, I feel the group's acceptance rather than our leader's condemnation.

After I finish, Bentley volunteers. He's talking about how he loved meth more than his wife and baby and is on the verge of tears, when the door flies open. It crashes against the wall, and Inez marches into the room. "What," she shrieks, "is going on in here?"

Jenica, who's facing the door, stares at the enraged woman, a shocked expression on her face. "You are interrupting a private session for group members only."

"We do *not* do private at this church." Inez shakes her clenched fists. "The Bible says to confess our sins. We don't hide our failures. We reveal them."

I don't look at the other program participants, but I feel the shared dread. It fires our nerves, constricts our muscles and suffocates our souls.

"This is a rehabilitation program, not a church." Jenica is calm but firm. "Confidentiality is of utmost importance."

"No, that's not how—"

With lifted eyebrows, Jenica asks, "Does this program receive state or federal funds?"

Inez glares at her without response.

"Dr. Hoffman, the director, will be here tomorrow." Jenica folds her arms, as if to suggest it's time for Inez to leave. "You can speak with him about your concerns."

"I know who the director is."

"We'd like to continue our *private* session, please."

"Men do not belong in the same classroom or group with women. I forbid it."

"That's for me to decide." Jenica's jaw twitches. "I–am–the–therapist."

"I'll have Ruby Jade speak with you."

"Please let her know mixed sessions are normal protocol Dr. Hoffman and I will employ from time to time."

Inez pivots and stomps out of the room, slamming the door behind her.

Jenica blinks, like she's trying to reconnect with reality. "Well, that was a surprise."

We shake our heads and shift in our seats.

"No?" She appears confused.

Samuel gets up, locks the door, and places a chair in front of it.

"Ruby Jade, Inez and Noreen believe we shouldn't have secrets from them," Joleen says. "Our lives are to be open to their scrutiny at all times. What we're doing right now with you is an affront to their, uh, leadership style."

"I don't mean to be offensive..." Jenica frowns. "They must realize this is a rehabilitation program, not a class at their church." Her hands and voice tremble.

I understand. Those of us counted among the Followers should have expected the melodramatic intrusion, yet it spiked my adrenalin, big time. I fold my arms across my chest to still my hammering heart.

"Whatever *they* think..." Joleen sits tall. "I trust you and Dr. Hoffman have a different approach." She looks around the circle. "You-all know what I mean."

"I agree," Marco's eyes flash. "We need a *safe* environment, one where they can't barge in on us anytime they get the urge or..." He gives Jenica a hard stare. "Or access your notes. What we say and do here should be confidential."

"I'm with you one-hundred percent." Jenica gives him a reassuring though shaky smile. "Not only does the state have laws and regulations in place to protect your privacy, confidentiality is a key aspect of our code of ethics. Whatever it takes, Dr. Hoffman and I will honor your privacy. Trust me."

"Thank you, Jenica." I get up and give her a hug to help settle her nerves. "You were great. Wish I had a video of what we just witnessed."

Sebastian is waiting for me at the usual time. When he steers toward town rather than Fellowship Neighborhood, I glance over at him. "Okay, Uncle Seb, what are you up to now?"

"Nothin'."

"Why aren't you taking me to work?"

"Like they say, never miss a good chance to shut up."

"Who is they?"

"So to speak…"

The way he's acting, I don't know whether to be frightened or excited. But the smile tugging at the side of his mouth probably means wherever we're going is good. Maybe he made an appointment with the judge. However, with T.W. now open for business, that doesn't make sense.

I decide to appreciate the ride away from FFOW territory, like I enjoyed my drive into town with Myrtle Mae yesterday. A twinge of guilt stabs at my conscience for how little work I've done lately. But then, whether I work or not, I won't get paid. And Ruby Jade's mother and property manager are the people who've been distracting me from my appointed job.

We pull into the parking lot of a bar-and-grill on the outskirts of town. Eric and I occasionally played pool there during our dating days. Now, I'm truly confused. "Is this where we're eating lunch?"

"This is where you're eating lunch."

"Without you?"

"I'll get your door."

He walks me to the restaurant door, matching his long stride to my slow one. I'm moving better now, but I'm not quite at my usual speed.

"So, you're just gonna dump me here?"

He chuckles and opens the door.

The smell of booze and frying burgers smacks me in the face. For some odd reason, the alcohol scent doesn't trigger a longing for a drink. That's first. But the thought of a big juicy hamburger is definitely tempting. I'm adjusting to the loud country music and dark interior, when the hostess greets us.

She's standing behind a podium with a wooden wagon wheel on the front. "How many in your party?"

"We already have a table in the far corner." Sebastian raises his voice over the music. "I'll take a couple menus, and we'll head on back there."

"Okay…" She sounds hesitant but hands him menus.

He leads me past the bar and the pool room, where the clash of billiard balls competes with piped-in music. From there, we walk between booths. Lowered window shades block much of the sunlight, and muted interior lighting barely dents the gloom.

But I can see the shelves above the booths are still lined with rusted, weathered cowboy memorabilia. Spurs, boots, hats, a pair of horseshoes, a barbed wire coil, a branding iron, a campfire coffeepot, a gun holster. On and on the shelves go around the walls.

The collection fascinated my husband. His grandfather, a Wyoming ranch hand, taught him to ride and rope. Eric loved to help him and the other ranch hands drive cattle to higher pasture for the summer and back down in the fall. He often said the cattle drives were the best moments of his teen years, and he never forgot the simple pleasure of eating chuckwagon stew and cornbread beside a campfire. After a fruit cobbler dessert, the cowboys would tell wild stories and sing old trail songs led by the harmonica-playing cook.

I can see my wide-eyed teenage husband taking it all in. The experience played a huge role in his art. His portfolio included several campfire scenes. Just before I was evicted from our apartment, I gave all the paintings and art pieces Eric left behind to his parents. I hope they kept everything. I'd love to see his work again someday.

Sebastian directs me to a table in the rear of the restaurant. But someone is already seated there. "We can't sit there," I whisper.

"Sure you can."

"But—"

"Here you go." He plops the menus on the table and motions to a chair. "Have a seat."

I glance at the seat and then at the person on the other side of the table. "Kip...? Kip! What are you—?"

He jumps to his feet, knocking over his chair, and wraps his arms around me. I hug him and hug him, like I've never hugged my brother before.

He squeezes me hard. "Happy birthday, Sis."

"What?" I pull away from him, staring into his blue eyes. "Birthday?"

"Yeah, it's your twenty-ninth birthday. How could you forget?"

I look at Sebastian, who's grinning from ear to ear. "Did you plan this?"

He shrugs. "How would I know it's your birthday, especially if you forgot?"

"Don't blame him," Kip says. "Mom and Dad and I planned this, once we had a couple phone numbers to work with." He reaches out to my boss. "Nice to meet you, Sebastian. Thanks for bringing Cassie."

The two men shake hands.

I thank Sebastian. "Without you driving me here, meeting Kip for lunch would have been impossible."

"Figured this is one place in town you won't run into any Followers." He chuckles and glances around the dusky restaurant. "Take your time. All afternoon, if you want. Just give me a call when you're ready for me to pick you up."

"I can deliver her back to her dorm." Kip's expression says he thinks his suggestion is totally logical, which it is.

"I'll let you know..." I eye Sebastian, who probably knows what I'm thinking. Should I risk being seen with my brother on the FFOW campus? I've been told unauthorized visits from family members tend to trigger Ruby Jade's temper, big time.

Sebastian tips his hat to Kip. "Good to meet you. That sister of yours is a jewel, but don't tell her I said so." He winks at me. "Later."

Kip rights his chair, and I sit across from him. He watches Sebastian go. "Nice guy."

"He's a lifesaver. I would be stark-raving mad by now if he hadn't brought some normalcy—and humor—into my life."

"That bad?"

"That bad." With my back to the other diners, I feel especially vulnerable. I swivel to check for Followers. This should be safe territory, but talking about FFOW in public makes me nervous.

A waitress with a long blond braid down her back and a tiny hoop in her nose comes with three glasses of water and sets them on the table. "Do you want me to wait for the other person to return before I take your order?"

"He left," Kip says. "But we haven't had a chance to read the menu. We'll do it right now." He points at me. "By the way, today's my sister's birthday."

"Kip..." I frown at my brother. *Please don't make a big deal about my birthday. I'll be dead meat if the Followers get wind of it.*

She grins at my good-looking brother. "I'll keep it in mind." With a wink, she adds, "I'll return in a couple."

Kip's hair is darker than mine, and he has blue eyes rather than brown. My skin is normally darker than his. However, thanks to the many hours he spends outdoors at high altitudes, he has a deep tan. Women always smile at him, having no idea he's oblivious to feminine attention. Mountain climbing is and has been his passion for years.

Kip opens his menu. "Order whatever you want, Cassie. It's your birthday, and I'm buying."

"I can't believe I forgot my birthday."

"I would have forgotten it, too, but Mom reminded me."

I smack his head with the menu.

"Hey, I retract my lunch offer."

"You're not getting out of it now." I grin. "I can't begin to tell you how good it is to hear you insult me again."

"My privilege." Kip peers beyond my shoulder. "Hard to see in this place, but I think that's our waitress headed this way. Quick, pick something."

I scan the menu. "Last time I was here, the hamburgers were good. I was with Eric and some friends, so it was a while back."

"Worth a try."

We both order a cheeseburger and a soft drink. I ask for sweet potato fries. He has regular.

The moment the waitress leaves, he reaches into his shirt pocket and pulls out a small white box. "Got a birthday present for you." Handing it to me, he adds, "Sorry I didn't wrap it."

"Ha." I snicker. "I don't remember you *ever* wrapping gifts."

"The paper gets thrown away almost as soon as a guy goes through the effort to wrap something. Seems like a waste to me." He shrugs. "Besides, my fingers get tangled in the tape and I make a mess. Go ahead, open it."

I lift the lid. Inside, nestled on velvet, is a silver kiwi bird on a silver chain. "Kip, this is adorable. Thank you so much." I don't have the heart to tell him I won't be able to wear the necklace for a year.

"I missed you in New Zealand and hated knowing you were locked away while I was having the time of my life."

"Very sweet of you. I thought of you standing on top of the world and wished I was with you." I flip the box to drop the pendant into my hand. "I love it."

"What's with your clothes?" Kip asks. "I've never seen you dressed that way before."

"You actually noticed?" Despite our mother's occupation, the only clothing items he knows anything about are jeans, t-shirts and outdoor sports apparel.

"This is May…" He lifts an eyebrow. "And you're wearing a long-sleeved shirt and long pants—and tennis shoes, not sandals. The sister I remember would be in ragged, faded cutoffs and a tank top."

"Yeah, I know." I sigh. "Let's just say the old adage 'when in Rome, do as the Romans do' applies to the group I'm with." I return the kiwi to the box and put it in my purse, wondering where to hide it. Between my mattress and box springs, maybe?

"Don't you want to wear the necklace?" He looks disappointed.

"I do want to wear it, really I do. But it might not, uh…" I glance behind me. "Be approved by the leaders, and then they'd take it away from me. I don't want it to disappear, like some of my other things disappeared."

"What?" He frowns. "I don't get it."

"Just part of the 'when in Rome' thing. After I graduate from the program, I'll wear it all the time. It's beautiful, and I can't wait to put it on, but I have to." I give him a sad smile. "I hope you understand."

"Not really, but you know better than I do what you're dealing with." He downs his water. "Mom and Dad wanted to be here for your birthday, but Sebastian said one person would be a safer bet. Not sure what he meant by—"

"He's probably right." I raise the shade beside our table to let in more light—and so I can keep an eye on the parking lot. I have no idea what I'll do if I see someone from the church, but I'd rather see them coming than be caught off-guard.

"Mom and Dad are worried about you, Cassie." Kip leans close. "First, they received a message from an unknown Montana number saying your phone is no longer in service. And then you sent a message from yet another number about emergency calls. When they found out coming for your birthday could cause problems for you, Mom overnighted a package. But when she tracked it, she saw it was refused."

Olivia. She couldn't miss one last opportunity to dig in her knife. I blow out a long breath. "Please tell them my move onto campus was unexpected and sudden." An understatement, for sure. "I only had a couple hours' notice." I lean across the table. "But don't tell them this part."

He narrows his eyelids.

"My former—I finger quote—*household guardian* hates me. Don't know why. Maybe because I came from the detention center. My guess is she's the one who rejected the package. Also, these people don't celebrate birthdays. From what I can tell, they don't celebrate anything, not even Christmas or Easter."

"What's a household guardian?"

"The person who controls your life when no one from Leadership is around to do it."

"Leadership? Are you talking about the leaders you mentioned?"

"Yes, the three women who run the place. And by that, I mean they run the church, the school *and* the rehab program. I call them the Fearsome Threesome."

"Are they qualified to do all those things?" He sips from the extra water glass.

"If the ability to relieve people of their paychecks and retirement funds is a qualification, then, yes, they're qualified."

He scowls. "Why are you still with the group?"

"Remember? A judge put me there."

"Yeah, but—"

"The judge who handles my case happens to be in cahoots with the leaders. He's not a part of the group, but he's funneling people like me into Transformation Way. As a result, the program receives state funds. My guess is he gets kickbacks."

"Wow, from what you've told me and what I read online, I knew it was bad." He rubs his jaw. "But I didn't know how bad."

"I haven't begun to tell you how awful the place is, Kip. It's all about fear and shame. And forget ever having a moment of relaxation or fun. They don't even play board games."

"What's wrong with board games?"

"One of my dormmates told me they're banned because Monopoly is played with dice like gamblers use, and the losers go bankrupt. The lead pastor, Ruby Jade, calls it a devil game. Yet, I've been told by people I work with that member after member has had to file for bankruptcy. They're expected to put lots of money in the offering plate, which is no surprise.

"They're also expected to drive late-model cars and wear expensive clothes, shoes and jewelry. The women have their hair and nails professionally done. Parents are required to dress their kids a certain way and send them to the FFOW school. God only knows what other expenses they have."

Kip starts to say something but instead, lifts his chin. "Here comes our food."

The waitress sets our plates down and brings silverware and condiments from another table. "I'll be back with your drinks." She smiles at Kip and takes off.

"Smells good," Kip says.

One bite of the hamburger, and I groan with pleasure. "I haven't had a real hamburger in forever."

"You've had fake hamburgers?" He snatches one of my sweet potato fries and pops it in his mouth.

"The last hamburger I had was in jail. It was half soy and half poor-quality meat. This is the real thing."

"Must have come from an organic, grass-fed, sun-kissed Montana cow."

"How would you know?"

"I don't. Ignorance is bliss."

The waitress brings us our drinks, promising to check on us later.

Kip sets his burger on the plate and picks up a straw. "How can Mom and Dad and I help you?" Stripping the paper off the straw, he adds, "And what makes you so sure that Sebastian guy is okay?"

I tell him what a great boss Sebastian is and how the few people I trust at FFOW trust him. I explain how he and Myrtle Mae encourage me when others treat me like dirt. One rabbit trail leads to another, and by the time I'm finished, Kip is ready to knock heads.

"Cassie, those people are worse than crazy. You can't go on living this way."

"I have to, Kip."

He pushes our empty plates aside. "Give me your hands."

CHAPTER NINETEEN

I do as he says, even though I don't remember ever holding hands with my brother, even when we were young, other than during family prayers before meals.

"I'll never tell my buddies I held hands with my sister," Kip says. "But I want you to understand how serious I am. You need to leave A-S-A-P, before they do something really bad to you. You can't ruin an entire year of your life living with those people."

"Where I'm living now is better than where I was before."

"But they can rip you out of the dorm without warning, right?"

"Yes, but—"

"Dad and Mom and I can put our heads together to figure this out. Or pool our funds to hire a good lawyer."

"Our parents have paid for too many attorneys already."

"And they'd do it again in a heartbeat. We love you, Cassie, and—"

"Well, well, what do we have here?"

We turn.

Vance is standing by our table, his expression as contemptuous as always. He yanks a cell phone from his belt. "I bet my mom would enjoy a picture of this illicit affair."

Kip releases my hands, shoves his chair away and stands. "Who are you?"

Vance backsteps. "Cas-*san*-dra can tell you all about me. She knows the power I wield."

A mixture of rage and frustration churns my belly.

Kip glances at me. "Is this guy for real?"

Vance stabs a forefinger at me. "You owe me."

"I don't owe you anything."

"It was your fault—"

"That you were drunk, broke into a home and landed in jail? It was your own stupid fault."

He grabs the table edge and leans close, his alcohol-infused cigarette breath a rancid miasma. "Like I said," he slurs, "your fault, an' you owe me." The vein along his temple pulses, as if emphasizing his words.

"Hey." Kip pushes Vance aside. "Leave her alone."

Vance shoves him into the wall.

I jump to my feet. "Stop!" This bar has seen many a fight, but I don't want to be in the middle of one.

Vance twists toward me. "Shut-up!"

Kip grabs his shoulder, spins him around and is about to slug him, when a gravelly voice behind me says, "You boys wanna settle it outside?"

The speaker comes alongside me. I glance over and recognize the wide-chested bouncer. He worked at more than one place I frequented in the past. But he doesn't appear to recognize me. Must be my Follower clothes and hair.

Kip releases Vance's shoulder.

Vance swings toward the bouncer, a snarl rolling off his lips. "Don't tell me what to do."

"Well, what d'ya know?" The man crosses his arms. His biceps bulge above his meaty forearms. "Mr. Longpre. Funny how we keep running into each other."

"What're you doin' here?"

"I'm here to tell you to get out before I call the cops."

"You can't—"

"I can. And I will." He pulls a cell phone from his back pocket. "I'm making the call in fifteen seconds. You can go now or get a free ride to jail. Your choice."

Vance glares at me through bloodshot eyes. "Ya did it again."

I clench my fists. "Time to take responsibility for your actions, Vance."

He stumbles away, and I fall into my chair, knees wobbling, heart pounding.

The bouncer watches him go before turning to us. "Longpre tends to cause trouble wherever he goes. What was it this time?"

"He was harassing my sister," Kip says. "Accusing her of stuff, getting in her face."

"The dude can't leave the ladies alone. He's either charming them or hounding them." He peers at me. "You okay, ma'am?"

"I'm fine. Just a bit rattled. Thanks for sending him away. My brother and I haven't seen each other in a while, and he interrupted our visit."

"Holler if he's dumb enough to return." The man turns to go. "I'll be in the pool room."

"Got it." Kip gives him a thumbs-up.

The waitress comes with the check and a tiny cake. I thank her and blow out the solitary candle with a shaky breath. Thank God, I don't have to muster the breath to extinguish twenty-nine candles.

As soon as she leaves, Kip asks, "What was that all about? You seemed to know the guy. And what was the name he called you?"

"His mother is the church leader, which is the reason why he thinks he rules the world. About the name, she gives everyone what they call an *approved* name. Mine is Cassandra. She even changed my last name from True to Turner."

"Ludicrous. Why in the world—?" He interrupts himself. "Don't answer. Let's eat the cake and get outta here. We'll find a park or somewhere that lets the sunshine in, where you can see your hand in front of your face."

I laugh and cut the cake, giving him two-thirds of it. "You have to admit, the hamburger was good."

"Yeah, the food is great." He digs his fork into the cake. "I might even come again. Next time, I'll bring a flashlight."

Assuming Vance went straight to his mother to blab his version of our encounter, I have Kip drive me to the dorm in time for supper. No sense adding another transgression to whatever story Vance concocts. I'm nervous about being seen with my brother, which is way crazy, but I want to spend as much time with Kip as I can and show him where I live. I'm relieved the gate code Sebastian gave me works on the first try, but Kip is incensed a church has restricted access.

However, I can tell he's impressed by the acres of lawn and the big buildings. "I'd give you a tour," I tell him, "but this place has cameras everywhere. The security guys would come after us. They even chased me down in a golf cart when I was walking in the cemetery and drove me back to my dorm."

He grunts and shakes his head, apparently lacking words to describe his reaction to FFOW.

We pass the dining hall, where the parking lot is half full. I ask Kip, "What day is this?"

"Wednesday. Are you so isolated you don't know what day it is?"

"The Followers, all two-thousand, eat together in that building every Wednesday evening."

"Two-thousand people?"

"Right. When they shout their mantra, 'praise God in heaven,' the building vibrates. I about had a heart attack the first time I experienced it. Actually, they shout an acronym, 'PGIH.'"

"Bizarre." He rubs the stubble on his chin. "All I can say. Bizarre."

"Yeah, I know."

Outside the dorm, we hug goodbye. I try not to cry, but my tears flow, anyway. God only knows when I'll be allowed to see my brother again.

"Keep us informed, Cat, and please don't cry." He hugs me one more time. "Whatever it takes, we'll get you out of this place. If you want, you can grab your things right now and come live with me in Washington."

"I've been told after a few months, a person grows numb and able to ignore the madness, at least most of it." I wipe my face with my sleeve. "If I make it through the program, Kip, I'll be free to restart my music career. That's my goal, to survive long enough to satisfy court requirements."

"After living like a holy roller zombie for a year..." He squints at me. "How could you possibly make music?"

"Only a year, Kip. Only a year. But pray for me. Pray I don't lose myself, that God puts a barricade around my soul. Some days I feel as if the real me is being sucked out of my body, and I'll never be able to retrieve it."

"I'll pray... And I'll come running the instant you're ready for me to remove you from this cult, which is what it is, Cassie. It's a dangerous, evil, mind-controlling, life-stealing cult."

I walk into the dorm and up the stairs. Eunice is in the hallway, coming my way. "Here you are," she says. "I knocked on your door. No wonder you didn't answer."

I appreciate the fact she didn't peek inside my unlocked room.

"Would you like a ride to the dining hall?" she asks. "I plan to go there in a few minutes, after I change my clothes." She looks at her snagged pants and worn tennis shoes. "Noreen took me shopping today, so I'd better wear something she picked out, even though…" Her voice trails off.

"Even though," I murmur, "your new clothes are uncomfortable."

She lifts an eyebrow, but her expression remains neutral.

"I'll change out of my Noreen-purchased work clothes and be right down."

Five minutes later, I knock on her door. She opens it, and I give her a thumbs-up. "You look nice, Eunice."

She makes a face, obviously not impressed with her "altogether" attire.

Her navy-blue pantsuit with white piping will fit right in with the Followers, although it doesn't mask the Vicks smell. Her glasses are still smudged, and her gray hair flips every direction. Noreen will no doubt tackle those fatal flaws soon.

On the short drive to the dining hall, I tell her Ruby Jade might single me out for some sort of disciplinary action.

Eunice's mismatched eyes widen behind her thick lenses. "Why would she do that?"

"My brother came to town today and treated me to lunch for my birthday."

"How nice."

"Yes, it was wonderful. But Followers don't celebrate birthdays, so I'm not sharing the reason for his visit. Anyway, I hadn't seen Kip in a long time. That's the good news. The bad news is Ruby Jade's son, Vance, saw us there."

"A son, huh? She doesn't seem the motherly type." She pauses. "I don't remember a wedding ring."

"I've heard her ex lives in California. Their son is a spoiled thirty-something who uses his connection with his mother to make life miserable for church members. He also has a drinking problem." *Such a nice way to describe a drunk. I wonder how many times it's been said of me.*

"I'm sorry to hear it." She pulls into the mostly full parking lot. "I can drop you off at the door, if you want."

"I wasn't on my feet much today. I can walk from wherever you park."

Eunice finds a space near the back of the lot. We get out and trail others toward the building, keeping a distance between us and them. "Back to Vance," I whisper. "He got kicked out of the restaurant because he'd had too much to drink and picked a fight with my brother. But he blames me, the same way he blames me for another alcohol-related incident. From what I've seen, his mother believes whatever he tells her, so God only knows what I'll be accused of tonight."

I stop, struck by the fact she parked her car and she's walking alongside me rather than returning to the dorm. "Are you going inside?"

"I told the girls to save us a place."

"I thought you didn't do church." The closer we get to the building, the stronger the smell of meatloaf.

"Ruby Jade says I have to do church…or lose my job." Eunice heaves a long sigh.

"Oh, right. Now I remember. Welcome to the club, Eunice."

Ruby Jade's prayer and comments before the meal don't include any mention of my latest offenses, thank God. When she finishes, she comes directly to our table. Everyone greets her with bright smiles—too bright. We're all faking our enthusiasm. By now, we know better than to reveal our true feelings. Even Eunice, new as she is to FFOW culture, has caught on.

Before I can put any food on my plate, our fearsome leader says, "Cassandra, come with me."

Eunice gives me a sympathetic but knowing smile, and Joleen squeezes my hand as I pass.

I follow Ruby Jade, who meanders from table to table. Her long red-satin dress crinkles and rustles with her movement. Smiling benevolently, she touches a shoulder here, a head there.

Everyone returns her smiles, but their focus veers away from me. Could be they don't want to be associated with whatever punishment awaits me—or, like at the Pritchards' house, I'm only a blip on their radar. Oh, well. I didn't expect the rehab program to be a popularity contest.

She leads me to a narrow side room. The only furnishings are a small table and two folding chairs. Closing the door, she indicates I'm to sit in the chair directly under the solitary fluorescent lightbulb. Funny how this reminds me of a police interrogation room. I'm sure the setup is no accident.

The chair creaks when Ruby Jade sits across from me, but she ignores it and gets right to business. "Are you enjoying the Transformation Way program, Cassandra?" Like the last time we sat this close, her gold-flecked violet eyes are wide, yet her pupils are mere pinpoints.

"What I've experienced so far, yes. Are you not eating?"

She flicks her hand. "Meatloaf and Jell-O. Are you kidding? I prefer filet mignon." Her rosewater scent permeates the room, making breathing difficult.

"So, why—?"

"Yours is not to question why." She scowls. "Do you want to continue in the program, to graduate from the program? To..." She gives me a sly look. "To return to your music career?"

"Yes." I cringe inwardly. Where, oh, where is this going?

"For what you did today, I could return you to jail, and you would not discover the gift of God within you."

My stomach clenches. I give her a questioning look.

"You know full well what I'm talking about."

I don't respond because I have no idea what she's thinking, and I refuse to second-guess her crazy logic.

"You went whoring after a Gentile this afternoon." Her eyelids narrow. "A dark-skinned Gentile."

Whoring after a Gentile? All I can do is stare at her. *Rodrigo has dark skin, but I didn't—*

"Don't play innocent with me." She leans near, drilling me with her purple eyes. "My son saw you with a *man*." The way she says *man*, you'd think it was a dirty word.

I take a breath, nearly choking on the stale air. "Vance saw me eating lunch with my brother."

"Not what he told me."

"I don't know what he told you, but I'm telling you the truth. My brother surprised me." I don't mention my birthday, the gift Kip gave me, the cake we shared... "I didn't expect him to come to Bozeman today."

She slams her fist on the table.

I jerk away.

"You did *not* have my permission to meet him."

I swallow and clasp my hands in my lap. "I had Sebastian's permission."

"Absurd. He may be my butler, but he has no status in this church. I, Ruby Jade Paradise, am the senior pastor. All requests for meetings with Gentiles come through me."

He's not a Gentile. He's my brother. "I didn't know. I thought because Sebastian is my boss..." My stomach growls.

"If you were in tune with God, you would have known. And I wouldn't have to waste my precious time telling you what you should already know."

Because not all rules are written.

Fingers intertwined, she begins to twirl her thumbs. Today she's only wearing three rings. They sparkle each time they catch the fluorescent lighting. "Vance saw you go into a bar with a Gentile," she says. "He would have taken a picture, but you eluded him."

"Vance was already inside the restaurant." I know better than to argue with Ruby Jade, but I feel the need to defend Kip, as well as myself. "He came to our table half-stewed and tried to pick a fight with my brother. I suppose he might have gotten a photo of us, if he hadn't been kicked out."

She rears back, blinking as if she might be considering my words. But then she yells, "That's a lie straight from the pit."

I fold my arms, mostly to keep my hands from shaking. "Your son has a drinking problem. The deputy said he was drunk when he broke into the Pritchards' house. Vance needs help."

She sucks air through flared nostrils. Like the Hulk in the comic books Kip collected in junior high, her chest rises, and she seems to expand before my eyes. "You *hussy*." She scream-spits the word at me. "You have no right to tell me what my son does or doesn't need."

I'm in too deep to back down now. "Because of my past..." I search for inoffensive language. "I'm, uh, sensitive to people with similar issues."

"Oh, pshaw." She blows me off with a flick of her wrist. "Stop spreading lies about my son and stop calling Sebastian 'uncle.'" Her purple eyes flash. "Those are orders."

Aha. As I suspected, the Fearsome Threesome read my texts. "He asked me to call him *uncle*."

"I doubt it. He would never be so ridiculous or inappropriate." Her dark eyebrows knot. "My neighbors will be scandalized."

Since when does she care what people think of her? Besides, her neighbors are acres away from her house. They can't hear me, and if they did, how would hearing me call Sebastian *uncle* scandalize them?

The end-of-meal buzzer interrupts my vain attempt to make sense of what she just said.

"Go help the others." Ruby Jade pushes from the table and makes her way to the door. Hand on the knob, she says, "And stop wearing those stupid shoes and socks in public."

When I don't respond, she stomps back to the table and bends so close her face is inches from mine. "You may think you pulled one over on the Pritchards, Cassandra Turner, but you can think again. God and I know you're the twofaced snitch who ruined their lives. You *will* confess to betraying Olivia and Owen. I guarantee it."

Yanking the door open, she rushes out, and a loud clatter rushes in. The diners are already dumping their silverware and plates into the bins. Trembling from head to toe, I slowly get to my feet. Good thing she left so quickly. I was about to bypass caution and launch into a tirade about ruining children's lives.

On my way to my dormmates' table, someone drops a fork at my feet. I kneel and reach shaky fingers to pick it up, but the church secretary, Evelyn, beats me to it. She leans against my shoulder. "Just so you know," she murmurs, "we sent a message to families, telling them participants' phones are out of service. Pass the word."

I can barely hear her above the din. "Your parents have been calling the office. I'm only allowed to say someone will get back to them. Never happens." And then she's gone, fork in hand. A teen boy rolls a big trash bin between us. I slowly stand.

No wonder Mom and Dad were worried. I straighten and shuffle through the chaos. Thank God my parents now have Myrtle Mae's number as well as Sebastian's. And Kip can tell them I'm okay. Knowing I have a caring family offsets Ruby Jade's threats, at least to some degree.

By the time I reach my table, my dormmates have finished their cleanup and are pushing the chairs in. "I'm so sorry you missed dinner," Shakyra says. "Here…" She opens her purse and digs around. "This energy bar is old, but it's better than nothing."

"Thanks." I unwrap the bar and take a bite. "Remind me to tell you-all something later."

"Eat it fast." Merikay scans the Followers hurrying through the doors to the next building. "You can't eat in the sanctuary."

Together, the seven of us drift across the dining hall. My friends chat. I chew. Outside the church doors, I swallow my last bite and stuff the wrapper into my pink purse. Snapping it shut, I follow the others to an empty row and collapse into the end seat.

Maybe I can gather my wits before the service starts and Ruby Jade hits us with more craziness.

I haven't been in my chair thirty seconds, when someone taps my shoulder. I turn.

Noreen is standing in the aisle, her phone in her hand. She crooks her finger. "Come with me."

Again? Twice in one night? Does Leadership know it's my birthday? Are they intentionally trying to ruin my day, like I supposedly ruined the Pritchards' lives?

She leads me down to the front row, which sits way too close to the stage for my comfort, and points to a chair. I sit, cross my legs and look around. Now what? I should have accepted Kip's offer to take me to Spokane to live with him. I hate being in the front row, and I hate to think what the Fearsome Threesome are planning. It can't be good.

I close my eyes. Kip is praying for me, and I know my parents, Myrtle Mae and Sebastian pray for me—and Corban. Whatever is coming, God will get me through it.

CHAPTER TWENTY

When I open my eyes, Logan is sitting in the front row of the men's section. His face is pale, and his arm is in a sling. What happened and why is he in the hot seat?

Before I can make eye contact with him, Inez's voice blasts from the pulpit. "Good evening, Followers."

Behind me, the Followers thunder, "Good evening, Inez."

"We have a wonderful service planned for you tonight," she declares. "But before we begin, I must explain why Mr. Logan Dahlstrom and Ms. Cassandra Turner are seated—seated separately, that is, on the front rows."

Is Logan, like me, wondering what concocted story he'll hear about himself?

"This morning," Inez proclaims, "while mowing church property with the church's newest riding mower, Logan Dahlstrom let go of Jesus and rolled the mower, causing five-hundred dollars in damage. Because we are a responsible organization, the mower is insured. However, we have a five-hundred-dollar deductible. Logan Dahlstrom, stand and face the congregation."

He does as she requested. Pain is written all over his rigid body. He should be in bed.

"Because you need to learn responsibility, you will immediately see to the repairs and pay the deductible. When completed, the mower must appear and run like new. Turn in the receipt to the office to prove you did as instructed, so we can notify our insurance company."

She leans over the pulpit. "Do you understand?"

He nods.

"I can't hear you."

He turns toward the pulpit. "Yes, Inez." His eyes are as lifeless as his voice.

"You may be seated." She doesn't even mention his injured arm. I wish he'd spit in her face, walk out of the building and never return.

Inez turns to me. "Stand, Cassandra Turner, so the congregation can see you."

Facing the FFOW flock, I search the crowd for familiar faces. Other than my wide-eyed dormmates, the women are pokerfaced mannequins. Eunice's mouth is open, and her eyes behind the round lenses are even bigger than usual. I warned her, but Inez's heartless behavior would shock even a FFOW veteran.

On the men's side, amidst a sea of males who appear to stare right through me, Corban offers a hint of a smile and a half wink. Another man gives me an encouraging smile. I try to place him and realize it's Joseph, without his goatee. His eyebrows are bunched, as though he's leery of Inez's intentions. I know the feeling.

Logan's head is down.

In the middle section, the married section, a woman in a wheelchair is parked in the aisle beside a gray-haired man. She glances from Logan to me and then to Logan again. Both the man and the woman's shoulders are tense, their jaws tight, their eyes narrowed. The woman's hands are folded below her chin, as if she's praying. Mr. and Mrs. Dahlstrom, perhaps?

Vance and another brawny man are at their posts, the doorways on each side of the sanctuary. As usual, Vance's arms are folded across his broad chest. From my vantage point, I get the impression he's using his knuckles to push his biceps upward, maximizing their bulge. The expression on his haughty face says he can't wait to see me skewered like a hot dog on a willow stick.

"Cas-sandra." My fake FFOW name hisses from the huge speakers hanging from the sanctuary ceiling. "You brought shame upon this church today by eating and drinking with a Gentile in public. And not just any Gentile—a man." Similar to Ruby Jade, she says "man" like she's spitting filth from her mouth.

Evidently, Ruby Jade's little talk with me was a waste of time, like she said. Taking a deep breath, I square my shoulders and prepare for the attack. First thing I'll buy if I ever get a paycheck is stronger deodorant. Mine can't handle the stress this church generates.

"And not just any restaurant..." Her shouted words ricochet off the sanctuary walls. "A bar that serves alcoholic beverages and blasts carnal country music over loudspeakers. You, an alcoholic, not only entered a bar, you ate and drank with an outsider with whom you are having an immoral affair. Admit your sins to the Followers. Confess."

The word echoes above our heads. "Confess...confess...confess."

Brows furrow. Mouths turn downward. Gazes come alive and drill into me.

My first instinct is to ask, "Since when is eating lunch a sin?" But I remember Corban once admonishing me to pick my battles and to pick them carefully. "I ate lunch with my brother," I say, hands clasped, "at a restaurant he chose." No sense bringing Sebastian into my confession. "I had a Pepsi. He drank a Mountain Dew."

"Your *brother*? I don't think so." The sneer in her voice is unmistakable. "Our source tells us he was a good-looking man, so he can't *possibly* be *your* brother."

I blink and then blink another time. That's a new low, even for Inez. I should be angry, but I remember Myrtle Mae suggesting Inez is jealous of anyone who puts her aging features to shame. Her catty insults aren't worth a response.

A slight movement on the women's side catches my eye. Marcela. She lifts her chin, twice, as if trying to encourage me. I'm so happy to see her, I have to bite my lips to repress a grin.

The congregation's focus flickers, and fabric swishes behind me. Glancing over my shoulder, I see Ruby Jade approach the pulpit. She mutters, "Get on with it, Inez. We'll deal with her later." The contemptuous look she gives me could melt rocks.

I turn my gaze forward again.

"From this moment on," Inez barks, "you will sit on the front row during services. Do you understand, Cassandra Turner?"

I nod. "Yes."

"Sit down."

I sit.

Vance's raucous laughter shatters the stillness like a machine gun burst. After a moment of stunned silence, a unison intake of Follower breath whooshes from wall to wall.

Ruby Jade swivels his direction. "Vance, that's enough!"

He laughs a maniacal laugh, spins into the hallway behind him and takes off.

Inez gathers her papers to the sound of his smug though fading laughter. God only knows why Ruby Jade cut short my inquisition, but I'm grateful. I slide my feet under my seat. If she doesn't see my shoes, maybe she won't rant about them.

The podium lowers, and Ruby Jade steps behind it. "This is a special night, my beloved Followers. We have much to discuss."

Discuss? Who do you think you're fooling? I concentrate on her animated face, striving to keep my own features impassive and to slow my pounding heart. Discussions aren't allowed, only abject obedience to her idiotic decrees.

Evidently, this is important enough in her mind she's skipping the music tonight. No big loss. Of course, I wouldn't say such a thing in public because I don't want to insult the musicians. The orchestra members do a phenomenal job of making Ruby Jade's songs almost singable.

"First, I want to emphasize the importance of our cleanse sessions." She steps to the side, resting an elbow on the pulpit. "Some of you believe cleanses are solely for other people, an opportunity to drag dirt and demons from other Followers' soul. Such false beliefs are straight from the devious devil."

The acrylic stand wobbles. She blinks and straightens, eyes wide, but she doesn't miss a beat. "Confession is an integral component of the process. As James says, we must confess our sins to one another in order to experience true healing.

"Never forget." Bending toward us, she metronomes her finger back and forth as she talks. "Sickness in the body comes from sickness of the soul." Tick-tock, tick-tock. "That's why some of you are sick or dead."

I almost laugh. If they're dead, they're not here, enduring her sermon. Lucky stiffs. I chuckle inwardly, laughing at my own joke. But then I remember Eric lying in a windblown Wyoming grave. How can I even think of joking about death?

She folds her hands over her belly. "Due to countless cleanse sessions in my youth, which included much confession and crying out in deep repentance to the Lord, the devil's demons no longer torment me." Her thumbs begin to circle. "Dirt is no longer allowed to reside in my soul."

I'm thinking, *That's a bunch of hooey*, when she jabs a long fingernail at me. "This means even our front-row sinners, Cassandra Turner and—" She points at Logan. "Logan Dahlstrom have the potential to ultimately reach the state of sinless perfection I have already attained."

If you represent perfection, we're all in trouble.

"We can help you, but you must work hard, submit to authority, give of your time, allegiance and finances, confess, repent—and yield to cleanses again and again and *again*. In time, God will draw the gift he planted within you to the surface, so you can serve him and this church with your body, soul and spirit."

Stepping behind the pulpit, she says, "I will be visiting each of our households to ensure you understand and correctly implement cleanses, beginning with the Transformation Way households." She lifts her eyebrows. "To be clear, the men and women's dormitories will be visited separately."

Without warning, she slaps the pulpit, rattling the speakers. I jerk, and I'm sure everyone behind me does the same.

"Enough family business," she says. "I've titled tonight's talk, 'When We Must Speak Falsehoods to Protect the Things of God.'"

I sit back, hands on my knees. This ought to be interesting.

"Adam and Eve's son Cain, who killed his brother Abel, is an example of when not to lie." Eyes narrowed, she adds, "In fact, he lied directly to God by telling him he didn't know what happened to Abel." She does the metronome thing again. "Not a wise move on his part. Yet, other times in Scripture, lying was not only required, it was essential for survival. A prime example occurred while the Israelites were in Egypt, and the pharaoh commanded their midwives to kill all baby boys born to Hebrew women.

"But the midwives feared God above a pagan ruler and did not do what he ordered. Being a man whose pride was threatened—that gets to male egos every time—the pharaoh summoned the midwives to his court. He asked them about all the baby boys toddling around Israeli neighborhoods. His soldiers must have reported seeing dozens of them."

I resist the urge to scratch the mosquito bite on my neck—or to cross my legs. Instead, I do the FFOW squirm—infinitesimal muscle movement to relieve stress and discomfort, careful to appear like I'm paying attention but to never look directly at Ruby Jade. I've had enough eye contact with her for one evening.

"Their response?" She lifts her dark eyebrows. "They said the Hebrew women were vigorous, unlike the Egyptian women, and they gave birth before the midwives arrived at their homes, an outright lie. Yet, the midwives saved God's people for eternity with their fibs.

"And then there was Jael in the book of Judges. She led Sisera, commander of the Canaanites, to believe she was a friend, not a foe, and then proceeded to pound a stake through his temples."

Someone behind me groans, probably the same girl who couldn't handle the Jezebel story in Inez's Sunday school class.

Ruby Jade chuckles, apparently amused by the thought of a woman daring to do such a dastardly deed. "Similar to those who went before her, she was protecting God's people.

"I could go on and on," she says, "but I'll provide one more example—Jacob's wife, Rachel. When her father searched her tent for stolen household gods, she sat on the idols and told him she couldn't get up. She was *indisposed*, she said, as happened monthly to women of that time."

I stifle my incredulity before it hits my face, or at least I hope I did. Monthly indisposition doesn't happen today?

"By doing so, Rachel defended God's chosen people. She was one of the founding mothers of the nation of Israel."

I'm confused. God surely did not condone theft or appreciate a founding mother revering pagan gods so much she stole a set.

"The good news, the bless-ed good news..." Ruby Jade leans toward us. "This very church is the New Israel. These women, through godly deception all those many centuries ago, secured the future formation of Faithful Followers of the Way, hallelujah!"

With a great roar, the Followers jump to their feet. "Praise God!" they shout. "Hallelujah, PGIH!"

I hurry to join them, clapping and smiling my biggest, fakest grin and mouthing, "Rubbish, rubbish, rubbish."

In time, the din subsides and the Faithful plop into their seats.

"To be clear," Ruby Jade says, "honesty is what we expect within the Followers. In fact, Leadership will never tolerate dishonesty. However, if you find yourself in a situation in the community or with your Gentile relatives where you need to defend FFOW with deception, don't hesitate to do so."

I groan inwardly, ashamed to think I've done that very thing.

"We, the Faithful Followers of the Way, are God's chosen people. We have our own truth to safeguard. When we come under attack, we must use every means at our disposal to shield this body of believers from the enemy and establish God's kingdom on earth. This is our calling, our high and holy calling—to bring God's kingdom to earth."

She raises both hands high. "I, your beloved pastor, prophetess and psalmist, will lead the charge, hallelujah, hallelujah!"

Once again, the Followers are on their feet. I'm so blown away by Ruby Jade's twisted logic, I can barely stand, let alone clap and cheer. But I don't have a choice, especially in the front row.

She lowers her hands. "Dismissed." With that, she leaves the stage. Something tells me she actually believes what she said.

I glance behind me. The others look as confused as I feel, but the lights flicker, which is the signal to go home. People gather their things and file into the aisles.

Thursday morning, I settle into the classroom circle along with the other participants. "From what I hear," Doctor says, rubbing his hairy chin, "this has been a week of storytelling for you, relaying your personal stories, first to your church leaders and then to Jenica. This morning, I'm asking you to tell them one more time."

Samuel groans.

"Hear me out." Doctor raises his palm. "This time, anyone in the group can ask a question. We won't give advice—that includes me. But we can interrupt the storyteller with questions to seek clarification or ask the reason for a thought, a mindset or an action, or maybe how a person handled a certain situation. Those kinds of questions."

He places his hands on his knees and looks each of us in the eye. "You've all been in therapy groups before, so I don't need to remind you what we say in this room is confidential. However, because I get the impression confidentiality is lacking within the church, I will remind you the Transformation Way rehabilitation program is *not* the church. It may be supported to some degree by the church, but it is a separate entity. Any questions?"

He glances around the group.

Joleen says, "Makes perfect sense."

The rest of us nod.

"I will make you two promises." Doctor stands, goes to the door, closes it and locks it. "First, we will not have another interruption like the one you endured yesterday. I have made my position clear to the church staff." He positions two chairs in front of the door, either to show us he's serious or because he doesn't trust Leadership any more than I do.

"And, two..." He returns to his seat. "Your conversations with me and with Jenica will remain confidential. Any notes we take, whether on paper or electronically, will remain with us. We will *never* keep files in this building or share our findings with the church staff."

"Whoo-hoo!" Shakyra shouts, hands in the air.

We all clap and cheer.

"Glad you approve." He smiles. "Now, who wants to go first?"

A quarter after twelve, I crawl into Sebastian's dusty-smelling pickup and run a finger across the dashboard. "Been driving on dirt roads?"

"You caught me red-handed." He grins. "Took the long way over here. I do my best thinking when I'm bouncing over washboard roads."

"If you say so."

He hands me a sandwich and an apple. "Ready to work?"

"You mean no more time off to play?"

"No more time off, at least this week. But Myrtle Mae wants you to be sure to stop by for tea. She has a surprise for you."

"I've had a lot of surprises this week."

"One more won't kill you."

I laugh. "They've mostly been good surprises, really good. How's her kitten doing?"

"She's a feisty one, for sure. I tried to introduce her to the boys, and she scratched Fenwick's nose. The dog yelped bloody murder."

"Must have been quite a scene."

"Myrtle Mae felt terrible. I told her it was a surface scratch. But the glare Ruby Jade gave me when she saw it could blister a cow's hind end. She adores those dogs, like they're her children."

"What did you tell her?"

"I said he must have stuck his nose into something he shouldn't have."

"Ah, so it's not only Followers who feel they have to lie to your boss."

"That's not exactly a lie."

"Yeah, right. And not exactly the truth, either."

As soon as breaktime comes around, I drop my gloves by the bush I've been trimming and walk to Myrtle Mae's house. I know she's anxious to see me, and I'm always happy to see her. She's a bright spot in my murky FFOW existence.

The moment I knock on her door, she calls, "Come in, come in." Inside, we hug, and I step back to check out her black slacks and red blouse. "What, no muumuu?"

She giggles. "If you want, I'll dig out our dresses, and we'll go another round downtown."

"I don't think Bozeman is ready for another round of Hawaii babes quite yet."

The kitten meows from the other room.

"You poor baby." I step into the living room. "Your owner has been neglecting you, I see."

"As if she'd let me." Myrtle Mae snorts. "Citrus is a demanding little creature who can be very vocal, considering her size, especially at night. Can't get a thing done."

"Demanding, are you?" I kneel beside the box and lift the kitten out. Placing her in the crook of my arm, I run my fingers over her small body. She immediately begins to purr.

Carrying the cat into the kitchen, I say, "She seems happy now." Her soft fur and kitten smell are a balm for my scorched soul.

"Of course, she's happy. You're holding her."

"Are you sorry you got Citrus? It was my idea."

"Oh, no, not at all." She smiles. "I adore her. She's good company, a real cuddler, for sure. I tend to grouse now and then, but I don't mean anything by it."

"She'll get easier as she gets older."

"Like a child."

"Like a child." I don't remind Myrtle Mae her daughter and grandson have become more and more difficult as time passes. She's plenty aware of the sad fact.

"What kind of tea do you want today?"

"Your concoction, please. I love it."

"Coming right up. Care for a bowl of peaches with a little cream? A friend gave me a jar she canned last fall."

"How could I refuse? Sounds delicious." I sit at her kitchen table. The kitten curls in my lap.

Myrtle Mae sets a cup and saucer in front of me. "But first, I have something for you." She retrieves a brightly wrapped package about the size of a book from her counter and hands it to me. "Happy birthday, Cassie!"

CHAPTER TWENTY-ONE

"How sweet of you to think of me, Myrtle Mae." I hug her waist with one arm. "Sebastian must have told you."

She sits across from me. "I know how it is with birthdays in the church, so I thought I'd sneak you a little something on the sly."

"You are quite the crafty woman."

"Practice." She laughs. "Lots of practice. You're not the first, uh, shall we say, object of my affection."

"I enjoy being an object of your affection." After sliding the ribbon off, I slip my finger under the tape, trying not to tear the paper. She might want to use it again. Inside is a plain brown box. It smells like cardboard and gives no hint as to the contents.

I lift the top and gasp at the sight of my husband's face smiling up at me. "Myrtle Mae, how did you…? Where did you?" I blink back tears.

"You told me your parents sent a family portrait that included your husband. But you only glimpsed it before your roommate told you to put it away."

"And then Olivia stole my stuff, so I never had another chance to look at the picture." Wiping my wet cheeks with my sleeve, I touch the glass that covers Eric's framed features. He's holding a trophy. "Where did you find this picture?"

"Sebastian took me to the university. We knew your husband was an artist, so we went to the art department and asked if a student named Eric True had won any awards. We figured it was a way to single him out from the other art students. The young woman at the desk searched in her computer and, sure enough, he had. When she turned the screen around to show us the picture, Sebastian asked if she could print a copy for us.

"At first, she said she wasn't allowed to provide copies of student pictures. But after I told her Eric had passed away and we wanted to surprise you, she said, 'Under the circumstances, I'd be glad to do that for you.' Although I was prepared to pay whatever she asked, she didn't charge me."

"Nice of her." I lift the picture. "This must be when his wolf sculpture won a statewide competition and a Helena bank bought it for their lobby. We celebrated with a cross-country ski trip to Yellowstone, where we saw real wolves, five of them, running through the snow."

"Oh, my." Her lavender eyes widen. "Must have been a frightening experience."

"We were in our car at the time. They were less than thirty feet away and didn't seem to notice us. We could see their breath. They were beautiful and powerful and a confirmation for Eric regarding the direction he was going with his art. One wolf was pure white, like his sculpture."

I clasp the frame to my chest. "I hadn't seen this picture before, but I love it. It's the most wonderful gift ever. Thank you so much." I look down at the cat. "I'd hug you again, but then I'd disturb Citrus. She's sleeping so peacefully."

"You can hug me later. Right now, I'm appreciating the quiet." She drops one of her tea balls into my cup and adds hot water. "I have to admit I gave you the picture knowing you can't display it."

Despite the delicious cinnamon aroma rising from the tea, disappointment lumps in my throat. "I should have thought of it."

"I did think of it, and here's my solution." She pours water into her cup and sets the teapot on the trivet. "If it's okay with you, I'll place the photo at the back of the towel shelf in the bathroom. Anytime you want, you can go into my bathroom and peek at your husband."

She holds up her hand. "I know it's a *terrible* place for his picture, but if I put it out and my daughter happens to stop by…" She sighs. "A highly unlikely possibility. But you know she'd ask a dozen snoopy questions."

Myrtle Mae comes around the table to study the photo, her head tilted to see better. "I'm sorry I can't display his picture. He was a rather handsome young man."

I hold the frame at arms' length. "Yes, I definitely have to agree. This is a great shot of Eric. He didn't smile big like that after he got sick."

"Another potential problem…" Myrtle Mae goes to the refrigerator. "I'm concerned the picture could make you miss him more than ever. You've had enough heartache. I don't want to cause you additional pain."

I smile, knowing she'd never intentionally hurt me. "I'll be okay. Yes, it's wonderful to see my husband's face after so long. However, he's gone, and I can't do anything to bring him back. Took me a few years, but I believe I've truly accepted Eric's death."

"Good." She divvies the peaches into two bowls, pours cream on top and brings the bowls to the table. Handing me a spoon, she says, "Dig in. These peaches are too good to let sit."

I snap the support arm from the back of the frame and set the picture on the table, where we can both see it. "How's that?"

"Perfect." She sits across from me.

I cut a peach slice into thirds and take a bite. "You're right, Myrtle Mae. This is scrumptious. I haven't had fruit this good in a long time."

She takes a bite and lowers her spoon. "You have a third issue to contend with."

"I do? This is a complicated photograph."

"Only one more issue."

"Are you sure?"

She wipes cream from the side of her mouth. "A certain Mr. Dahlstrom appears to be quite fond of you, Cassie. And if I read you right, the feeling is mutual."

"I don't..." I blush. "I mean, he's a nice guy and all, but..."

"But what?"

"But I'm married, or I was married, to the love of my life." I glance at Eric's picture.

"Which is my concern, sweetie." Myrtle Mae reaches across the table to pat my hand. "Don't let this photo, which is *only* a photo, confuse you. Your husband is no longer with us. I wish I could have met him. But that will have to wait till glory. In the meantime, you're no longer married. You're free to love again."

"My brain knows it, but my heart... Sometimes I feel as though it's in a tug-a-war between the past and the future, maybe even a future with Corban." I duck my head.

"You couldn't have picked a finer young man. I've known the Dahlstrom brothers since they were young. They've been through hell and high water, but they've come out shining, no thanks to my daughter."

"Were you at last night's service?"

"No, I don't usually attend. Bad food followed by an hour of bad preaching doesn't set well with me."

"I can't believe you don't enjoy your daughter's preaching." I pretend to be shocked.

She makes a face.

"She's more like you than you think, Myrtle Mae. I found out last night she's not a fan of Wednesday-night food, either. But what I wanted to tell you is Logan and I got sent to the front row before the church service started."

"Good grief. What now?"

"I'm being punished for meeting my brother for lunch without Leadership permission."

She rolls her eyes.

"Even more disturbing is Logan had an accident on one of the church mowers and was injured. Yet, he was at church when he should have been in bed. His arm was in a sling and he was in obvious pain. But did Inez offer sympathy, like a normal person would do?

"Of course not. Instead, she chewed him out in front of everyone. *And* said he has to pay for the repairs because the five-hundred-dollar insurance deductible is the exact amount of the damage."

Closing her eyes, Myrtle Mae whispers, "This has got to stop."

"I agree, but how?"

Later, I'm with Sebastian when he calls Eunice to tell her I'll be working late and will miss supper. He's leaving tomorrow afternoon, so he wants to make sure the premises are "up to snuff" before he goes. He also wants to show me what to do while he's gone.

He puts the call on speaker phone. After a moment's hesitation, Eunice tells him I'll miss household night, which could be an issue if she has to report attendance to Leadership. She and the girls have permission to prayer-walk around the Transformation Way campus, not including the men's dorm.

Sebastian grunts. "If someone has a problem with my employee's work schedule, Eunice, they can talk to me about it."

"Thank you."

I picture my dorm mom sighing with relief.

By the time we're done, the shadows have lengthened, and Sebastian and I are both tired. "Mind if we do fast food tonight?" he asks. "I need to get home and pack a couple things for the trip." He sighs. "Don't know how long I'll be there."

"Fast food sounds great right now. I'm starved." I put my hand on his arm. "I'm sorry you have to go through this, Uncle Seb. In addition to watching your brother's life fade away, you have to take care of his business *plus* deal with Ruby Jade and Vance. Has to be tough."

"Thank God, Quentin has good lawyers and an accounting firm to walk me through the maze." He looks so sad my heart goes out to him.

Back in the quiet dorm—everyone is either working or in bed—I wash my face and brush my teeth. Before I go to bed, I kneel before my bedroom window to breathe in the night air and pray. The curtains flap with the breeze. Tree shadows dance in the cemetery. Why I, of all people, find peace and comfort in a cemetery, I don't know. But I do.

If I had Eric's picture with me, I'd trace his features in the moonlight and put it—glass and all—under my pillow while I sleep. Folding my arms on the windowsill, I rest my chin on them. Myrtle Mae is right. I can't center my hopes and dreams on my deceased husband, with or without his photo. But I can't focus on Corban, either. Jesus is my hope and my salvation, not a man.

I rest on my heels, wondering when I'll see Corban and how Logan is doing. If I had Corban's phone number, I'd call him on Myrtle Mae's phone. "Wait," I whisper. "I bet Sebastian has his number." I'll have to get it from him to put on her phone. Because the Dahlstroms do lawncare for Ruby Jade, Corban's number on her mother's phone shouldn't be a big deal.

While Jenica is setting up her computer Friday morning to show us a video about the science of addiction, I inspect the room. Does T.W. not have a projector? Even the jail had projectors in the classrooms. Like the lack of music books for Corban's class, educational supplies for the rehab program don't appear to be at the top of Leadership's shopping list.

Following the video, we read an article about substance dependence and discuss what we read. From previous rehab programs and jail classes, I already knew addiction is considered a brain disorder because it changes the brain circuitry involved with stress, reward and self-control. But I'd forgotten those changes linger long after a person has stopped using drugs or alcohol—not what I wanted to hear.

When Jenica announces breaktime, I hurry outside for a dose of sunshine and fresh air. The reminder that time doesn't necessarily heal addiction is discouraging. I'm sure she didn't mean to dash our hopes for recovery, but I hate the hopeless feeling that's come over me.

I pace the sidewalk in front of the center, whispering Philippians 4:13 over and over to settle my soul. *I can do all things through Christ who strengthens me. I can do all things through Christ who strengthens me.*

But then I stop. I can make it through the program with Christ's strength, but I can't fix my brain. Alcohol damaged it, and the damage might never be undone. Sometimes people recover from substance abuse. Sometimes they don't.

"Jesus," I whisper, "when you walked this earth, you healed all sorts of sickness and disease. You can heal me, too, if you choose. I'll trust your plan and your power and not get stuck in regret and fear. Thank you for the healing you've already done."

After a year of sobriety, I not only feel better, I think better. And I have a more positive outlook on life. I'm grateful for good health and the hope I have in Jesus.

On my way back to the classroom, I pass the tall reception desk, which remains unmanned. The office behind the counter is dark and locked. Hearing a phone, I peer through the small window on the door.

The room has a desk and a chair but no other furnishings except the ringing telephone on the desk. After several rings, it stops, probably picked up by Evelyn in the church office. My guess is the caller is some participant's relative wondering what happened to their loved one. I'm glad my family has some idea of what's happening in my life. But I'm reminded I need to tell the other participants what Evelyn told me.

Shakyra sidles up next to me, bringing a subtle whiff of perfume. "Ever wonder why that room is as empty as Jesus' tomb?"

"Yes, I do wonder. Looks as if it's never been used."

"As far as I know, the program has never had permanent staff. My guess is the lack of office workers is not only about money, it's also about maintaining control from on high.

"When someone comes from the state to check on the program, Ruby Jade switches Evelyn from the church office to the reception desk out front. Another person sits in this office with a screen in front of them. Last guy she sent over didn't even know how to turn on a computer, let alone use one." She rolls her eyes.

"Does the state ever do surprise visits?"

"I've never seen it happen, but I'd like to." Her dark eyes sparkle. "Can you imagine the panic, the rustle of satin, the scramble of stiletto heels?"

On the drive to the Bozeman Yellowstone International Airport outside Belgrade, both my window and Sebastian's are down. The highway noise makes talking a challenge, but it doesn't stop Sebastian, who lists his pickup's idiosyncrasies. "Penelope weaves a bit," he yells over the wind whipping through the truck, "so hold tight to the steering wheel and don't get distracted."

"Penelope?"

"Yeah. Penelope the Persnickety Pickup."

"I never heard you call your truck by name before."

"Didn't have a reason to." He taps the instrument panel. "Keep in mind she doesn't have air conditioning."

"Oh, yes, she does." I hold out my arms and my long sleeves flap with the breeze. "I'm about to blow away."

"Don't take corners too fast, or she'll fishtail."

"Okay."

"The clutch slips a bit, so you'll have to—"

"I'll be fine." I pat his shoulder. "If I could drive our old clunker of a truck, I can drive yours... Whoops." I cover my mouth. "I didn't mean your truck is a clunker. I only—"

"You can't hurt my feelings." He chuckles. "But Penelope, well, she's another story."

"Sorry, Penelope." I pat the dash. "I didn't mean to compare you to—what did we call our truck? Oh, yeah. A mule. We called it a stubborn mule."

"See, you named your truck, too."

"Well, sort of."

We've just merged onto the highway, it seems, when he slows for the airport entrance. Belgrade is only about ten miles from Bozeman.

"If I have questions, can I call?" I ask. "Or will you be too busy for interruptions?"

"Call anytime, for any reason."

Stopping in front of the terminal, he shifts into neutral, stomps on the parking brake pedal and gets out. "I trust you have your license with you."

I hold up my pink purse. "In here."

"Good. Slide on over."

I maneuver beneath the steering wheel.

"After you adjust the seat, you might take a spin around Belgrade to get the feel of her before you head back to Bozeman." He reaches behind the seat for his bag and closes the door. "She has plenty of gas."

"One more thing." He rests an elbow on the doorframe of the open window. "Ruby Jade and Vance will head for this airport in a couple hours, if you get my drift."

"I'll make sure we don't cross paths."

Cruising the interstate with the windows lowered and Sebastian's favorite country station cranked high, I sing at the top of my lungs, "God Bless the USA." Freedom, glorious freedom. My heart dances with the current that whisks in and out of the truck.

Do the Followers celebrate Independence Day? It's all about America, not bunnies or Santa Claus. Surely, it's not deemed a pagan holiday. I downshift and take the next exit. I'll find out soon enough, but I hope they do. I love fireworks.

When I'm fairly certain Ruby Jade and Vance have left the house, I drive all the way to the back of the property and stop beside Myrtle Mae's carport. I'd rather park there than in her daughter's garage. After I give my sweet friend a quick hello hug, I get to work, determined to keep the weeds under control and the bushes trimmed while my boss is out of town.

Dinner with my dormmates is quiet. We're all tired and ready to plop in front of a television with popcorn and hot chocolate, not that watching TV is an option in the dorm. As soon as we finish eating, the others climb into a van to be driven to a work project. God only knows what time they'll get home.

I decide to try for another stroll in the cemetery. The evening is cooling but comfortable, and though the shadows are lengthening, enough light remains I can see where I'm going. I want to find the greenhouse and peek inside.

I avoid the cemetery entrance, as Hank suggested, and climb the low fence. Swinging one leg then the other over the top rail, I step inside the graveyard. No lights flash, no sirens blare. But it doesn't mean I'm undetected. Time will tell.

A gentle wind dances through the cottonwoods, rattling the leaves. A fox hunkers behind a headstone and a squirrel dashes up a tree trunk. Feeling as though I stepped from the city into the country, I make my way onto one of the gravel paths that crisscross the grassy expanse.

Similar to Ruby Jade's backyard, the well-tended burial ground has an abundance of bushes and flower gardens scattered among the trees. I'll have to ask if the cemetery has a maintenance crew. I'd be happy to volunteer for that work crew.

Air currents waft around me, alternating between the warmth rising from the soil and the evening breeze that floats down the mountainside, bringing a fresh pine fragrance. The only sounds are muted birdsong, leaves rustling above me, and the crunch of my tennis shoes along the gravel path. I feel more relaxed than I have all day.

Catching sight of a parked white car in the distance, I slow my steps. How strange. Someone must have gotten permission to enter the cemetery. But why are they here so late in the day?

Curious, I crouch and make my way toward the car, slipping from bush to bush, tree to tree. The car is similar to Noreen's, but I'm fairly certain it's not hers. When I get close, I hear a voice and duckwalk behind a tall bush. Peering between branches, I see... Inez?

Faced my direction, Inez Curtis is standing above a grave, hands on her waist. She's talking to someone or something. The headstone, maybe? I don't see any people around. She sounds angry.

CHAPTER TWENTY-TWO

I suck in a breath. Inez is the last person I expected to see in the cemetery. Actually, I didn't expect to see anyone. I sink so low I can barely see between branches. The wind dwindles, and the birds stop singing.

"I waited, Charles Allen Yates," she's saying. "I waited and waited for you to leave that homely woman. You didn't love her. We both knew it, but you kept dragging your feet. And where did it get you?"

Her voice grows louder. "Here in this grave. I told you if you kept eating her greasy cooking, you'd keel over from a heart attack. And sure enough, it's exactly what happened. I was right, as usual."

She paces between plots, her features twisted and hazy in the twilight. "You could have had everything with me. Prestige, money, travel, eating at the best restaurants, a five-thousand square-foot three-story home…"

Her moan dissolves into a whine. "Your house is the size of a postage stamp, Charles. You loved escaping all those bratty kids and relaxing beside my pool—my Olympic-size pool—with Restaurant des Delices cheesecake and their most expensive wine.

"You could have had such luxury *every* evening. WE could have had it. But no, you were determined to stick with your marriage vows. You didn't mind sleeping in my bed when she took off on all those mission trips.

"But the minute she returned…" She glares at the stone slab. "Then you were suddenly all about being Mr. Married Man. And now I'm stuck with a ridiculous abduction charge, and you're not here to defend me in court."

My mouth drops. This is the woman who called me a slut, who told the entire church I was having an affair? A woman who'd apparently been sleeping with a married man for years? As shocking as the news is, the more important revelation is that she was charged with kidnapping Zachary, unless this is about another child. *Thank you, Jesus.*

"I'm done with you, Charles." She stomps her foot.

My mouth drops even farther, if it's possible. She's telling a dead man she's done with him? Has she lost her marbles?

"I know, I know. You're dead and all that, but if your spirit is hovering here…" She glances around, and I deepen my squat, nearly touching the ground.

"Be assured…" She shakes her fist at the headstone. "I am finished with you. No more crying in my pillow, no more rereading your love letters, no more tear-stained journal entries about how much I miss you. I–am–done."

For a moment, she appears triumphant, but then her shoulders slump and she turns away. Must be hard to break up with a dead man.

Just when I think she's going to mope her way to her car and drive slowly home, tears dripping down her face, she whips around. From what I can tell through the growing gloom, all sadness has left her face. It's now contorted with rage.

"I will have my revenge," she screams, "and it will be *sweet!*" She waves her arms. "Sweeter than my double-chocolate cheesecake brownies you love so much, sweeter than the strawberry wine we bought in Canada."

She begins pacing again.

I'm dying to know what kind of sweet revenge she thinks will jolt a dead man.

Tromping over graves, she stomps to her car and returns with a handful of papers. "These…" She holds the pages high, waving them in the night sky. They glow white against the twilight. "These are photocopies of your sappy letters, every last one of them. When I'm good and ready, I'll mail them to your wife.

"You can be sure, Charles, my name will be blocked out, except where you call me Pookie. But she'll recognize your sloppy handwriting. And she–will–go–*nuts*, absolutely *nuts*, trying to figure out who Pookie is.

"I can't wait. Maybe she'll even come to me for counseling. Now, wouldn't that be sweet revenge? My chance to tell her she's the one who killed you."

If it doesn't happen…" Inez shrugs. "I'll find a way to let her know."

When she returns to her car this time, she starts the engine and drives away.

Dusk settles deeper on the cemetery and I plop onto the grass, which is now cool to the touch. Seated with my legs crossed, I try to get a grip on what I just heard. I can't believe Inez blames her lover's wife for his death. Actually, I can. Poor Mrs. Yates. Those letters will give her the shock of her life.

Or, maybe not. Maybe he was the kind of jerk who had affair after affair and she was sick of it—and glad he died. I'll probably never know the rest of the story, but if I ever get a chance, I'll let Mrs. Charles Allen Yates know any man who'd have an affair with Inez Curtis isn't worth mourning.

The next morning, Saturday, I dress in layers and take off as soon as breakfast is over, determined not to get sucked into a FFOW work project. I have another doctor-ordered week of healing to go, but certain people might not accept her order as a viable excuse. After all, I can walk and drive a truck.

Careful not to exceed fifteen miles per hour, I make my way through the church grounds toward the exit. Hardly daring to breathe, I pray no one will run out into the road to stop me. I'd rather spend the day in Ruby Jade's backyard, deadheading flowers and hanging with Myrtle Mae than working alongside brainwashed Followers.

Maybe she needs to grocery shop or run errands. I could drive her. Or maybe she needs a kitten break. Whatever the day holds, this is a rare chunk of freedom I plan to enjoy to the fullest.

Once I've parked the pickup and said, "Good morning," to Myrtle Mae and Citrus, I walk across the grass to Sebastian's hideout to get the tools I'll need. I'm shedding my long-sleeved blouse and polyester pants, when I catch sight of the "I Am the Cat's Meow" t-shirt Sebastian bought for me. Lifting it from the shelf, I shake out the folds. What better day to wear the shirt than today?

I take off my t-shirt and slip the new one over my head. It still smells like a department store and is a perfect fit. Too bad Sebastian won't be around to see it.

I plop the hat on my head, grab tools and gloves and am stepping out of the shed, when Corban and Logan come around the corner of the house. "Hey, you two," I exclaim. "I'm so glad to see you."

Their faces light up, although Logan still looks a bit wan.

Corban eyes my t-shirt. "Nice shirt, Cassie."

I glance at the striped cat on the front. "Sebastian gave this to me, but this is the first chance I've had to wear it. Ruby Jade and Vance are in California with him. If I had a phone, I'd send him a picture."

Logan asks, "What happened to your phone?"

"Noreen took away all the program participants' phones.'

"Bet she enjoyed doing that." He scowls. "They love to isolate people from their family and friends."

"I'll take your picture." Corban pulls a phone from his pocket.

"Thanks, but if Ruby Jade and Vance are with Sebastian and they happen to see—"

"They won't. We have a private way to communicate with Seb. Besides, he's super careful."

I'm mulling all the potential problems when he says, "Pull the hat over your face. If anyone else sees this, they won't know it's you."

"Perfect." I rest the hand holding the gloves on my waist, and with the other, the one with the clippers, I tip the hat so all I see is the brim.

Click.

"Was that your phone?" I ask.

"Yeah. It has a camera sound. Hang on a sec. I'm checking the pic." A moment later, he says, "Looks good. He'll get a kick out of this."

I raise my head and readjust the hat. "Can I see it?"

Click.

"Corban, did you take another picture?"

"Sure did." He laughs. "This one's for me."

"For you?"

"Ha." Logan chuckles. "Smooth move, bro."

"If you don't mind, that is." Corban comes over to show me the photos. Both of them turned out surprisingly good. "You've been so sad since you came," he says. "I like seeing you happy."

"But..." I frown. "Now you have two pictures of me on your phone, which isn't safe, for either of us."

"Watch this." He touches the screen. "I'll send the first one to Sebastian, and the message will disappear in ten seconds."

I look over his shoulder, enjoying his closeness, his soapy smell and the fact he wants a picture of me. The message is gone within seconds.

He deletes the photo from the phone. "The second picture goes to my computer before I delete it, if it's okay with you." Corban turns to me, and we're almost nose to nose.

I think of Eric's photo hidden at the back of Myrtle Mae's bathroom shelf but decide now is not the time to mention it—or the person to mention it to. "I'm honored you want my picture, but I don't have one of you."

He grins. "You don't want my ugly mug in your dorm room. It'd give you nightmares."

Before I can respond to his wisecrack, he turns serious. "If Leadership ever saw it, we'd both be flogged."

"I hate to interrupt you two," Logan says, "but we'd better get to work." He gives me a funny look. "Hey, since when do you work on Saturday, Cassie?"

"Since certain people are out of town." I aim my chin at the house. "I also needed to escape the dorm. Sebastian said I can drive his truck while he's in California, so I'm taking advantage of having wheels, for a change."

"Any idea when the nasty duo will return?" Corban asks.

"I don't know about those two." I shrug. "But Sebastian could be gone a long time, taking care of his brother and his business. All three flew to California yesterday afternoon."

"Maybe Ruby Jade and Vance will like it so much they won't come back," Logan says.

"Dream on, dude." Corban snorts. "Remember, Ruby Jade has a mansion on Catalina Island. But like a homing pigeon, she always returns to Montana."

"A house on an island must have cost a fortune." I survey the big house that looms above us. "Any idea how she pays for her fancy places?"

Corban gives me a knowing glance. "Your guess is as good as mine."

"On an even more appalling subject ..." I aim the clippers at Logan's sling. "I'm so sorry about your arm, Logan, and what Inez put you through at church."

"Thanks." He adjusts the sling. "I considered the source. I hope you did the same."

"I did. But still, she was vicious. And you looked like you were about to fall over."

"That's how I felt."

"Something good came out of it," Corban says.

"I can't imagine what..." I give him a doubtful look. "Other than a like-new mower for the church, at no expense to Leadership."

Logan blows out a long breath. "Yeah..."

"As you might imagine," Corban says. "Our parents were furious. Dad said he wanted to grab Inez by the throat and shake her till her puny brain fell out her ear. And Mom, well...she's a mom. She cried and yelled a lot. Anyway, they're finally ready to leave the church."

"Oh..." I try to smile. "How wonderful for you, but... I mean, will you two go, too?"

Corban surprises me by wrapping an arm around my shoulders. "Exiting FFOW is a process, Cassie, a long process. Discreet goodbyes need to be said, gifts exchanged, tools returned, secret phone numbers shared, debts paid or collected—"

"I had no idea." My first instinct is to slip out from under his arm, but then I remember what Myrtle Mae said. *You're no longer married. You're free to love again. You couldn't have picked a finer young man.* I can't believe how good it feels to have someone hold me, even if it's only a traditional FFOW side hug.

"We have to do this together," Logan says. "If something happened to Dad, we'd need to be available to step in to help Mom. If we were in and they were out, or vice versa, we wouldn't have a clue what was happening with them."

"To leave Mom at Ruby Jade's mercy—or lack thereof—is unthinkable," Corban says. "Without a doubt, she'd take advantage of Mom's physical limitations."

"A nice way to say she'd make life hell for Mom." Logan's face darkens. "She's done it to plenty of other people. Even tied them to their beds for days and tried to scream the demons out of them."

"How awful." I feel sick to my stomach. "What about their house? You said Ruby Jade has a lien against it with an early payoff penalty."

"Their lawyer says he's fairly certain he can get them out of the contract. As soon as they give him the green light, he'll get on it. Seems anxious to go head-to-head with Ruby Jade."

"That's great, but I'll miss you guys." I'm not sure I can face the next year without them. "I've already lost Marcela and Zachary."

"Hey…" Logan waggles a finger at me. "You can't get rid of us so easily. We'll be around 'cause we want to take as many friends with us as we can when we go."

"Which includes you." Corban squeezes my shoulder.

"But the rehab program…"

"We'll cross the program bridge when we get to it," Corban says. "Right now, we'd better get to mowin'."

"'Cause the grass won't quit growin'." Logan grins. "Good one, if I do say so myself."

Corban groans. "Just for that, you get to buy lunch, dude." He pats my back. "Be thinking what you want to eat, Cassie."

They take off on the mowers and I dig into the flower beds. I'm so happy to be outside on a sunny spring day and away from FFOW craziness I find myself singing *Heavenly Sunshine*, a Sunday school song from my early childhood. Startled by the sound of my voice rising above the mower noise, I sit back on my heels. I haven't sung out loud since I was incarcerated.

"Yes, you have," I murmur. "You sang along with the radio in Sebastian's truck and you sing in church." If you can call it singing.

I yank at a foot-tall prickly weed, which must have sprung up within the last couple of days. The roots release their hold, and I fall backward. Followers don't sing, they yell, in unison.

Still gripping the weed, I stare into the bright blue sky. *Thank you, God, for giving me this day and this time to sing, really sing, to you.*

CHAPTER TWENTY-THREE

At break time, I bypass the picnic table and hurry to Myrtle Mae's house to ask her for water. I haven't had a drink since I left the dorm. But she's a step ahead of me, coming my way with a stack of plastic drinking glasses in one hand and a pitcher of water in the other.

I take the water from her. "This is so thoughtful of you, Myrtle Mae."

"I'll go get the iced tea." She hands me the glasses, and I deliver everything to the picnic table.

About the time Corban and Logan arrive on their mowers, she returns with the tea, along with cookies and apple slices. The four of us sit at the table, the guys across from me and Myrtle Mae. They're as ravenous and grateful as always, and I can tell Myrtle Mae is pleased she hasn't forgotten the key to a man's heart.

I down two glasses of water before I reach for a piece of fruit. "I didn't realize how parched I was."

"Thanks, Myrtle Mae." Corban sets his tea on the table. "This is great."

"My pleasure." Her lavender eyes twinkle.

"Cassie..." He waves an apple slice at me. "How was your first week in the rehab program?"

"Has it only been a week? Feels like forever."

"How it is around here." Logan grunts. "Was it bad?"

"It was okay, except for Monday, when Leadership graced us with their rosewater presence. The worst moment was when Ruby Jade humiliated the dorm mom, who's new to the Followers."

Myrtle Mae frowns. "One of these days, my daughter will understand people respond better to honey than vinegar."

"Any good moments?" Corban asks.

"The highlight was when the therapist kicked Inez out of our private session."

"Oh, my..." Myrtle Mae chortles. "Sparks must have flown."

Logan laughs, but Corban's forehead creases. "Did they fire the therapist?"

"No. In fact, before the group session the next day, the director locked the door and placed chairs in front of it. Then told us he'd informed Leadership the church is a separate entity from FFOW, and they'd better keep their noses out."

"Uh-oh." Logan pounds the table. "No one, and I mean *no one* tells Ruby Jade what she can and can't do. She'll fire 'em both, and the program will fold, again."

"It's possible." I sigh. "However, the director has leverage. First off, thanks to a tipoff by someone you and I know and admire, the judge ordered them to open the T.W. doors ASAP. Leadership was so desperate for staff, they hired two people who are not Followers and whose practices are in other cities. If they fire them, they'll be at odds with a judge who sends participants to the program. Secondly, the church receives state money to pay the fees for most, if not all of us in the program."

"Ahh..." Logan nods. "I get it. It's about the money."

Corban grabs another cookie. "Isn't that always the case?" He brandishes the cookie. "What do you want for lunch, Cassie?"

"Why is it my decision?" I turn to Myrtle Mae. "Corban says Logan is buying lunch today. What sounds good to you?"

"Huh-uh." She shakes her head. "I distinctly heard him ask you what *you* want."

"But I like everything. I'm not a picky eater."

"Come on, Cassie." Logan aims both forefingers at me. "You choose or we all starve."

"What food did you miss most while you were in jail?" Corban's eyes are soft, and his expression is similar to Eric's when he wanted to please me, to make me happy.

"Well, I can think of one thing..."

They all lean a little closer.

"We had Mexican food at GCDC—tacos with fake meat, dry beans and equally dry rice, but we never had fajitas, something Eric and I both loved."

"Fajitas, it is." Corban gives me a thumbs-up. "We know a place that makes amazing fajitas."

"What kind?" Logan asks. "Steak, chicken or shrimp?"

"More choices." I groan. "I like them all."

"There's your answer." Corban punches his brother's arm. "Order all three. I might even chip in a dollar or two."

"I'm holding you to it." Logan pulls his phone from his shirt pocket.

Later, at lunch, I smile at Logan over my steak fajita. "This is the best fajita I've ever eaten. It tastes as good as it smells. Thank you."

"You're welcome." He elbows his brother. "Corb paid half."

"We'll have to take you where we got these one of these days," Corban says. "It's a small cafe, where the smell of sizzling meat, onions, peppers and spices smacks you in the face the moment you walk in the door."

"Sounds heavenly. I'd love to go with you. But you have to promise me Vance won't show up to ruin the meal, the way he did when my brother came." I turn to Myrtle Mae, who's seated beside me. "Sorry. He's your grandson. I didn't mean to—"

"He's a brat." A fierce expression darkens her eyes. "Way too old to still be a brat. I love him, but I do believe time behind bars might do him some good, help him grow up." She puts her hand over her mouth. "Oh, dear. Now, I need to apologize for insulting you, Cassie."

I give her a quick FFOW side hug. "Not everyone benefits from incarceration, but I can say my experience was an eye opener. Might be good for your grandson."

Corban places another tortilla on his plate and spoons shredded chicken onto it. "Speaking of being locked up, did the Pritchards return your guitar when you moved to the dorm?"

"Are you kidding? Olivia gave me a half hour to pack my things and then practically shoved me out the door, promising to burn anything I left behind. I can only hope it doesn't include my missing stuff."

He lifts an eyebrow. "Only one way to find out."

"Which is…" I put my fajita down.

"Go looking for it."

I study his face, considering the risks. "I don't think so."

"Hey, dude." Logan high-fives his brother. "Great idea."

"You guys are nuts. My boxes could be anywhere."

Corban rests his forearms on the table. "Most Follower homes, but not ours, have a keypad entry. Makes it easy for Leadership to walk in anytime they want. Do you remember the Pritchards' code?"

"Are you serious?"

"As a matter of fact, I am." He grins.

My heart flip-flops. How can I resist that smile? I sigh and recite the code. "You realize Olivia will blame me. Right?"

"She'll never know we were there," Logan says. "Right, Corb?"

I glance from him to Corban and back. "Sounds as though you two are experienced."

They shrug their shoulders, grins tugging at the corners of their mouths.

"Speaking of time behind bars…" I want them to understand this isn't a game. "Breaking and entering is illegal. If you're caught…"

"Hasn't happened yet." Corban twists his glass round and round. "You said the basement has storage cabinets."

"Behind the laundry room, which is beneath the garage. But the cabinet doors are locked. I checked."

"If they're typical cabinet locks," Logan says, "they'll be easy to pick." He pretends to jiggle a lock with a pick.

"Oh…" I fold my arms. "You two don't merely do break-ins, you pick locks."

"We didn't say that." Logan smirks.

"Of course not." I elbow Myrtle Mae. "What do you think about these guys, Myrtle Mae?"

"Well, dear…" She rests her elbows on the table and her chin on her clasped hands. "I say, you gotta do what you gotta do."

"Myrtle Mae Fleming." I scowl at her. "I can't believe what I'm hearing. Here I sit, trying to go straight, and right in front of my eyes, you're encouraging these two reprobates to do something illegal."

"I'll have you know…" She sits taller. "Retrieving your stolen possessions is not illegal. It's the proper thing to do."

"Are you going to tell that to the judge when these guys end up in court?"

"It won't happen." She winks. "Because they're Montana's finest."

"Tell us about the entries," Corban says. "I assume the garage has a keypad, and a door in the garage, which leads into the house. How about front and back doors? Low windows?"

"The front door opens onto a wide porch that shades the big living room window. It's low enough to step into, but it's a picture window. You'd have to break it to get in, which I don't think you want to do. The kitchen door on the opposite side of the house leads to the garage. It has a side door exiting onto the backyard. That's all the—"

And then I remember the door I used to escape the basement when Olivia and Owen were searching for me. "The house has one other door. It's at the side of the house opposite the garage and has a flight of stairs leading down to the basement. From there, you can go directly…"

I stop. "Why am I telling you this? Now, I'll be an accessory to your crimes."

"No, no, not crimes." Myrtle Mae pats my arm. "They're doing what you can't do, dear—finding your things and returning them to you."

Logan turns to Corban. "Okay, so when they're all at church, we'll park away from the neighborhood, some place where we can hide the car, and hike in. Then we'll sneak around the—"

"Hold your horses." I raise my palms. "Walking along the road carrying two big boxes would look suspicious." Part of me wants them to find my stuff, but a far bigger part of me wants them to avoid jail. If Olivia senses any connection with me, she'll make sure they spend the rest of their lives behind bars.

Myrtle Mae clears her throat. "I believe…"

We all turn to her.

"I believe you should drive to the front of the house," she says, "open the garage door and drive in as if you have nothing to hide, like you're supposed to be there."

Corban cocks his head. "Okay…"

"You could wear uniforms," I add, "and pretend you're deliverymen or repairmen." I make a face. "I can't believe I said that."

"Brilliant," Logan exclaims.

"Not really. I mean, you're talking about Sunday, when no one makes deliveries, especially to FFOW homes."

"I wear uniforms for my job." Logan continues, his face alive with excitement. "We could each wear one and strut around like we're on a mission."

"Which we will be," Corban says.

"Reminds me," Logan says, "we name all our missions. What shall we call this one?" He points at Myrtle Mae. "You're on it, Myrtle Mae, I can see it. What are you thinking?"

She twists my direction, her eyes twinkling.

I make a vain attempt to look stern. "You're enjoying this way too much."

"Just trying to help a friend. How many boxes are missing?"

"Two big boxes, one sort of tall and square and the other longer and not as tall." I spread my arms to give her an idea of the sizes.

"Okay…" She considers the information. "How about Twin Towers?"

"Hey, good one," Logan says.

"I like it." Corban nods his agreement. "Operation Twin Towers, it is."

I sit back. "I'm beginning to grasp the beauty of this crazy idea…if you succeed, that is."

Myrtle Mae raises her eyebrows. "I think I know what you're going to say."

"If or when Olivia discovers my boxes are missing, she won't report them as stolen because they don't belong to her." I pause. "But she might tell Leadership and…"

Corban's brow creases. "And the dragons will breathe fire down your neck."

"Which means I can't put the boxes in my dorm room."

"I know." Myrtle Mae grabs my shoulder. "You can keep them at my house."

"Thank you, but…if your daughter ever ran across them…"

She lowers her hand. "You're right."

"We'll keep your things," Corban says. "As long as you need." He checks his watch. "I'd better get to my job, the one with the paycheck."

"Before I forget," Myrtle Mae says, "Cassie, can you help me with my new phone? Sebastian said I should check it every day for messages."

"Sure, be glad to."

She hurries to her house, and I help Corban and Logan pack the leftovers. "Thanks again, both of you. This was an amazing, delicious treat."

"You can have the leftovers," Corban says.

"I appreciate you thinking of me." I return his kind smile. "But my room doesn't have a fridge, and we're expected to eat in the dining hall. I'm sure you'll be able to get another fajita or two out of the leftovers."

He closes the Styrofoam container. "I'm serious about taking you out for fajitas one of these days."

"And I was serious when I said I'd love to go." I grin, already anticipating a night out with Corban. I have no idea how it will happen, but it's a possibility to ponder.

Myrtle Mae returns, phone in hand. "I pushed the power button," she says. "I can do that much."

Before the brothers take off, we share hugs all around. Corban gives me an extra squeeze and murmurs in my ear, sending chills all the way to my toes. "This is the best day I've had in a long, long time, Cassie True."

I turn my head to whisper, "Me, too, Corban Dahlstrom." He smells like gasoline, cut grass and sweat. I breathe deeply, wishing I could linger in his arms. Surprised by the thought, I step away.

Corban winks.

I blush and quickly glance at the front house through the branches that overhang the picnic table. Knowing Ruby Jade and Vance are gone has lifted our restraints. Yet, I'm fully aware a maid or whoever is caring for the dogs, which I haven't seen all day, might be watching us—and they might tattle, because it's what Followers do.

Don't be so paranoid. I wave goodbye to the brothers. If someone rats us out for eating together or touching, Myrtle Mae will vouch for our innocence. Even so, I miss Sebastian's buffering presence between us and Leadership.

Taking Myrtle Mae's phone from her, I type "MT1babe" on the big keypad and see she has three voice messages. The first is from my dad. "Cassie, I hate to tell you this…" His tone lacks its usual joviality. I suck in a breath, steeling myself for bad news.

Myrtle Mae grasps my arm.

"Your grandmother is failing," he continues. "The staff suggested we ask for hospice care for her, which we did. She's stable, for the moment. But if you want to see her before she passes, you'll need to come right away." He pauses. "I love you, Girl, and hope to see you soon."

"That was my dad," I tell Myrtle Mae, "about my nanna. She's not doing well." I blink back tears, but they fall anyway.

"I'm so sorry." She squeezes my arm.

"There are two other messages." I wipe my cheeks. "I can tell one is from my mom and the other is probably Sebastian. He's the only person outside my family who has your phone number, right?"

"Right. I haven't told anyone else about the phone yet."

I click the icon and am about to hand the phone to her, when I hear him say, "This is for Cat. Please tell her to call home. Her parents need to talk with her."

I delete his call and listen to my mom's message. "Cassie, sweetheart, I hope and pray you get this. Your grandmother is about to board the glory train. She still knows us, which is a miracle, but she looks around the room, as if she's searching for someone. When I tell her you and Kip are on the way, she seems to relax. Please let us know when you can come. I love you and hope to hear from you soon. Bye."

Hearing my nanna is waiting for me makes me cry even harder. I sink onto the bench seat. "She, my grandma...she's dying, and if I want to see her before..."

Myrtle Mae sits beside me. "Must hurt to be so far away."

I sniff and swipe at my nose with my sleeve. "My parents said I should get there fast..."

"Take my car."

"That's sweet of you to offer." *But I don't have gas money, and I can't leave without permission.*

"Call your mom. Tell her you're on your way."

"Okay..." I try to shake the cobwebs from my head. "Sorry, I'm in a fog."

"Understandable, dear, but you need to pack a few things and go. Tell your mother you have a reliable, insured car to drive, plus money for gas and food."

"You don't have to do all that. My parents will wire—"

"I have an emergency stash I'm happy to share with you. This is truly an emergency."

I hand her the phone. "You are so good to me." I've always enjoyed road trips, and this one should be long enough to clear the church craziness from my head. I want to be focused on my family when I get home, not on this place.

She gives it back. "You'll need this for the trip as well as the battery chargers. Sebastian had me buy one for the house and one the car. I told him I wasn't planning any trips, but he thought I should buy both anyway, just in case. And here we are, at the junction of 'just in case' and 'Cassie takes a trip.'"

I smile through my tears.

She gets to her feet. "I'll take the lunch things inside and be right back."

"Okay if I call Sebastian to ask his permission to take off work? If both of us are gone, the weeds could get out of control." I slide the water pitcher to the edge of the table. "I'll carry this to the house when I'm done."

"By all means, talk with Seb," she says. "But don't worry about the yard. And don't let him put my daughter on the phone."

"Oh, Myrtle Mae, you make me laugh."

He answers after the third ring. "Hello, Myrtle Mae."

"Hi, Uncle Seb. This is Cassie."

"Good to hear from you, Cat. I assume you got my message to call your parents."

"Yes, thank you. Did Mom tell you my grandma is receiving hospice care and probably won't live long?" Tears spring to my eyes again.

"No, but I got the feeling something serious was goin' on."

"She said she's about to board the glory train."

"Good way to put it. I'll keep the thought in mind when Quentin departs this earth. Could be any day now."

"How sad. I'm glad you can be with him right now."

"Sorry about your grandmother. You gonna go see her?"

"That's why I'm calling. Myrtle Mae—sweet, generous Myrtle Mae—offered me her car to drive to Oregon. But I thought I should get your permission to leave, since you're my boss. I mean, you're gone and the yard—"

"Stay as long as you need."

"Ruby Jade might—"

"I'll cover for you, and I'll pray for you and your family."

"Thank you." His kindness makes me want to sit down and bawl, but I swallow my tears. "I'll breathe easier knowing you're guarding my back."

"My privilege. Speaking of bosses, R.J. and Vance are at the airport, waiting for a flight back to Bozeman."

"Already?"

"Already. My brother finally told Vance he's not his father and he won't be receiving an inheritance from him."

"He's not? How did Vance get his last name?"

"You'll never hear R.J. tell it this way..." He pauses. "I'll fill you in on a little family history, but you'll have to keep it under your hat."

"I won't tell a soul. I promise."

"Not even Corban or Logan. Or Myrtle Mae. She doesn't know the whole of it."

"Oh, okay..."

"As soon as R.J. graduated from Bozeman High, she headed to Hollywood to become a singing, dancing actress. She'd starred in a couple school musicals and thought her name, which was Marilee Fleming at the time, would be on marquees all over the country within months."

He snorts. "Actually, her dancer name appeared on the nightclub marquee where she worked as a pole dancer, supposedly the only employment she could find."

"That's..." I try to picture Ruby Jade in a skimpy outfit, swaying seductively around a pole, but my imagination won't go there. "I never would have guessed."

"Not a pleasant visual." He chuckles. "However, she was a few pounds lighter back in the day. After her dances, customers occasionally wanted more entertainment, if you get my drift, and she would accommodate them, for a substantial fee."

All I can think is *wow, what a hypocrite*. Same as Inez, she's a fraud. She makes such a big deal about kinky behavior and her sinless perfection, yet—"

"One thing led to another..." He pauses. "There's more to the story, but it's not an alley to travel down right now. She got pregnant, quit the nightclub business and started a bookkeeping business. The woman is good with numbers, especially when it comes to money. Quentin, who was developing his business at the time, responded to an ad she'd tacked to a telephone pole. Happened to see it while he was walking his dog.

"Long story short, they made a deal. He'd let her give the baby his last name, and she'd set up his books and do his bookkeeping for one year without charge. Evidently, she thought a different name on the birth certificate would suggest her child was legitimate. She even wore a gold band on her left hand. I saw it. But Quentin was solely into the relationship for business purposes. They eventually formed a partnership but not a marriage."

"Interesting." I lean against a tree. "So, she doesn't know who Vance's father is?"

"Supposedly, she has no idea."

"Seems a little late to tell Vance."

"Quentin had no intention of assuming a father role after Vance was born. But R.J. insisted on referring to him as 'daddy' in Vance's presence. My brother didn't want to confuse the kid, so he played along. Also, when he realized Vance had a narcissist for a mother, he tried to give him some balance in life."

Myrtle Mae comes around the corner of her house. I lower my voice and move farther into the trees. "I'm actually beginning to feel sorry for Vance."

"Don't." Sebastian growls the word. "All Vance ever wanted from him was stuff—expensive toys, cars, electronic devices—and money."

"But, to find out now…"

"When Vance and R.J. promenaded into Quentin's hospital room, they were sweet as pecan pie. One on each side of his bed, they fawned over him like a couple syrupy southern aunties."

He blows out a long puff of air. "Picture my poor, helpless brother, Cat. He's flat on his back, a skeleton of the man he used to be. I doubt he weighs a hundred pounds. Then picture those two marching in, so pompous and sure of themselves, filling the room with their aftershave and perfume stink.

"Somehow, he mustered the strength to tell them to skedaddle. But instead of leaving, Vance leaned over Quentin and said, 'I *can't* leave. I'm your son. Even if you're too sick to talk, you're my father, and I'm your sole heir.'

"The threat and arrogance in his voice raised my hackles. I was about to physically throw him out of the room, when R.J.

said she was Quentin's ex-wife and he owed her years of alimony payments plus half the business proceeds."

I gasp. "You're kidding."

"Wish I was. Couldn't hold my tongue any longer. I told Vance to back off. Then I told R.J. she might have once been my brother's business partner, but it was years ago and no longer the case. And she was *never* his wife. I would vouch for that in court."

CHAPTER TWENTY-FOUR

"Whoa." I interrupt Sebastian's story. "You actually called Ruby Jade on the marriage thing?"

"Cowboy wisdom says, 'speak your mind but ride a fast horse.'" He grunts. "However, I wasn't about to leave my brother at their mercy."

"Did she take it okay?" I turn in time to see Myrtle Mae walk back to her house. Good. I'm glad she's not waiting for me at the picnic table.

"You know better than that, Cat. She was like an enraged bull, nostrils flaring, face as red as a bullfighter's cape. Before she had a chance to erupt, Vance yelled, 'It's not true.' I think he would have clobbered me, if I hadn't been on the other side of the room."

Sebastian huffs a quick breath. "Would have been okay by me. I was ready to beat the tar out of him, but I kept my trap shut. When I didn't respond, he turned to his mother. 'Sebastian is lying. You and Dad were married. Right, Mom?'

"She lifted her chin in the snooty way she has. 'We didn't have a ceremony, Vance, if that's what you mean, but we were together for years. I'm entitled to palimony and—'

"Right then, Quentin raised one of his bony hands off the bed and said, 'We were *never* married in any sense of the word, and I am *not* your father, Vance.'

"Vance's eyes about popped out of his head. 'Yes, you are. We have the same last name.'

"Quentin sighed, as though he was weary of the whole mess. 'I would've told you years ago, but your mother wanted to continue the charade.'

"'Charade? What do you mean?' Eyes as big as an owl's, Vance gawked from Quentin to his mother, his expression waffling between thunderstruck and furious.

"I said, 'They were young and dumb, Vance. They made a deal.'

"Oh, no," I whisper. "I bet that made Ruby Jade even madder."

"I thought she was gonna sprout horns."

"What did Vance say?" I pace the path Corban and I walked together.

"He was incensed, which I admit is understandable, and yelled, 'You made a deal? About my name?'

"R.J. turned all motherly, which, believe you me is not her norm, and reached out to him. 'Honey, I didn't want you to be...'

"Vance knocked her hand away. 'You didn't want me to be *what?*' Bending nose to nose with her, he said, 'Illegitimate? Is that it?'

"Being the shifty person she is, R.J. said, 'We're not here about your name. We came to make sure everything is in order for your inheritance.'

"But Vance wasn't about to let her throw him off course. 'Tell me the truth, Mom. I want to know the truth. If he's not my father, who is?'

"That's when Quentin piped up again. He barely spoke above a whisper, but when he said, 'You've already received your inheritance,' they stopped arguing and stared at him like he'd lost his mind.

"I could almost see the wheels spinning in R.J.'s noggin. She got this innocent look on her face, pretending to be a caring person. But I knew better.

"'Oh, dear,' she said, 'the sickness has gone to his head, Sebastian. He's not able to make rational decisions.'"

"A change of tactics?" I ask. Above me, birds are singing in the tree branches and feathery clouds float across a deep-blue sky. I hate to think of Sebastian and Quentin trapped in an airless hospital room with those two heartless crazies and their overpowering colognes.

"Right." Sebastian pauses. "You can bet your life she was suggesting he's not mentally fit and, therefore, not competent to dictate who gets his money and who doesn't. But Quentin ignored her and pointed to a chair beside his hospital bed. He told Vance to sit, and for once in his life, Vance did as he was told.

"Quentin looked him in the eye. 'It's true,' he said. 'Years ago, your mother and I were in business together for a short time. Our partnership ended when she drained the company bank account and took off for Montana. Your mother already has your inheritance, Vance.'"

"Oh, wow, that must have sparked fireworks."

"Yeah, fireworks and tantrums. R.J. waved her arms and yelled, 'Liar. All I did was take my share of the proceeds.'

"'We both know what you did.' Quentin's voice was fading but firm. 'You're not pilfering another penny from me.' Then he pointed a bony finger at Vance. 'You might have my last name. However, you have *never* been my heir.'

"Vance bristled like a cornered porcupine, but Quentin, who sounded as if he was about to breathe his last breath, kept talking. 'I might have made you an heir if you hadn't been such a greedy, demanding, pigheaded jerk. All my efforts to help you become a decent human being failed. As a result, the bulk of my estate goes to an organization that helps individuals like your ex-wives escape controlling groups similar to your mother's so-called church.'"

Despite the heat, my skin prickles. I gasp and come to a halt on the path.

"Yep," Sebastian says. "Vance and R.J. did the same thing. Vance said, 'What about my ex-wives?' And R.J. said, 'My church is a real church, Quentin. You shouldn't be meddling with my members.'

"Quentin grinned the biggest grin I've seen on him in months. 'I'm proud to say...' He even managed to lift his head for a moment. 'I helped both of your exes make clean breaks, Vance.'"

Once more, I interrupt Sebastian. "Did you have anything to do—?"

"Don't ask."

"Got it." I start walking again. Whatever happened, I'm relieved to know they safely escaped Vance and his devious-as-the-devil mother.

"As you can imagine," he says, "that's when all hell broke loose. Vance jumped up. 'I have your last name,' he shouted. 'You owe me my inheritance. Where did you send my wives? You should have left them alone.'

"R.J. started screaming something about being a common-law wife and he was going straight to hell because he subverted her priestly authority. I was stepping closer to protect Quentin in case they got physical, when a nurse came in, saw what was going on and told them to leave. They refused, so she called in the security guys, who ended up calling the police, who escorted them out of the hospital."

"Unbelievable." I shake my head. "Except, I can totally see those two doing exactly that. I'm sorry you and Quentin had to endure their wrath, Uncle Seb. Must have been horrible."

"Yeah, but it's over."

"Thank God you were there for your brother. How's he doing?"

"As you might imagine, they exhausted him. But after he got some rest, he said he was glad he told the truth. He'd always tried to be an honest businessman, yet he hadn't been honest with Vance. Now, he says, he can go to his grave knowing a three-decade falsehood was shattered."

I think of Vance. I can't stand the guy, but his mind must be reeling. His world has been twisted like a double helix. My guess is he's sitting at an airport bar, nursing his wounds and trying to make sense of life. Or, maybe he and his mother are plotting a backdoor way to get their hands on Longpre money.

I tell Sebastian I'm happy for his brother. "Did defending him cost you your job?"

"No matter how angry R.J. is, she won't fire me." Sebastian's chuckle is grim. "I know too much."

"Good. I don't want to lose you as my boss."

We end the call and I give my mom a quick call before I drive Seb's truck to the dorm, where I hurry into the white-white foyer and tread the white-white steps. I don't see or hear anyone. They must all be working.

In my room, I remove both layers of clothing and stuff my jeans and t-shirt into the oversized tote bag Myrtle Mae loaned me. My work clothes are sweaty and stinky, but I don't dare leave them here. Certain nosy people would find them and throw away my only comfortable clothing. And then punish me for having them.

I put the polyester pants and long-sleeved shirt back on, add another shirt and pair of pants plus underwear and toiletries to the bag and snap it shut. I haven't packed much, but I can borrow clothes from Mom or use her washer and dryer.

Before I drive to Myrtle Mae's house to exchange Sebastian's truck for her car, I find the director's phone number in my class notes and dial it on my borrowed phone.

He answers right away. "Dr. Hoffman speaking."

"Hi, this is…" For a moment, I can't remember which name he knows. "This is Cassandra Turner." I keep my voice low so someone passing in the hallway won't hear me talking on a forbidden phone.

"Hello, Cassandra. What can I do for you?"

I explain about my grandmother and hold my breath, praying he gives me the okay to drive to Oregon.

"I assume if she passes, you'll want to stay for the funeral."

"Yes. According to my parents, it'll be soon, and they'll have a service right away."

"You should be there." He clears his throat. "Go with my blessing, Cassandra, but return immediately after."

"Thank you, Doctor."

I close the window, grab the bag and my purse, and hurry down to Eunice's apartment. She takes forever to answer my knock, and when she finally opens the door, I'm greeted by her ever-present Vicks aroma. Her pantsuit, though rumpled, is tasteful, in a Follower sort of way.

"Oh, hi, Eunice," I say. "I was about to leave you a note. I thought you might be babysitting this afternoon."

"The mom wasn't feeling well and left work early." She pushes her glasses up her nose. "When she walked in, the baby didn't want anything to do with me, so I decided to come home and take a nap."

"Good for you. I didn't mean to wake you, but I need to tell you'll I'm leaving for a few days. My grandma isn't expected to live much longer…" I blink back tears. "I'm hoping to get to Oregon in time to see her one last time."

"I'm sorry about your grandmother." She scrunches her eyebrows. "But I have to ask. Do you have permission to go?"

"Yes, from Doctor Hoffman and also from my boss. His boss is Ruby Jade."

"Okay." She pats my shoulder. "Be careful and Godspeed."

Because Sebastian asked me to park his truck in Ruby Jade's garage, I stop there, instead of driving back to Myrtle Mae's bungalow. I don't relish the idea of going inside Ruby Jade's garage, but Sebastian was gracious enough to loan his vehicle to me. I can be gracious enough to park it where he wants it parked.

Not knowing which door to use, I push all the buttons on the garage-door opener, and all four open. My heart stops. Ruby Jade's black Lincoln and Vance's silver sportscar are side-by-side. Then I remember Sebastian saying their owners were at the airport, about to fly home. Even if their plane left already, they wouldn't be here by now.

I leave the keys in the pickup, close all the garage doors and exit through the side door, locking it behind me. The big tote hanging from one shoulder and my purse from the other, I walk to the back of the property and knock on Myrtle Mae's door. As usual, she greets me with a smile and a hug.

When I thank her for making the trip possible, she says, "I'm delighted you can be with your family, and I'll be praying you'll be able to spend time with your grandmother. She'll be so happy to see you."

"I wish you could have met her, Myrtle Mae. You would've been the best of friends."

Citrus is meowing from her box in the corner. I lift her and snuggle her between my cheek and my shoulder. "By the time I return, you'll be running all over the place, little one."

"Don't give her any ideas," Myrtle Mae says. "She's already a handful."

"I can tell she's stolen your heart." I set the kitten by her milk bowl.

"That she has." Myrtle Mae hands me a thermos, four water bottles and a grocery sack.

"What's this?" I ask.

"Snacks for your trip. You said you were going to drive all night, so I made you strong coffee and added espresso powder to the brownies. I also threw in a mug, so you don't have to drink out of the thermos lid."

"You're spoiling me. I should be riding high by the time I reach Salem."

"I don't want you to fall asleep and ruin my pretty car. Oh, and here, take my foldable travel hat. You might need it. I hear it rains a lot in Oregon."

"Thank you, Myrtle Mae, thank you for everything."

I wait until I'm outside city limits before I switch the car radio on full blast. I listened to Sebastian's radio when I drove his truck, but I kept the volume low, fearing a Follower might be in the next lane. Now, windows down, hair blowing in the afternoon breeze, I can enjoy music I haven't been able to hear for months.

The freedom to be driving away from FFOW, to be headed home to my family, is marred by a painful sadness, which grows stronger with the miles. I try not to cry because tears blur my vision, but they leak out anyway. I love my nanna, and I could have spent time with her during these last few years, if I hadn't been pickled in alcohol or locked in jail. Now, she might not remember me, or she could be comatose or gone by the time I arrive.

I'm grateful Myrtle Mae's car has cruise control. With twelve hours of travel ahead of me, I don't want to chance being stopped by a patrolman. I'll be driving halfway across Montana to Spokane, Washington, and from there, south to Portland and Salem.

When I called Mom to tell her I was on my way and that I'd have Myrtle Mae's phone with me, she said she'd pay for a motel in Spokane. I told her I wouldn't be able to sleep. The sooner I get to Grandma, the better chance I have of saying goodbye to her.

I love Montana—its plains, its mountains, its trees and rivers, its big blue sky and abundant sunshine. Mile after mile, I revel in the state's beauty and the fact I'm driving through the majestic Rocky Mountains, the West's best feature, in my opinion. The amazing north-south mountain range, a collection of a hundred mountain ranges, runs from upper British Columbia, through Colorado and down into New Mexico. If I remember geography class, the Rockies I'm seeing right now lie somewhere in the middle. They're gorgeous.

I drink in the radio music, when I can catch a station. My parched soul absorbs the intricacies of voices and instruments melding into harmonious tunes. Predictable beats are an additional nice touch I've missed these last few weeks.

I stop for gas in Missoula as well as to use the restroom and stretch my legs. While I'm filling the gas tank, I check the phone for messages. Nothing. So far, so good. No bad news from mom and dad. No threatening FFOW messages. Thank God, Myrtle Mae isn't on Ruby Jade's texting list. I couldn't bear to read another of her dumb directives right now.

The phone rings. I jerk and almost drop it. Stepping into the shade, I peer at the screen. Kip. I recognize the number. Smiling, I answer the phone. "Hey, bro, where are you?"

"Almost to Portland. Where are you?"

"Just stopped for gas in Missoula."

"Bummer. If I'd known you were driving, I would have waited for you."

"I didn't hear about Nanna until earlier this afternoon."

"What are you driving?"

"A friend's car, the same friend who owns this phone."

"I'm glad you have a sane friend in that crazy place. I'll tell Grandma you'll be there soon."

"Thanks. I love you, bro."

"Love you, sis. Have a safe trip."

I fill the coffee mug and grab a couple of Myrtle Mae's brownies before I get back on the highway. Missoula is a beautiful town. Someday, I'll spend more time here. I won't just pass through on the interstate. Someday.

A pair of hawks ride an updraft in the distance, apparently unfazed by the semitrucks, buses and cars navigating I-90 far below. Oh, to look at life from above, from God's perspective, and not become embroiled in daily challenges.

Leaving the hawks behind, I begin a long, slow, winding climb up a mountain. Myrtle Mae's car doesn't hesitate. "God bless that sweet woman," I whisper. "She's a gift from your heart to mine." I bite into a brownie and sigh. It's beyond good.

Sunshine flickers between pine trees, falling in stripes across the highway. The air cools. I roll my windows most of the way up and check my watch. Though the sun is lowering, the days are long, and nightfall is still hours away.

The radio begins to crackle and fade in and out just as the news comes on. "A Montana church located outside Bozeman is in the news again," the announcer says. "This time, three individuals, one of whom appears to be a key leader in the Faithful Followers of the Way church, have been charged with kidnapping and—" Static shreds the woman's voice into intermittent syllables.

"Don't stop." I pound the dashboard. "Come back, come back." But all I get is more hissing and crackling. I fall against the seatback. FFOW has not escaped scrutiny, after all. I should've watched television with the other women in jail. If I'd kept abreast of the news, I might have been forewarned before I got suckered into the Followers.

But what's done is done. No sense in working myself into a tizzy, as my dear Grandma Hunt would say. I push FFOW to the back of my mind and think about all the good things in my life. I'm homeward bound. The road before me is smooth, and traffic is light. Myrtle Mae's coffee and brownies are delicious. I couldn't ask for a more pleasant trip.

My brother's phone call makes me even more excited to see my family. I hate that losing Nanna is the reason for our gathering, but I'm grateful for a chance to be with my loved ones. Maybe I'll get to see some of my cousins.

I crest the hill and see flashing lights ahead. Cars slow. Taillights flare. I follow suit and steer to the side when sirens sound behind me. Coming up the incline are more emergency vehicles of some sort. Must be a bad accident ahead. I pray for the victims and those helping them.

A patrol car pulls in front of my parked car, one pulls even with it, and one stops behind it. My heart thuds my ribs. *What's going on?* Two patrolmen appear, one on each side of the car. I look from one to the other, my breath coming in ragged gasps.

They want *me*. But why? I never exceeded the speed limit, not once.

Gun in hand, the nearest officer barks through the window, "Turn off the engine and hand me the keys."

I do as he says.

"Unlock the door."

Again, I obey.

"Put your hands in the air."

I lift them above my shoulders.

He opens the car door. "Step out slowly, one foot at a time, hands raised. No sudden movement."

I comply. Out of the corner of my eye, I see another patrolman materialize near the back of the car, handgun aimed my direction. Do they think I have a trunk-load of drugs or what? My heart pounds. I fight to control my breathing.

My back against the car, I keep my hands high and my questions to myself. Vehicles pass at a snail's pace in the far lane. Despite the alpine breeze, exhaust fumes fill the air. The passengers stare, curious expressions on their faces. I'd like to tell them I'm as clueless as they are.

"Can you produce a valid driver's license?" the officer asks.

"Yes."

"Where is it?"

"In my purse in the car."

"Registration for the vehicle?"

"In the glove box."

The officer on the other side of the car finds both and comes around the front, my license in one hand and the registration in the other. "What's your name?"

"Cassie Anita True." My heart beats faster. Did I give him the correct name? I'm so rattled, I'm not sure.

"Is this your car?"

He's looking at the registration. He knows the car isn't mine, but I answer anyway. "No, this is not my car. The owner, Myrtle Mae Fleming, loaned it to me to go see my grandmother in Oregon. She's dying."

"This car is registered to a Myrtle Mae Fleming *and* a Ruby Jade Paradise."

My heart sinks. Ruby Jade's tentacles reach farther than I imagined.

"Miz Paradise says the car was stolen from her mother's home."

I swallow a groan. Ruby Jade rarely bothers to visit her mother, but now she's concerned about her missing car? How did she even notice?

"Can you please contact Myrtle Mae?" I plead. "She'll tell you what I said is true. I've got to get to my grandma before it's too late."

The man gives me an "are you kidding" glance and turns to the other officer. "Want her in your car or mine?"

"My parents are expecting me." Hands still in the air, I spread my fingers wide, emphasizing my words. "They'll be worried if I don't make it to Salem tonight."

"You know the drill. Call them from the detention center."

I cry all the way to Bozeman. This is too much, just too much. I should have known better than to lower my guard, to enjoy the trip and act as if I didn't have a care in the world. Only hawks can float above the chaos. That must be where God is because he's not down here where I need him.

CHAPTER TWENTY-FIVE

I've called my parents from the GCDC phone room each time I've been incarcerated. But this is the hardest call ever. I'm sick to my stomach over the thought of not seeing my nanna before she passes, not to mention missing her funeral.

"Cassie," Dad says, after he accepts the call. "How's my girl?"

"Not good." I lean on the kiosk and close my eyes.

"The detention center message threw me off," he says. "I thought you were on the way here."

"I was, until highway patrolmen surrounded me north of Missoula. Evidently, my friend's car has a second person's name on the registration papers. That person, who rarely has anything to do with my friend, reported the car as stolen. You wouldn't believe the production the officers made of my arrest out on the interstate. You'd have thought I was a drug runner." I'm still trembling from the shock and frustration.

"Can't your friend vouch for you?"

"I doubt she even knows about my arrest. She loaned me her phone, along with her car. Plus, the other person has a lot of influence in this town. When I have more time, I'll explain. Right now, we only have five minutes for this call."

"Any chance we can post bail and buy a ticket for you to fly here tomorrow? Your grandmother is failing fast."

"It would take a miracle, Dad." I gulp back tears. "The best-case scenario would be to get an arraignment hearing first thing Monday morning with a compassionate judge. But even if a judge happened to set reasonable bail, plus allow me to travel, who knows when I'd actually walk out of here."

"We'll pray about it."

"If you think it'll help." I'm beyond prayer, way beyond. But maybe my family's prayers will do some good. Can't make things any worse.

The cell doors are open until bedtime, and inmates are free to move about or sit in the common area at the center of the pod. A hum of feminine voices reaches into my cell, where I'm slumped on my bunk. Elbows on my knees, chin on my crossed arms, I stare at the wall. I thought I was done disappointing my family. Yet, at the worst of all times, I've blown it again, like I did when Grandpa died.

My parents would have gladly bought me a ticket to fly home. I would have been there by now. But Myrtle Mae's offer was so gracious, and a road trip with just my thoughts and the radio turned high sounded heavenly.

I was so happy to be going home, to see my nanna one last time, to be with my family. And then, without one iota of warning, I'm back in jail. *It's not fair, God!* Not that he cares what I think. But why take me to a mountaintop, literally, and then knock me into a ditch again? Why did he let Ruby Jade notice the missing car? Why does he let Leadership do nasty things to people, in his name? Is it because he doesn't care?

Someone calls my name, my FFOW name.

I turn my head. A woman with dark-red hair and brown eyes is standing outside my cell. Though she's wearing orange, she looks vaguely familiar. But whether I knew her at college, met her during my last jail visit or saw her at FFOW, I don't remember. "Hi. Do I know you?"

"Not really." She smiles. "I'm Trina Russell, Zachary's mom."

"Oh, right." I flip around, step off the bunk and walk over to her. "Couldn't place you for a moment. When I lived at the Pritchards' house, I saw you the morning the deputies—" I narrow my eyes. "How do you know who I am?"

"Like you saw me at the Pritchards, I saw you at church the night Inez had you go to the front."

I shudder. "An unpleasant experience, to say the least."

"Yeah, she was brutal. But I was glad to have a face to go with your name. When we first brought Zachary home, he couldn't stop talking about Cassandra, how you were kind to him when no one else was, how you helped him when his classmates were mean to him at school." Tears spill over her eyelids. "The therapist said having someone show concern and care for my son made the experience less traumatic for him."

I thought I'd emptied my tear ducts on the return trip to Bozeman, but tears fill my eyes.

"Don't get me wrong." She wipes her cheeks. "What he experienced was horrible, and it was my fault for letting them take him away from me. I don't know if I'll ever be able to forgive myself."

"Zachary is a sweet little guy." Picturing his cute freckled face makes me smile. "I adore him."

"He told me you promised you'd find me and bring me to him."

I glance around. I know cameras are everywhere in the pods. Do they have microphones? If Leadership were to get wind—

"Don't worry," she says. "I haven't said anything to anyone. All I did was put two and two together from what Zachary said."

"I thought you left FFOW and the T.W. program."

"Yeah, well…" She sighs.

"Why are you here?"

An officer comes toward us. "Do your visiting in the common area."

We nod and take the metal walkway to the open stairs leading down to the common area, where women clustered around tables are talking in low murmurs. You'd assume it was a coffee shop if they weren't all dressed in identical orange outfits and brown boots.

Women at the nearest table look me over, gauging the newcomer. One of them, an older woman I remember from before, whispers to the others. I know exactly what she's telling them.

Trina uses her commissary account code to buy us each a decaf coffee from the caged vending machine. We carry the hot paper cups to an unoccupied table at the far end of the room and sit across from each other.

Blue chairs and orange uniforms stand out against the common area's sterile white walls. You'd think we were at a Denver Broncos football game—Eric was a big Broncos fan. But the chairs are a nice touch. They lessen the severity.

I thank Trina for the coffee, which smells better than I remember, and ask how Zachary likes his new school.

"He loves it." She grins. "He has lots of friends, but it makes me sad how shocked he is they like him. The kids at Triumphant Way School must have treated him terrible."

"The teachers are as much at fault. I was only there a short time, but it appears they encourage the kids to beat on each other. And Olivia Pritchard? She resented Zachary, for some weird reason, and made no attempt to hide her feelings."

Trina frowns.

I quickly add, "But thank God the nightmare has ended for your son. Warms my heart to know he's happy now." *God knows I need something to warm my cold miserable heart tonight.*

"Thank you from the bottom of *my* heart." Trina tears up again. "I'd hug you, if I could."

"Hug accepted." I test the coffee. It's still too hot to drink. "So, what were you saying about FFOW and the program?"

"I can't return to T.W. The judge is finding a different program for me. But a couple friends talked me into attending the church services."

"Zachary's not supposed to—"

"He goes to church with my brother and sister-in-law, who don't want anything to do with FFOW. In fact, they were upset I went back. I tried to explain how I didn't want to return, but I was scared not to. They didn't get it."

"Scared not to return?"

"Ruby Jade says people who leave FFOW get terminal cancer or have deadly car accidents. I didn't want my son to lose me again. Even worse, ex-members go to hell when they die. I couldn't stand the thought of not being in heaven with Zachary."

"And you believe her?" I try to temper my incredulity. How an entire church can buy into Ruby Jade's hogwash, as Sebastian calls it, is hard to comprehend.

"Well…"

"Do you have a Bible with you?"

"All I have is one of those little New Testaments the Gideons give to inmates. It's the King James Version, but Ruby Jade doesn't approve of the Gideons. I can't remember why."

"Perfect." Ruby Jade doesn't like anyone who might somehow usurp her authority. "Read your New Testament from cover to cover. Then you'll be able to compare FFOW teachings with the truth." Here I am, ready to give up on God, yet I'm telling her to read the Bible. I should take my own advice.

"Good idea," Trina says. "I'll start tomorrow morning. I need something to unravel all the confusing thoughts banging around my brain. I hate being with the people who abused my son, yet I feel I *have* to be there." She grimaces. "Makes me crazy, as if I have a hurricane in my head. In fact, it's how I landed in here. I couldn't handle the turmoil and overdosed."

"I'm sorry." I give her a sad smile. "I know how it goes. I'll pray for Jesus to calm the storm for you, and I'll also pray for Zachary. Actually, I've never stopped praying for him." I take a sip of coffee. "I hope you don't mind me saying this, but losing you after his life stabilized must be terribly unsettling for him. He misses you so much when you're not in his life."

"I promised him I'll never do drugs again." Trina bows her head. "I know...promises aren't enough."

I don't respond. She sees what she's done to her son and wants to change. That's a start.

Swiping tears from her cheeks, Trina lifts her chin. "Now you know why I'm wearing orange. How about you? I heard you stole Ruby Jade's car. Is it true?"

"Wow, word got out fast."

"This town thrives on Ruby Jade rumors."

"Even in jail?"

"Even in jail."

"I don't remember hearing rumors about her when I was here before."

"You didn't travel in the right circles." Trina swirls her coffee.

"The truth is, I've been in before, several times," I tell her. "But this time, I didn't do anything wrong."

She lifts an eyebrow.

"Yeah..." I shrug. "Everyone says they're innocent, but when you hear what happened, you'll understand."

By the time I've finished explaining how Ruby Jade ruined my chance to see my grandmother before she dies, Trina is furious. "That's low, so low." Her eyes flash. "But it's not the first time. She doesn't want us to hang out with our families. Says it's selfish. We're not serving God when we're with them."

"Evidently she wants total control."

"She says friends and family members outside of FFOW are all liars. She doesn't want us to listen to their lies."

I'm facing the officers' station, a tall curved desk with two officers seated behind it. A third deputy enters from a door at the rear of the compartment. He glances at us, takes a second look and drops his gaze.

"Something going on?" Trina asks.

I murmur, "Your fiancé just walked in."

She twists, eyes him for a moment, and then turns back. "My *ex*-fiancé. You haven't heard what happened to me and Lawrence?"

"How would I hear? My circle of FFOW friends is small, very small." And I'd forgotten Officer Manning's first name was Lawrence.

"He was livid when he found out I started attending FFOW services. What they did to Zachary put him over the edge. He didn't understand how I could go back, and I couldn't explain to him why I couldn't stay away."

"I don't understand, either, but I'm sorry you're no longer together. Maybe later you two—"

She cuts me off. "We didn't know each other very well. Ruby Jade was the one who decided we should hook up, yet she didn't let us spend much time together." She glances at him again. He's turned away from us. "He would have made a good dad for Zachary." She sounds wistful.

I'm about to tell her Officer Manning was excited to become a father, but then I remember she doesn't know we met. "I heard him tell the social workers he wanted to go to the parenting classes."

"Yeah, Lawrence got right on the parenting thing." Trina's tone changes. "He told me he'd check Zachary's new school every day to make sure he was there, and I hadn't sent him to the FFOW school." She juts her chin. "He should have known I wouldn't do that."

"Followers convinced you to return to the church, so why wouldn't they convince you to transfer Zachary back to their school?"

"Well, for one, DSS wouldn't let me."

"I'm not taking sides." I lift my palms. "I'm only trying to show you what he might be thinking."

She swivels just in time to see Manning walk out the door he entered moments earlier. Trina sighs. "You win some, you lose some."

"Have you talked with him since you've been here?"

"He doesn't normally work in the jail, although he sometimes subs for sick or vacationing officers on his days off. But I did call him to say I'm done with drugs, so he wouldn't get all freaked out about Zachary."

"What did he say?"

"He said he's keeping his eye on both of us, and we can talk when I leave FFOW for good. Then he hung up."

"Hey…" I give her an encouraging nod. "Sounds as if he still has hope for your relationship."

"Conditional hope."

I want to tell her the Followers are all about conditional acceptance, conditional love, conditional hope…

A prerecorded voice comes over the loudspeakers, announcing it's time to return to our cells for the night.

Trina says, "Thanks for talking," and stands.

"Don't forget to read your New Testament." I get to my feet, cup in hand. "Matthew, Mark, Luke and John will tell you the truth about Jesus. Acts and the other New Testament books will tell you how real Christians live and how *real* churches are supposed to function."

The night is endless. I could blame Myrtle Mae's stout coffee and espresso-laced brownies, but I didn't get a chance to enjoy much of either. I'm mostly too disturbed about the mess I'm in to sleep.

When I close my eyes, Ruby Jade's purple eyes flash before me. "You have the mark of Cain," she shrieks. "You're a cursed woman." I flinch. Truth be told, right now I feel cursed—and haunted. Will I ever escape FFOW?

I open my eyes and try to pray, but my stark surroundings trigger a mental replay of my arrest and how disappointed my family must feel right now. I envision my sweet nanna in her nursing home bed, surrounded by my parents and my brother, yet searching the room for me. "Dear Lord," I moan, "I meant what I said to Trina about the Bible, but I'm not sure you hear me right now. If you do, please…"

After an oatmeal-and-banana breakfast Sunday morning, I take a shower, hoping to calm my jittery nerves. I'm sliding an orange t-shirt over my head, when I my name and number are called on the loudspeaker. "True-Twelve-Seventy-Two. Report to the desk."

My heart somersaults. Good news or bad news, what will it be? I slip on pants and shoes and dash down the metal stairs to the desk, my wet hair bouncing on my shoulders.

The nearest officer glances from a computer screen to my ID tag. "Miz True. At eight-forty-five a.m. tomorrow morning, Monday, you will be escorted to Judge Bock's chambers for a nine-fifteen arraignment."

Hearing a court appearance is scheduled and that Judge Bock, not Judge Snow, will be the presiding judge is a balm to my jangled psyche. I release the breath I didn't know I was holding. *Thank you, Jesus.*

"If you have an attorney—"

I shake my head. "I don't."

"In that case, a public defense lawyer will be provided for you, unless you decline. What is your wish?"

"I would appreciate an attorney, please."

"I'll note that."

"Thank you."

He types something on the keyboard. "Be down here ten minutes before the appointed time."

"Yes, sir."

Back in my cell, I sit cross-legged on my bed, trying to decide how to pass the time until the phones are available. I'm glad my cellmate is the quiet type because I don't feel like talking. I could go to the chapel for the Sunday service, but I'm not in the mood to worship God or to face the chaplain and the humiliation of my return to GCDC. I could watch TV in the recreation room or find something to read. However, I'm too antsy to focus on anything for long.

Finally, I opt to go outside and walk the perimeter of the exercise yard. Stepping out of the windowless hallway into the sunshine, I sense a palpable release of tension. Just what I need—warm air to take the edge off the AC chill and movement to stretch my taut muscles and calm my mind. Arms swinging and legs at full stride, I start walking and don't stop until five minutes before the phone room opens.

I hurry to get in line, yet at least a dozen others are already ahead of me. The queue is extra-long because today is Sunday, and the work-release women have the day off. Rookie Roxie is near the front. She looks healthier than the last time I saw her. I pray she can stay clean when she leaves. A couple other women are familiar, but I'm surprised at how many new faces I see. I'd forgotten about the revolving door here, which is crazy because I've gone in and out several times.

I'm a nervous wreck by the time I call my parents' landline. Their church service starts in a half hour. If they're not home, I'll call Mom's cell phone.

Dad answers and accepts the collect call. "Hey, Girl. You coming home?" Someone must be teaching his Sunday school class for him. I'm grateful. His reassuring voice helps calm my spirit. I tell him about the hearing and then talk briefly with Kip. He's rooting for me, as always, and promises to pray for a miracle.

Mom is the last to talk. Before I end the call, she says, "No matter what happens tomorrow, Cassie, remember we understand, and we will always love you."

"Thanks, Mom. You're the best. I love you, too, and hope to see you soon."

Between meals, I walk the yard. If last night was the longest night of my life, today is the longest day of my life. I pace and pray, pace and pray. Occasionally, I stop to visit with someone.

Trina tells me she read three chapters in Matthew before breakfast and that her brother is bringing Zachary to see her during afternoon visitation. I ask her to give him a hug for me. Talking with her makes me aware one positive has resulted from the arrest. I'm not sitting in the FFOW front row, fake singing and trying to stay awake during Ruby Jade's erratic ramblings.

Monday morning, I'm ready an hour early. It's the most nerve-wracking hour of my life—and I've had plenty of tense moments. "Oh, God, oh, God," I whisper as I shuffle about the pod. "Please, please let me see Nanna before she goes to be with you."

Finally, an officer whose nametag reads "R. Ellis" walks me the short distance from the jail to the Justice Court, where he introduces me to my court-appointed defense attorney. Her name is Barbara Adams. She has short dark hair and doesn't appear to be much older than I am. I'm struck by the simple professionalism of her outfit—a white blouse, navy-blue jacket and knee-length skirt, something I wouldn't have noticed before I met the Followers and subjected myself to their weird dress code.

Barbara says she reviewed my case, but she has questions, which I'm happy to answer. I appreciate the fact she takes notes, as if my problem is a serious matter to her. She seems sympathetic to my situation, but maybe she always acts concerned, whether she believes she can help a client or not.

I glance around the small courtroom, one I haven't visited before. Like the other courtrooms in the building, oak wainscoting lines the walls. The judge's bench, the attorneys' desks and the onlookers' benches are also made of oak. I know that because I once told my escorting officer I thought the wood was beautiful, and he told me it was oak.

A hint of marijuana hangs in the air. Have the walls absorbed the odor from the hair and clothing of certain defendants and their friends? Or is it coming off someone currently seated in the gallery?

No Followers are present, thank God. Maybe Ruby Jade realized how ridiculous this is. With any luck, the judge will too. The handful of spectators are probably here for hearings scheduled after mine.

Judge Bock, a tall, graying man with wire-rimmed glasses steps in from a side door. He's wearing a black robe and has manila folders under his arm. The bailiff tells us to rise. We all stand in respectful attention.

Sensing a commotion behind me, I turn my head. Ruby Jade is swishing into the room in all her silky finery, arm-in-arm with a snooty-looking man with slicked-back hair. I recognize him. He's the man I saw her with when I was waiting for Sebastian outside the courthouse. Must be her attorney.

My heartbeat falters, along with my confidence. If she had any sense of fairness, she would have brought her mother with her to tell her side of the story. But fairness is not Ruby Jade's style. I face the front. *Help me, Jesus.*

The judge takes his seat, glances at me and opens a folder. He appears to be a kindly person, which may or may not be the case. But at least he's not Judge Snow, Ruby Jade's yes-man.

Judge Bock motions with his hand. "You may be seated."

We all sit.

He lifts sheets of paper from the folder, scans each of them, and then asks the attorneys to approach his bench. They talk softly between themselves for several minutes. Barbara's back is to me, but I can see Ruby Jade's attorney scowl and shake his head. His jowls quiver, yet his silver pompadour remains firmly in place. I get the impression he's arguing with the judge.

With a decisive jerk of his chin, the judge sends both attorneys to their seats. My lawyer sits beside me but says nothing.

Judge Bock lifts his gavel. "Case dismissed with prejudice due to lack of probable cause for arrest." He bangs the gavel on the striking block.

Ruby Jade shouts, "No!"

The judge thumps the wooden block. "Quiet in the court!" He extends his hand toward me. "Ms. True, please stand."

I stand, hands clasped behind my back.

"You are free to visit your grandmother. However..." He eyes me over the wire-rims. "I expect you to remain in contact with the Transformation Way program director and to return within three days. Two days for travel and one day for family time, a total of seventy-two hours."

He looks at his watch. "Beginning at midnight tonight. That'll give you time to make travel arrangements."

"Yes, sir." I fight to contain a grin. "Thank you, sir."

I sit in my chair behind the defense table, the judge's words ringing in my ears. "You are free to visit your grandmother."

Court spectators may think they understand how his statement affects my spirit. Of course, I'm jubilant, as one would expect. I want to hug Barbara, hop around, clap and shout hallelujah.

Yet, deep down, I'm struck by the knowledge I'll never be the same. God just turned evil into good, meanness into kindness. And he did it when I was ready to give up on him. He was faithful when I was faithless.

The judge removes his glasses. "Court will resume in ten minutes."

The bailiff calls, "All rise."

The judge stands and exits the courtroom.

Could be my imagination, but I sense Ruby Jade's angry gaze blistering my back. I refuse to meet her purple eyes, and instead, turn to the public defense lawyer at my side. "Words can't express how grateful I am for what you did for me, Barbara." I grin. "Thank you. You're a lifesaver."

"My privilege." She leans close. "I'm pleased the judge understood how ludicrous the charges are and wasn't afraid to—" Pursing her lips, she gathers her papers. "I apologize. That wasn't appropriate."

When all her documents are in her briefcase and she's snapped it shut, I murmur, "I understand the judiciary system here isn't always openminded when it comes to a certain organization. Must be difficult for you."

"Yes, but this decision…" She beams. "This will be the highlight of my month, maybe my year. I plan to celebrate with my husband tonight." With a quick glance at her watch, she says, "I'd better vacate for the next attorney and go prepare another case." Pushing her chair away from the table, she whispers, "I can't wait to tell my coworkers. They may want to join our little party."

We stand, and I ask, "What happens now?"

She signals the officer who walked me over. "Officer Ellis will escort you to the jail, where you can change into your street clothes and go through the checkout process for your release."

"Thank you." How I will get from the Gallatin County Detention Center to my parents' home in Oregon, I have no idea. But God vaulted me over this hurdle, he can get me over the next. "Enjoy your party."

"Thank you. We may break out the fireworks early." Barbara grins and shakes my hand. "Have a safe trip. I hope your time with your grandmother is good." She leaves the courtroom by a side door.

I check the back of the room. Ruby Jade and her attorney are standing near the public entrance. She's looking at her cell phone and doesn't notice me, but her attorney does. He elbows her and I turn to Officer Ellis.

"This way," he says. He leads me to the exit my attorney used. "Best way to avoid a confrontation."

I'm so relieved I don't have to face Ruby Jade I could kiss the man. But I don't. I also resist the temptation to spin around and stick out my tongue at the obnoxious woman who put me through this ridiculous charade.

An hour later, I'm standing in front of GCDC, my pink purse and Myrtle Mae's tote and cell phone in my hands. Everything was returned to me except her keys and her vehicle—and the snacks she sent with me. I pray her car isn't impounded and Ruby Jade doesn't confiscate it or sell it. I wouldn't put it past her.

The first person I call is my mom.

"Cassie, where are you?"

"I'm standing outside the detention center, enjoying the sunshine." A giddy giggle bubbles from my belly. "The judge dismissed my case, Mom! Can you believe it?"

"Hallelujah, praise the Lord." I love hearing the joy in her voice. "Wonderful news. I'm so happy for you. Can you come to Oregon now?"

"Yes. Judge Bock gave me two days for travel and one day for family time."

"That's all?" She sounds disappointed. "What about your grandmother's funeral? We know it's coming."

"One step at a time, Mom. Permission to travel is a huge first step."

"You're right."

"Dad mentioned buying a plane ticket…"

"I'll do it right away. How soon can you leave?"

"I'm packed and ready."

"From what I remember, the airport is only fifteen or twenty minutes from the jail."

"Right. I'll have a cab take me there."

While I wait for her to call back with flight details, I phone Sebastian to update him on the latest. He had no idea I'd been arrested out on the highway and is beyond angry. I picture steam lifting his cowboy hat from his head.

"R.J. has pulled some dirty stunts before," he says, "but that's lower 'n mud, down with the stinkin' snakes 'n' badgers." His grunt borders on a growl. "My grandpa used to tell me, 'When you're throwin' your weight around, be ready to have it thrown around by somebody else.'"

"I hope it happens, but..."

"But R.J. wields a lot of weight. Another heavyweight will have to take her down and that Goliath just might be God. Trust me, it'll happen. One of these days, she'll get her due."

I tell him I have Myrtle Mae's cell phone and can't call her. I'd like for someone to let her know what happened. "Can you ask Corban or Logan to talk with her when they mow?"

"Better yet, you can call one of them."

"I don't have—oh, I do have their numbers. I put them on this phone for Myrtle Mae to use."

"Right. I remember you doing that."

"Before I go, how's your brother?"

"Fading. He's in and out of consciousness, mostly in. Whenever he gets fidgety, the doc ups his morphine. As far as I can tell, he's not suffering."

"Must be really hard for you to watch him fade."

"It is, but Quentin and I stayed in touch over the years and we've had some good talks these last few days. He knows the Lord. I'm confident he'll be joining your grandmother on the glory train."

The idea of them traveling to heaven together makes me smile. "I'll pray for Quentin—and you."

"And I'll pray for you and your family. Losing a grandma is no small thing."

"She's a special lady."

I move under the portico shade and dial Corban's number next. The sunshine is great, but the day is warming fast.

"Hello."

Hearing Corban's kind voice makes my heart sing. Although I ate lunch with him two days ago, I feel as if I haven't seen him in weeks, maybe months. "Hi, Corban. It's Cassie."

"Hey, Cassie." He sounds happy I called. "Myrtle Mae told us about your grandmother. I'm sorry she's not doing good. Are you in Oregon?"

"No, I'm in Bozeman, standing in front of the Gallatin County Detention Center."

"What?"

"I know. Crazy. I was on my way to Oregon when the state police pulled me over and arrested me for stealing Myrtle Mae's car."

"She told us she loaned you her car. Was something wrong with the license plates?"

"The plates are fine, and the registration and insurance info in the glovebox are current. Here's the hitch. Guess whose name is on the title alongside Myrtle Mae's."

"Should have known." He groans. "That was nasty. If I were a swearing man—"

"Yeah." I blow out a long breath. "I spent two sleepless nights in jail and had a court hearing early this morning. Judge Bock not only dismissed my case, he said I can go home for three days—two travel days and one day to see my grandma and my family."

"Did the judge return Myrtle Mae's car to you?"

"No."

"How are you going to get to Oregon?"

"My mom is finding me a flight as we speak. I shouldn't talk long because she'll probably call soon. I was hoping you or Logan could tell Myrtle Mae what happened. When her car suddenly appears in her carport, she's going to have questions. Actually, it may already be there."

"Sebastian asked us to keep an eye on her, so I stopped by a few minutes ago. She had cookies in the oven and her teakettle was whistling, like she knew I was coming. She introduced me to her kitten, Citrus. Crazy name."

I grin but don't tell him the name was my idea. "Was the car there?"

"No."

"Good, but I hope it hasn't been impounded. She loaned me her cell phone, so I can't phone her to tell her I didn't make it to Salem. Would you be able—?"

"Be glad to. How are you getting to the airport?"

A female officer walks out of the building. She looks me over but keeps moving.

"I'll call a taxi as soon as we finish our call."

"I'd like to drive you there," he says. "Give us a chance to catch up."

"Don't you have to work?"

"I'll let my boss know I'll be late. She's not a Follower, so I won't have to explain or grovel."

"Speaking of the Followers…" I rub my neck. "What if someone sees us together without a chaperone?"

"I don't mind taking a chance, if you don't mind. What can they do? Kick us out?"

I hesitate. As much as I'd love to spend a few private minutes with Corban, the thought of leaving the program and starting over somewhere else is not appealing.

"Sorry, I forgot about T.W." Like a deflated balloon, his voice has lost its energy. "You don't want to get kicked out."

"I was thinking about the possibility. Actually, the director is the one who makes program decisions, not FFOW leadership. Dr. Hoffman already said I can be gone as long as I need. And the judge told me to stay in contact with the director. I'll buzz him right now, tell him about my arrest and court appearance—and that you're giving me a ride to the airport."

My phone rings. I glance at the readout. "Mom's calling. I'll get back with you in a minute, Corban."

Twenty minutes later, I'm seated beside Corban, on the way to the airport. Something about being in his car with him feels natural, not uncomfortable or like I'm betraying Eric.

"I'm glad your mom was able to find a flight for this afternoon," he says. "I know you're anxious to see your grandmother."

"Mom says she's still hanging on, so maybe I'll get to hold her hand and say goodbye." I clench my fists, determined not to cry. "I hope so." My voice betrays my resolve.

"Cassie, look at me."

I squint at him, blinking away tears. What's he getting at?

"It's okay to cry."

"Grandma…" The tears spill over my cheeks. "My Grandma Hunt is the sweetest, funniest, most lovable nanna ever. I have so many wonderful memories of her. But because I was either drunk or in jail, I haven't seen her in ages. And then when I try to see her, I'm arrested, again, and…" I cover my face with my hands. "It's all so awful."

I feel the car slow and turn, but I'm crying so hard I can't look up. The car stops, Corban releases both of our seatbelts—clink, clink—and then his arms are around me. I collapse against his shoulder.

"It is awful," he whispers in my hair. "You've been to hell and back in less than twenty-four hours, Cassie. Other people would have cratered and given up. But you're a fighter. And you've trusted God through it all."

"No, I haven't. I was ready to give up on him this weekend." I sniff. "Couldn't pray, couldn't see any light at the end of the long black tunnel." I lift my head and smile at him through my tears. "But my family was praying."

"And God answered their prayers."

"I never expected the judge…"

"We have an amazing God who loves you very much, Cassie Anita True."

I bury my face in his shirt, breathing in his masculine scent. "I don't know why." Corban's arms around me feel so good I never want him to let go. "I'm a poster child for how not to be a good person."

"We're all poster children for the dark side. That's why Jesus came. To save us from ourselves."

"Thank God."

"Yes, thank God." He leans his head against mine. "By the way, I didn't learn why Jesus came at FFOW. I learned it from reading my Bible."

We sit entwined until my sobs subside. Finally, I straighten and wipe my eyes with my sleeve. "Guess I needed a good cry. But now your shirt's wet."

"The shirt's no big deal." He smirks and slides a damp strand away from my face. "I like having an excuse to hold you."

I raise an eyebrow.

"I didn't—" His grin fades and he pulls away. "I hope you…I mean, I didn't—"

"Corban…" I wrap my arms around his neck. "You did exactly what I needed, what I wanted. In your arms, I'm at peace, I'm comforted…I'm happy."

Resting his forehead on mine, he whispers, "Really?"

"Really."

We're back on the road, headed for the airport, when Corban asks if he can hold my hand.

I offer it to him, palm up.

He interlaces his fingers with mine and settles our hands on the console between us. Though we're both smiling, neither of us speaks. Too bad the airport is so close. Our time together will be short. My plane doesn't leave for three hours, but Corban has to go to work.

We're slowing for the Airway Boulevard turnoff, when he says, "After you get your ticket, I'd like to buy you lunch at the Copper Horse and hang out until it's time for you to walk to your gate."

I've passed the restaurant on my way to and from flights, but I've never eaten there. "You and Logan bought the fajitas. I should pay for lunch. Myrtle Mae gave me travel money."

"Save it for your trip. You never know what you might need."

"This is traveling. Besides, I don't want to keep you from your work."

"My boss says business is slow today. Not many shoppers. I can get there whenever it's convenient." He grins. "Right now, it's *convenient* for me to spend as much time with you as I can—if you don't mind. After what you've been through, you might want to be alone."

"I'd much rather spend the next couple hours with you than sit by myself with nothing to do except replay all the madness in my life."

Snuggled into the far corner of the Copper Horse, we're surrounded by lingering whiffs of pancakes, bacon, sausage and eggs and a great view of the mountains. Corban and I grin self-consciously at each other across the table. Our relationship has turned a corner, and I'm not sure what to think. But if I've learned nothing else the last couple of years, I've learned to take things moment by moment, day by day.

After we've had time to peruse the menu, he asks, "Know what you want?"

"The Reuben sandwich sounds good. I haven't had one in forever."

"Neither have I. Believe I'll have one too."

A waitress brings us water, and we order Reubens on sourdough, coleslaw and a side of sweet potato fries to share. After she leaves, Corban says, "Mom didn't make Reubens when we were growing up."

"Maybe she thought of the sandwiches as restaurant food, not home food."

"Possibly, but I'm pretty sure it was because Ruby Jade doesn't approve of the name."

I cringe. "Should I ask the reason?"

"According to her, someone who has the audacity to put his name on a sandwich is filled with pride straight from the devious devil. Reuben, if such a person ever existed, doesn't deserve for people to eat his sandwich."

"Twisted logic, as always, but I have to say it takes an egomaniac to know one. Maybe she was jealous. The name is similar to hers but much more famous." I tear the paper off a straw and drop the straw in my water. "When did you bite into your first Reuben?"

"One rainy night about a year ago." He looks at the ceiling, a half smile on his face. "Logan and I had just reunited teenage twins with their parents and watched them drive away, determined to never return to FFOW. We knew we couldn't sleep, that we had to celebrate before we went home, so we stopped at this grungy place on the edge of town.

"When Logan saw Reuben sandwiches on the menu, he said, 'We gotta try these to signify our solidarity with ex-Followers.'"

"Sounds like Logan, but you must have enjoyed the sandwiches."

"Definitely." He nods, but his nod is more thoughtful than enthusiastic. "For us, they're the taste of victory. We also ate sweet potato fries for the first time. Ruby Jade abhors them, says they're unnatural. God only knows why. My brother will be jealous when he finds out you and I ate Reubens *and* sweet potato fries."

"You can take him some fries and half my sandwich. I doubt I can eat a whole one."

"Nah." He shakes his head. "You don't need to—"

"I can't carry food on the plane. I haven't gone through TSA yet."

Our time together passes fast, too fast. We talk about our families, our faith, our FFOW struggles—and how good our food is. The sauerkraut adds the right amount of zing to the corned beef and Swiss cheese, and the fries are crisp.

We share our career dreams. I want to return to writing songs and performing them. Corban, who has a music degree and plays several instruments, wants to be a middle school music teacher and also give private lessons.

"One of these days," he says, "you'll have to come over to our house to jam. We have a collection of banned instruments, plus a soundproof recording studio."

"Really? I can't believe Ruby Jade approved the instruments or the studio."

"She didn't."

"What? How did…?"

"While we were remodeling with her money…" He looks both ways and then whispers, "We enclosed a couple secret rooms in the basement."

I lean my head back and laugh out loud. Diners two tables away stare. I mouth, "Sorry," and turn to Corban. "That's the best news I've heard in a long time. What instruments has our fearsome leader banned?"

"Drums, tambourines, guitars, keyboards…" He pauses. "I'm sure I missed something, but those are—" He interrupts himself. "And saxophones. She says they have a sensual sound."

"Ridiculous." I roll my eyes. "But it explains the church's pathetic music." I cringe. "I don't mean to insult you, Corban. You do a good job, considering what you have to work with."

"Yeah, I know it's pathetic." He sighs. "Anyone with an ear for music or a sense of rhythm must suffer through the songs. I know I do."

"I admire you musicians for staying together and somehow not dissolving into a cacophony." I dip a fry in fry sauce and change the subject. "Jamming with you and Logan would be crazy fun. But about your career, why aren't you teaching music in a school right now? I mean, fulltime, with classes and lessons."

"Have you forgotten Ruby Jade is the one who decides who works where and when? She says the timing isn't right."

"Argh." I yank at my hair. "I want to bash my head against the wall to knock all the insane things she does out of my brain."

"You and me both." He takes my hands and lowers them to the table. "Before you tear your hair out, we need to talk about something."

CHAPTER TWENTY-SIX

I gaze into Corban's blue eyes, wondering what he's going to say. He looks so serious. Are we over, when we've barely started? Is this the end of the beginning? I'm tempted to pull away before he says we're done, but I like the feel of my hands in his.

"Even if we had Ruby Jade's approval for a so-called friendship," he says, "which I doubt she'd give because the idea didn't originate with her, she wouldn't allow us to spend time together."

No surprise there.

"We've been privileged to work with each other and share breaks. However, winter is coming. Logan and I will probably clear her walks and driveway, as we've done for years. I don't know what Sebastian can find for you to do." He purses his lips. "He's creative. Maybe he'll come up with something. I hope so."

"Me, too." The cloud descending on my soul lifts. Corban's *I hope so* gives me hope for our tenuous future. "I would miss you and Logan—and Sebastian and Myrtle Mae."

"We've had some good times," he says, "a rare treat for all of us. My guess is Sebastian and Myrtle Mae long for real friendship as much as we do."

"What about meeting in the cemetery greenhouse? You mentioned it earlier, and now I live next door to it."

"Hmm." Corban raises his eyebrows. "Has possibilities, between snowstorms. Tracks in the snow would be an issue, but I'll toss the idea around with Logan." Squeezing my hands, he says, "As much as I'd want to, I won't be able to hold your hand or put an arm around you. We'll have to be discreet."

"I understand."

He rubs his thumbs over mine.

"I would miss special moments like this." An urge to kiss him startles me. I blink. What am I thinking? "Things will change dramatically when I finish the program."

"I hate to wait so long to have a normal relationship, a real relationship, but I'm willing to wait. In the meantime..." He winks. "We need to devise some subtle signals we can send from across a room or a lawn."

"Like your half winks and ear tugs?"

He laughs. "I know those aren't the best, but—"

"But I love it and I get the message every time."

"For *I miss you*, we could tap our fingers together." He releases my hands and demonstrates.

"Okay. How about crossing our arms?"

Corban tilts his chin. "Meaning what?"

"I want to hug you."

"Nice." He grins. "And intertwining our fingers could mean I want to hold your hand."

"Sounds like a Beatles song."

"Beatles?" He assumes an innocent, wide-eyed look.

"Come on, Corban." I aim a finger at his chest. "You may have had a sheltered life, but you majored in music. We took similar classes, so I know—"

Tapping a beat on the tabletop, he sings the chorus so softly the people at the next table don't seem to notice.

But I notice. He has a nice voice, a beautiful voice.

"You'd better not tell anyone I listen to devil music." He fakes a scowl. "That would get me sent to the men's dorm for sure."

"I've heard it's bad."

"Badder 'n bad."

"I saw Rodrigo coming out of there a few days ago."

"Yeah, we gotta get him outa there." He checks his watch. "One more thing before you go. We need to download the secure app I told you about on Myrtle Mae's phone, so you and I can text while you're away. You'll also be able to have private conversations with Sebastian and whoever else you need to talk with."

"Okay." I hand him the phone. "Is that degree of privacy is necessary? I'll delete everything before I give the phone back to Myrtle Mae."

"If Sebastian were here, he'd say, 'A cowgirl can't be too cautious in these here parts.'"

I snicker. "You hang around him much longer, Corban, you'll have to get a horse and a saddle and some spurs for your boots."

He laughs. "I've always wanted a horse. After all, I live in Montana."

"Right."

He downloads the app, shows me how to use it, and then slips Myrtle Mae's flowery bag onto his shoulder.

"Are you sure?" I ask. "It's a bit feminine."

He grunts. "Real men carry women's luggage, no matter how humiliating it is."

"You don't have to suffer for me, cowboy."

"My pleasure." He walks the stairs with me to the second floor. Before I join the TSA line, we stop in the meet-and-greet area. He hands me the bag, and I give him the takeout container with the half sandwich and fries I saved for Logan. "Promise me you'll deliver this to your brother and not eat it yourself."

"Bummer, foiled again." He winks and twirls an imaginary villain mustache.

"Ah-ha. You not only listen to devil music, you watch devil cartoons."

"Well, maybe, before I saw the light."

"Yeah, sure."

He wraps an arm around me, looks both ways and kisses my cheek."

A man across from us yells, "Way to go, buddy."

Heat rises from my neck to my face, but Corban laughs. "Don't forget me while you're gone, okay?"

"How could I after your sneak attack?"

He grins. "I put the picture of you wearing the cat t-shirt on my computer, like I said I would. I look at it every chance I get."

I feel my cheeks warming again. "Not fair, Corban. I don't have a picture of you." I open my purse and pull out the cell phone. "I'll take a picture of you and erase it before I return the phone to Myrtle Mae."

"So that's what you think of me."

"That's what I think of you *and* Myrtle Mae. If Ruby Jade happened across your picture on her mother's phone…" I shake my head. 'God only knows what weird accusations would result." I give him a questioning look. "What about the new app? Will it delete the picture?"

"No, just texts."

I back away from him and raise the phone to eye level. "Smile."

His wide grin makes my heart do cartwheels. I tap the screen and check the photo. "Perfect."

"Can I see it?"

"Nope. It's mine, all mine." Shoving the phone into my purse, I tell him I'll text him and then I start for the TSA line.

"Let me know when your return flight is scheduled to arrive," he says. "I'll pick you up."

I turn around. "I'd love for you to pick me up, Corban, but if someone sees you drop me off at the dorm…"

"We'll cross that bridge when we get to it. Goodbye, Cassie Anita True."

"Goodbye, Corban Dahlstrom. Hey, I don't know your middle name. What is it?"

"You didn't show me the picture…" He cocks his chin. "I don't tell you my name." With a wink and a wave, he walks away, calling as he goes, "Have a good trip, and stay in touch."

One more wave, and I join the queue, regretting I didn't throw him a kiss. Maybe next time. If there ever is a next time. As Corban said, winter's coming. Yet, I will cherish this parting moment and the memories we shared today.

I reach the TSA official and show him my ticket and driver's license before I join the other travelers zigzagging toward the screening area. The entire time, I grin from ear to ear. I can't help it.

Thanks to a loving God, a kindly judge and sweet Corban, the depression triggered by my weekend from hell has been replaced by boundless joy. The bliss bubbling in my soul froths and fizzes and threatens to erupt in song. If I could, I'd shout and dance and sing out loud.

People around me are eyeing me like I might do just that. Ignoring them, I hum the words of an old hymn, every word straight from my heart. *Praise to the Lord, the Almighty, the King of creation. Oh, my soul, praise him, for he is thy health and salvation.*

I turn the corner to loop the other way. *All ye who hear, now to his temple*— Noreen? She and a man I assume to be her husband are standing near the back of the first TSA line, tickets in hand.

Spinning the opposite direction, I stare at the ceiling. Did they pass Corban on their way in? Did they see me? I swallow. What do I do? If we're on the same flight...

Taking breath after long breath and blowing out through my mouth, I fight to calm my spirit. Maybe the Nystroms are on the same flight. Maybe they aren't. And if they are, they can't stop me. I have a judge's okay to fly home. Still, they can cause a scene and make the flight miserable for me and everyone else onboard.

I remember Noreen once mentioned her husband's name. What is it? And, I ask myself, why do I care? Anyone married to her can't be a trustworthy person.

I pull the black travel hat from Myrtle Mae's tote and unroll it, pleased it has a wide brim. Exactly what I need. I settle it on my head and tilt the brim so it hides my face from Noreen. Again, my co-shufflers eye me with raised eyebrows. I'd explain, but they'd never understand my plunge from euphoria to paranoia.

At the X-ray machines, I lay my bag, purse and shoes in the bin.

The TSA official motions to me. "Put the hat on top."

Reluctantly, I take it off, do as he instructed and quickly turn to face the body scanner, through which I pass without incident. When my things come out of the X-ray machine on the conveyor rollers, I grab the hat and drop it on my head before I retrieve my other possessions.

Hurrying toward my gate, I make a quick stop in the restroom to use the toilet and see what I can do to alter my appearance. I've just pulled my hair to the top of my head and stuffed it under the hat when in the mirror I see Noreen scurry into a stall behind me, a perfume trail following close behind.

Hands shaking, I open the pink purse, pull out the sunglasses Sebastian gave me and slide them on. I adjust the hat and exit the restroom, head ducked in case her husband is standing outside.

I'm well away from the restroom before I lift my head. *Bruce. His name is Bruce Nystrom.* Now that I can see more than feet, knees and rolling suitcases, I'm surprised I only caused two near-collisions between here and the women's restroom. This airport is always busy, especially during tourist season.

I reach my gate with twenty-five minutes to spare before boarding begins. Slouched in the far corner, hat low, I watch travelers hurry both directions. Before long, the Nystroms come striding along the terminal, pulling their carry-ons behind them. She's wearing yellow-and-green stilettos with her lime-green pantsuit. Sure enough, they slow and settle into seats several rows ahead of me.

"Oh, no," I whisper. "How could they?" They'll be on the same flight. I have no idea how to avoid them.

When first-class boarding is announced, Noreen and Bruce jump to their feet and trot to the front of the line. My heart sinks. I should have known they'd fly first class. I'll have to pass by them to get to my seat in economy…way too close for comfort.

I tuck stray hairs into the hat and untuck my blouse. Followers are expected to keep their shirttails inside their pants and skirts to avoid slovenliness, a character deficiency straight from the devious devil. My face is devoid of makeup, thanks to jailtime and blubbering all over Corban's shirt. Whether or not a lack of lipstick and blush will aid my disguise, I don't know. I just hope my appearance is a far cry from the altogether look.

My final preparation is to shove the telltale pink purse into the already stuffed tote. I make sure the strap isn't hanging out, push the sunglasses up my nose, and wait for the Nystroms to step onto the boarding bridge. Not until then do I join the others waiting to board the flight to Portland.

Stepping from the bridge into the airplane several minutes later, I pray one last time. *Please, God, make me invisible.*

The flight attendant, a thin Asian man with kind eyes, welcomes me with a smile.

I nod but keep my lips pressed. If nothing else about me catches Noreen's attention, my voice could give me away. I turn right and step into the cabin.

The Nystroms are seated on my left, third row back. They're both looking down at something. I tug the hat brim over my cheek and shuffle past. Noreen's perfume is so potent, I can taste it. Bruce is asking her which movie she wants to watch on his tablet. "The one my brother recommended or the—"

Stepping past them and out of first class, I'm caught in the noisy commotion of people fastening seatbelts and shoving carry-ons into the overhead bins. I don't hear the rest of the movie conversation, but it's okay. Like Ruby Jade and Inez, Noreen speaks with a forked tongue, as my grandfather would say. None of them follow the Follower rules, which supposedly came straight from God.

At this moment, I'm so relieved the Nystroms were focused on something other than me, I'm almost grateful for their hypocrisy. *You did it, Jesus. You made me invisible!*

I work my way to the rear of the crowded plane, feeling safer with each step that separates me from the church couple. My seat is by the window in the very back row, left side, which is fine with me. The fact I won't be able to recline my seat is a small price to pay for seclusion.

I stow my things under the seat in front of me, fasten my seatbelt and look around. A woman exits the bathroom behind the seats on the other side of the aisle. *Oh… I hadn't thought of the restroom being an issue. What if Noreen or Bruce can't get in the front restroom and come to use this one?*

Sighing, I rest my head on the seatback. I'll have to stay alert all the way to Portland, ready to pull Myrtle Mae's hat over my face, even though I am so–very–tired. My lack of sleep has caught up with me.

Two big black guys follow three chatting, grinning elementary-aged boys all the way to the back. The boys are carrying takeout containers from the Bistro. I'm pretty sure I smell hotdogs.

The boys take the seats across from me, one of the adults sits in front of them next to an older couple, and the other plops beside me in the aisle seat. He says, "Nice hat," and holds out his hand. "I'm Harmon."

I smile and take his big, warm, calloused hand. "Hi, Harmon. I'm Cassie." Something about him feels safe, though he's only spoken four words.

He leans forward to punch the other guy's arm. "Hey, dude, how'd you wrangle a seat that can recline? In front of a scrawny kid, no less. You can practically lay in his lap."

The other man waggles his fingers. "Magic computer fingers, bro. What it takes."

"Hey, I'm not scrawny," declares the boy across from my seatmate.

"Compared to me, you are." Harmon rubs the boy's head. "If your dad cramps your style, be sure to let him know."

The boy shrugs and opens his takeout container.

Harmon tells the boys to fasten their seatbelts and proceeds to fasten his. Turning to me, he asks, "You from Bozeman or Portland or neither?"

"Actually, I'm from both, Salem to be exact."

"Hey, cool. We're from Portland. Just finishing a family fishing trip in the Montana mountains."

"Did you have a good time?"

He turns to the boys. "Did we have a good time in Montana, boys?"

Their cheers and shouts cause heads to turn. "Montana's the best!" declares the boy by the window. "I want to move here." The closest boy says, "God sure knew what he was doing when he made Montana."

Harmon high-fives him. "You got it right, buddy."

"I agree." I smile. "But Oregon is nice too."

The flight attendants walk through, checking seatbelts, rearranging luggage in the overhead bins and noisily securing the covers. The plane taxis onto the runway.

I look out the window. *Goodbye, Corban. I'll miss you. I hope you didn't run into the Nystroms and get chewed out because of me.*

"Have family waiting for you in Portland?" Harmon asks.

I glance over at him. "Yes, I'm excited to see them."

He studies me with his serene brown eyes. "You look weary and worried, Cassie."

"The last few days have been rough." I sigh. "And the days to come will be hard."

"Can I pray for you?"

"I'd appreciate it, a lot."

He takes my hand again and bows his head.

I lower my tired eyelids.

"Father," he says, "dear Cassie is precious in your eyes." Though Harmon's voice is rich and resonant, it's not loud. "As Zephaniah said, you delight in her, you sing joyful songs over her."

I grin. My favorite verse. How did he know?

"You calm her fears with your love," he continues. "Help her to hear your music, feel your joy and bask in your love. May she give her worries to you. And may she receive your rest, strength and peace. In your sweet Son's name, amen."

He squeezes my hand.

I whisper, "Thank you, Jesus," and open my eyes. "And thank you, Harmon. That's exactly what I needed."

Palms raised, he declares, "God's got this flight, and he's got whatever awaits you in Oregon."

I remove the hat, close my eyes and lean back.

Yes, he's got this.

DISCUSSION QUESTIONS

1. After much agonizing, Cat has Deputy Manning return her to the Pritchard household. What kind of welcome does she receive? Discuss what this decision cost her. If you were in her place, would you have made the same choice? Why or why not?

2. As Cat drifts off to sleep after tending her shredded feet, her angst over Zachary's predicament resurfaces. She forces her eyes closed and tells herself, "God's got this." Share a time when you did all you could do and had to rely on this truth. When has God rescued you? Are you still waiting to be rescued?

3. Along with Cat, Candice observes Zachary's rescue and Olivia's arrest. When she suggests they call Leadership, Cat says, "Olivia has to be the one to break the news. She needs to feel the full weight of her crime. Believe me, I speak from experience." Share a time when you had to face the full weight of your actions. How did you get through it? How did facing the consequences benefit you?

4. When Marcela explains Zachary's "timeout" to Cat, she adds, "Ruby Jade says God's law is above man's law." Do you agree or disagree? When might this be true? What is wrong with applying this logic to Zachary's treatment? Is Ruby Jade referring to the Ten Commandments or other decrees?

5. Home alone on Easter, Cat reflects on Jesus' dual gifts of salvation and his empowering Holy Spirit. "I'm not powerless and life isn't hopeless, even when my circumstances might suggest otherwise." What circumstances in your life make you feel powerless and/or hopeless? How do these gifts from above encourage and strengthen you? How can you encourage others?

6. Both Zachary and Cat endure a "cleanse." Describe what happens during a cleanse. What feelings did this process evoke in you? What is the stated purpose for a cleanse? Do you think it accomplishes that purpose? If not, what does it accomplish? Do you know anyone who has experienced something similar?

7. Joleen describes the contradicting messages T.W. participants received from program staff and FFOW leadership. "[Previous staff would] tell me I'm a beloved, gifted child of God. But at church, I'd be subjected to a cleanse or called an addict, a loser, an embarrassment, stupid, a waste of humanity." Have you struggled with the same conflicting messages? Where do these messages come from? How do you get off the rollercoaster? How can you resist the negative and embrace the positive?

8. Ruby Jade, Inez and Noreen do not have to abide by the same rules, written or unwritten, as rank-and-file Followers must obey. List lifestyle benefits only those in the inner circle enjoy. Who decides who is in this select group? Does a similar scenario play out where you work, live or worship?

9. Fear and desperation suck Zachary's mom, Trina, back into FFOW. She hates being with the people who abused her son, yet she feels like she has to be there, and the "hurricane" in her head causes her to overdose. Has fear or desperation ever driven you to do something you regret? Why is fear so powerful? How do you combat fear?

10. God uses Judge Bock to turn Cat's arrest, which Ruby Jade instigated, into good when he allows Cat to continue her trip. He even orchestrates an intimate lunch with Corban. Describe a time God turned something meant to harm you into good. How has God provided for you when you thought all was lost?

Questions crafted by Pat Watkins

RELIGIOUS CULTS

"Truth is stronger than lies, and love is stronger than fear. If you are involved with a religious organization, keep in mind that God created us with free will, and that no truly spiritual organization would <u>ever</u> use deception or mind control, or take away your freedom."

("Combating Cult Mind Control: Guide to Protection, Rescue and Recovery from Destructive Cults" by Steven Hassan)

"Cults can be hard to identify. They're not freakish, otherworldly groups that set off all your internal alarms right away—if they were, no cult could ever gather enough followers to grow and survive. Instead, cults often feel like intensely hopeful and promising utopian communities that just might save the world."

(Escaping Utopia: Growing Up in a Cult, Getting Out, and Starting Over" by Janja Lalich and Karla McLaren)

"In abusive churches, compulsory confession serves the leadership. It erodes the health of the church community and hurts the person who confesses. Safe churches, however, respect the privacy and dignity of their members, and never compel them to confess private sins in a public or group setting."

("Spiritual Abuse in The Church: A Guide to Recognition and Recovery" by Kenneth J. Garrett)

"Destructive cults behave badly. They deceptively employ tactical thought reform, which quells independent thinking and engenders dependency in an effort to attain compliance. This is all done with little regard for collateral damage, which destructive cults rationalize as a necessary evil. Cult leaders instead seem to be relentlessly focused on their own needs and fulfillment; that is the hidden agenda of most, if not all, destructive cults."

("Cults Inside Out: How People Get In and Can Get Out" by Rick Alan Ross)

"Church abuse happens when a religious leader uses his or her spiritual position to control, manipulate or dominate a person or group of persons. The leaders of these groups employ control-oriented autocratic leadership. I'm not saying they do it insincerely, but they use their position as prophet, pastor, elder, priest or whatever they may call themselves to manipulate and control people's lives. It is spiritual intimidation."

(Ronald Enroth, author and retired professor of sociology at Westmont College; quoted in a *Catholic Sentinel* article by Ed Langlois titled "Narcissism a Hallmark of Religious Abusers")

"The mindset of the abusive pastor is set on one purpose, that of meeting his own desires for significance, security, and satisfaction. The church's members, programs, ministries, reputation in the community, and material wealth, etc., are all simply the tools that the abusive pastor uses to serve that one, exclusive purpose. ...They are dedicated to the promotion and care of themselves through the subjugation of their followers, and theft of their material and immaterial resources. These resources are consumed by the narcissist and thrown into the bottomless pit of his own unfilled, unfillable soul."

("Spiritual Abuse in The Church: A Guide to Recognition and Recovery" by Kenneth J. Garrett)

"The thief comes only to steal and kill and destroy; I have come that they may have life and have it to the full." (John 10:20 NIV)

CULT AWARENESS

Disclaimer: The below links are provided for readers who desire to research cultic organizations. The list is not exhaustive; however, these websites offer a wealth of information. As the author has not searched the entirety of any of the websites, she cannot endorse the contributors or their statements.

Advocates for Awareness of Watchtower Abuses: http://aawa.co/

Cult Education Network: https://culteducation.com/

Cult Research: http://cultresearch.org/

Cults in America Article: https://bit.ly/32Yro6q

Ex Mormon Christians United for Jesus: http://www.unveilingmormonism.com/

Ex Mormon Files: https://www.exmormonfiles.com/

Facts about JWs: https://www.jwfacts.com/

Families Against Cult Teachings: https://familiesagainstcultteachings.org/

Freedom of Mind: https://freedomofmind.com/

Holding Out Help: https://holdingouthelp.org/

International Cultic Studies Association (ICSA): https://www.icsahome.com/

MeadowHaven: http://www.meadowhaven.org/

Open Minds Foundation: https://www.openmindsfoundation.org/

Religious Cults Info: Resources, Answers and Hope: http://religiouscultsinfo.com/

Safe Passage Foundation: https://safepassagefoundation.org/

Spiritual Abuse Characteristics: http://thewartburgwatch.com/2013/07/18/spiritual-abuse-and-common-characteristics/

Watchman Fellowship: https://www.watchman.org/

Wellspring Retreat: https://wellspringretreat.org/

TANGLED TRUTH
ACKNOWLEDGEMENTS

I don't know about other authors, but I need a team to produce a book. Birthing *Tangled Truth* was no different. As always, my gracious husband, Steve Lyles, plowed his way through the gnarly rough draft. Our daughter, Alissa Ketterling, and her husband, Jim Ketterling, did a *final* final edit for me. And like she's done so many times before, Pat Watkins patiently read a couple drafts and wrote the discussion questions.

My critique group fed me ideas, bounced around titles and provided cover input. Amber Bennett, Laurie Bower, Val Gray, Lisa Hess, Marguerite Martell, Michelle Netten and Kathy Schuknecht, you keep my brain oiled. As with *Shattered Dream*, Laurie Bower went the extra mile to line edit *Tangled Truth*, twice!

In addition, several kind generous friends served as beta readers and proofreaders. Sharol Aranda, Lori Charlier, Pat Cory, Gail Harmon, Norma Hubka, Mary McGuire and Linda Newport—I'm so glad you joined the *Tangled Truth* team. Couldn't have done it without you!

Want to know what happens next to Cassie and Corban and gang? Turn the page for a peek inside "Hidden Path," the third and final book in the PRISONERS OF HOPE SERIES.

HIDDEN PATH

REBECCA CAREY LYLES

My excitement grows with each step I take along the busy terminal. I can't wait to see my parents and my brother again. But, oh, how I wish Grandma Hunt's impending death wasn't the reason for our gathering. Like I've been praying since I learned my nanna doesn't have much time left on this earth, I once again ask God to help her hold on until I can say goodbye.

I also wish Noreen Nystrom and her husband weren't somewhere ahead of me in the airport. Their unwelcome presence has tarnished my homecoming, to say the least. She's the one who tricked me into joining the Faithful Followers of the Way church and rehab program.

Noreen and Bruce were seated in first class on the flight from Bozeman, Montana, to Portland, Oregon. I was at the back of the plane, slower to disembark, and don't see them now. But still, they can't be too far away.

Scanning the crowd, I try to remember how many years have passed since I last saw my nanna. Life blurred after Eric's death, and I lost track of everything important. A sharp pain stabs my heart. Eric, my sweet Eric.

If he were here, we'd have so much fun with Mom and Dad and Kip. And maybe even with Grandma Hunt. She and Eric loved to tease each other. His farewell would have brought a smile to her lips. But we lost my husband early, and she had to say goodbye to him. We all had to say goodbye to him.

For the millionth time, I pull myself from the self-pity brink. I can't risk being sucked into alcoholism again, which is what self-pity does to me. I want to enjoy my family and celebrate the wonderful woman I call "Grandma" and "Nanna."

Nearing a bathroom, I adjust my sunglasses and check for Noreen's husband, Bruce. When I don't see him waiting outside the women's restroom, I pull my borrowed hat low over my eyes and step inside. The smell of hand soap and hairspray mingles with the subdued urine stench common to well-used public bathrooms.

Head down, I hurry into a stall, determined to maintain my disguise until I'm safely out of the airport and on my way to my parents' home in Salem. In theory, Noreen can't stop me from seeing my nanna. A Bozeman judge gave me permission for this trip. But I wouldn't put it past her to make a scene in the middle of the airport and have me arrested on a trumped-up charge like Ruby Jade, the church leader, did.

I can hear Noreen scream my FFOW name. "Cassandra Turner!" And see her stomp her stilettos. "What are you doing here? Ruby Jade didn't say you could leave. You belong in Montana!"

I don't want to risk a confrontation with her, if for no other reason than the fact she'd steal precious minutes, maybe hours, from court-allocated time with my loved ones. I'm anxious to be with my sweet family again. They'll hug me and welcome me home—and call me by my real name, Cassie Anita True.

I hang my purse, the hat and the flower-covered tote I borrowed from my friend Myrtle Mae on the stall hooks and take a brush from the bag. Running it through my hair, I think about the last time Mom and Dad saw me. They'd traveled all the way from Salem to Bozeman to visit me in the Gallatin County Jail, where I was a stringy-haired resident dressed in orange, bemoaning my two-year sentence.

I drop the brush into the bag and twist my hair on top of my head. I'd rather wear it down. But for now, I add the hat and angle it over my eyes.

My purse on one shoulder and the tote on the other, I cautiously open the door and survey my surroundings via the mirror across from the stall. Women and girls come and go. Suitcase wheels clatter against the tile floor. Toilets flush. Stall doors open and close. Water splashes in sinks. Hand dryers roar.

When I don't see Noreen, I hurry to the mirror to check my disguise. I'll be shocked if my family recognizes me, and not just because of the hat. Though I hate to admit it, thanks to Faithful Followers of the Way, I look less scary, more human than when my parents last visited. I've even put on a little weight. They should be pleased.

A woman leads a child into the stall behind me. The little girl jabbers, eager for her first airplane ride all the way from Portland, Oregon, to San Francisco, California.

Grandma Hunt loved to fly. She would have told the little girl to look out the window and count the farms. My grandparents were farmers who were quick to inform anyone who'd listen that family farms are what feed America, not General Mills or Conagra.

"Love your hat." The woman at the next sink is smiling at me.

I return her smile. "Thank you."

"It's very cute on you. You must be one of those women born to wear a hat."

"You think so?"

She smiles and turns to go.

I follow her out of the restroom. Was I born to hide my real self, like the FFOW leaders expect? Or does my true self shine through the façade the church forces on us? I hope so. Corban Dahlstrom seems to like the real me. Or does he only see the Follower version? And do I only see his Follower persona?

I look both ways before I step into the crowded terminal. When Corban and I work together away from the church, he's relaxed and fun, transparent. At the church, he's polite but guarded—and distant. The easy-going side of him is definitely my favorite.

Hat pulled low, Myrtle Mae's flowered bag on one shoulder and my pink purse dangling from the other, I weave between travelers to access the moving walkway. Once I'm on it, I hurry ahead at a pace just under a jog. Noreen and Bruce are probably down at baggage claim by now. Thank God I didn't check any luggage.

I'm meeting my family at Mom's favorite pre-security coffee shop, Portland Roasting Company. But like Corban, I can't let down my guard, at least not yet. The Nystroms might decide they need coffee before they go wherever they're headed.

Or… I stop. They might not have bags to claim. I could run into them anywhere along the way. My heart begins to pound, and I start walking again. Please, God. Don't let them see me.

The kind man who prayed for me on the airplane, Harmon, assured me God not only "had" the flight, he "has" what happens in Oregon. Thanks to him, and thanks to God, I slept all the way here.

"Help her to hear your music, feel your joy and bask in your love," he'd prayed. "May she give her worries to you. And may she receive your rest, strength and peace."

You gave me wonderful rest, God. Now, I give you my worries.

Jogging past a couple locked in an embrace, I touch my cheek and relive the surprise kiss Corban planted there just before I boarded the plane in Bozeman. The sweet memory makes me smile. Fingers on my lips, I blow a kiss into the air. This one's for you, Corban Dahlstrom.

I love the new closeness in our relationship, dangerous as it is.

Hidden Path coming soon. Watch for it on my website http://beckylyles.com/ and my Amazon Author Page: https://amzn.to/31UUcNb

ABOUT THE AUTHOR

Rebecca Carey Lyles grew up in Wyoming, the setting for her award-winning *Kate Neilson Novels*. She and her husband, Steve, currently live in Idaho, the beautiful state that borders Wyoming and Montana, the setting for this series. Together, they host a podcast called *Let Me Tell You a Story* (beckylyles.com/podcast). In addition to writing fiction and nonfiction, she serves as an editor and a mentor for aspiring authors. *Tangled Truth* is the second book in the *Prisoners of Hope Series*.

Email: beckylyles@beckylyles.com

Facebook author page: Rebecca Carey Lyles

Website: http://beckylyles.com/

Twitter: @beckylyles

NOTE FROM THE AUTHOR

Thank you for reading this story and caring about those ensnared by religious cults. I hope you enjoyed *Tangled Truth* and will consider leaving a review or rating online wherever you share your thoughts about books. If you'd like to learn about future releases, I invite you to go to my website – beckylyles.com – to register for my rare-and-random newsletter. You'll receive a free eStory as my "thank you."

http://beckylyles.com/newsletter---freebies.html

www.ingramcontent.com/pod-product-compliance
Lightning Source LLC
Chambersburg PA
CBHW020517260626
47156CB00006B/2037